THE STRANGE TALES OF BRENN...

A BOY
AND
A
RAT

Published in paperback in 2022 by Sixth Element Publishing

Sixth Element Publishing
Arthur Robinson House
13-14 The Green
Billingham
TS23 1EU
www.6epublishing.net

ISBN 978-1-914170-30-0

British Library Cataloguing in Publication Data. A catalogue record for this book is available from the British Library.

Printed in Great Britain.

THE STRANGE TALES OF BRENNAN AND RIZ: BOOK 1

A BOY AND A RAT

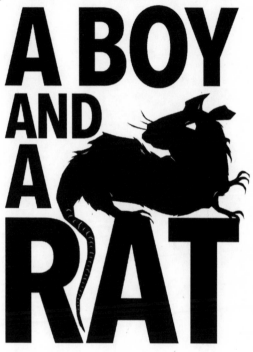

PETER JAMES MARTIN

CHAPTER 1
A MURDER TO BEGIN WITH

"Ow much longer do we ave ta be ere fer?" Riz asked, sounding very nasal.

I opened my pocket and saw him sitting there with his paw clamped firmly around his nose.

"Till we've got all the evidence, de-float the candles, and remove anything else that says this was anything other than your average human psychopath," I replied grimly. I was supposed to be helping by looking around, but I felt sick no matter which way I turned. A Rune that gets rid of nausea would have been handy.

Outside, the regular police were mucking around, making it seem like they were busy trying to solve the case, knowing full well that the killer was something out of their league, which to be fair, probably made them breathe a sigh of relief. After all, it wasn't going to be them fighting it, whatever it was.

It's a good thing I've got a strong stomach, otherwise I would have been rushing backwards and forwards to the toilet. In front of me was a scene from a horror movie. Blood dripped from a couple of bodies that were suspended from the ceiling, collecting into pots and pans from the kitchen. Another two bodies were draped over the settee, their necks slashed open at just the right angle so the blood looked like wings splattered on the opposite wall. The smell was horrendous, I don't know how Riz was able to keep it together, and Valarie had obviously seen those police programmes way too much, as she was taking pictures of everything important.

Perhaps I should explain... see, I'd had a call from Valarie a little over an hour ago, saying that she herself had been contacted by the Government to look into a case of supernatural dealings on their behalf. When she relayed that to me, I was expecting something different than what I ended up with. What she brought me to was a mass murder. A party of illegal squatters had all been killed in increasingly horrific ways. The ones who got their throats slit had had it comparatively easy.

Now, you may be asking yourself, what does this have to do with me? A guy with a talking rat who investigates paranormal shenanigans, and when no jobs are around, more mundane matters. Well, the murderer's masterpiece was in the hallway, and it was the first thing we saw. The body had been stripped and tied with small chains to several floating candles, with the chain links going through the flesh. The stomach had been opened and emptied, and moved somewhere else. In the now empty cavity was a fairy statue, taken from the garden and lavishly painted. The floating candles were a bit of a giveaway here. To make matters worse, they were scented candles, apparently brought to the crime scene. I've now lost any sense of attachment to anything to do with cinnamon.

The police, who were first on the scene, saw that, and straight away reported it to their bosses, who reported it to their bosses, who in a long series of passing upwards, passed it to the Government department that deals with this sort of thing. They are so secretive they don't even have an official name or an acronym, though, I would suggest WOS... 'waste of space'. These people then do what all those in charge do best... they shift responsibility. Citing lack of manpower, they contracted the job out to someone in the area, that someone being Valarie. She, in turn, hired us, not revealing till we walked through the door, the full details of what was going on. I can take one body, as gruesome as it was, but this many? With all those... pleasant smells, mixing together? I wished she'd hired someone else.

I heard her shout me from the back door, and then her gagging. I braced myself for whatever it was that was out there.

Valarie pointed to the back door.

"I think that explains a lot about this," she said, rather ominously.

I opened the door and was hit by the fragrant smell that was coming from what looked like a box used to transport white goods like freezers. There were a lot of flies buzzing round which did give a clue as to what was lurking in there. Every step I took over to it became heavier as my body begged me not to subject myself to any more gore or disgust.

When will I ever learn? I bent down to look in the box, and immediately turned to throw up. Even just trying to look at it for a second was too much. Inside the box, someone had made a makeshift scene of someone getting hung. Except all the parts used were the missing organs from the floating guy's stomach. The long intestines had become the noose, while the stomach was put through the loop with a face drawn on one end of it in permanent marker. That was supposed to be the person getting hanged. The large intestines had been folded and shaped, before being stuck to the stomach with pins, making the rest of the body. A solitary name hit my mind, and I threw up again.

It was another hour before we finished up in that place. Another hour before the normal police were allowed to do a sweep. As was protocol, we had to brief them on what we found, and what we knew about the perpetrator, if we could identify them or what kind of being it was. I let Valarie do the talking here, my mind too distracted to pretend to be polite. Riz was never polite in the first place.

Their conversation seemed to take place in a different building for all that I was paying attention, as things rumbled round my brain. The police officers were confused by the name, judging by the looks on their faces. I didn't register what they said they'd do now. If they were smart, they'd do nothing. This was a man, after all, who was thinking it's hilarious to do arts and crafts with people's internal organs, and using a dangerous kind of magic. The results would not be pretty.

They were still talking, which worked well for me. I started to back away from them, waiting to see if they noticed what I was doing, and when it became apparent that I wasn't going to be missed, I slipped out the front door, and started running. I estimated that with my fitness level, and the distance, it was going to be dark by the time I got there, to see him. Perfect atmosphere if you were into that kind of thing. Why I didn't tell Valarie and Riz? Because this is my fault.

What am I talking about? Well, it's a funny story, funny that it's also the story of how I met Riz.

CHAPTER 2
ENTER THE RAT

Twenty years ago…

Up until the point I met Riz, my life was run of the mill. I lived with my parents as an only child. My father, William Landis, worked all the hours under the sun, that's certainly what it seemed like anyway. His job as a delivery driver wasn't fancy, and it kept him busy, going here, there and everywhere, but it provided. He was gone by the time I woke most mornings, and would only appear briefly before I went to bed. The weekends were family time, and though he often seemed dead on his feet, we were all he wanted those days. Of course, his work meant I was closer to my mother, Mara Landis, who only got a job again once I was in full time school, and she did more hours the older I got. When I was thirteen, I saw her less and less. Throughout my childhood, she was there more. The weekends though, that was our time to bond, either out and about or at home.

Home itself was an end terrace house that backed onto a wide expanse of grass, a field of the sort that housing developers would normally love to bulldoze over. We lived in Thornaby, a town nestled along the banks of the River Tees, but we were lucky enough to avoid the flooding that other nearby towns got. It was a mixture of old and new housing estates, with the town having existed since the 1600s in some form or another, and then being home to a Royal Air Forces Aerodrome till it was shut down and eventually built on in the 1950s and 60s. This was how our little street came to exist. My parents often spoke of those olden days, and what the town was like before the A66 road cut through it. They had some nostalgia for that time, halcyon days long gone by, but when I was sixteen it didn't have any hold on me.

Now, I already said that my dad worked himself to the bone, and there was an additional reason, other than just paying the bills, and that was to make sure that my mum could afford to keep up with the one thing that she loved like a second child, her music. She owned many instruments, and could play them all to a canny degree. I didn't know it then, but there was a reason she could play, and that it was tied to the same reason I never saw her side of the family. The long and short of it was that my mum's side were arseholes. Anyway, as I was saying, we'd gather in the dining room on the weekends, and my mum would put on a performance with one of her instruments. Her gift was so that she could even take requests from me and my dad. Her playing was immense, especially on her favourite instrument, the violin. It was her pride and joy.

Of course, I tried my best to play. It seemed that my mother's skill didn't really transfer to me, but I did find some success with the saxophone, which, I'm not going to lie, I only wanted to play because of that Baker Street song. As I got older though, I saw less and less point in practising, as I wanted to distance myself from my failings. Why would I carry out this self-destructive behaviour? Why else? The treatment I was getting from other kids my age...

I have always been that lonesome figure, on the precipice of everyone's view, barely noticeable above the humdrum of normal everyday life if I kept my nose down and hid in the shadows. When that didn't work, I became a target. All my awkward mannerisms magnified under peer pressure. I'd say something without thinking and then that would be used to beat me into a sobbing mess for the rest of that term. It didn't help that I never fitted in. I wasn't athletic enough to be good at sports, and while smart, not smart enough to fit in with the brightest. If I'm feeling charitable about myself, I would say I was like the ugliest duckling. Riz has even used that to describe me, but with him, you can never be sure when a compliment is just a thinly veiled insult. This was me though from the time I started full time school aged five, to fifth year of senior school.

I don't want to drone on and on about this bullying but at the same time, it was a massive part of my life, and I tried everything to counter it. I ignored them, which was the advice I was given off everyone... which worked just as well as trying to put a fire out with petrol. I reported them to the teachers, which kept them off my back for about five minutes before things reverted. That's assuming anything was done in the first place. Then I tried to mouth back... yeah, that was probably the worst of all my options. I might have fared better if I had the mentality I do now, back then, but that's the way things fall I guess.

I managed to find a friend though, eventually. We bonded through a conversation I overheard and then pretended to know about. Yes, I was desperate. There were other things though that we started talking about naturally and our friendship grew. His name was Merrick Wenford, and he had a lot of qualities that I didn't have. He was a natural leader, charisma just oozed out of him and he was witty with no effort. He thought fast on his feet, thinking of comebacks on the fly and joked with everyone. He wasn't in the top sets for any subjects but that didn't bother him, to his friends that didn't matter, everything seemed to work out for him.

He stuck up for me, but as I learned much later, there were reasons behind this. I used to sit and watch him and some of his friends play football in break times. I was never good enough to play with them. For him, it was normal to be doing all these things: having fun with all those mates, being desirable to several of the girls in our year... I based my idea of normal on that, and judging myself by those values, I fell very short.

Okay, to put things into perspective, I know now that I shouldn't have compared things like that, but try telling the teenage version of me that. Normal is just what you're used to, the normal I deal with here in the present is dredging rivers for water ghouls, staking out the cellars of pubs for ghosts, and sharing a desk with a talking rat. Ah, the beauty of hindsight, we all must have done it at some point. Funnily enough, my sixteen-year-old self did it frequently, lying in bed, staring at the unforgiving ceiling, going over and over the day's events, or even events from a few weeks earlier, using hindsight to craft better scenarios.

This is another reason why I put so much into those small concerts that my mother performed... they took me away from all those thoughts I had, including the much darker ones where I questioned my life and the value in it. Her playing had the ability to soothe my mind, and even if it was just for an hour a week, it was bliss. I shared my mother's gift with Merrick of course, though actually, that's not true, he overheard my mum playing one time he was leaving and demanded to hear more. Her music calmed me, it completely entranced him. I could never get a coherent answer as to why it had that effect. He would look at me with the biggest smile on his face, saying, "Heaven doesn't sound this good."

That was a weird day.

Anyway, that's enough set up, the day I met Riz was a special one. Me and Merrick had just endured a school sponsored trip to a university for the week. I went because I was asked, and Merrick went because he was bored and wanted to be away from his parents. It was because of this that we didn't go straight home once the bus had dropped us off. We wandered around Thornaby, ending up at the beck, a little spot at the edge of the town, near the border with Ingleby Barwick. It was a nice August day, for once, the weather aiding us in Merrick's mission to avoid his house. We were at that age where the GCSE exams were behind us, and college loomed in the future, or at least it did in mine. I kept telling myself that college was going to be better, that I might finally learn to loosen up, and everyone would like me. It felt like an achievement just surviving the last five years. In a week or so, I'd find out what grades I got, which was nerve-racking when your parents made a big deal over it. They wanted a big future for me, wanting more from me then they did themselves.

I was their future, and it was a lot of pressure to put on my back. There were talks of what college courses I was going to attend and what university I would be aiming for, and where that would all lead me. They had a plan for me, one that I wasn't allowed to deviate from. Of course, compared to what the rest of the year had in store, the plan would go out of the window as the pressure ramped up.

As we meandered around, Merrick would stop to look at his watch, pondering where his family would be, wanting them out of his hair. That was the only part of his life that didn't seem perfect. I never knew what the issue was, or why they never got on. I was never brave enough to poke at it.

"Sometimes I think it'd just be faster for me to kill my family than wasting time like this," Merrick mused as he stopped and looked over the beck, a small trickle of water desperately wanting to be more.

"You need to work on your gallows humour," I suggested. "That really wasn't funny."

"Hah, well, I wouldn't open with that one obviously. I'll just use it when I think sarcasm has lost its bite."

This was typical of our exchanges. We'd share jokes about our lives. I hadn't developed my current sense of humour yet, so mine were never that funny compared to Merrick's observations. Now? Well, Riz has rubbed off on me, and I've been known to joke about murdering him, only ever seriously entertaining it once. In my defence, he was a prick that day.

No one else ever got this much talking out of me, and this included my parents.

Merrick shut up as soon as we heard the voices ahead, ones that were heading our way. From behind the bushes, four lads appeared, each with a peculiar smell around them, and the leader still with a cigarette in his mouth. I bet it wasn't tobacco that was in it, mind. They were in our year, but had barely been there, each having spent time out on suspension, a nice little holiday as they called it. To describe them would be to describe every stereotypical thug that ever lived and breathed, even on television. These were just some of the people who had made my school days a living hell. They were allocated to the lower sets, and wore that with pride. Every report they were put on, every detention, all of it fuelled their reputations and made their egos monstrous. Added to this was their connection with drugs, and out of school parties, involving the who's who of the school pantheon. They were the perfect opposite to everything I was. Had we known they were here, we wouldn't have ventured this far out. But it was too late now, they had seen us, and were already laughing as they made their way over.

"Wat yer doing, boyos?" the leader of the four said. His name was Darren, a name as rough as his looks. He blocked Merrick's path and, of course, his friends blocked mine.

I knew how this was going to play out. Merrick shot me a look confirming it, motioning me with his hand to stay back. He went to speak to Darren, wanting to calm any problem before it happened, which left me with the others. I wasn't as lucky as Merrick though, and I couldn't think as fast on my feet as I can now. It was because of this that I made a fatal mistake in how I answered the question one of the others asked, the same thing that Darren had said. This lad was called Paul.

"Wat yer doing, boyo?" Paul said. All the while standing very close to my face, intimidation his pride and joy.

My response?

"Going to see the beck?" Yes, I worded it like a question, so really when they went to push me into it, I shouldn't have been surprised. It took all my strength to avoid being hurled in, but my bag came loose in the struggle. It first dropped to the floor and then Paul grabbed it, seeing it as an easier target than me. This was how the bag was thrown to the other side of the beck, and into a bush. The lads thought it was hilarious, and once again, I was fighting back the tears and frustration. I was ready to go into a frenzy but knew it wouldn't end well for me if I did. Don't feel bad for me, it just makes it seem worse, and all this is pretty much ancient history. I had lost sight of the bag and was sure I was next when Merrick and Darren noticed what was going on, with impeccable timing. Thinking on it, my bag was probably an acceptable sacrifice for them. Made me wonder how they would have reacted if I was actually thrown in. Darren only called his lads off when Merrick changed tactics on the fly and held Darren by his collar. No surprises, they up and left, going god knew where.

Merrick came back over to me, back to his cool self. That burst of aggression was out of place for him, and only surfaced at certain points. I apologised to him, for having to get violent, even if none of it was my fault, but I was always apologising for something.

"Bren, stop apologising, or *I'll* throw you in the beck," Merrick said, patting me on the back. "On the upside, by the time we get your bag back, my family will definitely be out of our hair."

That idiot Paul had thrown my bag a fair distance, and it had come open, spewing some of its contents out, mostly rubbish that had been given to us by the folks at the university. I ran over to it and started just shoving it all back in the bag. Funny thing was, I didn't need any of it, but the way I was, I needed it all back where it belonged. My bag felt a lot heavier now, but I put that down to stress taking it all out of me. I also put the sound I heard down to stress... the sound of springs. Yes, you'll understand that more later, and why it makes me shudder even now.

Merrick had heard them too, but shrugged it off. Either way, we didn't hang around.

Merrick's place was gloriously quiet. The perfect environment for two teenagers to kick back and unwind after a somewhat stressful day. We laughed along with those comedy panel shows, practising our impressions. These moments were both meaningless and special for me. Not that watching these same things with a talking rat isn't unique or special in its own way, but it was a lost youth type deal.

I left Merrick's about ten, later than I would normally, but Merrick always wanted to watch one more show. The sunset was beautiful, from what I could see behind the houses, the sky tinged red. It wasn't a long walk really, not at the speed I was going. My senses sharpened so I could hear the slightest sound in front of me and behind me. All I heard was the hum of cars on the road. So all in all, it was quite pleasant, and I'd forgotten about how heavy the bag was.

Getting back into my parent's house, I darted up to my room and threw the bag on the bed before heading down to see my parents who weren't too surprised to see me home this late. It was a common thing these past few weeks. In some sense I think they were glad, as to them, I was acting like a normal teenager. The three of us exchanged the pleasantries that were part of our daily ritual. Nothing important was gleaned from anything said. After a little while, I returned upstairs, leaving my parents to whatever it was they were watching, and I heard a noise coming from my room. I got close to the door, which had been firmly shut despite the fact that I was sure I'd left it open.

There was someone talking, someone with a squeaky but gruff voice, which I'm still sure is an oxymoron.

"Oh, jump in der bag, datz a gud idea, dat will take yer where yer wanna go."

The words didn't make sense. Plus I didn't hear any other voice, meaning that whoever was talking, was having a conversation with themselves. This drew my attention to my observation about how heavy my bag was when I first picked it up. Perhaps, I should have gone downstairs, told my parents there was an intruder, you know, the obvious things that people who aren't me would have done. Thinking logically did not happen that night. Everything was hazy, like I had stepped from the waking world into a dream state, which I still think would explain things, especially if I woke up tomorrow and found out I'd been in a coma for the last twenty years...

I opened the door a crack and, not wanting to reveal my presence, I scanned the room but didn't see anything out of the ordinary at first, then I heard the voice again.

"Rite, ell dis place is shit, hope I'm not ere too long, get wat I need dun, nd blow dis place."

I opened the door wider, wide enough to get my head in and still couldn't see who was in here. The window showed no sign of forced entry, and it was impossible for someone to have gone in the front way while I was downstairs. I caught some movement out of the corner of my eye as something slipped under my bed.

With no other option, I slowly crept into my own room. Have you ever tried to be so quiet that you purposely take every step but somehow the floorboards creak even louder? Yeah, that was me right now. I knew that whoever was in my room must have been under my bed, so I got down on my hands and knees, and shuffled closer. All this was stupid, I know… it could have been a crazy murderer who could stab me in the head when I got down there. Well, I found something just as crazy.

The first thing I noticed was the tail, a tail that swished around like no one's business. Attached to this was a small brown body that seemed to be talking to a glowing stone that shone like the moon. I almost fell over in shock, which caused the rat to turn around and face me.

We both let out a cry at that point. The rat dashed forward to protect the thing it had been talking to, and I stood back up, unsure at what I was seeing. The rat came out a moment later, on all fours, as if it was just a normal rodent.

"Squeak," it said.

A few seconds of silence passed and its attempted disguise dropped as it stood up on its hind legs.

"Dis is a bit of a buggery, isn't it?" it said.

To my shame, this is the first time I ever passed out…

CHAPTER 3
NIGHT OF SPRINGS

I awoke to a voice, one that I had hoped to be one of my parents but no, it was the talking rat.

"Yer okay der, buddy?" he asked. I guessed it was a 'he'. It sounded like a 'he'.

It was hard to tell if the rat was being sarcastic, especially back then before I really became attuned to Riz's special blend of snark.

I didn't know what to say or do, any chance of it just being a vivid daydream dashed. Looking back, knowing a talking rodent was actually really cool, but my first words to Riz were not cool.

"I'm fine. How are you?" If this ever goes more public, I'm changing this bit.

"So yer brain's still workin den." The rat was sat looking down at me from the bed, my bed. He had made himself quite at home. I questioned how long I had been out for, something the rat must have sensed and then answered.

"It's been five hours since yer hit da floor," he said, scratching himself. Luckily for me, fleas always avoided Riz, showing that they did, in fact, make decisions based on taste.

"Five hours!" I sat straight up, and straight into a world of pain, as my head was banging furiously.

"Yer parents came in not long afta yer fell, mumbled sumthin bout yer bein tired so left yer dere."

That sounded about right actually. My sleeping pattern was terrible, so it wouldn't have been the first time they found me sleeping on the floor. When I was six and doing it, it was easy to put me to bed, not so much at sixteen.

"They came in, and they didn't see you?" I asked, Looking at it again, he was a small rodent who could have found plenty of hiding places in my room, so it would have been more surprising if he had let himself be known to them.

"I hid under yer bed again. It's bad enuff dat yer know bout me."

So far, everything was surreal. I was having a conversation with a talking rat sat on my bed.

"What are you?"

My first sensible question that night.

"Yer wudn't understand."

Riz's first avoidance that night.

"Okay, what do they call you?"

"Ma name is…" He stopped and thought of something before he continued. "Riz, call me Riz."

"Alright, Riz. What the hell is going on? What are you doing in my room?"

All I knew so far was what I had overheard, and one of the things there was about how he needed cover.

"I needed a place ta hide. I waz out near da river, gettin chased wen I saw yer bag. It waz a gud hidin place."

"Who was chasing you?"

Riz went silent. At the time, I didn't know if it was because the answer to the question was terrifying or what. Now I know that it was because he had heard something. I went to speak again, and he held a paw up to shush me.

"Quiet! Do yer hear dat?" he asked quietly.

I strained my ears in response to his request, and I did hear something, amongst the silence. The sound of springs, the second time I had heard it that night, and I made the connection straight away.

"Those springs again," I said involuntarily.

"Oh yer'eard dem earlier, did yer?"

The springing noise stopped quickly. My bedroom was at the

front of the house, facing the street, at least if the tree wasn't in the way. This tree had been a cause of annoyance to my family for a number of years. We constantly had kids trying to climb it to show off, and there was an overabundance of leaves every autumn. To top it off, there was a worry about the roots and what damage it could do to the house if allowed to grow unchecked. It was because of the tree that I couldn't really see much when I peered out of the window that night, trying to see the source of these springs.

"Yer don't need ta do dat," Riz advised as he watched me trying to get a better look outside.

"I want to see what that noise is."

Outside was what you would expect at this time of the morning, dark, quiet and deserted, which is how I preferred things. Then I heard the springs again, and from my limited vantage point I saw movement, just below the tree. Someone was in my front garden, snooping around. It was dark, and they wore dark clothing so, as you can imagine, it was hard to make out anything. Then I saw one of them jump. The figure bent down and then launched itself straight onto the roof. Riz had joined me to witness this as I fell away from the window, speechless.

"Der Spring Heels ave found me. Must ave seen me sneak in ta yer bag. Tho I wonder y it took dem dis long?" I heard another land on the roof, and then another. Three 'Spring Heels' were now doing who knows what on top of my house.

"W-what are those things?"

"Spring Heels're specially modded Bogies, a type of gobo. Yer know, a goblin. Yer heard of Spring Heeled Jack, aven't yer?"

I shook my head.

"Yer bout ta get a crash course in im. Jus hope der other Jack didn't tag along." Riz started looking nervously at my ceiling. There was a loft in-between us and those Spring Heels. Then a purple haze seemed to be etching itself across my ceiling, at which point, Riz leapt from the window sill, and darted towards my bag.

"What are you doing?" I shouted. I envisioned my parents

coming in and waking me from one of those waking dreams, but no, they stayed asleep. "What is that?"

Riz reappeared from my bag, clutching a pouch in his mouth, and he then ushered me to follow him, and together we legged it downstairs and into the back garden. I hadn't realised that's where he wanted to take me. It didn't seem smart going somewhere open. I wanted to voice an objection but Riz pre-empted it, something he did a lot of in the early days.

"Dey're in yer house now, dat mist in yer room, dat was dem breakin in magically. Dere boss musta giv dem der power ta do dat. We need ta get ta der field ova der fence. Dat shud be perfect fer my plan."

Riz ran up my leg and straight onto my shoulder.

"Your plan? When did you come up with that?"

"A moment ago, yer learn ta think quick in dis line of work."

"And what line of work is that?"

"Is dis important rite now? Dey aren't gonna be happy dat we're not in yer room."

He was right. The situation was getting too much for me and I lost sight of what was going on. What was more astounding was that he had decided that I was helping him, and apparently following his commands. I guess we were in this thing together, whatever it was.

"Let's get out of here then!" I said as I ran for the garden gate. Throwing it open, I ran down the short path and onto the field.

"Dat's perfect," he said, pointing to a spot just a bit further on.

I cast my eyes back home and saw three heads sticking out of the roof, each of them looking at me with glowing purple eyes that burned from sunken sockets. They started pulling themselves out of the structure, leaving no marks or damaged tiles. I ran towards the point that Riz gestured to, as springs sounded out and the Spring Heels touched down behind us.

Riz had already pulled out what I now know as a Rune. He was thinking several moves ahead of the goblins. Taking aim with the Rune, he uttered something in a language I still can't identify, and

I've searched through almost all of them. The Rune broke apart in Riz's hands, and the fragments shot out in the shape of an arc, covering most of the ground in front of us. The three Spring Heels were stood just ahead of this, their bodies constantly moving, their heads twitching as they observed us, small flames sparking out of their mouths as they breathed.

"What are they waiting for?" I asked, wanting this to be over quickly.

"Dey waitin on sumthin else." Riz then pointed towards the far end of the block of houses where another figure lurked. This one was taller than the Spring Heels, arms longer and there was a sheen to its hands that I never understood till it got closer. It was dressed differently to the Spring Heels, wearing a long coat and, amusingly enough, a top hat.

"Feckin hell! Can't I get a soddin break!" Riz shouted out.

"What? What is that one?"

"Kid, sumtimes yer betta off not knowin. Wat's yer name neway?"

"Brennan," I replied. I was a bit insulted. He could have asked for my name earlier than now. This strange lanky person walked over to us purposely and stood with the Spring Heels. A bit closer and I saw that it was unmistakably the same kind of goblin as the others, just, for some reason, taller. There was also intelligence in its eyes, oh and malice, a whole lot of malice.

"Boy, hand over the rat," it said. "He doesn't make a very good pet."

The English it was using was fantastic, with only the slightest hint of an accent coming through. It held out its hand towards me, like it was gesturing for me to place Riz in its palm, and that's when I saw that its 'fingers' were knife blades, bolted onto a metal hand that looked like it was forged in my nightmares.

"I'm not a pet, yer bastard!" Riz said angrily, not caring about the size difference or the fact that I was shaking where I stood.

"What's it to be, boy?" the goblin repeated, its friends getting increasingly agitated at the wait.

"Don't believe dem, Bren. Dey want us both ded. Yer seen

dem, nd dere leader doesn't care bout humans gettin caught up in dis."

My reaction was the following emotions, in order: panic, terror, annoyance. First two were self explanatory, the last one was because I had been dragged into this.

"I've only just met you and you're already going to get me killed!"

"Jack showin up surprised me, but we can still get outta dis. Jus got ta be clever," Riz said, before he dropped a Rune similar to the one he used earlier into my hand. I can still remember the weight of the Rune that first time I held it. Its touch was electric, and I felt static running up my fingers and then onwards up my arm. The symbol that had been etched into it was glowing with a faint light. I wanted to stare at it, while it was in my grasp, as the light seemed to be coming from deep within the Rune, far deeper than should be possible for an object that size. Those bad emotions I mentioned earlier? They were gone, and I felt stronger and braver. Back then, I had no idea what a Rune was, or its capabilities.

"What does it do?" I asked, despite the fact that this really wasn't the time to be asking questions.

"I'm gunna say a word'nd need yer ta repeat it, best yer can." Riz leaned in to my ear and whispered. I'll never forget what he said, but I've never been able to pronounce it as his voice turned to thunder, and echoed with sounds that no earthly being could replicate. He then looked at me, and my blank expression said it all.

"Okay, I'll ave ta use a different language den. Oh I know, dis one shud be a lot easier fer yer." He whispered it again, and this time I could repeat it, I mean, I could at least try and repeat it. I took a deep breath, only to get shushed again by Riz.

"Wen I give der signal."

At this, he turned his attention back to Jack, who was twitching just as much as the others.

"Well, dere yer go, yer stupid prick, I think yer got yer answer from der kid."

I heard a creepy laugh from all four goblins. Jack silenced the others.

"You are making the biggest mistake, boy. Don't think I will show you mercy because you are not a man. Give us the rat. Or I will take him over your blood drenched corpse." That was the most direct threat of this exchange, and I was at my breaking point, even with the Rune in my hand. The Spring Heels were preparing to jump at us. Jack didn't seem to be following this lead though, despite all the threats. He was just watching.

"Get ready fer it," Riz said.

I didn't know how this was going to work. The goblins had seen the Rune being activated, after all. From the way they jumped, I knew they could just land on us, and that would be it.

In one breath, the Spring Heels leapt at us, the sound grinding its way into my soul, which is an unfortunate feeling, and even now, all those years later, it's still there.

"Now, Bren!"

"Kelc'h Korrigan!" I yelled and the effect was instant.

The Spring Heels that were just about to land on us collided with a barrier made from a rushing wind that had the ferocity of a tornado and were knocked to the ground, springing the trap Riz had just placed.

"Gotcha, yer stupid pricks." Riz shook his paw at the fallen creatures, clenching it into a fist as he did.

The Spring Heels tried to get up but found the ground had become akin to quicksand, and very quickly, they were dragged down into unknown depths. First one went under, then another till there was only one left, struggling to leap back up. It reached out to Jack who looked at it bemused, and just when I thought it was going to help, this Jack took the Spring Heel's head clean off.

"You are a clever one, rat. Don't make the mistake of thinking this is over," Jack said, flicking the blood off his knife-like fingers. "By the way, boy, I'll be back for you later."

With that, the goblin sulked away, till I could no longer tell its silhouette from the shadows. It was obvious that the last part was meant to terrify me, but it was pointless, as I was already shitting myself. Afraid of what world I had blundered into. And believe it or not, this wasn't the worst that was to come either.

"We'll be alrite fer a while. Faine will ave ta create more Spring Heels. So, we'll be safe fer a couple of days, I reckon," Riz said.

Looking at him, I knew he enjoyed seeing those goblins end up like that. I felt queasy. Still, what they would have done to me if they had the chance...

I prodded the ground in front of me with my foot, wanting to make sure it wouldn't drag me down either, but Riz hopped down from my shoulder and darted across it in short jumps, proving that it was back to how it should have been.

"Da Rune waz targeted ta affect goblins only. We'ere neva in any danger from it, only dose morons. Now dat der danger haz passed, y don't yer show me round yer kitchen?" Riz started towards the house, and I followed, though I was still looking around for Jack. I realised that I was breathless, that I had been holding my breath for the entire encounter. I felt relieved but I couldn't deny the exhilaration I felt, for having just been part of it. I was scared pretty much to the brink of death, and certainly there was the chance that people would have found parts of my mangled corpse in the morning but I got a rush, one that I was only receiving the benefits of now.

"Yer get used ta der feelin," Riz said as I let him into the house, against all common sense and rational thinking. There was something – a strange sense this was right – kicking around in my head that I followed, that's the only reason I can think of as to why I went along with this, and everything to come. I don't believe in destiny, but I can't deny that this event could have been destiny getting impatient and coming to me and telling me to get a move on.

Whatever the case, everything inside the house was as it should be. My parents were still flat out asleep which was good, as explaining what I was doing outside would have been tricky. The kitchen itself was nice and warm compared to the coolness of the outside world. My eyes kept wandering over to the window, where I expected to see Jack staring back at me. Of course, there was nothing there but my reflection, and the reflection of Riz helping himself to the contents of the fridge and cupboards. Back then, as he is today, Riz was a glutton, he eats anything and everything. Being the polite boy I once was, I waited till he was done fattening himself up before asking about himself and the craziness I had become involved in.

"Okay, I want to hear it," I said, resolutely.

"Yer wanna hear wat?" Riz said, pulling his face away from a block of cheese.

"Everything. I want to know why you're a talking rat. I want to know why there's goblins with springs attached to their legs chasing you. I want to know who Jack is. Who this Faine is that you mentioned? What you were doing on that beck? Oh! And if there's time, what happens now?"

"Oh, yer wanna hear dat lot! Rite, but yer mite wanna get comfy first. I'm bout ta bore yer wit der details, nd if yer lucky, I won't charge yer fer der privilege," Riz said.

I was already involved in whatever this was. I couldn't change him hiding in my bag, I couldn't do anything about what had already happened. I was used to life screwing me over, but it had seemingly played a blinder here... and I wanted to know what else was coming.

CHAPTER 4
FOLKLORE

"Let's start with der basics. Yer know bout fairies nd gobbos nd all dat shit, rite?" Riz said, as he shoved a pawful of chedder into his mouth.

"Only from stories. I still can't get over all this."

"Save dat disbelief crap fer later. Rite now, yer learnin sumit. Neway, dere's different groups of dem, jus like dere's different types of animals," he said, almost sounding scholarly.

"Different groups of fairies and goblins?"

"Yeh, fer example, on der goblin side of things, yer got yer brownies, bogies, bogarts, red caps…" Riz started listing off all the different sub groups of goblins and I zoned out.

Then I remembered that I was sitting at an ungodly hour in the morning, in my kitchen, talking with a rat, who'd helped save me from four goblins, three with springs attached to them. Did I want any of this to make sense? That's what I asked myself then. I'm still undecided on that nowadays, and things have only gotten more crazy.

"Now, der fairies ave got different names but dat's not wat's important ta know bout dem. Wat's important is wat Council dey work fer."

"Council? What you mean like Thornaby Town Council?"

"Yer ejit, no!"

Riz reached over and tapped me on the head with his paw, and I was surprised at how much it hurt. He was a lot stronger than he should have been for a rat. I take advantage of that these days, as it means he can do more housework than he likes to admit. "When I say Councils, I mean der Seeley Council, nd it's counterpart, der Unseeley Council…"

"And what's the difference with them?"

"Easy, one likes humans, der Seeley Council. Der other one, doesn't, der Unseeley Council. How hard is dat ta get thru yer thick hed?"

What he said had shaken something in my brain, a nugget of information from a book I'd long since read, and clearly forgotten.

"So you're a Fae then? Working for the Seeley Council?"

Riz looked insulted when I said this, though it was only momentary, and quickly replaced with a smile that should have clued me in on his nature.

"Course I am, I'm der only hope against Faine Hedara, so I got a licence ta break every law goin till I brin im down."

"Is this guy that bad? Does he work for the Unseeley?" I asked, taking care to think of the questions slowly, otherwise I was just going to spew a word salad over Riz.

"Nah, dat's der thin, he's der first Fae in ages ta not be part of eitha Council. He's a propa bastard."

Riz had finished off the cheese and was looking for other food, so I gave him some biscuits from the barrel.

Between huge mouthfuls of rich tea biscuits, he continued. "He wants ta force humans ta worship der Fae, nd his brite idea ta do dat? Make yer scared of dem, so he's gunna kill a bunch of ya."

"What? What kind of stupid thinking is that? Why doesn't he just reveal himself? No one can deny physical proof like that!"

"One…" Riz held up one of his fingers to help his point. "Yer humans're stupid creatures nd wud happily explain der ghost of yer motha away if it kept yer sane." He then held up another finger. "Two, cuz he thinks dat even if he did dat, dere still wudn't be enuff dat wud believe in im. He thinks it's far easier nd moar effective if he jus performs sum, er, population control. Well, dat's wat he sayz neway. I think he's a psycho who's deluded imself." Riz was just pouring all of this information out so nonchalantly that it was scary. This was all normal for him... mundane.

"But why does he want to do that! Did someone stand on him or something?" Yes, at that point I assumed fairies were small creatures, like how they were often portrayed in movies or kids' cartoons. I hadn't read much folklore back then.

"Fae are bigger den yer think, ejit. Dey live in anotha dimension, one dat der experts call der 'Other' world. It's a borin place nowadays, used ta be a lot betta. Now dere's rules fer everythin! I ate goin dere."

I regretted then saying that I wanted to know everything, as by this point, I felt I knew nothing at all, even after he'd started talking, and the information wasn't sticking in my head. It was my fault, I should have asked for the explanation in the daylight hours, when I was more awake, and had more time to process that little encounter on the field.

"So, you told me about fairies."

"Or yer can call dem Fae, eitha's gud," Riz corrected me.

"Whatever. You told me about goblins, and about this Faine?"

"Oh! So yer're gettin it! Dere waz me thinkin I waz jus wastin my time wit yer."

"Why would they send you to fight this guy? Don't they have their own people?"

Looking at him, Riz was a rat, so he didn't look at all like a fighter. He had those spells, I suppose, but on his own, what good would he be? I don't take any pleasure in how wrong was I about this little furball. Even now, I don't know the half of what Riz is capable of but what I do know is if I sent myself back to me in that conversation, I wouldn't have asked that question, that's for sure.

"Cuz I'm der only one who can beat dis twat, dere own guys cudn't catch a cold if I sneezed on dem. Yer wudn't know of course, cuz yer a poor sod, but I'm big business! I handed Faine's ass ta him bout a hundred years ago, wen he hit up London wit dat Jack who yer jus met."

Jack? London? A hundred years ago? I made the connection

before I even thought about it in detail. What Riz was hinting here was that I had just exchanged a few words with the infamous serial killer, Jack the Ripper. That explained the top hat.

"Jack. The Ripper. Jack the Ripper Jack, that Jack?" My lip started trembling as the goblin came back to the forefront of my mind. Those knife fingers, and that way he killed his own friend… all traits you'd expect him to have.

"Yup, Jack der Rippa, yer know he started out as Spring Heeled Jack? Went round scarin people while Faine tweaked im. All der over Spring Heels, like der ones we fought earlier, were based offa him."

"Then why didn't he leap in to attack us after I used that shield thing."

"Cuz I hurt im!" Riz puffed out his chest, proud of what he was talking about. "Couple of days ago, we'd fought nd I used a Blast Rune ta blow his legs off. Faine replaced dem wit normal ones. Jack waz dere dis afternoon when I found yer bag. Lucky he didn't go afta yer nd yer friend."

Riz was right there. Merrick and I wouldn't have survived that encounter, though I wouldn't have minded if Darren and his mates had met Jack.

"We heard the springs, but we just didn't talk about it. I guess we got lucky."

"Aye, yer did," Riz rubbed his whiskers, the look that nowadays meant that his depraved, disturbed little mind was cooking up a scheme. "Let's hope dat luck sticks wit us as we go afta dem."

"Excuse me, we?"

I did a double take and I thought I'd misheard him. The rat, who I just met, was now wanting me to help him kill Jack the Ripper. Just going over that part again, seventeen years on, that still sticks in my throat. "Can't you call on the Seeley to help?"

Riz burst out laughing at such a ridiculous volume, that I thought he was going to wake my parents.

I shushed him.

"Don't shush me," he said. "But nah, we can't rely on dose twits, Dey barge in nd make a bigga mess, dat's y I came back ere alone, ta handle it ma way. Cuz I'm smart nd brave like dat. Normally, I wudn't botha askin fer yer help, yer look as much use as a teddy. I'm gunna cut yer a deal tho and let yer help me in wat I gotta do."

"This doesn't sound safe…"

"Safe? Nuthin is safe, kid, yer world cud end any second, of every day. Yer gotta live fer the moment! In dis moment, I need yer help ta deal wit a git of a Fae nd his murderin lackey!"

"Is this supposed to be a selling point?"

"Let me put it did way, wat choice yer got? Jack saw yer, he saw yer wit me, nd he likes wastin people like yerself. Yer don't help me, yer ded, yer help me, yer mite not die!"

"That's not an argument!"

"It wazn't an argument, it waz a fact, nd facts don't care. Face it, kid, yer involved now, like or not. Best way out of it is fer yer ta help me fer der time being!"

"Wait a moment, isn't this your fault in the first place for hiding in my bag? Those Spring Heels followed you!"

Riz rolled his eyes so hard that I swear I heard it clear as day. He let out a sigh, a forced sigh at that, as though he'd rehearsed this conversation already.

"Wazn't it yer fault dat yer bag waz dere in der first place? Coincidences do happen, yer know," Riz yawned. "Not like I planned thins ta go like dis, otherwise it wud ave gone far betta so I wudn't need yer help."

It seemed that the conversation was on the wane, and that I wasn't going to get any more details about how he came to be in my bag. Riz, oblivious, or probably not caring about my concerns, climbed the fridge, pushing it open.

"Got nuthin ta say ta dat den?" he asked, rummaging around, before reappearing with two cans of lager. You'll probably all have that as a mental image, and wondering how he managed it, but let me assure you, it's a sight you would never forget.

Still, I couldn't find the words to argue with what he said, none of it was what I wanted to hear. Riz basically admitted to fucking up my life. His act of survival changed my life, and doomed it, if you want to be cynical. Back then, I was angry but I also felt guilt over that anger. Now, I'm more or less at peace with this, probably helped by a few other things I've learned over the years, as well as some other things both me and Riz learned.

"Look at dis way, thru random chance we ended up togetha. Or yer can believe destiny nd dat shit, all der same thin ta me. Yer strike me as a kid who doesn't know wat dey want."

"What are you talking about?" I said in surprise at the shift in the conversation.

"Normal kids mite ave jus froze up at any point. Normal kids wud ave run at der sight of der Spring Heels. Yer did none of dat. Yer stayed wit me, yer listened to me. Wat waz it dat made yer stay? Y're yer still stood here? Yer cud ave went straight upstairs nd tried ta forget all of it." Riz necked one of the cans. "I mite be wrong, but I think yer got sumthin from doin it. Deep down yer enjoyed it didn't yer, dat rush yer got from der Rune, dat sense of danger."

"What are you trying to say?"

"Nuthin, jus dat if yer help me now, yer wud get dose feelings again, yer wud get ta prove ta yerself, nd everyone else dat yer matter. Let me train yer, nd wen Jack nd is friends come bak ta get us, we can get dem! Wudn't dat be sumthin ta remember? Yer wanna be prepared fer dat, don't yer?"

I remember being conflicted. He'd called it right, regarding how I felt, but I was still terrified. One wrong move, and it would be all over. That's a lot to put on a sixteen year old. That said though, I almost blurted out yes right then and there. Was I that desperate for a chance for my life to have meaning that I would throw my lot in with a talking rat? Look, you know how this is going to go, I'm telling you this story after all, but try and picture things as they were back then, not knowing how the future was going to turn out. I still debate whether I made the right choice, but that's the annoyance of hindsight.

"Do I have to answer now?" I asked.

Riz had just finished the second can. He shook his head. "Jus sleep on it. Wudn't start trainin yer rite now neway. I'm knackered." He bounced off the table and headed into the living room.

"Where do you think you're going?" I said, following him.

He went through the living room and then up the stairs to my room.

"Where do yer think I'm goin? I'm off ta bed. I needs ma beauty sleep."

The little git, without checking with me, took one of my pillows and dropped it to the floor, before jumping on it.

"Nite, kid," he said, shutting his eyes and instantly starting to snore.

Luckily for him, I was completely knackered so fell straight into an uneasy sleep.

CHAPTER 5
RUNES AND MORE MAGICAL LORE

My mother woke me up in the morning, at about nine, which was the usual at the weekend. Still half asleep, I looked down and was surprised and relieved to see only the pillow there, as though I'd knocked it off during my sleep.

"There's a cup of tea waiting for you downstairs. Don't let it go cold again," my mum said kindly, then she left me to sort myself out.

I lay back in bed and let out a sigh. Had it all been a dream after all? What do you think…?

"Wats fer breakfast?" Riz said, crawling out from under my bed. He went up to my bedside table so he could see me better. "Yer were moanin in yer sleep."

"I had very weird dreams. Do you know anything about it?"

My dreams were bizarre and terrible, yet each had a strange beauty about them. They were of far off vistas, with strange peculiar elements that were deeply unsettling in their intricate details. There were fluttering beings that shifted from humanoid-shaped with the most beautiful wings to lights with a haunting haze surrounding them. The sky… a mixture of colours that made a mockery of ours. Other locations appeared but these were far more alien and consisted of twisting ruins and entities that I couldn't grasp. The impression I got made me happy I couldn't see them. The thunderous language Riz had used earlier that night was the soundtrack to all this and reverberated in my bones. Of course, I explained all this to Riz, and his expression was one of remembrance.

"Oh yer saw all dat, did yer? Hah, interestin, wasn't expectin dat, othawise I wud ave slept in yer loft," he said like it was no big deal.

"You know what that was?" I asked, hiding my frustration.

"Yeh, don't worry, waz probs jus cause it waz yer first time dealin wit crap like dat, yer were sensitive. Yer know, like, psychic or yer get summit in yer blood."

"Will it happen again?"

"Maybe, maybe not, depends on how yer deal wit things. Anyway, breakfast time?" Riz replied, brushing aside my question with one based around eating. "Bring me back sumthin nice."

I knew I wasn't going to make any headway with that line of questioning, as apparently it wasn't a big deal in Riz's eyes. The dream thing did settle down the more Riz and I shared a room. But even now, it will flare up if something is bugging Riz. The images from those haunt me whenever I close my eyes, mixing in with all the shit I've seen. You get used to it... you have to.

I dragged myself up and got sorted... I hated going to breakfast in my pyjamas. As I went downstairs, I thought how crazy the situation was. In my room was a talking rat who I had helped fend off three goblins with springs and face down Jack the Ripper... And here I was, going to get him breakfast. This was a brave new world.

In the living room, my dad was sitting reading a book. I thought I could escape any comments but I must have creaked a floorboard because I hadn't entered the room fully when the book was lowered and my dad's gaze fell upon me. Was I in trouble? Had Riz been discovered? Were my parents awake during the fight last night? No, it was none of these things. My dad wanted to make a cheap joke at my expense. See, to my parents, I hadn't fainted, I had just fallen asleep on the floor like a child fighting back bedtime.

"Your mum called me upstairs when she found you. It's been about ten years since we last found you like that!" His tone was humorous, and I was thankful that I was spared a dad joke. "What did you do last night round Merrick's?" he asked, sounding curious but I also felt he may have been probing to see if me and Merrick had been doing anything else. We hadn't of course, and then, I would rather have him think I was drinking than know the truth.

"I was tired, been staying up too late these past few nights."

This wasn't a lie. I often stayed up later than I should have and still do now.

"Once you've started college, you'll have to start going to bed earlier. Not staying up late playing that computer of yours," my mum added as she came in from the kitchen, carrying hot drinks for her and my dad.

"I will, closer to then," I said as I went into the kitchen to get some food for myself, and for Riz. As I was preparing the food, I asked myself if I would be better off if they knew the truth, guilt beginning to gnaw away at me. I didn't like keeping secrets for this reason, yet here I was, with a secret so crazy that even if I told them they wouldn't believe me, yet if I had been a bit more confident, I might have been able to carry that. I was also terrified of what they would have said if they did find him, or if they learned about the attack of the goblins.

I quickly finished my cereal and turned my attention to what I could give Riz. I decided on a simple meal: toast. Nice, warm, buttery toast. My parents would think I was just hungry. Indeed, they didn't question it when I went back through the living room with the food. They only stopped me as I headed into the hallway.

"You're going back upstairs?" my mum asked. I suppose this was a break in my usual routine. Normally I would sit with them until we headed out or did whatever we were planning to do that day.

"Yeah, I'm looking for something in my books," I replied. It was the first thing that came out of my head. Although this just attracted more attention.

"What is it, like?"

Again, my parents knew me better than I thought, so anytime I would do anything out of the ordinary this would happen.

"Oh, it's just a story I was thinking about yesterday. Back

down soon!" With that, I hurried off, not wanting to drag out the interrogation any longer.

Riz had apparently spent the time I was gone making a mess on my bed. When I went in the room, he was sat on my pillow, next to an empty pouch and all those Runes strewn across the duvet. Some of them were grouped and there were eight in all. Only a few shared a symbol, and less shared a style that looked as though the symbol had been chewed out of the rock.

"Wat did yer brin me?" Riz asked without even looking at me.

I put the plate of toast down next to him, and before I could say anything, he dived on it. I waited for a thank you, but it proved pointless.

"Wat?" he asked as he put the final piece into his mouth.

"Didn't your parents teach you to say thank you?" I said, moving the now empty plate.

"Did yer parents teach yer ta talk ta rats?" he replied sarcastically. He went back to arranging the Runes, moving a couple to different groups, but without knowing anything about these things, it looked very pointless to me. I had wanted to talk to Riz about what we did now, I had an idea of what to do, but I wanted to run it by him first.

"Riz, I've got an idea on what to do next," I said as my eyes went over the Runes again, remembering the feeling when I first used them. I had an impulse to run my hand over the one nearest to me, to feel the symbol and the power I knew that was lurking in it, but Riz nudged my hand aside.

"Finish yer sentences!" he said, snapping me back to the room.

I took a step back from the Runes and cleared my throat.

"I think we should bring my friend Merrick in."

The sentence had an unusual effect on Riz... he looked like he was trying to hold back a sly smile. He coughed out of it, and started needling me for more details.

"Y wud we wanna do dat?" Riz asked, tilting his head as he looked up at me, making me feel even more nervous.

"I think, I mean, I think it would be best," I mumbled. I knew what I wanted to say but I wasn't getting the words out. I stopped and calmed myself. "What I mean to say is I think it would be best if I let my friend Merrick know what's going on. More help would be good right?"

"Well, I'm not gunna say no ta more help. More hands make lighta work nd all dat crap, yer sure he can handle der truth? Wudn't want im ta go crazy jus cuz I sed hello afta all."

"I don't know, but he'll listen to me, and I know if there's a way he can help me, he'll do it." If you're thinking I'm giving Merrick too much credit, then you're both wrong and right. When it came to me, he did give it his all to help, but for others, he did it for appearances sake.

"Rite, wen we gonna see did kid den?"

"We'll go round his this afternoon to talk about it."

"Gud, now we can get down ta sum learnin," he said, as he moved the piles of Runes closer together. "Shut dat door."

Door closed, I went back and sat on the floor so I could see what Riz was doing.

"So, der first lesson is an important one, it's bout dese." Riz waved his paw over the gathered Runes. "Yer remember wat dey're called, don't yer?"

"Runes?" I felt the urge to touch one again, and I reached out slowly, feeling drawn to one of the ones closest to Riz. He watched me closely, till I was about a hair's breadth away. Then the little git bit me. I pulled my hand back sharply.

"Keep yer hands ta yerself wen I'm talkin! Do yer know wat damage yer can do wit dese if yer don't use dem properly?" He straightened the Runes out. "Rite, let's begin wit der basic of der basics…"

What followed was the first lesson Riz ever gave me about Runes.

This lecture set the mood for all the rest that would follow in our time together. I suppose Riz found it easier to teach me like I was a five-year-old who needed everything spelling out.

"Runes're concentrated magic." The way he said 'concentrated' he stretched out each syllable, I think to make a point. "Der effect all depends on wat der symbol is." He tapped on the carved symbol on the Rune, and as he did, there was a pale colour, sort of like mist caught in the first light of dawn, that sparked out of it and into the gaps between his claws. "Dis one is a Light Rune… wen used, it creates a ball of lite. Useful fer dark places."

I counted five different symbols amongst the eight, and now I knew what two of them did at least.

"So where do you get them from and what makes them magic? Is it the stone? Or that symbol? Or is the tool that you use to carve the symbol."

I unleashed a barrage of questions, so quick that Riz was a bit overwhelmed at first. In fact, I suspect he had hoped that he wouldn't have to go further than that.

"One bleedin question at a time, yer jackass! Jeez, I can't answer all dat at once!" Riz stretched out, and I think he was going through the questions, looking for the easiest to answer first. "Der magic comes from der symbol, dere jus ordinary stones othawise, well dese wud be anyway. I crafted dese ones myself cuz I waz in a rush nd ad no cash ta get betta materials."

To clarify, these were just stones he had picked up from the ground and put the symbol on. How? I hear you ask. Riz covered that next.

"As fer der symbol, yer jus need sumthin sharp ta do der cuttin. I've got dese thins so I'm set." He touched his front teeth with his claws.

"You use your teeth to bite into rocks to turn them into Runes?" I asked, just wanting to make sure I hadn't missed anything so far.

"Yeh, how else wud I do it? Gud ta see yer gettin it so far tho, wud hate ta ave ta start ova. Neway, der Runes are only active once der symbol is on dere. It draws in dere power, nd boom! Yer got yerself a Rune. Wait. No, I'm missin sumthin. Wat waz it."

For reference's sake, this 'sumthin', he'd done as recently as the previous morning before he encountered Jack the Ripper at the beck and cowered in my bag. Turns out that this 'sumthin' was very important.

"Ah dat's it! Yer need ta direct der magical energy inta it, wit a ritual or yer jus got a fancy stone. Mite make a nice paperweight, but yer certainly wudn't take it on a job wit yer."

"Where does the energy come from?" I asked. I remember this being the only part so far that caused me to raise my eyebrow. Yes, I had a high tolerance for weird.

"Der air, yer ejit, sum of yer cultures call it chi, mana but most of der 'Others', especially der Fae, dey call it Aether. It generates itself by sum by-product but I leave dat stuff ta der researchers nd alchemists. As long as it's dere, I get ma Runes, so we're all gud."

That was the most technical I had heard him at that point, showing that there was far more knowledge lurking in his brain, far more than you would think given his appearance.

"So was it the fairies who first created Runes then? And did they give it to us?"

"Ha! Fae creatin Runes, oh dat is funny! No, yer freckin ejit. Fae were given der Runes, nd den dey passed it around cuz, dey're stupid morons who believed in unity nd other crap. Dey gave it ta der druids as well," Riz wiped the tears away from his eyes, after having rolled around laughing at my supposed stupidity.

I sat down and pondered what he'd said, wondering what it all meant for the world that I had taken for granted. In truth I was starting to get a headache again from thinking about all this.

"Wait, how many different groups did they give Runes to?"

"Lots, I don't know der full amount, I've neva been bothered ta learn dat. I mean, doesn't make much difference now, does it?"

He had a point, but it wasn't a great one. Learning more about the past is always worthwhile. I sort of still hold this belief, but events have tested it. I mean, clearly, some information should have stayed hidden, or should have been destroyed completely.

"So who was it that taught the Fae the Runes?"

"Yer can ask dem but dey don't share crap like dat." Riz said, turning his attention back to the Runes.

From what he said earlier, I'd assumed that the fairies were at the top of the food chain. To learn there was something above them scared me. I've since learned that fear was the right emotion. There's a lot out there, and almost none of it gives a crap about us. I know it's a worn out comparison, especially in this context, but we're ants to them, even less than that. It was just lucky that I never encountered them in the early days, otherwise I wouldn't be here now.

"Do you know much about them?"

"Bout who?"

"The ones who taught the fairies?"

When I asked that, Riz's demeanour changed just like the previous night, and I could see in his eyes how serious he was. "Just drop it, alrite?"

He worded it like a question, but I knew the intent, plus the way he said it… I had quickly worked out that he shortened words down and that was his personal thing, adding to his accent. Yet when he said that, he sounded the words out properly, and the accent was gone. In its place was a tone akin to that language I heard him use, that sounded terrible and ancient. The moment passed though, and Riz was back to his usual self, acting like it had never happened.

"While der Fae didn't invent Runes, dey did convert a few inta a special type of Rune. Der Eternal Runes."

"What's so special about the Eternal Runes?" I was thankful that Riz had changed the topic so quickly, for both our sakes.

"Yer remember der Rune I got yer ta use last nite? Nd how once yer used it, it jus broke apart in yer hand? Not all Runes get used up like dat. Sum work fer a while before dey break down, like der Healin Runes."

Riz hopped over to the other end of his Rune collection, bringing my attention to two Runes that shared the same symbol, except that on closer inspection, I saw that one of the symbols looked incredibly worn away, with cracks slithering away from the edges.

"Dis Rune ere as bout one gud use left in it, while dis one, which I've neva used, haz three ta four uses dependin on how yer use it."

"How you use it? There's multiple ways to use these things? This is a lot for me to take in."

I had forgotten that I needed to use an activation word with these as well, just to complicate matters.

"If yer gud, yer can Rune Craft dem, changin one effect inta anotha, nd changin der type dat a Rune can affect. Course, changin der Rune from a multi-use one ta anotha makes it weaker. Yer also ave ta be careful wen yer changin thins mind. One screw up nd yer can kiss yer ass gudbye." Riz made the hand movements to simulate an explosion.

The implication was clear and I learned a very valid point: do not mess around with these. So far during the course of this lesson, I had been surprised that Riz hadn't just listed the types of Runes and what they did. It seemed like an obvious thing to start with, but no, instead we had the history lesson. Admittedly this was important, learning about the race that gifted Runes to fairies and how they worked. It left me with more questions, and I still wanted to know what other things were out there, lurking in unseen places.

"What about other things out there?" I asked, hoping to fill in a bit more of the blanks.

"Der's all sorts out dere. Not jus gobs nd Fae. Yer got yer water ghouls, yer ghosts. Oh, nd yer dragons, of course," Riz said as he put the Runes away.

Apparently that was the end of that lesson, but that was just the first of many. Then my mind snapped back to what Riz had just said, about dragons.

"Urm. Did you just say dragons?"

"Yeh, wat bout it," he said, like it was nothing at all, typical Riz.

"Like fire breathing dragons?"

"Yeh, oh nd wurms, n wryvens, n wyrms of course."

"I don't… I don't know what they are."

"Yer don't need ta worry bout all dat, Faine is der focus, nd he's jus a Fae."

At that moment, my mum started playing her violin, and the atmosphere in the house changed instantly, a warm feeling spread into my room, carried by the notes.

I saw Riz's ears pick up instantly, his eyes enlarging.

"Who is playin dis… music?" he asked. He mumbled something else but I didn't hear it. I never pressed it, as my own will to speak was subtly repressed. It wasn't a sinister feeling at all, but one of comfort. God knows what Riz was feeling. He stood there with his little mouth hanging open.

I looked down at my watch, realising that time had passed us by. Merrick would have been awake by now. It's not that I didn't enjoy learning all I did, but Riz threw everything at me, seemingly not caring if I was going to take it in or not.

"Merrick should be up now," I told Riz, and he lit up with that sinister smile again, snapping out of whatever tranquillity he'd been enjoying.

"Let's go den."

CHAPTER 6
YES, MERRICK, HE'S A TALKING RAT

"Yer want me ta get in dat?" Riz stared at me as I held my coat out, pocket open ready for him to climb in.

"Well, you can't travel on my shoulder, can you?" I replied. "It would be weird to go out with my school bag now that school is finished."

I saw him look at the pocket again with resignation. He wasn't happy about my plan but couldn't think of anything better so he had no choice. He waited till I had my coat on before hopping in. The weight hit me just as quick.

"Why are you so heavy?"

The little twat bit me in response. Riz has always been very touchy about his weight. So there I was, in the summer, wearing my big coat, with the sun bearing down outside. Worst thing was, this was normal for me. I always had this thing about covering myself up, something that has relaxed as the years have gone by, but then I had this anxiety of people seeing my bare arms. I think it may have been because of how thin I was, a feature that always drew comments from onlookers, who gasped in astonishment that they could put their whole hands around my wrists with ease. I've never been stocky.

We went downstairs and I popped my head round the living room door, telling my parents where I was going, as was customary.

"You don't need a coat on in this weather," my dad said, as usual.

"I've told you, I feel more comfortable with it on," I said as I squirmed, getting a nudge from Riz for my troubles.

"Stop it! Yer shakin me around, yer daft bastard!" my passenger complained in a low moan.

"What was that?" my dad said in confusion. He moved to get out of the chair but I moved closer to the front door.

"Oh, it was nothing! Nothing at all!" I opened the door, turning back to see the puzzled looks I got.

"Bren, are you alright?" my mum asked, joining my dad in bewilderment.

"Yup, I'm just heading to Merrick's. Be back before tea!" With a smile, and sweating profusely from the heat and stress, I bolted from the house, letting the door shut itself.

I turned down the cut right by the side of the house, the same one I had run down the previous night, coming onto the same field. In the light of day, it looked completely different, but I could still make out the point where the Spring Heels had fallen into the earth.

Merrick lived about a fifteen minute walk away, and it could be a nice walk to his house, as long as the way was clear. Luckily, that day was a clear one. What didn't help however was that feeling of being watched.

Riz confirmed it.

"It's jus a watcher. Faine isn't goin ta let us go like dat, but don't worry, dat thin won't be a threat," he said, peering out of my pocket.

"A watcher? Is that another fairy?" I said nervously. Fearing being ambushed, I stuck to the roads instead of taking my usual short cut through Village Park.

"Yeh, think of dem like will o' wisp. Not exactly der same, but close enuff. Faine makes dem do grunt work. Jobs like dis, fer example. Dey don't ave any way ta attack us, even if it bloody charged us, it wud jus pass thru us. We're perfectly safe, plus it'll be scared shitless of me."

"They are afraid of you?" I said, wishing the street wasn't so quiet. I'd have settled for the kids playing football between cars right then.

"Yup, damn rite ta be as well. Everythin shud fear me, I'm der toughest thin dere is!"

I didn't voice my concern then, but I did wonder if I should have been afraid. The answer to that is mixed. I can look at some things and say with absolute certainty that Riz is something to be afraid of, then other times I see him huddled in his drawer, reading those romance novels, writing what could be charitably called stories, and shrug.

We came to Merrick's gate and I spotted the rest of his family getting in the car. This was perfect timing. While I was prepared to have to try and tell Merrick without him making too much racket, now I was free to tell him and let him make as much noise as he wanted. Also no one would notice if he passed out like I had.

"Oh Brennan! You here to see Merrick? He's just waking up." Merrick's dad was a plain sort, almost nothing like his son except for vague resemblance. "Here, I'll let you in the house."

"Yer got der perfect shtick wit dem aven't yer! Shame yer such a goody two shoes or yer cud rob dem blind." Riz whispered.

I just smiled as the front door was unlocked for me.

"I'm a good person," I whispered back.

"Make sure he has a shower, will you?" Merrick's dad said as he got back in the car.

I watched them drive off before I went into the house. It was there in the hallway where I thought about what I was actually going to say. How did you tell someone that you had met a talking rat? Tell them that you had been chased by goblins?

"Let me talk ta im," Riz suggested, as if I was going to be that stupid to just let him do all the talking.

Thankfully, I knew Merrick wouldn't hear any of this, as he tended to sleep like the dead.

"No! He's my friend, so I'll be the one to tell him. It's only right."

"From wat I've heard he seems like he's yer only friend. Don't yer ave any othas?"

Sad answer incoming… many of you would have seen it coming. In fact, I have already told you that.

"No."

"Wat a surprise, anyway, kick dat door down, nd let's get talkin wit im. We're wastin gud trainin time ere."

I climbed the stairs and crossed the landing, arriving at Merrick's door, which like normal, was shut. I wondered how best to wake him, and what state I would find him in. There was one time I found him asleep on the floor, having woken up and then just crashed again.

"He's sayin sumthin," Riz pointed out, sticking his head from the pocket and staring at the door.

I pressed my head against the door. Straining, I was able to make out Merrick's voice, just short bursts. This wasn't new to me as I had slept over numerous times. I hadn't paid any of it any heed then, though really I should have. See, those first times, I had never really heard what he was saying, just that he was saying it. Here though, it was crystal clear, as was the fear and terror in his voice.

"No! I'm… I'm not Adam." Then came a lot more mumbling and words with syllables I will never be able to understand. Then he lowered his voice, before shouting, "NO! IT WASN'T ME! WHY? EVERY TIME! I HATE YOU!" That last part, that fear I mentioned before, it had turned instantly to hatred.

I went to go in there but Riz bit me.

"Yer can't go in dere wen he's goin on like dat! Did no one eva tell yer not ta wake sumeone up wen dey're talkin in der sleep." Riz put his paw to his mouth as though he was deep in thought. "Yer knew he did dis?" he asked me. I assumed he was trying to gauge how much I knew.

"I didn't think it was an issue, to be fair," I replied, waiting for the moment that I could go into the room. It had gone quiet again, but there was some slight murmuring that softened further.

"Yer shud be gud ta go now."

I steadied myself and knocked on the door, then I knocked again, and again. That time, I got a response.

"I'm… I'm up!" Then I heard the sound of feet hitting the floor, and the bedroom door opened. Merrick greeted me, thankfully in his pyjamas. The face he wore though… it was one of those rare times where you saw the real him, and especially after that little outburst of his, it was haunting. Those eyes that radiated death, not outwardly, but inside. Merrick spent his life up to now living personas to fit in with what other people wanted. Figuring out the real him was like solving a puzzle, blindfolded and having to do it with your tongue. As soon as he registered it was me though, the mask went on, the eyes switched to kinder jewels, covering up the holes in his soul. If you would believe it, this was worse when we first met. He admitted one time, during those bare-your-soul sleepover conversations, that I was the calming influence on him, that things were tolerable when I was around, making my useless jokes.

"Bren? What are you doing here? You normally ring first." He returned to his bed and sat down, allowing himself to wake up fully. "Plus we weren't supposed to be doing anything today, I…" He stopped mid-sentence to yawn. "I might have been doing anything."

"I had to come and see you." I took a deep breath. "Something happened last night."

"Look, those dreams are completely normal. Things will get better once we get you a girl," Merrick said, brushing off my first attempt to get this reveal off the ground.

"No, nothing like that." I went all out with the second attempt. "Last night I was attacked at home by goblins with springs attached to their feet!" The sheer craziness of how this sounded would get him to take notice of me, and by the look on his face, it worked.

"Dude, what the actual fuck are you talking about?"

"I've got proof, as I also met someone last night, who helped me survive that encounter."

No turning back now… this was the moment of truth. I didn't leave Merrick any chance to speak and his eyes widened when I pulled Riz out.

"What are you doing with a rat in your pocket! You just carrying it around for a walk? What the hell, man?"

"This isn't a normal rat, Merrick! He crawled into my bag yesterday when we were at the beck." I brought Riz closer to him, and in return, he leaned back.

"Get that vermin away from me! I hate rats!" He tried to push me aside, but Riz bit him. "See! Fuck off out of here with that stupid thing!"

"Yer stupid git! I'm not vermin! Nd I'll do more den bite yer if yer keep talkin ta me like dat!" Riz shouted out.

What happened next was quite hilarious, because it didn't happen to me. Merrick pointed at him, looked at me, and then back at Riz, before toppling backwards onto his bed. He should have counted himself lucky, he at least landed on something soft.

"Nd yer didn't want me talkin ta im, y?" Riz asked as he jumped out of my hands and onto Merrick's bed. He started prodding him. From the angle I was looking, I think Riz might have been smiling again. Something about this clearly amused him.

"That could have gone better." Actually, I said that, but really, it went as it always would have. It took Merrick half an hour to come round, during which time Riz explored all his drawers and wardrobe.

With a groan, Merrick sat himself back up again, and remembered what had just happened. He ignored me and fixated on Riz with a mix of bewilderment and horror.

"The rat. The rat spoke," he stammered, as he backed up to the far corner of his bed.

"He's not dangerous. He's a good guy. He more or less saved my life," I said.

"More or less?" Riz asked, not caring at all how Merrick was adapting. "Try: I wudn't be alive at all unless Riz waz dere to save me."

"Now isn't the time for all this!" I snapped back.

"Why is the rat talking? What is going on?"

Any illusion that I had of Merrick being this cool, streetwise person had been broken and the remains trod on repeatedly by this encounter.

"I'll try to explain it best I can if you just calm down first." So I gave all the details this time, sparing nothing.

"You were attacked by people with springs on their feet?" Merrick asked, picking on the most random element to question.

"No, we wer attacked by gobs wit springs in dere smeggin feet," Riz said, his impatience dripped from his words.

"Gobs?" My friend asked, this was turning into a bit of a loop.

"Yeh, goblins. Yer know, little creatures, sum of dem can be really nasty."

"Do you even know what you sound like? Do you honestly expect me to believe all this!"

Merrick was trembling. I knew Riz had doubts about this, but now I was seriously doubting myself for suggesting this. Through my plan, I had broken my best friend. Now I look back and half laugh, and half wonder how much I was to blame for all that followed.

"Uh, I have a talking rat with me? Do you think I would fake that?" I asked and he shook his head.

"Am I high right now? What the hell, Bren? You turn up and just drop all this shit on me! Why?"

He really was freaking out over this, as perhaps most normal people would, when faced with a talking rat.

"Listen up, butta cup! Ma name is Riz, nd yeh, I'm a talkin rat. I'm not yer mind playin soddin tricks, I'm not a freakin puppet. Bren hasn't got his hand up ma arse."

I lifted both my hands up at this point to confirm it.

"Yer in on dis secret now, so deal wit it!"

Merrick sat on his bed, and rubbed his hands over his face and through his hair.

"This, this is insane. Why did you bring him here?"

"B-because…" I froze, all my reasoning about why it was important to bring Merrick in on the secret was gone. Like being in the spotlight and getting stage fright.

"He brought me ere, ta get yer ta help us! Nd I'm prepared ta make it very much worth yer while, if yer know wat I'm sayin." Riz winked at Merrick, in the universal language of you scratch my back, I'll scratch yours. This line of thinking has gotten me in a lot of trouble over the years as Riz had a history of not following up with these. Guess who has to deal with the fallout.

"What are you offering? Exactly?" Merrick said, clearly interested to hear. His voice wasn't back to its normal tone, but it was getting there.

"Depends on wat yer really want. Fer der trouble of helpin me wit Faine nd Jack."

"Jack?" Merrick said, interrupting the rat, whose eye started twitching.

"Yeh, Jack der Ripper, interrupt ma again, nd I'll bite yer, already bit dis ejit fer less!" Riz pointed at me.

"Jack the Ripper? Why not! Anyone else to bring in this on this chaos? There is nothing you can offer me that will make this better!"

"Oh I can offa yer summit gud alrite, yer want treasure nd shit. Or I can do summit even betta, like how bout bein taught ta use magic? Eh? Dat get yer interest? A little bit of magic ta keep yer crazy dreams away?" Riz got closer to Merrick, wanting to tempt him further.

I was a little bit put out about how the rat was wording things here. He made it seem that I was getting taught as a practicality in dealing with Faine and his lackeys. It was getting spun to Merrick as one of the finest rewards you could ever hope to get. I wasn't about to question him on this here, not when, methods, aside we needed Merrick.

"Magic, eh? Well I was just wondering about what we can do with a talking animal, all those TV shows we could hit, but magic? The power to do whatever I want?"

It was Riz's turn to interrupt Merrick, returning the favour from earlier.

"Yer don't think I wud ave already tried der TV circuit? Gud grief yer got no imagination!"

Merrick glared at Riz, but I gave him my best, 'please' look. His face softened, and his anger seemingly diffusing.

"Right, how about this, you give me a few minutes to talk it over with Brennan, in private, okay?" Merrick sighed.

Riz nodded, somewhat respectfully.

"Yer want sum time ta waste before yer accept ma gracious offer. Dat's cool, yer try ta learn magic off sum 'Other' loser nd it wud cost yer an arm nd a leg."

You might think that Riz is talking about the financial cost of learning magic from anyone else, and you'd be right. However, he's also being literal, as some of the magic users we've had to face down could testify. Riz then left the room, but as I knew, and I think Merrick knew, Riz was a rodent with big ears. Even whispering, he was going to know what we were talking about.

"Okay, Bren, first things first, this is completely batshit insane. I don't think I'm ever going to be completely okay with this, as you know, he's a talking rat."

Merrick did make a brilliant point.

"I'm not exactly thrilled with this but, you know what they say about once in a lifetime chances," I said, coming off meek.

"Well, that was going to be my second point, yes, this is insane. However, learning magic, now that..." Merrick put his hands together as he spoke, his pointing fingers resting against his nose as he thought. A smile crept over his face, one that looked a little less then stable. "That I can work with. Making money off the talking rodent would have been a passable option, but the ability to make all my problems disappear? Who wouldn't take that, especially with proof walking about!"

A switch had been flipped in my best friend, one that I was familiar with. This occurred when he got a new idea that he thought was the bee's knees, rewriting whatever apprehension he previously felt. He would throw himself at this with reckless abandon if it brought him closer to accomplishing it. He looked even more enthusiastic with this cause than I did.

"What do you want to use magic for then?"

At the time, I thought this was an innocent question. Magic

48

had been the catalyst for his decision regarding Riz, so it made sense to ask.

"To get what I want. Isn't that why anybody does anything?" A little bit of Merrick's other side peeked through, his eyes giving off the stare that I usually got if I talked to anyone else, or if anyone had the audacity to show me kindness. It was rare that I got that vibe during normal conversations though. If you could call this a normal conversation.

"W-well, what I m-meant was…" I started stuttering due to nerves. I couldn't think of a better response to that statement.

"I told you before, I can't understand you when you stutter," Merrick replied, flicking his hair out of his face. "It doesn't matter, does it?"

Merrick was back to his jokey tone.

"You said you fought these goblins before, didn't you? What's our chance of making it out of this alive? I mean, what's the point of learning magic if you're going to end up dead?" he said. I had to really think about this. I could have lied through my teeth and said it would be a cakewalk, but Merrick was good at catching me out. Made playing the card game cheat difficult. If I told him that we'd be lucky to make it out alive, then he would do what every sensible person would do and tell us to get lost. Wasn't a win-win situation for me.

"Well, I came out alive?"

This was the best take I could give on it. I wasn't lying, was I? Merrick looked me over for a second, and I could see the gears in his head cranking over.

"If you survived, then it shouldn't be a problem for me, if we leave the leader of whoever it is we're fighting to the rat. Fine, I'm in, but only because you are, and for us to learn magic." He put his arm around me. "When we learn all the magic the rat can teach, we're going to be unstoppable!"

"Ain't dat easy, mate," Riz said, pushing the door open again. He'd obviously heard the good news and came in to confirm it. Both him and Merrick were wearing the same smile, and it was downright creepy.

"Perfect timing, Roz, was it?" Merrick said, trying one of his oldest jokes on Riz, who fake laughed it off.

"Sorry, I thought der kid told me yer were gud at jokes, not seein dat wit tricks as old as I am," Riz gave a subdued reply. Had I tried that nowadays, he would have straight out bit me. Heck, I don't even have to make a joke and the little twerp bites me.

"I'm all in anyway, rat. As long as you give the magic training, that is," Merrick announced. I felt a tension between the two of them, a clash of egos forming already. What was the worst that could happen?

"Yer want der trainin? Well, yer in luck, cuz it starts now, poncey boy. Go get yerself sorted!"

Merrick smiled smugly, then headed out to the bathroom, leaving me and Riz, who winked at me.

"Yer can try nd appeal ta der betta nature all yer want, kid, but no one can resist learnin magic!"

CHAPTER 7
RUNE TRAINING FOR BEGINNERS

Once Merrick was dressed, Riz was ready to explain the next step.

"Alrite, now we got all dat talkin out der way, nd yer both ready fer dis, let's get ta der fun stuff. We need ta get sumwhere wit lots of space, nd I wud prefer it if it waz quiet."

"The beck where you climbed in my bag might do, unless you don't want to go there in case the Spring Heels turn up again," I suggested.

"I told yer earlier, dey won't be quick in comin back, not till Faine made more of dem, nd Jack is goin ta be choosin his moment, so I'm not worried bout dem. Dat place will do fine."

"What you going to be teaching us then?" Merrick asked.

"I'm gunna teach yer how ta pull a rabbit outta yer hat. You're gonna be fightin, fer cryin out loud! Wat do yer think I'm gonna teach yer? Yer first lesson, is gonna be how ta blew shit up. Alwayz a crowd pleaser," Riz said, almost a little too happy with his own speech.

"This is going to be better than I thought!" Merrick joined him with glee. I felt out of place in that moment. Blowing things up is kind of fun, especially if you want to relieve some stress, but I never got the same amount of joy in it as Riz. I preferred building things, not ending them. Unless there was no other choice of course, or if it was called for, I mean, we all have those lines that shouldn't be crossed.

"Yer kidz ready?" Riz asked, causing me and Merrick to nod

like those dog ornaments you could buy for cars. "Den let's get goin, boyz!"

The trip to the beck was uneventful. I discovered that you quickly get used to the feeling of being watched. You could still tell of course but it loses all its unnerving power. Merrick and me walked side by side, neither of us talking about what we clearly wanted to talk about. In between, I was also having a little discussion with Riz, talking in hushed whispers so people didn't think I was crazy talking to my coat.

"Don't yer get bored livin ere?" Riz asked, sticking his head out. "Dere's nuthin ere!"

This was his observation about Thornaby, and though we had only walked up Thornaby Road so far, it was an accurate one.

"I don't go out a lot. Well, not on my own. I only go to school, or Merrick's house. If I'm with him, I go wherever he wants. Otherwise I stay at home, where I'm safe."

"First off, yer give im too much control, secondly dat's even more borin! Dere's a whole world out dere. Several, in fact."

"Yeah, those worlds are filled with things that want to hurt me or outright kill me."

"Heh, we'll see wat yer think once I'm through wit yer trainin."

I imagined him rubbing his paws together at that point.

The beck was nice and quiet, just as we'd hoped for, and Riz jumped out from my pocket and began scavenging rocks.

"What's he doing?" Merrick asked.

Remembering what Riz had already told me, I knew he was gathering up the stones to turn into Runes for our training. Of course, Merrick knew none of it. Riz came back over to us, carrying an impressive ten palm-sized stones of varying degrees of quality.

"Rite, our first lesson in Rune magic, how ta make thins go boom!" Riz started biting the stones, using his teeth to grind and cut away at the centre of them.

"I'm confused already," Merrick said as he bent forward to see what Riz was doing. He had gotten too close though. Riz jumped at his face and caused him to fall backwards.

"Don't yer know wat personal space is? Wait till I'm ready!"

He got back to work while Merrick picked himself up.

"Dese are makeshift Runes, I let yers loose on der proper ones nd yer mite kill yerselves, wudn't want dat. Dese ones're lightly powered so yer get a bang but dats it."

"So you use these things to do magic? Beats a wand, I suppose," Merrick said, although I didn't know if he was disappointed that he wasn't using a wand.

"A wand? Dis is Rune magic yer ejit, wat wud yer be usin a wand fer? If yer not takin dis seriously, yer can piss off."

Riz joked about it here, but we have met people who used wands as part of their magic. Fighting someone like that is, different, let me tell you.

"Kay, Bren, yer already got a chance ta use Runes last nite but dat waz wit me guidin yer. Dat won't happen next time, yer gotta be ready ta use dis on yer own. Nd as fer u," Riz turned to my erstwhile friend. "Dis is all new, so yer get ta experience yer first touch wit der Rune. Sum people can't handle dem."

"I'm not afraid!" Merrick said, puffing out his chest, making himself appear braver in a comedic fashion.

I was also eager to hold a Rune again, my hands twitching while I remembered the rush of feelings that made me bolder and that electricity that went through my body, all starting at the Rune in my hand.

"Yer first, kid." Riz chucked one of the Runes my way, but Merrick sidestepped in front of me and caught it.

"He's already tried one of these. I think I should go first."

He clenched the fist that had the Rune in it and there was a visible arc of lightning that ran from his hand and up his arm and shoulder. He wasn't put off by that, while I had reservations. Riz on the other hand laughed it off.

"How are you feeling?" I asked Merrick, who was staring into space.

He looked fine especially once the lightning died down. He looked better than that in fact.

"Yer enjoy dat den?" Riz echoed my question, but he was less concerned, and acting more like the friend who was egging someone on,

"I like this. So, rat, how do I make this thing pop?" Merrick was acting more arrogant than usual.

"Cuz yer new ta dis, like im last nite, I'm teachin yer the Breton language mode, it's a gud compromise fer dese. Der word fer dese is Tarzhadem, nice nd simple."

"Let's do this!" Merrick posed with the Rune out in front of him as he yelled the word, "Tarzhadem!" The symbol in the heart of the Rune glowed and then it burst apart with all the fury of a shook-up bottle of lemonade. Merrick wore a bemused expression on his face, he turned back to me and Riz. "So how much stronger are the real ones then? Are we talking ten times stronger? A hundred times stronger?"

"If yer listen nd do wat yer told, yer mite see fer yerself. Bren, it's yer turn now," Riz said, and when he called out my name, in that shortened way, I saw the first spark of jealousy in Merrick's eyes. It faded fast when he saw the rat catapult one of the Runes into my forehead.

"What was that for?"

I rubbed my temple, and picked up the fallen Rune. I felt that buzz of electricity again, but in a more subdued fashion. That was it for a moment, till I had the feeling of someone trying to pull me away, not in the physical sense, but at my spirit, or whatever you'd want to call it. The sensation didn't last long enough for me to see, or experience, anything else.

"What you looking at me like that for?" Merrick asked.

I wanted to ask why he was looking at me in the first place, but I ditched that line of thinking, as I realised it was just going to lead to a circular argument.

"It's-s fine!" I sputtered. It took longer to get the words out than it should have. Everything did feel normal again though, which was nice.

"Yer felt a pull, didn't ya?" Riz showed that at least he was paying attention.

I nodded, and the rat nodded in return.

"On der brite side, dat'll stop wen yer fired ova a hundred of dere thins, so look forward ta dat." Riz's reply didn't exactly cheer me up. "Rite, get a move on, same word as I told yer friend, put yer arse in gear!"

I took a deep breath. I had already used them and these were far weaker than those. I just had to concentrate and say the word properly.

"Tarzhadem!" I said the word, and the Rune popped just as it did for Merrick.

"Gud, neitha of yer screwed up wit sayin der word. Wud ave been a rite pain in ma arse ta ave ta find more help!"

"Can we have stronger ones now?" Merrick queried. His tone implied that he wanted to get out there and cause some real destruction.

"Yer still got more types of Runes ta try! You're gunna try a different one, nd dis one needs ta be aimed but again, it's jus a weak version."

Riz went to hand out the next few Runes when we heard the sound of springs uncoiling. The look on the rat's face said it all.

From above, a Spring Heel landed in front of us, and then two more behind it… a trio of goblins with springs for legs. Seeing them in the daylight revealed them to be more horrific as it was clear that the new legs had been put on quite crudely, and the metal rusted.

"We come for revenge," the lead one announced, shifting from one position to the next.

"Faine told us not to go but we want revenge," another added.

"Yer shud av listened ta yer boss," Riz said. He had been caught out, which I now know is one of his biggest pet peeves.

Merrick stepped forward, ostensibly to protect me, and a laugh escaped his lips.

"Better hurry up with the real ones, rat. Looks like we have to put them to use…"

CHAPTER 8
FIGHT AT THE BECK

The three Spring Heels stared at me and Riz, looking right through Merrick, who had his palm open, and ready to take possession of the Runes we both thought Riz had on him. Logically, we should have both also seen through this.

"Yer can keep yer and dere all yer want, but yer gunna be waitin! I don't ave any propa Runes on me at der moment!" Riz announced through gritted teeth.

"And you didn't think we would be attacked while we were in a secluded spot?" I said, my panic not yet having reduced me to a quivering mess. I had reached the anger stage.

"I figured Faine wud wait a while! He normally doesn't waste is cannon fodda dat ez!" Riz sighed.

"We hear you!" one of the Spring Heels yelled out.

"We already tell you!" its friend said, fire coming out of both its mouth and nostrils, like a demented looking dragon.

"Master Faine told us no, we sick of listening! We come to end this!" the third added. It was hard trying to tell each of them apart. All three of them even unfurled their clawed fingers in unison, which wasn't helping in telling them apart.

"Okay, rat, this is the type of thing you wanted back up for. What's the plan?" Merrick said, acting like he was simply going to beat up the school bullies again.

"Der plan fer der moment? RUN AWAY!" Riz fled the scene, quickly followed by me and by Merrick. From behind, came the sound of springs again, mixed in with only a little bit of goblin laughter.

"Running away! That's your plan!" I gasped. I willed my legs to move faster then they ever had, something which would become quite common throughout my illustrious career.

"I sed fer der moment, didn't I! Who do yer think yer talkin to anyway? Dey got der jump on us, but dey're gunna learn dat it won't save dem. While yer two keep dem busy by not dyin, I'm gunna make sumthin dat will blast dose gobs inta itty bitty pieces!"

I wanted to object furiously to Riz's plan, but I couldn't, as I was interrupted by the creaky coil of springs overhead.

"I'll tak dat silence as a yeh!" Riz peeled away from me and Merrick, running to the side and under a bush, as we more or less crashed into the three Spring Heels. They reached out for us, and Merrick tried to do what he always did in a fight, punching one of them in the face. To his credit, the goblin did fall back, a weird ooze trickling from its nose. I assumed then it was blood. Now whenever I think of it, I picture blackcurrant crumble filling. As the other Spring Heels stood their friend up, the damage Merrick did was even more impressive, his lucky punch, as he deemed it later, did more than break the goblin's long nose, it also tore its upper lip off and caused its left eye to bulge out. It staggered forward and fell again. Neither me or Merrick wasted this opportunity and we split the scene again, diving into an overgrown bush once we were sure they couldn't see us anymore.

Merrick's hand shot over my mouth as we heard the springs again.

"Sshh," he whispered.

The Spring Heels leapt past, looking around for us, the one Merrick had hurt clearly having issues, wobbling a lot more than the others, its breathing hard.

"I find him! I find him, I gut him!" it managed to say.

"They good hiding, but we get them," one of its friends said. I got the impression that they shared some sort of comradery. The display surprised me, though Merrick was just as dismissive of it as I guessed Riz would have been.

"Heard the way they're talking? Idiots," he said in a low voice.

The moment was getting tense, and at one point, a Spring Heel looked directly at me, but all three moved on. Me and Merrick let ourselves breathe easy.

"Where did the rat go?" Merrick asked, getting his composure back.

"I don't know. He said he was off to make some Runes."

"Fantastic. He's probably ran off, knows what's best for him, I bet."

I didn't agree with that assessment. I couldn't explain it, but I felt that Riz was going to be true to his word here. Yes, you read it right, Riz could be decent, as long as his self interest was involved somehow.

"H-he'll be back," I stammered. "H-he'll be back with those R-Runes!"

A twig snapped nearby, and a Spring Heel landed dramatically next to the bush, its head twisted as it twitched his long nose. This was clearly not the one that Merrick had attacked, though it shared the hatred in its eyes.

Neither Merrick or I dared say anything else, as the goblin prowled next to us, coming closer and closer to where we were.

It only took a second for the situation to get worse as the goblin's head spun a full one hundred eighty degrees, its beady eyes focusing on us.

"Found you!"

The Spring Heel's voices were already high pitched, yet this one broke even that limit, unleashing a howl that could sunder steel. Naturally, we ran again, and the Spring Heels started the chase up anew.

I remember the rush I felt, the peril reaching the peak that it had last night. We humans have the whole fight or flight thing going on for us in terms of survival mechanisms but I had to wonder if that was true of the 'Others', the Spring Heels that were chasing us included. I still don't have an answer to this question but thinking back to that day, could a different reaction to that response have changed things? The whole time we'd been running, Merrick had actually been working on something else, a plan to evade the goblins. It hadn't escaped his notice that the goblin had only found us by pretty much standing directly in front of us, its senses either being dulled or just handicapped for whatever reason.

"I've got an idea, mate," Merrick said as we were running, before barging into me. The impact knocked me straight through the branches of a low hanging tree. Through the leaves I saw Merrick calling to all three Spring Heels, capturing their attention. Then, he led them away, leaving me alone, under the tree's cover.

I sat there, unsure of what to do, even the spring sound got distant, and I didn't hear any yelling, or screaming. The tenseness I felt wasn't easing up, and the aura of doom that was pervading my thoughts wouldn't let me believe that I was safe, even if it looked like Merrick had sacrificed himself to do just that.

I didn't wear a watch at that time, so I had no idea of how much time had passed, how many seconds had elapsed between me sitting there under the tree, and when I stood, feeling brave enough to venture out. I probably should have waited longer.

As if proving my sense of foreboding, I didn't get to hear the Spring Heel before its razor sharp fingers scratched across my back. Fabric, wool, skin, bone, none of it mattered as the 'Other' dashed past me, leaving its mark. I collapsed to my knees, the pain's intensity grounding me. I thought I was going to die. May sound melodramatic, but let's put you in that situation and see how you fare.

"You bleed like weakling!" The goblin laughed. It went in for another attack when Merrick tossed a stick, which moved through the air like a javelin, having the perfect luck, though not as lucky for the Spring Heel, to become impaled in the goblin's eyeball. As it howled in pain, Merrick hauled me up by grabbing my shoulder, and dragged me into a run.

"Just bumped into the rat," he said, breathless, though he looked at me with those dead eyes, like I'd done something wrong. Didn't have time to question it. Not when my back was hurting, and I was getting tired, the adrenaline draining from my body. If I could have gotten away with it, I'd have happily gone to sleep.

"W-what did he say?"

At that, Merrick forced three stones into my hand.

"Two of them are those blast Runes he told us how to use. The ones that used the word, Tazhardem."

"And the other one?"

"That one is called Arrow. Its word was…" We both stopped at the howl of a Spring Heel. I guessed it was the one that Merrick had injured. "Here they come again."

Distracted, he then remembered what he was telling me before. "Word for arrow is Saz-eh. The rat said that aiming is important on that one."

A Spring Heel landed between me and Merrick forcing us apart. It was quickly followed by its kin, and I can only assume one of them went after Merrick as well. Now that I was armed, it was now or never for me.

I took a deep breath, the biggest one I can ever remember taking. It hurts my chest to even talk about it now. I stepped forward, purposely snapping a twig. The goblin instinctively turned to me, looking very surprised, with its intact bulging eye showing its expression. I spoke first.

"Tazhardem!" This scene I remember in slow motion. I know it didn't happen that way, ending in a flash, literally. My memories though allow me to examine the rush I felt when the Rune burst in my hand, all its concentrated energy shooting forward in a powerful blast that sped towards the Spring Heel. The rapidly changing blue of the blast lit the area up for a moment, and must have been the last thing the poor goblin saw before its head blew apart. I was riding a high after the body fell to its knees. In a survive or die situation, I had survived.

There were just two things I didn't think about after that. One was the fact that I was just stood gawking into thin air at that point. The other was I had just made an awful lot of noise, and that was one of the ways these things were hunting us.

A sound made me quickly turn, and without even checking to see what I was firing at, I shouted out, "Tazhardem!" The shot went wide though, as the Spring Heel that had come to investigate, reacted quicker than its comrade. He caught sight of the headless Spring Heel and rushed me. I went over and dodged again. He caught me though, grabbing my leg and cutting into it. Oddly enough, I didn't feel any pain then... no, that was to come in a minute or two.

I only had one Rune left to use and it was the one I hadn't got any training in, but I was in a risk-taking mood. The sound of another explosion not that far away provided me with the moment I needed. I held my arm out and remembered what Riz had started to say, and the little bit Merrick had just said. I had to aim this one, which I took as meaning that this Rune was going to create a smaller and more powerful shot, just like an arrow. I aimed and got ready to shout out when the Spring Heel leapt away from me, seemingly knowing what I was going to do. I held back, and staggered to my feet. I may not have felt any pain, but I certainly felt the effect of the leg wound now, and I couldn't stand straight.

"I kill you!"

This Spring Heel was determined, or maybe mad with rage. Despite knowing that I had killed one of its allies, it ran at me again. I should have found a way to retreat and regroup. I had already dealt with one of them, and I hoped that Merrick had killed the other one. Against all three of us, the Spring Heel may have fled. With that option not being available, I had to dig deep and unearth all the cunning I had to get a good shot in.

I darted around a tree as the Spring Heel leapt for me, missing me by an inch. Using this break to the fullest, I ran from tree to tree, building up some distance. I thought of the position that I needed the Spring Heel to be in, and worked out where I had to be to get the best shot. It would be a simple matter to get it where I wanted. Having taken a quick glance around the area, I'd found a large tree whose roots were sticking out of the ground. Bushes either side of it that provided some cover. I couldn't have asked for a better location, and felt my luck was changing.

I spied the Spring Heel round the last tree, and threw myself against the roots. Reminiscing like this, I picture it as if some

Hollywood mogul decided to film it, even down to the framing of the scene. The Spring Heel came straight at me, with no room to evade. It was now or never and I allowed myself to feel a bit smug. After all, there was no way the goblin could escape this, and they'd soon be going to wherever it was that they went to when dead. Fun fact: goblins believe in reincarnation apparently, according to what Riz has told me.

"Saz-eh!" I said the words just as Merrick had told me, and the Rune burst apart but the shot didn't go the right way. Instead of going forward and striking the goblin, it went backwards. I said before that I didn't feel my leg getting attacked, well let me tell you, I felt everything as my right arm was torn apart by the magical bolt that exited through the bloody ruin that was my shoulder. My chest contracted as shock took hold. It was a miracle I stayed conscious. All this must have been amusing to the Spring Heel as he just stood there, laughing. I couldn't even lift my other arm now, death seemed moments away and my life haphazardly played out in scenes. At last, the Spring Heel took a step towards me, but you know how they say that every dark cloud has a silver lining? This had one, though it could have easily gone the other way.

"Die!"

The Spring Heel looked ready to pounce till it was ripped in half. I never saw the bladed hand moving, let alone stab through the goblin's back. The top half flopped around while the head looked around to see who had killed it. I ended up holding my breath again when I saw it was the same threat from the night before, Jack the Ripper. The larger goblin smiled as he plunged his left hand into the Spring Heel's head, like scissors into a bath sponge. Jack then observed me.

"Aww, I wanted to be the one to leave you in pieces, boy. This is the fate of all those that side with the rat. Enjoy your choice." I didn't know if he was going to say more but we both heard something. Car doors slamming, and then footsteps. Jack didn't look amused by this interruption, perhaps he wanted to gloat more.

"Time's up, no matter. We'll meet again, unless they cut you up."

Jack disappeared shortly before the first other humans appeared, men and women in black suits. I didn't see much more. As these strange people advanced on me, I fled into the convenient comfort of unconsciousness.

CHAPTER 9
ALL THE GOVERNMENT'S MEN

I woke up facing an unknown ceiling, but that wasn't what my first thought was. No, if I remember right, my first thought was 'I have an itch yet cannot scratch'. Profound, I know. A few seconds more, and I realised that I wasn't hurting anywhere. I scanned my body and found with great relief that every part was intact. The sight of my arm being a bloody ruin was etched into my brain with all the shock that it brought, but here, I was flexing it.

Someone had changed my clothes for me, subbing them with normal hospital wear, and I could see my tattered clothes, which did show the brunt of the battle. There was even the splatter of my blood on the t-shirt. Memories are funny things, especially if the last one you had compared so markedly different to what you were like currently. A wave of disconnect came over me, linking that fight in the forest to me in this hospital room. If I wanted to, I could have easily shut everything out and made the past just a feverish dream while being sedated for whatever. The clothes were the flaw of course, as was the creepy guy standing in the corner of the room. I almost leapt out of the bed in surprise.

"Who are you? How… how long have you been there?" I asked. Had I been like I am now, my words would have been very different. For starters, I would have sworn a lot more.

"It's good to see that you're awake, Master Landis. You've been unconscious a few hours," the man said as he stepped into the light.

He was wearing a slick business suit, the same as all the politicians I'd seen on the news. He was balding with more hair behind his ears than on his head. Thick rimmed glasses sat perfectly on the bridge of his nose, and he kept adjusting them mechanically, like he had been programmed to do it at set intervals. Let's be clear, I had nothing at hand to defend myself, and Riz wasn't anywhere to be seen. I was completely at this weirdo's mercy.

"Wh-who are you?" I asked again, the only words that I could grasp then.

"How rude of me! Let me introduce myself, after all I know who you are, Master Brennan Landis."

It didn't occur to me then, but he kept referring to me as 'Master', even though I was over sixteen years old then. I should have been a Mister! I didn't point this out as I wasn't in a position to speak up about it.

"My name is Lionel Marr. I'm a minister in the Ministry of Other Worldly Business."

"MOWB?" I honestly replied with this, much to Lionel's surprise, and annoyance.

"Please don't turn it into an acronym, some things are just meant to be said separately," he said, his eye twitching slightly. "Or, if you prefer you can refer to us as the Department of Other Worldly Business." Lionel then caught me doing what he must have known I would try to do, given what had literally just happened. "Don't even bother yourself turning that into an acronym either."

"H-how did you know my n-name?"

"We checked your wallet."

If you think this is a mundane answer, since he was trying to portray himself as some mysterious entity, then yeah, it was endemic of everything the Ministry did and was.

"W-what do you w-want with m-me then?" Now, as I'm telling you this, it'll seem obvious that this is the question I should have asked first.

"I want to discuss your recent contact with the 'Others'. I must warn you any attempt to lie will be met with extreme punishment.

And let me tell you, I've already filled out the paperwork in advance. I've had a rather testing day."

"W-which ones d-do you mean?"

I could ask you to bet on who he was going to ask about, but it's fairly obvious, and I'm not going to insult your intelligence.

"Let's get straight to the point. What's your relationship with the being who's dubbed himself, Riz the rat? The little twat that he is, God's grease filled blister of a pimple."

I think Lionel forgot that he was asking a question at this point, instead opting to just insult Riz.

He continued, "Riz, the little prick, a conniving bastard with the ego that would dwarf the sun but with the charisma of a dead slug. A creature that would find better use being tied to a cat's scratching post, one that has done more damage to the world than any weapon we humans could ever create."

"I-I didn't-t k-know you h-had met." My stammer got worse the closer Lionel got.

Lionel pulled out a notebook, one that clearly marked Volume 86, and continued his tirade.

"There are hundreds upon hundreds of recorded incidents bearing that git's name, among other names, as he's gone through a lot over the years. At one point, he even bit the queen of England! Along with every member of the Ministry at least twice."

"He met Elizabeth the Second?"

"No, well, yes, and Elizabeth the First, though let's not get into that story," Lionel said, putting the notebook down, seemingly remembering what this was about.

"S-sounds like you d-don't need me to tell you about R-Riz!"

"Oh we do. After all, you might be able to shed some light on what he's up to, why we're getting reports of him, along with goblins with bloody springs on their feet!" Lionel pulled out a photograph from the book, a picture of Riz running along, and above him, a Spring Heel. Without context, you might be forgiven for thinking that they were working together.

"H-he's fighting them! N-not working with t-them!" I shouted out. Rookie mistake.

"Oh, so you definitely do know more then! Good, start talking… the rodent is up to something and it's my job to find out what it is, work out if it's a threat to us, and if it is, stop it."

I decided to co-operate because of the fear aspect that Lionel was radiating, plus, I figured that if I told him that Riz was trying to stop Faine from killing us all, then it might gain us an unlikely ally.

"R-Riz is trying to s-stop a Fae called Faine, w-who wants to cull us so we b-believe in all the old tales again, i-including belief in fairies. Th-the goblins with springs are f-foot soldiers of Faine, and th-they're led by J-Jack the Ripper," I took a deep breath before continuing. "Despite w-what you might t-think, Riz is f-fighting on your side."

My plea fell on deaf ears, as Lionel laughed his ass off at what I'd said.

"On our side! That's the funniest thing I've heard all day! We're aware of Faine and his schemes, but it'd be a cold day in hell before we trusted that fiend again. The best result for us is if they kill each other off!"

Lionel was still laughing later, as I processed what he said, and what it meant for me, and this line of questioning.

"Th-there's n-nothing left to say! Th-that's the truth!" I pre-empted him asking me once more about what Riz was up to.

"There's plenty left to say, I believe. For instance, what's your involvement? What's the rat getting you to do? What role has he got planned for you? Are you a patsy, or are you going to be a warrior, willing to die for his glory? What's it to be?" Lionel leered. He picked up a flask from a bag on the floor and unscrewed it, taking huge gulps of whatever drink was inside. Tea or whisky, take your pick.

"I-I'm n-not going to s-say! I t-told you w-what he wants! H-he w-wants to stop F-Faine!"

"But why? Have you asked him that? Hmm? Do you know what Faine's current objective is? Word on the street, if I may borrow a vulgar phrase," Funny, him considering that a vulgar phrase, considering what he had already said about Riz. "Word on the street is that Faine is after a body to steal, at least that's what our investigators and translators have said. A special someone in this bottom dweller of a town, someone who has whatever Faine wants and/or needs. Did the rat tell you that?"

"N-no," I said meekly.

"Well, clearly, the rat isn't using you because of your brains, or brute strength," Lionel started jotting things down in the note book that he'd picked back up. I spotted the words cannon fodder and meat shield.

"What about associates? Who else other than you is the rat working with? A being like him isn't just hanging around with a nobody like you."

It hadn't escaped my notice that he hadn't mentioned Merrick. This gave me hope that he'd managed to escape from all this.

"I'm n-not a nobody!"

"Of course you are! You're clearly not from a family with money, otherwise you would be dressed better and have money to your name. The majority of people in this town are trash, so it's safe to assume the same of you. You should be honoured that we choose to heal the damage that had been inflicted on you. I was overruled as I said we should have let you go armless." Lionel made it painfully clear what his morals were, cementing him as a complete and utter jackass to me. At least I had my answer as to why I had my arm back and all my wounds were gone. I couldn't see the Rune from where I was laid, so I assumed it was under the bed.

"Th-thank you!" I spluttered, I didn't know what to say, and that seemed like a good fit.

Lionel rolled his eyes at my expression of gratitude.

"Yeah, they all say thank you. Thank you for not letting me die, thank you for allowing me to continue living a pointless existence, living at the bottom of the food chain," Lionel sighed. "You've not told me anything I don't already know, maybe I shouldn't have delayed the Cleaners after all. What a pain."

"Th-the C-Cleaners?"

"Yes, they are the ones we send in to clean up an incident, so that the dumb majority of the population can continue getting on with their lives, serving the mechanisms that run the county."

I'll add a bit more to Lionel's explanation since he just gave me the bare minimum then of what the Cleaners really were. In essence, they were a paramilitary group solely at the disposal of the Ministry of Otherworldly Business. They use whatever means necessary to maintain the secrecy of the incident they're dealing with, though this has limits. I've dealt with them on many occasions, trying to keep them from destroying a key bit of evidence, trying to stop them from removing some new Other I'd befriended, or just generally trying to stop them being gigantic dickheads.

"I think I'll get the Cleaners to come and take care of you. I'm sure you wouldn't want that though, would you?" Lionel took another swig of his drink, part of it sloshing out of the side. The way he drank it you'd think it was alcohol.

"N-no! Y-you can't!" I cried out.

"Can't I?" Lionel lifted a black briefcase from the floor besides the bag. Its shine told me that he took more care of this briefcase than anything else. He tapped it lovingly.

"In here is all the paperwork I need to have you turned from a problem to a footnote in the obituaries. As I said before, I've already taken the liberty of filling it in. I'll show you."

Lionel put the briefcase on his lap, undoing the locks and opening it, his smug grin turning into frantic.

"It's empty! Where's all my paperwork? My Thatcher signed pens!" Lionel said, panicking.

"Dose pens tasted terrible, paper waz gud fer wiping ma arse tho," Riz laughed as he crawled out from under my bed, clutching what I guessed, at that point, must have been the Healing Rune.

"You! Give that Rune back! That is government property!" Lionel leapt to his feet, and I honestly thought that he was going to try and step on Riz, who just held the Rune up to stop any attempt at that nonsense.

"Yeh, yer even try dat shit nd I will wreck yer. Not even jokin, it'll be u lyin in dat bed, not der kid," the rat smiled, and I knew, just as much as he did, that Lionel wasn't about to do anything other than back off.

"How long have you been in here?" Lionel asked, trying to put his anger back in its box. I could still see it in his eyes though.

"Long enuff ta hear yer threatenin a kid, nd I thought yer dumbasses were supposed ta be mild mannered." Riz worked his way up so that he was sat by my side.

"He's a British citizen and a minor at that. He's under our protection. We are acting within our remit."

"Hah! Protectin im? Tell me a'other funny one! Tho if yer wanted ta know wat I waz doin, yer shud of jus asked. I mite ave told yer if yer weren't so stupid!"

"You have no right to be acting on British soil!" Lionel launched a new offensive, but not one I understood. At least, not at that moment.

"Like I giv a crap bout yer laws! Dey'll change again before too long, jus like all der otha times! Get's borin afta a while havin ta deal wit suits like yerself."

"I am here under the authority of the Queen herself!" Lionel's face had started to turn red, his mannerisms resembling that of a primate, jutting his shoulders forward, his hands closed fists.

"No yer not!" Riz howled with laughter. "Yer ere cuz yer manager told yer ta get yer ass ere, nd he only did it cuz is manager told im! Nd as fer yer Queen, she doesn't care wat yer do! I bet she doesn't even know wat yer job is!"

If Riz laughed any harder, he'd have ended up on the floor again.

"You are really pushing me, rat! I have tricks up my sleeve for you, as well as dealing with this punk!" Lionel's forehead vein was starting to protrude more and more.

"Yer got sumthin like dat, den use it! Come on den, let's see wat yer got, tossa!"

All my fear had drained away while watching this argument unfold. Lionel seemed less a figure to be afraid of, and more one to mock.

"I'll get you for this, rat!"

"Dat's wat yer sed wen I bit yer! Still waitin fer yer revenge dere! Yer all bark nd no bite, do yer need me ta giv yer notha demonstration?" Riz bared his teeth and Lionel jumped back.

"This isn't over! Mister Landis! If you carry on working for this… this scum, you'll end up dead! Mark my words!"

"Oh, bore off, yer vacant starin jackass!"

With Riz's final insult, Lionel timidly moved forward for his stuff and then stormed out of the room.

"Wat a twat," Riz crossed his arms, sighing.

"Riz! You're alright!" I said, instinctively hugging him. That was until he bit my hand.

"Neva do dat again, rite? Y wudn't I be alrite anyway? Yer 'ere der one who got is arse handed ta im, by yerself I mite ad."

"I got the word wrong, didn't I?" I laid back in disgrace, expecting Riz to have something to say about it.

"Yer'd be surprised by how often dat happens, kid," he said, in an almost tender way. "I knew a lot of wannabe magicians, propa pros at der job as well, who blew demsleves up cuz dey were too stupid ta remember der word."

"Really?"

"God yeh, it waz at it's worst in der 30s, wen yer ad magicians settin up schools, nd der teachin der wrong frickin word ta der class. Imagine how dat went!"

I didn't have to imagine it, I'd felt it. In my mind, I pictured a magic school, like in the movies, but all the students blowing themselves up.

"Wat I'm tryin ta say is don't worry bout it. Yer didn't waste a valuable Rune, nd yer still alive, so move on. Tomorrow is anotha learnin day."

Another nice thing for Riz to say, in his own special way of course. What would his reaction had been if it had been a rare Rune that had backfired? It'd probably involve him biting me. Luckily, that hasn't happened yet, I'll let you know if it ever does.

This touching scene couldn't last forever though, and we both heard voices from beyond the door, voices that belonged to my parents.

"Now that the specialist is gone," someone was saying, "you

may see him. I'm told he's fine so we'll discharge him soon to clear the bed out."

"Thank you, doctor."

That voice was my mother's, and just hearing it brought on all the guilt of putting myself in this situation, and what my death would mean to her and my father. My father, by the way, was doing a worse time of trying to hide his emotions.

"Th-thank y-you!"

Yes, my dad stuttered the same as me when under pressure.

"I'd betta skaddle den, leave yer ta yer parents. I'm expectin a lot of tears nd a lot of raised voices, gud luck!" Riz scurried away as the door opened. I didn't see where he went, but my focus was on my parents as they rushed me. True to what Riz said, there were tears and finger wagging. I was glad they didn't know the full truth about what happened, but I had started to wonder how long I could keep it all secret for.

CHAPTER 10
HOME SWEET HOME

Like the doctor had said, I was discharged from the hospital that night, and it was only close to midnight. While I had assumed that was far too late for this sort of thing, I reckoned that Lionel, the prat from the Ministry of Otherworldly Business or whatever it was called, was causing trouble because that was his only form of revenge. I took it in my stride though as I welcomed the thought of sleeping in my own bed, in my own room, and not have to worry if a confused patient was going to think my room was a toilet. You laugh, but sadly, this has happened to me. Anyway, the trip in the car home felt a bit weird. I flexed my arm, the one that only a few hours ago had been a bloody mess, and it felt completely normal, as if nothing had ever happened to it. The Healing Rune that had performed this miracle was still in Riz's clutches, as far as I knew. The way he went on about it, I didn't see him letting go of it anytime soon.

As we drove through darkened streets and pitch black countryside, I strained my eyes, looking for any sign of Jack the Ripper and his Spring Heels. The fact that I didn't see anything out there wasn't much of a relief, as each shadow took on new meaning. I think my parents were idly chatting, maybe they had even asked me questions. Questions that I ignored. The excuse for what had happened and the explosion that was heard for a mile around? Gas leak. Yes, that's right, a gas leak. And what was worse? Most people believed it, as they simply wanted an explanation, and to get on with their lives. Of course, anyone with half a brain might have questioned how I managed to be at the epicentre of a gas explosion and come through unscathed. Truth be told, my parents' reaction had surprised me, and scared me a little, as they hadn't questioned anything at all. I get they were happy I was okay, but surely they should have been more curious as to what happened. Since getting in the car, they hadn't spoken about the incident, instead either talking about other hospital visits, and other mindless small talk. I didn't engage with any of it, as I just wanted to sleep.

Not that I was able to get straight to sleep, as no sooner had I got into the house, went upstairs and collapsed on the bed, Riz started scratching at my window like a demented cat.

"Oi! Don't start playin sicky now, yer prick! Let me in!" he demanded.

"Do you have to be so loud!" I said, opening it a crack for him to slither in through.

"Yer wudn't ave let me in anywayz!" Riz said, and I was struck by a memory that popped into my head from what Lionel had told me earlier. As an instant reaction, I bopped the rat on his noggin, taking him by surprise.

"Wat der bloody ell waz dat fer?"

"That was for not telling me what Faine was after around here! Looking for a special 'someone'. It's me, isn't it? That's why you snuck in my bag!" I said in the loudest, angriest, whisper.

"Fer cryin' out loud! No! It isn't u! It really waz a mistake ta crawl inta yer bag, I thought I'd made dat really clear!" Riz retorted, looking insulted. "As fer der reason y I didn't tell yer, wud it ave made a difference? Faine only wants dis twat ta use im nd abuse dem. Wud yer want dat ta be u? Or wudn't yer ratha it be sumone else who get's tortured! Wat's dat sayin, betta u den me!"

"Are you really that selfish? Don't you believe in putting others before yourself?"

"Do I ave ta answer dat? Yer live as long as me, yer learn ta only look out fer one person… yerself. It's really ard ta fuk dat up."

As angry as I was getting with Riz's attitude, at the same time, I saw the increased futility in continuing. I didn't know then how long Riz had lived for, but I knew the chances of me changing his mind were slim to none. My dad always made a point to tell me to only argue when I could prove my point, otherwise I'd just be wasting energy. Apparently, this was why he never argued with mum that much. It was clear to see who the boss of the house was.

"What happened to Merrick?" I asked, changing the subject and lowering the tension. The change in subject even caught Riz by surprise.

"Merrick? Oh, rite, well I tried ta keep track of im afta yer blew yerself up but he slipped away. I mean, I waz also tryin ta dodge dose twats from der government."

"That's good then. I was lucky I had you to come to my rescue, I dread to think of what they would have done if you hadn't. If they had captured Merrick…" I trailed off.

"If dey captured him, dey wud ave used im as leverage ova yer, so I'm pretty sure he's safe. Now, how bout yer show yer gratitude by frickin feedin me!"

"Now you're making me go downstairs again," I groaned.

"Dam rite, don't ferget der cheese!" Riz shook his little fist at me, as I trudged away for the midnight snack. I may not have looked it, but I was pleased that Riz had returned. Though, I would have much preferred to have gone to sleep.

The next morning, I woke up with a buzz, not like a bee buzzing in my ear, but a buzz of energy. Maybe it was how close to death I was before, maybe it was because I realised that with everything that had happened, I'd gotten away with it, by being both still alive, and not restrained by the government. I jumped out of bed, getting dressed super quick. I felt wide awake, powered by a million coffees, which was funny, as I hated coffee.

"Riz! Wake up!" I said, rocking the set of drawers I knew he was sleeping in. I'd spotted his tail hanging out of one of them. Getting no response, I shook it with all my strength, almost causing all the books and crap on top of it to fall off.

"Wat der ell! Wat time is it!" Riz opened the drawer with a start, and looked over to my bedside clock. "Y re we up at dis time of mornin? I waz enjoyin ma beauty sleep!"

"I'm ready to get back with the training!"

"Howz bout dis, yer piss off downstairs nd I'll get on wit it wen I wanna!" Without so much more as another word, he slammed the drawer shut. I'm not quite sure how he managed that, but it was just one of those things you didn't question.

A bit dejected, I went downstairs on my own, leaving him to sleep off whatever mood he'd found himself in. My mum was in the living room, drinking a cup of tea, in a far more dignified manner than what Lionel had been like towards the end of our encounter.

"You're up early!" she said, looking up at me with some bewilderment. It was rare that I was up before 9am if I didn't need to be. Had my life been as I had expected it to go after the end of my GCSEs, I wouldn't have crawled out of bed till 11. If that.

"I didn't want to waste the day," I replied. I couldn't tell her the truth, so this seemed the next best thing to tell her. She looked at me with her inquisitive eyes, that had in the past been able to suss out anything I'd tried hiding from her, no matter how good a poker face I maintained. A spark in her eye told me that her suspicions had been roused but to my relief she never prodded any further. A knock at the door distracted both of us.

"Expecting anyone?" I asked.

"No, not at this time of morning," My mother swiftly went to the door, opening it ajar. I saw the surprise on her face, and I was just as surprised when I heard Merrick's voice.

"Oh hi, Mrs Landis. Is Brennan up?" he asked.

"Actually, he's just come downstairs." My mum looked back to me.

Merrick's eyes followed hers to mine.

"Brennan!" He said that with more enthusiasm than I think he meant, as my mum turned to him with that inquisitive look again.

"I mean, hey Brennan, how's things?" Merrick quickly got his composure back to form.

"Thing's are fine," I lied through my teeth. I couldn't say otherwise with Mum hovering nearby. I needed to get Merrick away from prying ears to really discuss what was important.

"Did you want to come in?" I offered, but Merrick must have read my mind as he had a counter offer.

"Nah, I was wondering if you wanted to come to the shops with me? Got to do some stupid errands," He put his hands behind his head and gave his best grin, acting as if nothing had happened, and everything was still normal.

"Hell yes." He didn't need to ask me twice. I didn't even give my mum chance to say anything as I left the house.

"Do you really need stuff from the shops?" I asked, once we were a little ways away.

"No, I just knew we wouldn't be able to talk about the rat or what happened in front of your folks. I mean, I'm guessing they don't know what happened?"

"If I did, would I be here now? They'd probably lock me away in my room for my own safety. And Riz? Dad would flatten him with a shoe!"

The mental image of my dad chasing after Riz with a shoe was a good one. To this day I still think of it, as a what could have been memory.

"Good point." He closed his eyes, satisfied with that answer, before continuing with what he wanted to say. "I saw it happen, and it was like it all went down in slow motion, from the words you said, to your arm exploding. I was in shock, mate. I almost got taken out by one of those things as I was so distracted."

There was a lot I wanted to say about this, but one thing jumped out at me, above all others.

"You saw what happened to me?"

Merrick looked taken aback, like he wasn't sure about what he'd said, or what he should say next.

"Yeah, I wasn't that far away by the time you used the Rune. I was circling my way back to you from where I'd ran. Wasn't just me though, the rat saw it all. It was him who saved me from the Spring Heel. That was weird though, didn't see him at all till he blew it up. Then it turned out he was stood right next to me!" Merrick skipped over what I'd asked, and focused on what he'd wanted to talk about.

"I swear there's more going on with him than he's telling us." Merrick's words echoed thoughts I was having at the time. I shared with him what Lionel had told me, what I had already told Riz off for, having hid Faine's objective here in Thornaby.

"He wants someone?" Merrick said.

"Yeah, that's why Riz was prowling round. He was trying to figure out who it is, and get to them first."

"And what was he going to do when he found them?"

That was a very good question that I hadn't stopped to think about, instead jumping to conclusions that I might have been the one that Faine wanted. I didn't tell Merrick that part, and he didn't reach that conclusion either.

"I don't know, Riz didn't tell me when I confronted him over it," I explained, then going into more detail about the conversation I had with the rat the night before, excluding my theory of course.

"This is why I think the rat is up to something, Bren! I mean, stuff like that? You have to tell us!"

"I know. Maybe he still doesn't trust us?" I suggested.

"Or maybe we're just disposable to him… if he is a him!"

"What are you saying?"

We'd stopped walking now. Our little journey had taken us up the road and towards the little area near the two council flats that stood lonely in the skyline. Despite the town centre being a stone's throw away, there weren't many people making their way through here.

"I'm implying that we don't know what he even is. I don't think he's a rat, or a real one anyway. I may not be smart, but I know rats lack the vocal cords to render speech like he can! Then there's the dexterity with his hands. Look, I feel stupid just explaining this."

Merrick started pacing, his frustration radiating with each step.

"Maybe he was a person who got cursed?" I said. "Like in the stories? I mean, if goblins and fairies are real, and dragons…"

This was when Merrick interrupted me, like after the past couple of days, what I'd just said was a bigger bombshell than anything else we'd discussed.

"Pardon me, but dragons? Breathing fire type dragons?"

"I think so, Riz told me. Along with a lot of others, you wouldn't believe how much stuff is actually real."

I misread the room here, well, forgiving the fact that we weren't in a room.

"And you didn't share this information yesterday, why?"

"Did it matter considering how fast things went yesterday?"

Merrick had to think for a moment, I saw him ticking it over, his eyes moving from left and right.

"Okay, might not have had time for it yesterday, but were you going to tell me? I feel like that is something I needed to know, especially if there's a path from this where I'm going to get eaten by a flipping dragon!"

"I think you're being a bit silly, Riz didn't even say where the dragons are."

"Riz didn't tell us that Faine was after someone in particular though. Why would he bother to tell you where these monsters were? I mean, outside of that little rat body of his, he's probably a monster too!"

I tried imagining Riz looking like any of the creatures he mentioned, and none of them seemed to fit. You're probably sat there thinking this is a stupid thing to say, and that Riz was quite capable of being any of these things. None of them met with Riz's approval, he had comments about their looks that has gotten us into a lot of trouble. You already knew that though, didn't you, or at least, you guessed correctly.

"Bren, do you really think he's got our best interests at heart? The rat wants us to fight for him, when he's more than capable, from what I saw, and what you told me."

"Does that mean you don't want to help him?" I put the question to Merrick.

He shook his head, before flicking his hair off his eyes with his hand. This move normally melted the heart of any girl watching, and didn't he know it. It had no effect on me, but the few times he'd done it outside of school, when no one else was around, I realised it was a gesture for him to calm himself. As such, where his talk before was far from rational or neutral, as he preferred it, it was back to a pleasant sounding tone.

"No, I said I'd help, and I'm not going to go back on that. Plus the little furball said he was going to teach me magic, and that's not a prize I'd just walk away from, especially after seeing what it can do."

It was a relief to hear him say that, even if it wasn't the most selfless of reasons.

"Though I'd understand completely if you wanted to back out," he added. "I mean, it's easy for me to say I'll help, I didn't have my arm blown off! Mistake or otherwise."

"I…" I had to pause for a second. It should have been easy to say what I'd already told Riz, what I had already decided in my head. However my resolve faltered, which Merrick took for an answer, not even letting me finish what I was going to say.

"Have you told the rat you're not helping anymore? I'd be careful how you word it, knowing his secret and all, he could try something. I wouldn't put it past him to kill you. Though if he tried it, I wouldn't be quiet. He'd have to kill both us in that case!"

"Th-that's a bit extreme, isn't it?" I said, getting caught up in what he had deflected the conversation to, rather than correcting him.

"Bren, we're dealing with a shadowy government department, a talking rat, Jack the Ripper. There's no such thing as too extreme anymore. Maybe…" Merrick himself stopped, seemingly deep in thought. "Maybe, we should have our own contingency plan in case he tries anything. You know, secret messages left for others, or we tip those government guys off so they can avenge us."

"Th-they're afraid of h-him. I don't think they w-would be any help in d-dealing with him!"

"Are you nervous, Bren? Has he said anything to you? He hasn't followed us, has he?"

I don't know why he thought that I would know if Riz had followed me, I thought, like I was losing the conversation.

"No! He hasn't followed us at all!"

"Good, the mood I'm in right now, it wouldn't have been pretty for him."

"I don't mean that either!"

"Bren, you're starting to get a bit crazy."

A bit crazy? I was starting to seem a bit crazy while we were discussing a talking rat potentially turning murderous on us. If I was a bit crazy, what did that say about him? Don't answer that. I think contact with Riz brings out the crazy in everyone eventually.

"O-okay, let's j-just calm down!" I pleaded. I breathed heavily as if I'd been running a lot, despite having not moved an inch since we got to this point. "W-what I m-meant was that I'm n-not giving up o-on Riz. I'm g-gonna help h-him as long as I can!"

I'd finally said what I should have said about five minutes earlier. Merrick let me finish what I was saying this time, and he gave a look which I could only describe as respect mixed with heavy disappointment.

"That's fair, you got guts, you know that?" He laughed, slapping me on the back as he did it. "Just between you and me though, let's try to keep those guts on the inside this time, right?"

"O-okay!" I sounded too enthusiastic when I said that but it didn't change the mood.

"I still think we should have a contingency plan though, end of everything, we can't trust him. He's still hiding too many things from us."

Merrick turned back to face the way we'd come and started walking.

"We're not going to the shops?"

"Nah, I think we've said everything that we need to for now. We're united in helping him, as long as he doesn't stick a knife in our backs. Seems fair, doesn't it? So, let's go home, and by that, I mean, I'm going home, you can do whatever the feck you want!"

I watched Merrick take a few steps ahead, before I caught back up with him, retracing the steps we took earlier.

"If he asks what we talked about," Merrick said, "just tell him that we were confirming our commitment to him giving us ultimate power!"

I think I laughed.

As we walked down our road, I saw Riz looking out of my window, staring at me and Merrick. All the way to the front door.

"Better be careful, Bren, he's starting to act like a stalker! Later, mate!"

Merrick hit me on the back again, and then left me, turning to walk down the cut that led to Baysdale Road.

I didn't go in immediately, instead I talked myself through everything that had happened so far. Merrick had put the thoughts into my head about what Riz was, and what his plans were going to be for us at the very end, once we'd exhausted our purpose. I wasn't amused by the feeling that I was helping what could turn out to be a bad guy. This led me to think of the person that Riz swore blind was the 'bad guy', Faine. Was this a matter of choosing the lesser evil? The Fae was using Jack the Ripper as a minion, who seemed as bloodthirsty as you'd expect given the name. If Riz wasn't lying about his motivations, he was only doing it to save his people. Wasn't that a work of a good guy?

It wasn't going to do me any good thinking about it outside, so I sighed and went into the house to deal with Riz, not realising that an even bigger disruption was on the horizon, and by that, I meant barrelling her way towards me like a freight train.

CHAPTER 11
AND VALARIE MAKES FOUR

The atmosphere between me and Riz wasn't fantastic after my little jaunt with Merrick. He'd asked me what we were talking about, and I repeated back what I had been told to say. Not convincingly, mind you. I knew he didn't buy it, but at the same time, I couldn't tell him what we were really talking about, as that would have really soured things. So we made small talk instead:

"So, what's it like being a rat?"

Yes, I really had nothing better to ask him, well, okay, I couldn't think of anything better to have said. Back then, I wasn't good at being spontaneous, not like I am now.

"How do yer think it feel's ta be a rat? I don't know how der actual rats do it!" he said rudely, which I took in my stride.

"Why are you a rat?"

My next doozy of a question. I was brilliant at thinking these up, wasn't I? I will never know if I was going to get a sarcastic response from Riz, or if he would have just straight up bit me, as heavy pounding on the front door stopped us. To be clear, this was the kind of knocking you'd expect the police to do if they wanted you. Riz raced from my bed to the window still, pushing his face against the glass to see what was going on.

"Dere's a lass! It's a lass makin all dat racket!"

Funnily enough, I think my dad was thinking the exact same thing downstairs when he shouted up to me, "Bren! Do you know this strange girl who's trying to break down the door?"

"No! Never seen her before in my life!" I shouted back.

"Looks pretty enuff. Yer sly fox, yer neva told me yer ad a lady friend," Riz said, nudging me in the ribs.

"I don't have a girlfriend!"

I took a look out of the window again, carefully peeling the curtains back so I could get a better look at her. The first thing that stuck out to me, aside from her long hair that flowed with the wind, was the old polaroid camera she was wearing round her neck, and the bag by her side, that looked set to burst open. Her outfit set her apart from what I'd seen girls my age wearing, being more practical than stylish, though from appearances, she was definitely at least my age.

"You keep knocking like that and you'll be paying for a new door. Can I help you?" I heard my dad say, finally answering the door.

"You can't, but your son can!" she said, her voice sparking with an energy that made you envious, pointing up to my bedroom window. "He's just been staring out at me, so I know he's up there."

"Urm, Brennan? There's a girl at the door for you!"

I'm sure he yelled this extra loud on purpose as if to prove a point to anyone who may have been listening to the loud banging.

At my dad's request, I came down the stairs, not before instructing Riz to hide in case either my mum or dad went in my room while I was downstairs. Not that I thought they would venture upstairs, not if I was talking to a girl on the front door step. They would be far more interested in that.

"Good luck, kiddo." My dad patted me on the shoulder as he went back into the living room, where I imagined he would join my mum in listening in behind the door.

"H-hi?" My voice went into automatic stammer mode as I faced her for the first time. Her eyes caught my attention, and then I got the camera shoved in my face, as she took a quick snap. With the flash of light blinding me, I stumbled back a bit, almost falling over, but she grabbed me by the neck of my t-shirt and pulled me towards her.

"Brennan. Brennan. Is it okay if I just call you Bren?"

"Actually-"

"Bren it is! So, my name is Valarie. Valarie Turner. Smile!" She threw her arm around me and put her head close to mine as she took a picture of the two of us.

Even though she had let go of me, I could tell she seemed ready to explode with excitement.

"Valarie? Wait, what are you doing here? How do you know me? Do I know you?"

A torrent of questions left my mouth, and this wouldn't have been Valarie if she didn't have answers for them already to go.

"In reverse order, nope, why wouldn't I know you and I'm here to talk to you of course!" She pulled a notebook and pen from her pocket and skimmed through it. "So, let's start at the top. Aren't you going to invite me in? You can't just leave me sitting on the doorstep looking pretty." Valarie fluttered her eyelashes at me before laughing. "If that doesn't work, I have something else I can offer you and your partner." She whispered the last part, so that no one with their ears to the door could hear it.

"My partner?" Due to the shock, I almost shouted this part out, which would have done me no favours.

"Yeah, you know, the rodent who has many names, most of which can't be said in polite conversation?"

"Oh! Okay then, please come in." I panicked and let her in. It wasn't as if she was threatening me now, but I didn't want her talking about Riz at all, even in guarded whispers, within earshot of my parents. I did not want that conversation.

"Great!"

She walked in like it was her house and, as I closed the front door, started looking around, peering behind the corners and up the stairs. She was surveying the place, a custom that I'd get used to and rely on when working with her in the years that followed, but for the first time, it definitely seemed like she was looking for things to steal.

"Well, you going to show me to your bedroom?" she asked in the most forward way possible. I gasped at it, and I heard a thud from behind the living room door. I wasn't the only one who was shocked.

"Urm," I mumbled, and my mind took this opportunity to run for it, leaving me resembling a drooling moron.

"Your room straight up the stairs? Is it on the left or right?"

"Wh-what! W-wait!" I lost the ability to form complete sentences. "D-don't...!" Fragments being the only thing in my vocabulary.

"I suppose I've got a fifty-fifty chance, right?" She started up the stairs, with me red faced, unable to get my thoughts in order to go after her.

"That's your parents room clearly," I heard her say from the top of the stairs. "Which means that one of these should be yours!"

"W-wait!" I shouted again. I tore up the stairs after her, just as she went into my room.

"Bingo!" She cheered. "Now, where's the rat?"

I closed the door after me, my chest hurting as bad as it did yesterday facing down the Spring Heels.

"H-how do you k-know about h-him?"

"Relax, will you," Valarie said softly, with her back to me. She turned with a gentle smile. "I'm on your side, trust me."

That was something that I wanted, but found it hard to do. Not a lot was being done to earn it.

"H-how do I know that th-though?" I replied, more of the truth showing then I would have wanted.

"Because it's the old saying, isn't it, 'You'd be dead if I wanted to kill you'."

The way she said that while smiling was very unnerving. As much as my trust was in free fall, I knew, without a doubt, that she was telling the truth there.

"Anyway," she lightened up again. "Hurry and tell the rat to get out of his hiding place. We've got a bit to discuss, like his vendetta against Faine Hedara."

Saying that name brought Riz straight out of his drawer.

"How der blazin ell does sumone like yerself know bout im?" he spat out.

"There he is, the infamous rogue himself! It's nice to meet an animal of such distinction!"

"Answer der flippin question! Nah, actually scratch dat, answer how sumone like yerself knows who I am! I'm like der VIR of everythin supernatural! Not sum common scum dat every Tom, Dick nd Harry talk bout!"

"VIR?" I interrupted Riz's big rant with that little question, and the look I got back off him in return made it clear I should have known what it meant.

"Very Important Rat, fer smeggin sake, Bren. Keep up!"

"I see you're just as polite to everyone and not just the girls then," Valarie observed. "Does my knowledge rattle you?" She proved once again that when she wasn't talking, she was listening. Watching.

"Plz. I know one who's far worse den yer wud every hope ta be, yer a tot in comparison!"

"We're thinking about the same person," Valarie nodded, and I saw a shiver run down Riz's spine, the first time I ever saw one. For fun, saying the name out loud, even now, will have the same effect.

"Betta start talkin or I'm gunna start bitin! Who're yer, nd who sent yer! I know it's not er who put yer up ta did as she's happy wen I'm payin."

"As I told your partner, Bren, my name is Valarie and I'm working with my uncle, a man called Colin. We investigate all kinds of supernatural goings on. Just like you!" Valarie shared a couple more details.

"I don't know eitha of dose names so y shud I care?"

Riz being ever so blunt.

"Because 'she' is one of ur patrons, and a great family friend. She's already said I'm like the daughter she never had."

I was lost already. I had no idea on who this 'she' was. Or why she was so important at that time. The way this person had seemed to have gotten under Riz's skin was interesting to me though. The rat wasn't fazed by going up against Jack the Ripper yet a name made him tense up.

"So wat, she sent yer ta do her dirty work den? Sounds like yer jus a bossy bitch jus like er! No wonda it sounds like yer both get along. Yer wud be betta off jus mindin yer own freakin business!"

Up to now, you may have noticed that Valarie wasn't as antagonistic to Riz as you may have been accustomed to. This is the moment where all that started. I would say it was a love-hate relationship, but I'd be lying as it was clearly a hate-hate relationship. What did Valarie do in response to Riz's outburst? Well...

"What did you call me?" She said those words with a cool confidence that gave no clue what she was about to do. Which is and will always be my excuse as to why I didn't immediately rush to Riz's rescue.

"I called yer a bossy bitch!"

The last part Riz mumbled so you couldn't almost hear it.

"I thought so. Bren, do you mind if I use your bathroom? I need to freshen something up. I'm surprised you haven't noticed. It's stinking up your room." She smiled, and I didn't click what she was referring to.

"Oh, go r-right ahead."

"Wat, yer runnin away already afta one insult?"

Famous last words.

"Who's runnin, Rat?" Valarie bent down and caught Riz unawares, grabbing him by his tail and picking him up. "I was told I might have to put my foot down with you. Though I'm not as harsh as her to step on you, plus I don't want to get my shoes dirty."

"Valarie? What are you going to do with him?" I said, in a bit of shock at how easy she had subdued him.

"Like I said, I need to freshen something up. What? You didn't think I meant me, did you?" She winked and then carried Riz off into the bathroom. I crept to the door and watched from afar as Valarie flushed the toilet and then lowered Riz into the swirling waters.

"Ya bitch! I'm gunna get yer fer dis!"

This was the start of their long running battle, one that will likely never end, and more often than not, drags me into a vortex of pain.

"Maybe next time you'll think twice about calling someone a bitch then."

Valarie then dropped him to the floor where he tried to shake off all the water. "I'm not all bad, at least I flushed the toilet first, and I wouldn't have done that if you were an ordinary rat. I don't hurt animals."

I'd never seen Riz move as fast as he did when he rushed back into my room, taking position next to me, trying to look threatening while also being sopping wet.

"Get rid of her, Bren! She jus tried ta kill me!"

"I gave you a bath. See, you smell a lot better now."

She walked back in and leant against the wall casually.

"Don't mak me use ma Runes on yer!" Riz carried on, throwing out threats.

"You sure you want to do that? Especially since I can help you with what you want."

"Goddamit…" Riz said, proving that he was never going to pass anything up that could help him.

CHAPTER 12
DOWN TO BUSINESS

"H-how can you help us?" I asked. I could see that Riz was still sore about what had just happened, but he wanted to know.

"Go on den, tell us wat yer know bout Faine. Den I'll see if it's worth bein nice ta yer ova."

"Hold up, it's not that easy, quid pro quo, rat. I'm sure you're familiar with that!" Valarie said, putting her hand in front of Riz's face.

"Yer want sumtin in exchange? Ell tell us wat it is yer know den we'll hear der crap yer want in exchange, dat's fair rite?"

As if anyone with half a brain wouldn't be able to guess what he would do instead of listening to her.

"No, that's not how it's going to work. So, what I want. See me and my uncle have a few difficult cases, one which is bearing down on us. We've exhausted all our usual contacts, so we went to you know who, who told us to track you down. So here I am!"

I had several questions already, mainly how she, a girl little more than my age, had gotten involved in this business, and who this person was she and Riz kept mentioning, but it didn't feel the time to interrupt, not with us poised to get some new information, even if the rat had to give something up first.

"Nd wat case is dat? I know a lot of thins, so don't expect me ta remember every stupid obscure thin, kay? Since yer not gunna tell us nethin, just spit out wat yer want already."

"What I want is to know where has Artemis dropped off to?" Valarie asked, poised to write down whatever came out of Riz's mouth.

"Y do yer want ta speak ta dat bitch?" Riz answered.

"Because I want to? My uncle and her go way back. She even provided us with a few bespoke items that I bet you would love to get your paws on."

Valarie made it look like she was going to open her handbag up, even letting Riz loom in close, desperate, it seemed, for a peek. As he got close though, she shut it on his nose.

"As if I would show you that easy, not with those sticky paws of yours."

Being naïve at that point, I thought she meant his paws were dirty. Yes, you may pity me.

"If yer won't tell me wat yer want Arty fer, den I'm not tellin yer diddly squat bout er. Yer mite be huntin er or sum sick nd twisted shit."

Riz would want you to believe that he was doing this for the wellbeing of a friend. I suspect it was more that he was just wanting to be an awkward twat.

"To make sure she's okay. We've been dealing with something dangerous and personal and I know you want to squeeze all the gossip out of this, but it won't work. If you want information on Faine, then you're going to tell me where you last saw her. I don't want her dealing with anything on her own."

Till this point, Valarie had seemed to keep to a jovial tone, never hinting at a serious side, but this comment, almost precisely to put Riz in place, showed her at her most stoic. Given the atmosphere, I almost didn't want to put my hand up, interrupting things, but I wasn't able to follow most of what was being said.

"Who's Artemis? The way you're both talking about her, she sounds quite important."

"Yer familiar wit der Greek gods, yeh?" Riz asked.

"Yeah?"

"Den yer wud be familiar wit Artemis, yer plank! Now shush… der adults ar talkin!"

I got the implication there. I didn't believe it at first, but I took what he was saying.

"Anyway, so if I tell yer wat I know bout Arty, yer gunna spill der beans on Faine rite? Den ye'll bugga off?"

"Well, I don't know about that last part, but other than that… yes."

"Fine. Richmond," Riz rolled his eyes. Getting this simple an answer out of him was a mammoth task indeed.

"Richmond?" Valarie asked, furiously writing it down, and then stopping to question it.

"Yeh, yer know, der place, Richmond, got a castle nd shit. I met er dere fer sum supplies, she waz tryin ta lay low," Riz explained, again, making it look like every second he spent doing that was a second he could have spent doing other things.

"So we go to Richmond, we'll find her?"

"Maybe, maybe not, yer know wat she's like, she mite ave gone ta ground again. Wat's she got erself in ta dis time? Not fightin wit er father again, is she?"

"If you really, really have to know and won't keep your long nose out of other people's business, then Umbral."

"Oh, dat git."

"You're acquainted with him?" Valarie asked, her eyebrow raised.

"Yer cud say dat."

The name didn't mean much to me, like most of the names that I'd heard so far.

"Anyone want to tell me who he is?" I asked anyway.

"Not our business, kid. Jus know dat es one of dose sort yer neva want ta ave nethin ta do wit."

"I'd listen to the rat. I've had too many dealings with that monster," Valarie said, still with the serious expression on her face. "Don't feel sad for me though. There's a truth I'm searching for and I know it lies with him. I'll pry it from him, one way or another."

I didn't doubt that she would.

"Anyway, enuff of dis crap, I told yer wat yer wanted ta know, so u betta tell me wat I want!" Riz got closer to Valarie, which I thought was a dangerous position for him.

"Well, for starters, I'm going to ask you another question. Did you know fully what Faine wants in Thornaby? Why he'd come to this place?" Valarie shifted her positon on my bed, so she was laid on her front, head resting on her hand. A spark in her eye, where she knew something that she assumed you didn't.

"Yeh, he wants one of der kidz from ere. Cuz powas or sum daft thin, as if anyone wud side wit im," Riz answered. The Riz I knew would have believed he'd jumped over Valarie's gotcha attempt. Of course, it didn't work.

"It's more complicated than that. What if I told you that he was gathering an army? Hmm? Did you realise that? Well?" Valarie was enjoying every second of this. Don't blame her. If I had that much information that Riz didn't have, I'd enjoy it as well.

"Wat?" Riz's face dropped a little, then he quickly got his composure. "How der ell wud yer know dat? Nd how does dis kid factor in ta shit!"

"She was right, you really don't like getting caught short in knowledge, do you?"

"Answer me damnit!" Riz demanded.

"W-why does Faine n-need an army? Is h-he going to war with us? J-just to make us b-believe?"

The weight of the conversation dropped on me, making me even more nervous than I was before.

"From what I've been told, it may have started out as a way to make us all believe, but when a certain someone kept stopping him, things have escalated." Valarie rolled her eyes till she was looking at Riz.

"Yeh, blame me, y don't yer! I waz fightin dis twat long before yer daddy was a glint in der milkmen's eye! Dat's even if yer can tell yer family tree apart from a pack of mice!"

Riz seemed more defensive here. Even going after Valarie's family, which at that point, we knew nothing about. There was a change that came over her, her eyes turning darker and the mood in the room turned chilly. I fidgeted as I sat, fighting the urge to move away from the violence that I knew was surely coming.

"I'd watch what you're saying about my family, rodent. Otherwise, getting flushed down the toilet will be the least of your worries."

Valarie's words left us both stunned. It wasn't so much what she said, but the way she said it. I saw Riz's whiskers move, like he'd caught the scent of something in the air. Though he neglected to tell me what was going on.

"Ain't dat interestin," I heard him mumble.

"Now, let's take the discussion away from my family and back to where it should be aimed… Faine and his intentions."

"Don't see how yer can help wit dat. Bet yer don't even know who he's afta!"

"Better question is, do you?" Valarie smiled as she turned the question around. "I may not know his name, and it is a 'him', but I know that it's someone aged sixteen to eighteen, who isn't trained whatsoever and is not on the radar of any service!"

"Nd yer found dis out, how? Wait, don't tell me, it waz er wazn't it, back to er old tricks." Riz face palmed with his little rat paws.

"No, actually it was one of the Spring Heel clones. One of those rare ones with a conscience. Gave all the details it could before it died," Valarie explained, flicking through her notepad.

"Blimey, yer killed it?"

"No, you idiot!"

Valarie whacked Riz on the head with the notebook. "I came across him in my own investigation after Jack the Ripper attacked him. My uncle scared him off. I wrote down all of what he told me."

"Did it tell yer anythin useful before it died, den? Like where ta find dis kid, or wat Faine is gunna do if he get's im?"

"I thought it was obvious as to what was going to happen if he finds him, as I'm sure you're very much aware." Valarie looked at Riz from the sides of her eyes, lining him up like she was aiming to kill him. "His army will get someone very powerful, as this individual is full of Curse magic."

Curse magic, one of the pillars of magic that flow through the world. We'd already spoken about Rune magic, that Riz used and was teaching me… Curse magic was another source of power, as I'd come to learn. Valarie had said very powerful in her description of it, and she wasn't wrong. To put it simply, Curse magic is something that witches in stories dealt in, having power to turn people into other things, and to cast a spell that hunts people through their descendants.

"Nd? It wud be easier fer im ta get sumone from der Unseeley Council ta help im. Dey can use Curse magic, practically dere bread nd butta!"

"From what I learned, this person is far stronger than whatever the Unseeley could muster. Faine wants them to be a general in his army, and someone he can copy the power from for the next generation of Spring Heels, or whatever he'll call them."

"Y-you mean he'll try to clone them too?"

The thought of having duplicates made of me was unsettling. I knew that I wasn't Faine's target, from what Riz had said, and despite only knowing her for an hour, I felt safe to assume that Valarie would have informed me I was the target from the moment she met me.

"Not exactly. What the Spring Heel said was more along the lines of Faine cutting you open, tinkering around, taking the part he wanted, and replicating it in the new troops so they can do it too. You'll get stitched back up again. I mean, Jack did."

"Rite, I'm sick of dis talk, will yer get ta der point! Yer not told me anythin dat I didn't already know!" Riz shouted out, so loud that I was positive that it was heard downstairs. I think I got lucky though and didn't see any sign of my parents coming to see what was going on. "I mean, I told yer were ta find Arty! Nd yer jus tell me crap like dat! How is dat fair!"

"Maybe because I wasn't finished? Like news I got just this morning, about how Faine is zeroing in on his target?" Valarie fluttered her eyelashes, smirking at Riz, who had once again, obviously underestimated her.

"Y der ell didn't yer tell us dat in der first place!"

"Because you never asked?"

"Yer a freckin bitch yer know dat rite? While we've been sittin ere chattin, Jack cud already ave nabbed der bastard! Bren! We gotta split rite now!" Riz jumped to his feet, shouted again as he did. He jogged over to me, and started pulling my sleeve. "C'mon! Wat're yer waitin fer yer ejit! Let's go!"

"B-because Valarie is still here?" I said.

"Tell er ta piss off! We've got no time ta waste!"

How important this was to him hadn't gone unnoticed. I turned to Valarie, an apology already forming on my lips.

"Don't apologise, Bren. We'll see each other again!" Valarie smiled, and Riz stopped in his tracks, forgetting, in the moment, that he'd been wanting to be gone.

"Wat? I thought our deal waz dun. Yer got wat yer wanted ta know, nd yer told us wat we wanted. Dat waz der end of it, yer can sod off!"

"That certain someone we both know, told me to give you all the help I could, as in her words 'you'd only mess it up again'. Well, she didn't say mess, but I don't feel comfortable fully repeating what she said."

Now knowing who they were on about, I could only imagine what she really said, and all the extra bits that Valarie edited out.

"Does she really think I need a flippin babysitter!"

I was actively holding on to Riz at this point, not wanting this to explode further.

"It's not for your benefit! For his!" Valarie pointed at me.

"M-me?" I stuttered. Finally, I was involved in the conversation proper. Shame about the context though.

"Riz has a reputation with human apprenticeships, and not a good one, shall we say." Valarie gave the rat a hard stare. "Personally, I wouldn't trust him with a ten foot barge pole." She winked at me as she said that. That was both her subtle and not-so subtle way of warning me about him.

"Nd I wudn't trust yer eitha! If yer know er den yer already minglin in sum dark places dere, yer lay down in mud, yer get filthy!"

"In your case, it should be, lay down with rats, you get fleas!" Valarie shot back.

"Rats wit fleas? Oh! Yer makin a bubonic plague joke! Well, hardy har har! Der joke's on u as dat waz before I took dis form, bitch!" Riz replied. His smug grin didn't last when he saw Valarie making a note. "Wat u writin?"

"Just another piece of the puzzle in trying to work out what you are!"

"Oh, u fukin bitch," Riz snarled, not that Valarie took any notice of what he said.

"I do have to be off now, Bren, I'll be in touch very soon! I look forward to helping you with your problem." She looked at Riz as she spoke. "Oh, and helping you to bring down Faine, of course! I'll tell my uncle about where Arty is. I'll have to introduce you to him."

"Knowin yerself is bad enuff, not sure I wanna meet anyone else of yer family tree!"

Valarie ignored the comment and stood, straightening out her clothes as she did. I got to my feet as well, and she took hold of my hand, starting to shake it. My heartbeat started racing, making it resemble the drum beat of a dance track.

"Yer tongue is hangin out," Riz sighed.

As quick as she took my hand, Valarie let go, that smile she wore when I saw her downstairs now back on her face. For anyone who's guessed that I started developing feelings for her at this point, congratulations on seeing the obvious.

"Oh! Almost forgot!" Valarie pulled a small slip of paper out of her bag and shoved it into my palm. "My phone number and a Hotmail address you can reach me on."

The first girl's phone number I ever got. I'd never let on, but I still have it in one of the books that I have lying around the office.

"O-oh okay! I look forward to working with you!" I said, my shyness making Riz nauseous. Suffice to say, he wasn't a fan of Valarie.

"Yer can't seriously say yer trust er, can yer?" he moaned, but this time I joined in with ignoring him.

"Good luck, Bren, talk to you soon!" With the same enthusiasm with which she entered my life, Valarie then walked back out of it. Albeit temporarily. I watched her as she left my room, went down the stairs and out of the front door. While I had expected my parents to have been waiting in the hallway, they had spent the entire time in the living room, and they were anxious to know what had gone on.

As if I was going to tell them.

"Bren!" my dad shouted up to me. "Who was she?"

"Never mind that, Will. Is she your girlfriend?" my mum called out over the top of him.

"She's a friend! F-from school!" My response was as ill-conceived as the excuse itself.

"Oh really?" My dad had shifted into detective mode, resembling the ones he loved watching on TV. "You've never mentioned her before, you always said that Merrick was the only friend you had there? What aren't you telling us?"

Normally this would be the point where my mum would step in and get him to leave me alone, saying that they'd give me time. Not so much this time.

"What have you gotten up to with her?" My mum picked up the pace of the interrogation, and even though a flight of stairs separated us, I knew she was giving me the hard stare. I was also amused as to how their logic was working, as now they were convinced that me and Valarie were an item.

"Yer parents ar morons," Riz muttered, climbing into my underwear drawer. "So ar u fer trustin dat bitch."

Maybe he was right, but what did that say about me being willing to trust him? Something that was going to be tested in the worst possible way...

CHAPTER 13
JACK'S PLAY DATE

Riz didn't venture out of the drawer till three in the afternoon.

"Yer ejit, yer wasted a whole day of trainin!"

Yet he was the one who had been in a hissy fit, but of course, it was all my fault.

"We really should go and see Merrick, tell him about Valarie," I suggested. I didn't want to leave him out of the loop with any of this.

"Yer mean yer wanna brag bout yer girlfriend? Are yer dat much of a sad act dat yer need ta show off der bitch's phone number? Giv me a flippin break. I don't mind goin, but let's be clear dat yer jus wanna rub is face init."

"That's not true at all! Besides we're not together! Why do you and my parents think we are?" I protested. I wouldn't have complained if I was with Valarie at that point, but seeing as we had just met, it wasn't realistic.

"Fine, wateva yer tell urself. Maybe yer shud let me break der news ta Merrick while yer wait outside," Riz suggested, while stretching and crawling out of the drawer.

"Or maybe not? Given how you've been acting, you'll probably cause him to throw you out of a window! Just like Valarie trying to flush you."

Over the years I've known Riz, I think it's a good thing that I've only ever thrown him out of a window twice. Wait, no, four times, with one of those being to save him from a burning building, only to be told that he could have handled it.

"Considering how much yer struggle ta talk ta people, Me handlin all dat is one of der betta ways ta tackle dis. Yer can be der muscle, nd I can be der brains. Like always."

Nope, Riz didn't have an ego at all, can't you tell? Yes, the way he was speaking was wearing on my nerves, even then, but I didn't think you could argue against him. He had an aura of indestructibility that made it seem that nothing I did would ultimately matter, and that he was always right.

To clarify, he's right some of the time, but spends too much time gloating about the other times to notice all the things he's wrong about.

"I-I'm not so sure," I said meekly.

"Even u aren't sure bout arguin against it! It's a brilliant idea, nd perfect time ta see Merrick! I'll do der talkin, while yer just stand outside nd look pretty."

I should have been concerned that he wanted alone time with Merrick, but I didn't see it then. What I saw was Riz wanting to sideline me to the role of his personal carrier. I'm over egging it here but it wouldn't be far off the truth.

While I said good bye to my parents, Riz hid himself in my coat pocket again, not that I was looking forward to wearing that coat today, the temperature was high, and that coat made me feel like I was sweating my life away. Honestly, I never know how Riz didn't complain about how hot it was, the pocket must have been like a little microwave, yet he never had an issue.

"I'm off to see Merrick," I said, sticking my head through to the living room door. My mum was reading a magazine, while dad was watching one of his favourite detective shows. Neither looked surprised that I was going out again, as it was custom for me to be out with Merrick most days when I wasn't in school.

"Will you be out for tea tonight?" My mum asked, without even looking up from her magazine.

"No idea, depends on what happens. I'll ring if I'm going to be out," I replied. Again, this was all standard stuff. Nothing I was saying would give them reason to think I was up to anything. Yet, my mum still slowly turned so her eyes were staring at mine.

"Don't get into any trouble, okay?"

Her words struck me, and while reasonable to assume it was just because I'd spent time in hospital, I felt that they meant more.

"I-I won't!" I quickly shut the door to put some distance between me and my mother's stare.

"Wat took yer so long?" Riz moaned as I put my coat on.

"I had to tell my parents where I was going!"

"Nah, all yer ad ta tell dem waz, 'I'm leavin, bye'!"

He made it sound such an easy thing to do. Well, I suppose it would be easy if you were a bastard.

"Just shut up, we're going now, aren't we?" I replied, hushing him as I left the house.

We had only made it to the bottom of Baysdale Road when Riz, gave me the most unwelcome news you could get when you were dealing with the 'Others'.

"Dey're followin us."

I didn't need to question how he knew this, and neither did I have to ask who he was talking about.

"Where are they?" I looked around but only saw the random person walking by, cars driving past, and all the houses around me. A bus turned the corner onto Humber Road, the brakes giving a striking addition to the soundtrack of the scene.

"I don't see anything," I added.

"I don't care if yer don't see nethin, dey're out dere nd dey're clearly followin us!"

"That's not what I meant! I'm not saying I don't believe you, just I can't see them!"

"Dey is gud at hidin."

I did get the impression that I was being watched, more so that I couldn't pass it off as paranoia.

"What's the plan then? I can't lead them to Merrick."

"Yer rite, we can't! Wat we av ta do is get dem ta a secluded place, nd make dem very ded."

"I thought you said Faine would take a while to build more Spring Heels!"

"Less talk, more runnin!"

Riz bit me to get me moving, and I turned away from Humber Road, cutting straight across it and headed towards Redcar Road. This wasn't going to lead to a better place either. I knew that a right turn would take me up some green space, near Littleboy Park and up to the graveyard, which as stereotypical as it sounds, was always a good place if you wanted quiet. Not that the idea of fighting goblins atop the remains of the dead was appealing to me, but I was panicking.

With no better ideas, I ran towards it, keeping a nervous eye around me, in case the Spring Heels jumped me, or worse. While running, I realised how surreal it would be to watch this memory back, from someone else's point of view. Running away from an unseen threat in the blazing heat of a bright summer's day with a rat in my pocket. Couldn't write it.

"Think dey're gettin closa! Three ta four of dem, one of dem is slightly different. Shit. It's frickin Jack!"

That was news I didn't want to hear.

"Jack! You want me to fight Jack the Ripper!"

"Yer don't want im ta kill yer, den yeh, yer gunna ave ta fite im!"

Riz with the persuasive arguments again.

"We don't have any Runes though! Unless you hid some in my pocket?" I asked, hopefully.

Riz didn't talk for what seemed like an age. In reality, it must have only been three seconds, as I hadn't even reached Acklam Road yet.

"Yeh, dat mite be a gud idea ta start carryin dem around wit yer," he mumbled.

"Brilliant! I'll just send that idea to myself, three hours in the past! Riz, what're we going to do?" I shouted. It was supposed to be an internal kind of scream, but it ended up being vocal, and I don't regret that. Despite the odd looks from people walking their dogs to the park. I'd have gladly exchanged places with them. As I waited for the road to clear so I could cross, I thought I heard a metallic twang, evidence of Spring Heels, not that I needed to hear that.

Once over the road, I paused going in, fully realising what I was letting myself in for. I was going to face down not just a bunch of goblins with springs attached, but also Jack the Ripper. I was armed with nothing but a talking rat that would be the first thing I would throw at them. Yes, folks, the rat-a-pult idea was birthed here. Had I stayed out of the graveyard, I would have been safe, if even for a little while, but I could have also put others in danger. If they wanted to, they could have pried whatever information they wanted from my head, simply by threatening others.

"Get goin will yer!"

"Why are you pushing for this? We have nothing to fight with! Should we be finding some way to distract them till we can think of a plan?"

"Duh, do yer remember who yer talkin ta? I've got a plan! A very gud one in fact, so gud yer gunna be amazed nd glad yer got me ridin round in yer pocket!"

"Unless you're going to reveal you have a rocket launcher hidden somewhere here, then I don't see how I can be amazed!"

"Yer'll see, tho I'm gunna ave ta get yer ta do one thin fer me."

I didn't want to hear this. It doesn't take a genius to guess what I was going to have to do. Had I any sense I would have just chucked him into the graveyard and been on my merry way. Instead I walked in. I have no sense.

"W-what do you w-want me to do?"

"Hold dem off fer me, while I get wat I need."

He hopped out of my pocket, running as soon as his little paws hit the ground. Leaving me alone with the approaching sound of springs, which climaxed with two Spring Heels crashing through the trees. They didn't care about the grave markers they were knocking down, and admittedly, I didn't care about the graves I started to run over in the effort to get away from the goblins. It's not something I would repeat nowadays, being far more knowledgeable about what could happen when the resident takes offence.

"You can't run!" one of the Spring Heels hissed. The other was too busy spitting in rage to say anything.

"And you can't catch me!" I shouted, still running deeper into the graveyard. Here, nature ruled supreme over the forgotten tombstones, where time had rubbed away the names of those entombed. From here, no one would see the fight that would go down, unless they were in that same section. Oh, and the squirrels, which Riz hated, for reasons that he has told me, but I've long since forgotten. If you're curious, just think of something that Riz would hate someone for, and you wouldn't be far off.

"Stop running, boy!" Jack roared as he leapt down in front of me, stopping me from going any further. That was a good thing, mind, as I was running out of graveyard in that direction to run to.

"J-Jack!"

It was time to mix it up. I'd just done the first part of running, so now it was time to stall with talking. In encounters like this, you can always tell that the enemy wants you alive if they haven't killed you on sight. Like this Jack could have killed me before I had even realised he was there. They wanted me alive, which gave me an advantage.

"What do you want from me?" I yelled at him

"You? No, it's the rat we want, you're just the fleshly delivery device. I imagine the rat choose a skinny brat like yourself because you would do what he wanted, like his little servant," Jack said, never taking his eyes off me. Every time he exhaled, embers of fire came from his mouth. Of course, he didn't know the half of what was going on with me and Riz, or that I was far from his obedient transporter.

"So you want me to hand him over, and you'll let me go?" I had to make it sound like I was open to an offer, if it meant me living. I mean, if I wasn't convinced he would have killed me anyway, I would, maybe, have taken it.

"Let you go?" Jack threw his head back in laughter, proving me right. "No, we won't be letting you go, but you do have your choice of a quick death or a slow, agonising one."

How predictable. For your information, for those of you keeping track of these things, I think this is said to me every week or so. Sometimes they try to keep it fresh with maybe an original torture method… doesn't matter though.

"That's not very fair, is it? I have what you want, and I could hand him over right now. I'm not liable to do that if you're just going to kill me anyway. Who would take that deal?" I argued, trying to keep my confidence high. Jack wasn't buying it. He didn't look fazed in the slightest. On the contrary, his smile was getting bigger. He started walking towards me, flexing his fingers, which, like those of the smaller Spring Heels, were knives with serrated edges. As he got closer, I could see the multiple scars and stitches, the metal braces that had been seared into Jack's flesh. Each one was a reminder that he was a constant experiment for Faine, a monster forever undergoing modifications. Had he not been advancing on me, intent on killing me, I might have sympathised with him.

"D-do you want h-him or not!" My confidence shattered here, as you can tell.

"Yes, and I'll take him from you when I've ripped out your spine. That is, if you actually have him." Jack clearly didn't care if I did or didn't have Riz. And I didn't have him. The Spring Heels around me weren't doing anything but watching at this point, sharing in my fear it seemed. After seeing what Jack had done to some of the Spring Heels, it wasn't much of a surprise.

"M-maybe w-we c-can talk a-about this some more!" I was edging backwards, but at a slower rate than how fast Jack was coming up to me.

"I think your fear is proving that the rat has already fled. You're just buying time for him, aren't you? Another weak-willed human turned cannon fodder for his ambition. How many of you have to die for him?"

I didn't give him an answer as I was distracted by a light from a bush, one that was getting brighter and brighter.

"What are you looking at?" Jack followed my gaze and leapt back as an arrow of light leapt out and vaporised the head of an unfortunate Spring Heel.

Riz crawled out of the bush, holding several Runes that he'd just crafted, none of them uniform in size or shape, even the symbol lacked his usual finesse. The effects spoke for themselves.

"We ave jus begun ta fite, yer twat! Keep yer soddin mitts off ma property!" Riz said. I was now stood in the middle of Jack and Riz, feeling like a gooseberry between the two, and increasingly useless in the fight that was brewing...

CHAPTER 14
DARK HORSE

"Yer gunna start dis dance, den?" Riz taunted.

"Riz!" I wanted to make him aware that I was still in the middle of the two of them, a place I'd rather not be.

"Will yer get outta der way, Bren! I'm tryin ta be all heroic by savin yer ass."

Riz trying to be heroic, there's an oxymoron if ever you heard it.

"Boys! Give this lad some fun, will you? I don't want any interference while I deal with the rat. Mess this up, and I'll let you tell Faine what happened!" Jack leapt over me as he spoke, making me seem useless even as an obstacle. The Spring Heels, hearing the threat, obliged, and the remaining three came at me. I had to roll out of the way to avoid being torn up by their claws. Riz was now engaged in a fight with Jack, as the pair had wanted. I wished Riz had been more sharing with his plan, as he neglected to tell me how I was going to fare against three Spring Heels, unarmed. All I could do, as I had been doing previously, was run. I knew the chances of it working this time were slim to none. There wasn't much ground between us, and with those blasted springs of theirs, a single bound would catch me. Seeing how Riz had gotten me into this mess, I'd use him to get me out of it.

I duly ran, but towards the Spring Heels, who were momentarily confused, just as I had wanted. I jumped through an opening in between the three of them, and when I was back on my feet, I ran to where Riz was. Reading this, you may be picturing my movements like a slick Hollywood scene... I assure you it wasn't anything like that. A fact I only noticed at this point was that the Spring Heels' movements were strangely slow, nothing at all like the ones we'd dealt with a day or so ago. I had all the time I needed when I'd hit the ground to get back up again, before they'd fully registered what I'd done. Not that I thought this at that split second of time, but I'm helping to fill in your gaps of my experience.

"Bren! I told yer to get outta my flippin way!" Riz repeated his comment from a moment ago. I didn't listen, as I was too busy focusing on picking up some of the Runes he'd made and he was hoarding to himself. So far, he'd failed to land a single shot on Jack, though it had kept him away.

"I'm taking these!" I said, after I took them. In the scant time I had, I grabbed the Blast Runes, because they were the only ones in the pile that I was confident enough to use. The Arrow Rune was the one that had ended up putting me in hospital, so there was no way I'd risk that again. Knowing my luck, it would have killed me outright this time, making Jack's job even easier, or I'd be stuck with Lionel at the hospital. Don't need to tell you all how bad that would be.

"Oi! I'm usin dem! How do yer expect me ta thwack dis ejit if yer take ma stuff!"

"Less talking! More blasting!" I shouted at Riz in between heavy breaths. My unfit body was starting to fail me, feeling the chest pains that came from heavy exercise, and my legs turning on me. According to fitness instructors, you're supposed to push past this pain barrier, but try telling that to my sixteen-year-old self. It wasn't happening. Naturally, I slowed down at this point, and turned to face the Spring Heels that were behind me. When I say behind me, I was sadly being literal, as when I spun round, one was only a few inches away, already in the motion of jumping at me. For reference, its claws were the closest thing to me.

"Tar'Hazdem!" I got the words out in the middle of a breath. Both the Rune and Spring Heel burst apart in blast of purple magical energy. That was new. Normally it was a blueish white.

"Der colour is jus cuz I ad ta make it outta crap stones!" Riz managed to shout out, reading my mind apparently.

The last two Spring Heels jumped at me again, caring not for their fallen friend, which, given my past encounters with them, should have been obvious. Clearly, these weren't made with concern for their fellow goblins, or themselves. I wasn't overly afraid, mind. When in possession of Riz's Runes, I felt braver, stronger. I had already transformed one goblin into ash, and still had two Runes left to turn the others likewise. I may have smiled at this point, but can't remember exactly. With a Rune in each palm, I pictured myself as if it was one of those cool Hollywood movies, where I was wearing dark sunglasses in the middle of the day, and had quips for every time I blew away a foul denizen. The two Spring Heels came at me, and I held my hands up with a mighty roar of, "Tar'Hazdem!"

The two energy blasts leapt from my hands into the faces of the goblins, killing them both instantly.

"Well wud yer look at dat, Jack, yer prat! All yer followers ave been wiped out!" Riz gloated. "Nd dis is y Faine shud come take care of thins himself, cuz yer jus useless!"

"You think I would turn up to a fight like this with so few troops? I just wanted you to use up your Runes before committing myself." Jack clicked his fingers, sparks flying from his knife fingers. At his command, a horde of Spring Heels landed on the ground. There was easily ten of them now, and all that confidence I'd earned through being brave, standing up to Jack, killing those other Spring Heels, was wiped out.

"Hah! Yer think dat scares me! Me nd Bren ere aren't afraid of yer damn gobos!" Riz said, though I failed to see how he could back up such a statement. The rat only had one Rune left that I could tell, though the symbol did look a bit different. I didn't see how that alone would change our fate in this battle.

"Riz! We're c-completely outnumbered n-now!" I said.

"Nd? Dis is rite where we want dem!" Riz turned away from me, and back into Jack, who was standing there bemused at our conversation. He knew that the balance of power had swung back in his favour. He hadn't even ordered the new Spring Heels to do anything yet, and they just stood there, drooling with mouths agape.

"We're right where you want us? Interesting. Pray tell, what did you plan to do next? Was it requiring both of you, or can I take apart your human servant?" Jack threw a stare in my direction.

"Yer not gunna ave a chance ta lay a finga on im! As I sed, dis is y Faine shud ave dun is own dirty work!" Riz was trying to taunt Jack again, probably wanting to make him mad so he'd make a mistake, a classic tactic that only had one failing as far as I could tell. Namely that Riz's anger management was woefully short.

"Faine doesn't need to dirty his hands in dealing with you. That's why he trusts me to do it for him." Jack started flexing his arms, as if he was getting ready for an exercise session.

"Trust yer? Afta dis, yer gunna be a world record holda in failure! Yer cudn't catch a cold, let alone deal wit me, I'm der reel deal!"

There was Riz running his mouth off again. As if this scenario was going to be made any better by him doing that.

"Enough. There will be plenty of time for us to talk once you're strapped to a little table, and we're extracting all that information from your skull." Jack jumped at us, causing the rest of the Spring Heels to move in.

"Kid! Get ere now!" Riz shouted at me, but I froze as the sun was blotted out by the Spring Heels jumping down, knocking me over, and holding tight on my arms and legs. I felt the steel of their claws on my body, cutting through my clothes.

"U ejit!" Riz yelled. He may have called me some other, less polite names, but I didn't hear them. "I told yer ta get ova ere! Now I got ta save yer arse too!"

Great to hear that I was making things harder for him, that was totally what I meant to do. With my head being forced to the ground, I lost sight of Riz and Jack. I assumed they would be back to the fighting, but feeling the cold edge of a knife against my throat meant that Jack had found a new way to fight Riz, using me as the weapon.

"What's this one worth to you, rat? Is he like the others? Will his death mean nothing to you? Or do you have some semblance of loyalty to him? It's been a one sided test up to now, hasn't it, and I know insanity is the act of trying something and expecting different results, but what's one more roll of the dice, eh? Let's go for test thirty-five? You going to give yourself up? Or do I kill him?" Jack announced, putting his head close to mine. I couldn't see his face, but felt his breath on the side of my face, and the warmth of the embers that sparked against my skin.

"Do I ave ta decide now?" Riz asked, which made my heart stop. There was nothing I'd learned about him at that point, which would have made you believe that he'd have chosen to help me over himself. Why I thought that this might be that time he found a heart is a mystery to me. Maybe I was naïve, or probably just scared and stupid.

"Maybe that would have been funny if you hadn't used that joke the first ten times I killed your workers," Jack's retort cut deep. To me that was, Riz didn't seem fazed.

"Riz! Help me!"

My plea fell on deaf ears.

"If yer ad listened ta me in der first place, yer wudn't be in dat mess wud yer! Got a lot ta learn, kid." Riz literally ran his paw over his face as if frustrated with what had happened to me. I still get ribbed about this from him, not much, but it still gets brought up. I tell him to shove it.

"Now is not the time for this!" I cried out.

"The boy is right, now isn't the time for you two to be arguing. Make a choice, rodent."

I think Jack was getting impatient with us. He was starting to show it as I felt his finger blades more keenly against my skin. I didn't dare breath in case it ripped my throat open. In my attempt to keep my neck away from the sharp implements that Jack called his fingers, I saw Riz's whiskers twitching.

"Tar'Hazdem!" another voice called out, sending out a short blast that took down two of the Spring Heels that were holding me down. The remaining ones all leapt back to confront the new foe. I couldn't tell who it was. Being freed, I crawled on all fours till I was next to Riz, who was looking in the direction of my saviour. He didn't have a disgusted look on his face so it clearly wasn't Valarie. God, would he have hated that. This left one person who it could have been. How this was the case, I would yet learn. I sat up and stared in the same direction as Riz, confirming that the one who had saved me was Merrick.

"No one touches my friend like that. I don't care if you are the bleeding Ripper! I'll blow you up too!" he said, striking a pose with his outstretched hand holding onto a Blast Rune.

"Dat's one of der ones I giv yer last nite! So yer kept hold of dem, eh? Pretty tricky." Riz sounded impressed with him holding onto what were incredibly dangerous weapons.

"Merrick!" I gasped, relieved to see him, though not as much as Jack was, till that joy turned to anger and hatred.

"You! What the hell are you doing! Throwing your lot in with the rat? This isn't right at all!" His words didn't make sense.

"Not that it's any of your goddamn business but I'm here to help him, and since he's helping the rat, well, I guess he's my problem too!" Merrick was aiming at Jack alone at this point, but the Spring Heels weren't moving on him, a change in behaviour considering what they had done to me.

"Your problem? Your problem! Your problem should be that you're fighting on the wrong side, Cursed One! Faine brought us here for you! Everything that has happened here has been in order to bring you into the fold!"

Jack's words shook me, and I know they must have shaken Merrick too. Riz, however, wasn't fazed, and as I looked down at him, he yawned, till he realised what I was doing, then he wore that fake look of shock that fooled no one. It became clear that the rat had known all along about Merrick, about what he was, and that he was Faine's target. Riz had told me that it was by accident that he ended up in my bag, and I knew what he'd meant now. He'd meant to get into Merrick's bag, go back home with him, presumably drawing him completely in the fight, leaving me behind. My heart sank as I thought about it, almost making me lose focus on the fight.

"What are you talking about!" Merrick yelled out. "Answer me! What do you mean I'm cursed! Tell me what you know, right now!" He started to advance on Jack, who hesitated. The Ripper looked back at Riz, then towards Merrick who was getting closer, his face bulging with rage. He then did what no one expected.

He and his Spring Heels fled...

CHAPTER 15
REVELATION'S AFTERMATH

None of us that were stood there could believe what we had witnessed, let alone what we had just heard. Jack the Ripper, one of the most fearsome killers in history, along with a rabble of Spring Heels, had fled the battle. Given the choice to either fight the person he'd wanted to meet, or run, he'd gone with the latter, leaving his target in the clutches of the supposed enemy, ie. us.

Merrick was still in a state of combined shock and anger, one that didn't want to subside quickly.

"Did you know about this?" he said. I thought he knew me well enough to know if I was being honest or not. I was a terrible liar, and I'd gotten out of telling my parents about Riz by not talking to them at all. If I had known about Merrick's important role, I'd have done something about it. Riz on the other hand...

"Leave im alone. He didn't know diddly squat." Riz jumped up to my shoulder so he could look Merrick in the eyes, crazed as they were.

"You mean you never told him anything? You two weren't talking about me behind my back?"

I shuffled on my feet. Technically, we never discussed this as a possibility, but at the same time, we did talk about him in some other fashion. I kept my gaze away from him, in the hope he didn't sense my guilt and assume the wrong thing. It didn't work.

"Really, Bren? This is your answer? You meet the rat and suddenly bitch about me behind my back!"

"Merrick! We need to talk about this! Let's calm down, and if it's at all possible, can you put the Runes down, please?"

As we were talking, Merrick had been inching closer to me, the Runes he planned on using on the Spring Heels, aimed at my direction, or maybe at Riz, but given he was on my shoulder, it was a moot point. Merrick took a deep breath, looked at his hands, and pocketed the Runes. That was one danger out of the way, not that we were out of the woods yet, literally and metaphorically. I wanted to get away from the accusation phase of the conversation as fast as possible, as it was not going to help. This is despite the fact that it was a dick move by Riz to withhold the information like that. Playing Devil's advocate though, I could see a case as to why he would have kept it from us. At first, that is. After the beck incident, where I almost died and I learned the government was sniffing around, warning me about Riz, incidentally, then yeah, he should have told us. I did wonder if Valarie knew anything as well. If she had, she'd kept that card close to her chest. The fact that we were off to see Merrick about Valarie entering the picture had been pushed to one side because of this revelation.

"Why didn't you say anything when we first met?" Merrick asked, now calmer and more reasonable.

I should point out that my brain was screaming the moment that the Spring Heels and Jack left. I hated confrontation, always have. I wanted the earth to swallow me, to save me from having to deal with the justified anger radiating from Merrick, like the luminous glow from those cheap glow in the dark toys. I wasn't going to get that relief, sadly. Best I could hope for was Merrick not trying to blast us all to kingdom come.

"I didn't tell yer cuz I didn't know der measure of yer yet. I cud of told yer den found out dat yer were already in league wit im! Or maybe it wud ave made yer go nd seek im out. I cudn't risk dat! So I wanted ta lay down low, nd find out wat kind of person yer are." Riz's explanation was quite considerate, and made sense… from his side.

"You didn't think it wise to tell me that I was a target?" Merrick responded. "Or to tell Brennan that you were just using him to get to me?"

"Wud it ave made a difference? It waz soddin yestaday! Nd look, yer know now, wat can yer do bout it on yer own? As fer usin Bren? He chose ta help me! His involvement is all on im!"

Like that, the ball was passed back to me, and I felt like I had to say something, as one of those blasted awkward silences was rapidly descending us.

"I just wanted to help... I-I..." I couldn't think of anything else to say. It was daft that I had to defend myself when, in the context of the original problem, I had nothing to do with it. I had no idea that Merrick was the original target of Faine's plan, whatever that was. I didn't know Riz was keeping that secret. I'd only known the rat for a couple of days at that point.

"Do you know what I am then? If you knew he wanted me, you should know why?" Merrick asked, sounding exasperated again.

"Well, duh, cuz yer full of Curse magic." Riz laid it out all so simply.

"Oh, that all?" Merrick laughed. "And what does that mean?"

"It meanz wat I sed it means. Curse Magic, very powerful stuff. Nd dat's y Faine wants yer fer is crusade. Want's ta get yer ta use it fer is advantage!"

I glanced nervously at Merrick. I didn't know how he was going to react, and while I could never claim to know what he was thinking at the best of times, he was a complete mystery here.

"Help a genocidal fairy, or stick with an egotistical rat who's hiding more secrets than a young girl's diary? Well, those choices are very difficult." Merrick moved his hand to his mouth, posing to look like he was contemplating an insanely difficult problem.

"Say wat yer want bout me, but at least I'm not tryin ta turn yer species inta meat!" Riz replied, missing the humour completely in what Merrick had meant.

"Settle down, rat! No one said I'm throwing my lot in with Faine and his stooges," Merrick sighed. "Is that how little you think of me?"

"Do I ave ta answer dat now? Tho ta be fair, der only one I think highly of is ma self," Riz admitted, to no one's surprise at all.

"Be that as it may, I'm not joining forces with Faine, not while my friend is still by your side. Besides, you have a deal to uphold. You're going to teach me magic!"

"Uh…" I said, putting my hand up.

"Ah, right, you're going to teach us both magic. You've made a start with these Runes but I want to know everything! I also want to know all about what makes me so special. If I have a power that Faine wants so badly he'll make multiple attempts to get it, even in broad daylight, then I want to know how to use it!" Merrick announced, with one of those smiles that makes you think twice about if this is a good idea or not. I looked to Riz, wondering how he was going to take such a request. I remember Riz's face clearly as he mulled over what Merrick wanted, and what he himself wanted from this whole encounter. I can say that with some accuracy as this is Riz we're talking about. He never decides anything without first thinking about what's in it for him.

"Teachin yer Curse magic? Yer really wanna go down dat route?" the rat asked.

"Just think about what I can do with that! I don't see a downside here."

Merrick was being dead serious about this, which was making it worse. The question of what he'd do with the power didn't cross my mind back then. I was too busy working out what I would do with that premise. Depending on my mood at the time, there would have been few survivors.

Riz offered one of his best explanations yet. "Der downside is der curse itself, moron! Like not dyin peacefully, or bein driven blinky bonkers! Der curse mite activate wen yer turn twenty nd start rottin yer bones from der inside out! Yeh, yer can gain dat power fer yerself, but yer still doomed by it!"

"And? Still better then what I got at the moment."

"Is yer life really dat bad? Cuz all it looks ta me is it's borin," Riz said, calling it as he saw it. "Neitha u or Bren ere lead excitin lives." At my expense, of course.

"You have no idea what it's like to live up here…" Merrick patted himself on the head, as if to emphasise his point. "I have bad dreams where I'm hunted for something I never did, waking up to a life that wants nothing more than me to conform to its expectations. I have to hide myself with masks just to fit in and be who everyone expects me to be. Magic, any kind of the stuff, feels like it will be the thing to break my chains, let me be who I want to be. Before the bad dreams come again."

This was the most truthful I've ever seen Merrick be. We'd had sleepovers before, complete with the philosophical questions that occur late at night when you should be sleeping, but even they didn't go quite like this. The only part that he touched on which I'd heard before, was that of masks, the ones he used to gain favour with each of the cliques back in school. The thought that ran through my mind was asking myself what the real Merrick was, and if I could ever be sure if I was talking to him, or just another mask. There wasn't any real answer to that, of course, I just had to trust that he was only ever being the real deal when I was alone with him, that I gave him no reason to retreat behind a mask. Contrary to this though was the idea that maybe, just maybe, I was just a means to an end for him, whatever end that would turn out to be. Certainly wouldn't have been the first time a friend used me. Given how much I needed friends though, it wasn't a thought that I allowed to dominate too much.

"So, lemme get dis straight, yer want me ta teach yer der dangerous magic, so yer can feel free? Dat rite?" Riz asked.

"That's right. Don't I get to feel that way? You seem to be like that all the time," Merrick observed. His eerie insight here was regarding how Riz was. While he never said he was working for anyone, or any organisation, it was definitely not the government, Riz didn't seem to abide by anything. Heck, he didn't seem to have much in the way of feelings about the aftermath of his actions. It also meant that Riz didn't have a leg to stand on in terms of denying what Merrick had said.

"Godammit," Riz muttered.

"Is that a yes? You owe me, rat. You could have avoided all this by letting me in on what Faine wanted, but you didn't! And I'm going to remind you of it every chance I get unless you help me now. In fact, you don't help, me and Brennan will leave you high and dry."

I had managed to stay out of it by and large, till now, when Merrick dragged me in on his side.

"Oh, is dat a fact?" Riz raised his little rat eyebrow. "Nd yer both agreein ta dis den, are yer?" The rat then looked at me, and I think he saw the hesitancy in my face, as he had the smile of someone who knew to call the bluff. Merrick followed his line of sight, till he was looking at me as well.

"Bren, are you with me or not? Don't say you're going to side with the rat."

"Th-this is b-between you and R-Riz! I'm n-not involved!" I threw my hands up, and stepped back, I couldn't think of any better way to show my neutral stance. This was a bad move.

"Bren! What the hell! We're a team!" Merrick stared at me in horror, like I'd just said something insidiously evil.

"Wait a minute, yer talkin bout me keepin secrets, but how did yer know how ta find us!" Riz burst the moment apart, taking the heat off me and putting it firmly back onto Merrick who floundered at first.

"Well," he started to say but quickly lost the words.

"Yer knew where we were, nd knew ta come packin! Say wat yer want bout me, but dat jus screams dodgy!"

"What made you think of that?" I asked Riz. I was relieved to have the pressure taken off my shoulders. It was interesting to see that the pendulum had swung back in the other direction.

"Jus popped inta ma hed wen I waz thinkin bout wat happened ere. I mean, it's not like we were anywhere near hiz house. It waz more likely dat der women yer met today wud ave turned up ta help out, mite ave been betta if she ad ta be honest."

This is important, this is probably the only time where Riz thought favourably to Valarie fighting alongside us. Universally, he rather have someone set his fur on fire repeatedly, while trapping his tail in clothes pegs.

119

"What woman?" Merrick asked, which of course has been the literal reason we had been heading to his in the first place.

"Answer ma question first instead of tryin ta change der subject!" Riz snapped. "How did yer know we were ere!" he repeated.

"Fine, I knew you were here because I saw you both here in my sleep, heading up here, watching what you were talking about. Is that woman the same as why you were heading my way?" Merrick's expression darkened.

"You saw us in your sleep?"

I made a mental note that I would think more carefully before saying anything in the future. I then noted that for the first time, Riz himself had been confused, his jaw slightly hanging loose.

"Der ell… How did yer do dat den?"

"Like I know!" Merrick laughed. "This has been happening for years and years!" There were tears forming in his eyes, as he finally seemed to admit a secret he'd keep hidden. "I think I might have seen it all, you know. And everything I see, stays with me. Words have torn open my heart." He seemed to have gotten more poetic as well.

It would be easy to dismiss what he was saying as over-dramatisation. I won't forget the look on his face though, that's what sold it to me. Haunted eyes told their own story. Riz tilted his head, something was bugging him, so he pressed further.

"Yer say it's been happenin, den shudn't yer ave expected ta see me?"

"I don't choose what I see, and I didn't see you till after Bren brought your miserable self into my life. After that, you're always there."

The mood had reached a point where it was more tense than when Jack and his Spring Heels were there, at least they were a menace that was easily dealt with. With what Merrick was saying, I couldn't see an easy way forward, to reconcile what knowledge we'd gained, and the consequences that we couldn't see yet. This had been a turning point of sorts, and while no middle ground had been reached between the three of us, it didn't mean that certain wheels weren't turning.

CHAPTER 16
FROM THE FRYING PAN AND INTO THE FIRE

A week had passed since the day that we learned that Merrick was Faine's target all along. After that event, I told Merrick all about Valarie… what little I knew anyway. At first he was suspicious but he took a dismissive tone when he learned that I had her phone number. Still, he agreed to meet her, though we were undecided if we should let her know about his curse. Speaking of which, Riz had dodged the issue of getting Merrick to use it, sticking to teaching us other Runes instead. Obviously I was okay with this arrangement. Merrick though, not so much, as you might imagine. It meant that I got an earful from both directions whenever the other wasn't there.

The increased visits from Merrick, and my frequent trips out hadn't gone unnoticed by my parents, and their suspicions meant more room checks. It was normally my mum that did these, and I was getting paranoid that they knew what was going on. I had a brief conversation about this with Merrick, during a lapse in training, waiting for Riz to make some more Runes. His response wasn't encouraging, and he seemed annoyed that I had asked it when he was in the middle of rant about how the rat wasn't giving in to him. As you would think, Riz wasn't much better when I brought it up with him, and all he had to offer as advice was, and I quote, 'Dey shud be happy dat I ad a teacher as gud as im.'

This was not helpful. At all.

The highlight of the week, though, was the lull in activity by Faine. Every night I lay awake in bed for a while, listening to the silence, and waiting to see if the sound of springs would pierce the ambient noise. It never happened though, saving me from having to face the Spring Heels or Jack. That was something else that got me a bit of bother, from both Riz and Merrick, my reluctance to want to fight the Spring Heels.

"I have to agree with the rat. I don't get why you're still worried about fighting them," Merrick had said, playing catch with the Rune, checking it every time to see which way it landed.

"Yer killed tonnes of dose thins now, yer a pro at it, if such a thin existed, yer shudn't be worried bout dem now." Riz held up another stone, checking it over before taking his teeth to it.

"If I screw up, one of them can kill me!" I replied, not sharing their confidence.

"Yer ejit! Stop worryin!" Riz threw the Rune at my head, and all I could think of was that it was going to leave a mark that my parents would see.

"I'm scared, okay? Isn't it okay to be scared?" I admitted.

"Not of dose runts. Yer keep yer wits bout yerself, nd it'll be fine," Riz turned his attention to another stone.

"I can't do that to my parents."

"Your parents? What? Like the fact that you're already lying to them? You hid what really happened at the beck? I bet you never even told them about how you don't want to go to college!" Merrick laughed, prodding me in the arm. I don't know if he was trying to cheer me up, or just put a sadistic smile on his own face.

"Yer don't wanna go ta college? Gud, plenty of otha ways ta make cash!" Riz chimed in. "As fer yer parents, I'm not gonna stop yer tellin dem, jus be prepared fer all der crap dat will brin, I mean, dey ain't gonna like it, nd dey'd ave yer hauled away fer soundin crazy!"

"Maybe we're both crazy for agreeing to work with you for no gain, rat," Merrick said snidely.

"Yer goin on bout yer stupid curse again? Maybe I shud jus cure it instead! See how yer frickin like it! Yer can jus be a borin sod!"

"Cure it! Hah! If you could do that, you would have done it already!"

Anything I had to say was lost as Merrick and Riz started arguing again, neither of them that interested in my problems.

Things weren't going to be any easier for me that night, as I had previously arranged for Valarie to come over, to meet Merrick and see if anything new had been turned up. As would become the norm, she was right on time, even though we were late.

"Bren! There you are! I thought you were just making a lady wait for the fun of it!" Valarie joked, as she leaned against the front door. I saw curtains twitching in the front room, which told me that my parents were also aware that she was here.

"Sorry, we got carried away. Come in and we can talk in private."

"Private? Wat, yer want sum time fer her nd yerself do yer? Get sum kissin dun?" Riz shouted, making sure that we all heard what he said.

"Is he in there?" Valarie asked quietly, without breaking her smile. She pointed at the pocket with the big bulge, obvious to those who knew where to look. I didn't have to answer her, and with a nod, she kicked it. I was in shock, Valarie was pleased with herself, and Merrick burst out laughing.

"That was perfect! Can I get a go?" he questioned, using his charming voice.

"Sorry, and you are?" Valarie blinked in confusion.

"Merrick? Hasn't Brennan told you about me already? I'm kind of a big deal."

I'd seen this performance before. He only ever did with girls, and the usual routine was that they'd fall for the charm, swoon for his cool. Most of the girls who hung around in his group fancied him, even fighting amongst themselves for his approval.

It should go without saying that Valarie was not that type of girl. She took one hard look at him and yawned... a new reaction I hadn't seen before.

"Oh, that's you? A loud mouth. You fit in well with the rat."

This was not the best first impression.

"Oi! Bitch! I'm gunna get yer fer dat! I don't care dat yer protected from she who mus not be named!" Riz squeaked. I don't think he meant to squeak, but it did make it funnier.

Merrick didn't laugh though, that comment Valarie had made didn't pass him by unnoticed.

"Loud mouth?" he questioned, and I saw that annoyed twitch in his eye, the one that appeared in the rare instance that someone didn't fawn over him.

"Merrick, let's just find out what's going on, okay?" I replied, trying to calm him down before anything major happened. It was probably too late for that though, as Riz was now out of my pocket and running towards Valarie, who pretty much beckoned for him to try it. The fight was as short as you would expect, as although Riz bit her, she got him by the tail again, and made sure to hold him far away from her face.

"Hey! Merrick, was it?" she said, grabbing his attention, before throwing an irate Riz at him. "Catch!"

I could probably point out now that there was only one thing that Merrick and Riz had in common, a shared feeling, if you would. That feeling? A hatred of Valarie. Like I already said though, she wasn't the type of girl to care what anyone thought of her. This just confirmed it. She put her hand on my shoulder and winked at me.

"You going to let us in then?"

I involuntarily blushed. She was nothing like any other girl I'd met, and it'd been a long time since a girl would even think to talk to me at a level approaching friendship. It was hard to think clearly on the simple fact that I'd known her for only a week.

I opened the door and was happy to find that my parents weren't window twitching, no, they were upstairs, with muffled talking showing them to be in deep conversation over something. This meant that going to my room was a no-go, as if any arguments arose, my parents would clearly hear it. So instead, I optioned to have the meeting downstairs, under a strict quiet voices policy. It should have been all so simple.

"Right, first things first, why the hell did you throw the rat at me? Is that how you say hello to people!" Merrick hissed. I saw the temptation in his eyes to say worse things, but gladly he never followed through. I had often tried to curb that in him, getting him to think things through instead of just mouthing off. Sounds like I'm talking about Riz there, doesn't it?

"Yeh! Wat der ell yer playin at throwin me at a dick like im!" Since the revelation that Merrick was Faine's target, and the one that Riz had been trying to get to first, he'd rarely said much about him, so this was a surprising choice of words from him, again, one that didn't go unnoticed.

"A dick? Coming from you who tells me I'm this all powerful being but then won't teach me how to use it? That's the qualities of a dick!" Merrick argued back, his voice rising.

"I thought we'd agreed ta cure yer fer der greata gud!" Riz snapped back, continuing the trend of louder voices.

"When did we agree that! You used it as a threat but that was it, you stupid rodent!"

I was losing control of the conversation quite quickly. Matters only calmed down when Valarie spoke up.

"What are you guys talking about?"

Riz and Merrick both remembered what we'd decided about telling her, and as they'd already blown the secret, I thought it made sense to tell her.

I kept my reply short and sweet. "Merrick is the one that Faine was looking for."

"Wat did yer tell her dat fer!" Riz moaned.

"Because you and him fighting told her it anyway! I rather have everyone on the same page at least."

"So it's true, then? Well, I didn't know what to expect with who it was, but to find that it was connected still to you two, that's an interesting development." She got closer to Merrick, and started to prod him, like a scientist with their research.

"I had it in my head that he wanted one of those lucky sods with an inbuilt magic connection. What can you do?" Valarie asked, furthering what she knew further.

I had thought that we'd gone quieter again, but no, Merrick had to get angry and raise his voice again.

"If the rat had shown me how to do it, I'd curse you for a million life times!"

"Fer der last time, I'm not showin yer how ta use yer fukin Curse magic! Yer can see thins otha's can't, jus run wit dat already!" Riz threw his paws up in the air.

"Oh? That's surprising to hear," Valarie said, genuine surprise in her voice. "I had you pegged for someone who didn't have any cares or worries. You really won't show him how to use Curse magic?" she asked, repeating Merrick's question that he'd been asking or a week solid now.

"Rune magic is where it's at. As sumone who talks ta she who will not be named, I thought yer wud know dat." Riz crossed his paws and smiled.

"Well, duh, of course I know that, but my impression of you was that you were a black-hearted little bastard that would do anything and everything in order to get what you wanted. At least that's what I gathered from speaking to you know who, and my relatives who know you."

That last part caused Riz's ears to twitch.

"Yer family know me…" He tilted his head in confusion, an act that both me and Merrick replicated.

"Yeah, so I know a lot more now than I did a week ago. Don't think you can say the same, can you, rat?"

"I found out that this twat was the one Faine wanted ages ago! Last week yer didn't tell me anythin I didn't know!" Riz shouted in reply.

There was no point in shushing them now. My mind quickly started cycling through excuses to tell my parents, after all, there wasn't any way they didn't hear what the stupid rat said. Trying to explain his voice away would take an epic level of swagger.

Much to my relief, and something that shifted the tone of our impromptu meeting, my mother's violin music started to play. Much like Riz's experience, the music entranced Valarie. She stood statue still listening to it. We were all listening, mind, you couldn't ignore the music, no matter your mood.

"Luv dis piece, mournful, like a banshee's wail," Riz pointed out.

"You know music?" Valarie asked, momentarily breaking from her trance.

"I've been ta a few music halls in ma time, hung out wit dose great composers, nun of dem can hold der drink, mind," Riz boasted.

"How old did you say you were again?"

That was Valarie's follow up question. It's also been one that's often repeated in an attempt to trip Riz up, prying the answer from him.

"I neva sed in der first place."

No matter how he words it, it's not much different than that.

All four of us sat listening to my mother's recital as she cycled through a small selection of the songs in her repertoire. I knew every piece she played, having heard them countless times before, and even now, I hum the melodies, remembering each note and the memories that clung to them. I said before about my mother's musical ability, but while I had always appreciated it, knowing it was that thing that made our family special, it was only at a time like this, where there were more people present, that I got to share that. Merrick, Valarie and Riz, the three of them partaking in this haunting experience.

After the sixth song came a pause which allowed our little group to resume whatever it was we were doing before, not that there was much appetite to do that. Instead, I think we all reflected on different things. I know I did. Given what they said next, I can imagine they were the same.

"A lot has happened, hasn't it?" Merrick said, in a rather unusually sombre tone.

"It ain't ova yet," Riz said. "Not till Faine is taken outta der picture."

"Till the next one shows you up, you mean," Valarie sighed.

127

"You deal with him, there will be someone else threatening everything. That's how it usually is."

"Let's focus on im first, rite?"

"Well, how are we going to get him?" I spoke up, causing them all to look at me.

"Dat… I don't know yet, I'm still workin on it. Tho now he knows dat we know he wants dis git," Riz pointed up to Merrick, who then asked, "And that helps how?"

"Easy, we gots sumit dat he wants."

"So, I'm bait? Thanks, nice to know I'm an important and valued member of the team," Merrick said, though I wasn't sure if he was being serious or sarcastic.

"Not much of a plan from where I'm looking," Valarie said, which wasn't super helpful either.

"Leave it wit me, nd I'll come up wit a blinda of a plan. I've beaten Faine before, nd I can damn well do it again!" Riz said triumphantly. This signalled the end of the meeting.

"Okay then, I'll leave this in your ratty paws. Let me know when he gets a plan, Bren," Valarie said, packing her stuff away.

"Wait, a question fer yer before yer bugga off. Did yer find Arty?" Riz asked, the smile on his face hinting that he knew what Valarie's answer was.

"You know we did. Though, she's got a message for you actually, apparently you owe her big time?" Valarie replied, with a comment that in hindsight Riz should have known was coming as he was in debt to everyone, it seemed. I've run myself ragged trying to sort them out. Why? Because I'm an idiot, that's why.

"Goddammit!" Riz headbutted the sofa in frustration, much to Valarie's amusement.

"See you soon, Bren," she winked and walked out.

I think I mumbled a goodbye, and Merrick could tell that I was smitten. Not that it was hard to see.

"Really? Her? All the lasses you could have chosen, and you go for her?"

I couldn't deny the accusation, instead I looked away.

"I-it's not like th-that!"

"Yer cud ave fooled me." Riz rolled his eyes as he spoke.

"Y-you're not helping!"

"Well, unless the rat is going to change his mind and teach me how to use this Curse power…" Merrick waited to give Riz a chance to interject, but he never said anything. "I'm going to go as well. See you tomorrow, Bren!"

As fast as Valarie had left, so had Merrick. This left me and Riz alone on the sofa. I'd managed to regain my composure at this point, and as I was getting more used to the rat, the way I spoke to him evolved as well.

"Why won't you teach him? You know it would be easier for us. If he's as powerful as you said before, then wouldn't it be a good thing?"

"Nuthin gud comes from Curse magic. All I wanted ta do, waz keep im from Faine. Curse magic shudn't exist. Now I got a question fer u…"

I was fully prepared for him to say something about Valarie, just as Merrick had.

"All dose pieces yer mum plays, dey're gud nd all, but y doesn't she do der vocal parts? It's only ever der violin bits!"

I wasn't expecting this.

"I don't know, maybe she doesn't have a good singing voice?" Not a convincing argument, I know.

"Dat's a load of crock nd yer know it!"

"Why don't you try asking me yourself?" my mum said, standing in the doorway.

You could have heard a pin drop as I took in what was going on…

CHAPTER 17
THE RAT IS OUT OF THE BAG NOW

I noticed that behind my mum was stood my dad. While my mum was looking as serious as could be, with a stern expression to match the mood, my dad, on the other hand, was looking less thrilled with the reveal of a talking rat. Admittedly, this was not how I envisioned my parents finding out about Riz, and what I'd been up to. I actually thought they would have fainted on the spot. To see my mum, standing there as if all she'd caught me doing was smoking, was surreal.

"M-Mum! D-Dad! I… I mean… Wh-what I'm t-trying to s-say is," I struggled to get my words out, fearing what was going to happen next. I looked down at Riz, hoping for some sort of guidance, but I got nothing from him. Instead, he was just staring back at my mum, as if he was trying to figure her out.

"Yer not scared of me? A talkin rat?" he asked her. It was odd to hear the curiosity in his voice.

"Yes and no. I'm not scared of a talking rat, but I know you're more than that, aren't you? My family have tales about stuff like that," my mum said, mentioning her side of the family tree for the first time in what seemed like years.

"Family, eh? Must be sum family if dey got stories of me." I saw his whiskers start twitching, as he sniffed the air. "Wat's yer story tho. Yer know how ta keep yerself hidden." He sniffed the air again. "I mean, are yer even hum-!" Riz didn't get to finish the sentence as my mum wrapped her hand around his snout, keeping it firmly shut, and ensured that she had his full attention.

"If I were you, I'd keep thoughts like that to myself," my mum said in a passive yet very aggressive tone, that dared you to test her warning, yet made sure that you wouldn't. Evident here, since Riz didn't attempt to finish what he was saying. Instead, he changed tack.

"So, secrets out, big shocka! Yer son is workin fer a talkin rat," he started to say.

"Working for?" I interrupted, forgetting that I was on the spot as well.

"Shush, let me handle dis." Riz turned back to my folks. I had no idea what his angle was going to be.

"Anyway, so secrets etc, etc. Yer seem like reasonable folk, nd I gotta say, yer can play a mean violin, lady."

"Mara, my name is Mara. If you're going to talk about me, at least use my proper name," my mum snapped.

Dad had ventured a bit closer. Seeing the way mum had dealt with Riz's little outbursts had obviously shown him that the rat wasn't much to be fearful over. We didn't know the half of it then.

"I-I wouldn't have believed it if you'd t-told me," my dad said, speaking up for the first time. "A talking rat…" He looked at Mum, who looked back and sighed, sharing something that was more than a glance, thoughts on what to do next, proof of the bond that they'd forged well before I was born, and all that had happened to them. A lot of which I still have no idea of.

"Will, I think you owe me an apology," she said to my dad before turning back to me and Riz.

"Sorry for doubting you again," my dad said, "just I had hoped we'd left all that behind, yet… here we are. The more we run, the easier it finds us, it seems."

Their little conversation didn't seem to have anything to do with what was going on in front of them, though Riz was a bit annoyed to be grouped into events I was assuming he had no part to play in. Given his long, apparently infamous life, I'm not entirely sure I would have believed it.

"Oi! Don't know wat yer chattin bout, but it's got nuthin ta do wit me. Now if yer got nuthin ta say bout me or my arrangement with Bren, then leave us alone."

"I wouldn't be so rude, rat. And no, I don't think you've got anything to do with what's gone on before. This is just a case of bad luck." Judging by the expression on my mum's face, I think she was biting her tongue in order to move on the conversation. "Brennan, can you tell us how this all started, and how you ended up with someone so foul mouthed?"

"Well…" I took a big breath.

I recounted every aspect of the story so far. I was already in deep enough trouble as it was, there was no sense in keeping any detail back or hiding anything. This meant telling them the truth about what happened at the beck, the visit from Lionel at the hospital, and how Merrick fit into all this. They also now understood about Valarie's little trips, though it didn't do anything to dissuade them from the notion that she was my girlfriend.

Throughout my presentation, my parents didn't say anything, showing no reaction to what I said. Riz just put his paws over his eyes and ears, likely waiting for the carnage that was going to follow once I'd stopped talking. I decided to end on a positive note that, while wouldn't sway anyone, I'd hoped would soften the blow.

"Of c-course, everyone loves your m-music!" If I went back in time, I wouldn't say this. It added nothing to the discussion, did nothing to improve anyone's mood, and it was akin to a lead balloon.

"So, ever since a week last Friday, you've been sneaking off behind our backs, living in constant mortal danger to help out this rat?" My dad must have gotten more used to the situation as he was the one who took lead, my mum closing her eyes, as she often did when deep in thought.

"W-well… yeah…" I admitted. There wasn't any way I could have spun it to look good, not that I was that sort of person then or now. If I screw up, I'll own up. Unlike someone else I could mention who was also there, taking no responsibility whatsoever for what he'd instigated.

"Do you think that little of us that you didn't tell us?" he went on to say, missing the obvious reason that I'm sure many people would argue.

"I didn't t-think you'd believe me. I mean, goblins with springs in their feet, a talking rat, a genocidal fairy? Th-that's all crazy, isn't it?"

"Don't try that excuse, it's just a lazy way of trying to avoid talking. Brennan, I thought we brought you up better than that," my mum said, a disappointed tone entering her voice.

"I-I'm sorry." That was all I could say. The guilt that had been slowly building turned septic and started eating me away. I should have been relieved that my parents knew now, but I felt even worse.

"You lied to us, you almost got yourself killed, three times, and why? For the sake of this rat you barely know?" Dad added.

"I-I had to help! He needed someone and you always told me to think of others before myself. Riz needed the help, and I-I can't turn my back on him now!"

If anyone makes a list of the wrong things said at the wrong times, this is surely on there. I blurted it out with no thought, but fuelled by pure emotion. I didn't know what to say anymore. I knew my parents were hurt and they had every right to be. At the same time though, this one little week with Riz had changed so much for me, not even counting how it had shifted my world view. What I hoped was that the jumble that was my brain could filter out the right words, mix them together in coherent sentences, and feed them back to me, making a compelling argument that both assured my parents and allowed them to see this from my point of view. There were still some parts of this missing, mind, as to why my mother wasn't freaking out more, but all that was just white noise at the moment.

"You should have come and told us what happened in the first place. We don't keep secrets like that!" my dad said angrily.

I hadn't noticed till now, but his gaze when he wasn't talking to me, kept snapping back to Riz, as if making sure the rat wasn't up to something. It sounds bad when I say it like that, but I have a habit of doing the same thing nowadays, because I can't trust the little twerp when my back is turned… that he's not trying to help himself to things he has no right in touching. Sadly, this is most of the time.

"Will, we both know we have no right in going that far. We can be angry, yes, and of course we are, but saying that will just make us look like hypocrites in the end," Mum sighed. Again, I knew nothing about what they were talking to. I never believed they were hiding anything till this conversation.

"I'm sorry, Mara, I'm just… I just don't know what to do now." My dad's admission hurt me deeply.

"If I mite speak up now…" Riz said, standing on his hind legs, as if it did any difference to the height levels between everyone. "I'm fallin ta see much of an issue ere cept is lyin, which is sumthin I'd neva do."

Yes, you read that right… he tried to claim he never lied. Less said, the better, as thinking on it now, several years down the line, still gives me a headache.

"Th-the issue is more then that!" my dad shouted back, his voice wavering a little bit as he directed his words at the rat.

"Is it? How so, yer lass dere adn't sed anythin bout wat he's doin, yer der one who brought up mortal danger, den went on a tangent bout yer family drama. Face it, I'm a positive change in yer son's life. Heck, I got im a girlfriend!"

That last part, I don't know why Riz included it, but I did see the distaste in his eyes. I can only imagine that it killed a part of him inside to say it, even as a throwaway excuse.

"Mum?" I turned to her. My inner voice was screaming and raging with a confusing mix of feelings, though my emotions were all in agreement that I wanted this confrontation to end at its earliest convenience. The sigh she uttered was one of the loudest I've heard, and I think she was already nursing a headache from this. Another reason for me to feel guilty.

"Are you using Healing Runes?" she finally asked, though I couldn't tell who the question was aimed at.

"Y-yeah, that's how I was healed at the h-hospital," I said, before Riz could get a word in.

"Mara, what are you saying?" my dad asked, finally taking his eyes off Riz to look at my mum with eyes full of shock.

"I'm not saying anything yet, I'm just weighing up options, Will," she replied.

"I thought you were suggesting we let Brennan carry on working with... the rat." My dad sighed, waving his hand towards Riz.

This presented an opportunity to assert myself, make a decision about my future. You may be sat there thinking that hadn't I already done that in spades with every action I'd undertaken so far? Clearly yes, cause and effect and all that jazz, but what I was about to suggest was far more important. Despite my fear of the life that Riz was living, the world he was part of was exciting to me. Again, this was before I knew everything about the life Riz led. I didn't trust him at this point, but I couldn't have guessed all the trouble that he'd bring. Not that I didn't get into enough of it myself along the way. Still, I didn't want the life that had seemed pre-destined for me. College, university, all of it. Knowing how I felt, I wasn't going to achieve the lofty goals that other people pictured for me. My parents talked lovingly of all I might have achieved, a good job etc. That was no longer enough. If my life was going to lead to mediocrity, then I wanted to do something different, something that might actually be worth a damn. I do miss the money I would have had from a good job though, can't deny that.

"Mum? Dad?" I spoke up as clearly as I could manage, drawing their attention back to me, and getting the sideways look treatment from Riz. "I want to ask something, and I don't want you to instantly shoot it down."

"That all depends on what it is, Bren," my mum said softly. I didn't know what she had been thinking about before, or why she specifically asked about the Healing Runes. Whatever it was had pushed her to a resolution she was committed to, or at least, made her look as though she was seeing things in a different light.

"Mum, Dad. I want to take a gap year. I know you want me to start college in September, carry on as though life is completely normal, but I can't do that. I've seen too much now to just slide back into that normal world." I stopped there for the moment, to let what I was asking sink in. Not that I gave anyone enough time to counter it yet. I wasn't finished talking.

"I only want the year, to explore this new world that Riz has shown me, to learn all I can from him. I said I would help him, and I intend to keep my word, even if you let me or not. You always taught me to help someone in need, after all."

"Brennan! What you're asking us to do… you can't be serious!" my dad said. He wore a sad and disappointed look, like I was breaking an item of his that he held dear.

"I am serious! I want to help people, and stopping Faine would certainly do that!"

"I don't even know who Faine is!" my dad shouted back.

My mum put her fingers in front of his mouth, getting him to stop and calm down.

"Bren, me and your dad are going to talk about this. Can you give us some time, please? What you've asked is very serious." Without so much as a second word, she led my dad away, leaving me and Riz to stew in the pain of waiting.

"Yer think dey're gunna buy dat crap yer sed?" Riz asked.

"Crap? I meant it. I don't have any faith in my own abilities, in terms of self-esteem. Mine is missing in action, and has been for as long as I can remember. The things I'm learning from you, the world that's slowly being revealed to me… makes me think that I might actually be worth something in the end."

"Even if it kills yer?"

"Honestly, as much as no one wants to die, if I died doing something worthwhile, or protecting someone, then great. Fighting alongside you, it gives me meaning."

"Gawd, I haven't drank enuff fer dis," Riz moaned.

I'll reiterate, despite how clichéd my words were, and they could have been ripped from any movie, not going to deny it, I meant every syllable. Really though, Riz had no room to talk about this, I think judging from the look I caught on his face, he was happy with what I'd said.

Seconds turned into minutes, and minutes turned into a half an hour. Then, me and Riz heard footsteps coming down the stairs, and the living room door opened again. My mum entered first, followed by my dad. I didn't know what they had discussed, and by the redness of their eyes, they'd both been crying, yet managed to piece themselves back together.

"Brennan," my mum started.

I tensed up, expecting to have to fight for my point of view again.

"After talking about it, and coming to a few realisations of our own, we've decided to let you have your gap year… with a few provisions."

This came like a bolt out of the blue. I was glad, but instantly suspicious and curious in equal measures over these provisions that would ensure that I got the change I wanted for my future.

"Wat're der provisions, den?" Riz asked. He really seemed to be doubting what he was hearing. It's the most I'd seen him interested in a conversation that wasn't about himself or money.

"First, any sign of imminent danger, you're to send him on home. You're not to purposely put Brennan in any danger for selfish reasons." My mum's provisions were so far predictable and based in common sense. I don't know if she trusted that Riz would keep to them or not. I certainly wouldn't have. Knowing Riz, he only has one escape clause, and it only refers to himself.

"Nd wat's der second one?"

"I will take over part of Brennan's training myself, including teaching him about the 'Others'."

This is the comment which floored me and Riz. I could only imagine that my dad must have done the same when they discussed it upstairs.

"Mum, what… what are you trying to tell me?" I became apprehensive about what I was about to be told. I don't know how many different possibilities there were over what she could have said, end of the matter was, I know what she did say. This was what she said…

"Brennan, there is something we've been keeping from you.

We could never decide on when the right time was to discuss it with you. I think we hoped that we would never have to bring it up, but luck was never on our side." My mum paused, and I saw her mouth moving, but didn't hear her say anything, which made me think she was practising what she was supposed to be saying.

"Mum, Dad... I..." Then it was time for my own words to fail me, as I realised there wasn't anything I could say to make this better.

"Brennan, there's a reason we never see my family back in Ireland. I'm a banshee."

I think my heart stopped completely as my world was turned upside down... again.

CHAPTER 18
THE NEW STATUS QUO

A month later...

"Brennan, pay attention, I'm trying to teach you something important!" My mum snapped the book in her hand shut with a bigger slam than I thought possible. It was now mid September, a time when I should have been a week or so into the first year of college, but now, here I was, sat in the kitchen, surrounded by every book that Riz had managed to procure. We didn't ask where they came from, it was deemed to be much safer that way.

"Sorry, I was distracted," I said. I had been daydreaming again but the mundane and boring answer was tiredness. Between Riz and mum, I was being worked like a dog, and it was catching up to me.

"Yer can think bout yer girlfriend later!" Riz quipped, thinking he was hilarious. What was funny was that, while I was in the kitchen being overloaded with facts, Riz was in the living room watching TV. Not having to hide anymore meant that he could take full advantage of the house and all its luxuries, namely the TV. Even funnier, my dad watched it with him. All those detective shows that my father adored, he found a second fan in Riz, the rat who he couldn't stand the sight of. Didn't take him long to warm up to him, though Mum still was sceptical, and trusted him far less.

"I hope he isn't thinking of her when he should be focusing," my mum scolded.

"I'm not! I swear," I said in my defence, not that they would have believed it anyway. I'd seen her every week so far, to 'check in' as she termed it. I wanted so much to tell her what I'd discovered, but as you'd expect, I had been disallowed to do that.

"We're almost done for the day, Bren. Can you just listen a bit longer?" My mum sighed, flipping the switch for the kettle. A cup of a tea was a perfect signal for the end of a lesson. I think my mum meant it to be a relaxer, a beverage to enjoy while the knowledge seeped into my brain. For the past month though, the knowledge was instead seeping out of it, and the bits that stayed started pushing other bits that were already there, out. Luckily, I don't think I needed any of that stuff. Well, too bad if I did.

I'd also seen Merrick during this time, of course. Riz was still teaching the pair of us the finer points of Rune magic, at a pace that was akin to a snail deciding to take it easy. Like with Valarie, I hadn't told Merrick what had gone on between my parents and Riz. All I told him was that they now knew about Riz and that was that. If you were wondering if his attitude had improved – as if I would have been that fortunate – it had gotten worse. Whereas before, Merrick would at least try and pretend to get along with Riz, now it was all business. I still got the usual banter though, when the rat or Valarie wasn't there. Yeah, he had a growing problem with her as well. That was harder to pinpoint a cause than it was with Riz. I didn't want to get in the middle of the two, so tried to keep them apart where I could, just for an easier life. That was getting harder to do as time wore on.

"Brennan! What did I just say?"

I scrunched my eyes as I realised that my mum had been talking all the time my mind had been elsewhere.

"I'm sorry, I'm finding it hard today," I admitted.

"Yer always findin it ard work, yer lazy sod!" Riz yelled again from the front room. "Stop slackin or I'll work yer arder!"

He really wasn't helping. The work that my mother was trying to drill in to me, was an examination of banshees in the complex framework of the 'Others', and how they interacted with the Fae. Banshees had formed the centre of what I'd learned, and for good reason. I was half banshee it turned out. Don't get excited though, it doesn't actually change anything about me because of my gender. Though it did explain a couple of things. Maybe it would be best to recap more of the conversation that we had, when she dropped that particular bombshell:

"A-a banshee? Wh-what are you s-saying!"

What mum had said had floored me, as it would anyone. I'd heard the myths of course, from TV shows and books, to hear it from the mouth of my mother though.

"Dat explains a lot," Riz said bluntly. "Tho, doesn't explain y I can't sense yer," He rubbed his chin in bewilderment.

"That is probably due to this." My mum opened the locket she had always worn around her neck. One that I always presumed to have either a photo of dad in it, or her family. I had been wrong on both accounts as what greeted me as I gazed into it was a Rune, not unlike the ones that were upstairs in my room. This one was fashioned out of dark marble, the colours inherent in the stone blended into black near the symbol, which glowed a brilliant blue. Riz's eyes shot up as he saw it, and he immediately went to grab it. The predictability of the move was evident when mum just took a step backwards, letting Riz hit the laminate flooring.

"Where der ell did yer get dat Eternal Rune?" Riz spluttered as he picked himself back up, crawling back to the position next to me.

"It was a gift from a woman down in London. I think her name was…" Mum didn't get to finish as Riz put his little rat fingers in his ears and started shouting, "Do not ell me it's er! Do not say er name!"

"What was her name?" I asked, ignoring Riz, which was to my peril as being a little git and all he bit me.

"Don't ask dat! Yer say er name nd she finds out bout it!"

Given the way Riz had reacted to a mere mention of who this mysterious woman was, I connected it to Valarie's benefactor.

As if to spite Riz, and his strange behaviour, my mum, without any fear, answered the question.

"Her name was Alice, and she helped me and your father when we really needed it."

"Gah! Wat ya sayin er frickin name fer! Now she'll be watchin us! Den she'll come at me fer my cash!" Riz panicked, which was fun to watch.

"What is the Rune then?" I asked, taking another look at the high craftsmanship on display.

"It hides my presence from 'Others', meaning we can could live our lives without any worries. Not that it's helped that much." My mum glared at Riz.

"Ey, I didn't come ere fer u. I didn't even know who yer were!"

"She didn't suggest you did, more that the 'Others' find their way to us despite that locket," my dad added.

The excitement over the Rune, and Alice, had overtaken the news about my heritage, but Riz rounded back on the topic.

"Fine, dat explains y I cudn't sense yer, but wat bout im!" He pointed at me. "As a half-Other, I shud ave smelt im a mile off!"

My mum had a simple answer for him though.

"Riz, have you ever seen a male banshee?"

Well, a simple question. The rat had to think about it for a second, rubbing the hair on his chin.

"Fine, watevar."

That was him satisfied with what was going on, but I still had questions, too many of them. I went to stand up, but couldn't move from my seat.

"I don't understand what's going on…" I said.

Sensing my unease, my dad sat on the sofa with me, pushing Riz to the side with a book. "That's pretty much how I felt when I discovered the truth, son."

"Oi! Watch it!"

My dad's reaction here was to just drop the book on him. A smart move that I've copied over the years. Putting his arm round me, I could tell my dad was still a bit shaken, but he understood what I was going through.

"This is all part of the reason why we don't speak to your mother's family."

"I thought they didn't want you two to be together?" I asked.

"They didn't. It's more involved than that, but I think we've already got a lot to talk about." My mum came over and joined us, and standing next to me, she leant over and hugged me. "We'll talk about all of it though."

That she did, and I'd love to go through it all here, but I think I've given you the most important parts. I'll share the rest, don't worry about that.

Anyway, back to the makeshift class room in the kitchen. I was saved from any more learning, or jokes about Valarie, by a series of knocks on the front door, which coincidentally meant that Valarie was there.

"Girlfriend saved yer ass again," Riz gleefully prodded, as I passed him in the rush to get to the door. I caught a glimpse of what Dad and the rat had been watching, a classic noir film, The Big Sleep. I never learned why my dad had a fondness for noir films.

"Love dis scene." Riz had turned away from me, and back to the screen. As I had learned about my family's 'Other' connections, I also saw all the little human behaviours Riz had, much like his precious romance novels, the ones he still tries to hide from me. Dad was sat in the chair opposite, and while distrustful, I knew that he was warming up to the rat, because of moments like this. The knocks repeated at the door again, louder this time...

"Took your time!" Valarie said, barging past me without a word. The first few times she'd done it, I tried to protest, but now, all the will to fight had gone.

"I was in the middle of a lesson," I half lied.

"Hi, Mr Landis!" Valarie waved as she confidently crossed the living room and entered the kitchen. I need to point out here that I never confided in her regarding my heritage. I wanted to, don't get me wrong, but I didn't. Still, with her increased visits, Valarie was building a rapport with my family, Riz excluded of course.

"Hi, Mrs Landis. Is Bren still being a problem student?" She didn't mince her words, but there wasn't any malice in what she said, more a cheeky tone.

"How did you guess? Well, since you're here now, I may as well end the lesson early. You will do better tomorrow though, Brennan." My mum put the book she was carrying down, and walked towards the kettle, flipping the switch in an elegant flick of the wrist.

"He just needs more practise." Valarie laughed as she patted me on the back. "And you've got Rune practise tonight, haven't you? How you avoid the temptation to blow Merrick away, I don't know."

Oh, forgot to mention, Valarie and Merrick weren't getting on well either. This was harder to work out the cause for, but I did wonder if the whole situation was wearing on him, eroding his usual tolerances.

"That reminds me," my mum said as she left the kitchen, heading up the stairs.

"What did I say that reminded her?" Valarie was just as puzzled as I was. All I could do was shrug my shoulders. We got our answer a moment later, when she returned holding the bag that Riz used to hold his Runes. Of course, he must have sensed her touching his things as he came in the kitchen and jumped up to the table.

"Wat yer doin wit dem? Dey're my stuff!"

"If these are what you're using to train my son, then I have an interest in them." Mum's words brought dad to the kitchen as well.

"What's going on now?"

"Yer wife is changin der terms of our agreement! She taught Bren history nd all dat crap, nd I taught der gud stuff!"

"No, Riz, you are teaching Bren all the destructive Runes, the ones that require him to be up close and personal to the danger. Why aren't you teaching him the defensive ones? The ones that can be used to avoid a deadly confrontation?"

I'd never thought about what my mum pointed out. She was right, everything that I'd been taught, the primary use was to

144

create a blast of energy, in various ways and shapes, that would make the target dead. What he hadn't taught me at that point was how to defend myself, other than getting out of the way. Though that was fairly obvious.

"I start wit der important stuff. Der best defence is a smashin offence! He can learn dat stuff later." Riz tried to wave it off but no one was buying it.

"You haven't even taught him how to use the Protect Rune? That was the first one my uncle taught me!" Valarie giggled, pulling out what I believed was the Protect Rune.

"I waz gunna wen der time waz rite! Like I sed! Is no one listenin ta me?"

"No, Riz. Especially when you're sprouting crap," Valarie said with a smile, getting a growl in response.

"If yer think it's so important, den u can teach dose Runes to im!"

"Fine, I will."

I don't think Riz was expecting my mum's response. Everyone else though was trying their best not to laugh.

"Fine!" Riz repeated what Mum had said, but in a more squeaky way. "While yer doin dat, I can get back ta figurin out how ta take down Faine! Once nd fer all!"

"Have fun then." My mum used her sarcastic wit, the one that was normally reserved for when either I or my dad came out with a stupid comment. Was nice to see it used on someone else. Riz was stewing in his rage, at least, that's what it looked like from my angle. He sat there, front legs crossed, his back straight up, adding to his, already, odd appearance. He've must have known he was played. This mood was broken however, as, after my parents, me and Valarie shared a cup of tea, Mum retired to her room, and started playing the violin. Her haunting music made more sense now, in the wake of the banshee revelation, as did Riz's earlier question about why she didn't sing, as singing wasn't a thing she'd done since she ran away with Dad. I envied Valarie, for not knowing the truth that made me rethink every aspect of life.

"I love listening to her recitals. I wish I had her talent for music. Do you play, Bren?" Valarie asked.

"Sort of, I can play the saxophone," I said.

"Yer, not very ell," Riz butted in.

"Oh, like you haven't used that joke before. I've half a mind to use you as bait and go fishing!" What I said was supposed to be a threat, but it didn't come across that way. What it did do however, was turn a little light bulb on in his head.

"Bait, eh?" He rubbed his little chin again, the ends of his mouth being drawn up to the base of his ears. I don't need to tell you that this wasn't a good sign...

CHAPTER 19
CURSE'S ORIGIN

Another week passed before Riz mentioned about the plan again. The way it worked its way into the conversation wasn't standard either.

"Oi! Call Merrick up nd get im over ere!" Riz demanded, as he jumped on my chest as I lay in bed... happily asleep, I might add. My sleeping was getting less erratic as I got used to the weird dreams that Riz brought with him.

"Why?" I said, refusing to open my eyes. If I focused hard enough, I hoped that maybe he would disappear like a bad vision. Sadly, he was still there, jumping up and down on me, either trying to wake me up, or break a rib. Either was possible.

"Cuz I've got a job fer yer scrubs! Ye've dun nuthin dis past week! Dis is der least yer can do!"

This 'nothing' he mentioned was a full week's timetable of studying about the 'Others' and then Rune training. Each time I was pushed to my limits of endurance. I don't bother going to sleep on the nights anymore, I just let myself collapse on the bed instead.

"Can you tell me what the job is?" I enquired.

"I'll tell yer wen Merrick gets ere den yer both can piss off nd do it!"

I couldn't keep my eyes closed anymore with Riz spitting on me. I shot my hand out to grab him, but he jumped up, and landed on my arm, then launched himself from that to my head. "Nd get up!" he screamed at me.

"Riz? Want a coffee?"

That was my dad's voice, and it wasn't to make sure I was okay. I was confident that he'd heard Riz's rant though, he was just ignoring it.

"Yeh! I'll be down fer it! Jus sortin yer son cuz he's a lazee sod!" came Riz's reply, and I faintly held the desire to throttle him.

"I'm getting up!" I threw off my blanket, making Riz dart off, repositioning himself on my drawers.

"Still too slow, yer ejit! Yer need ta be fasta! Now go!"

There are drill sergeants who are less ferocious then Riz. I did what I had to though, getting myself sorted, before heading over to Merrick's. I did try to ring him, to wake him, but no one answered.

Walking around on my own was starting to become unnerving. Yes, I could feel countless eyes on me, but it was the silence that was bugging me. Most other times that I had left the house, Riz always accompanied me, hiding in my pocket. Like how it is nowadays, I didn't get a moment's peace.

The walk should have been tranquil, but I had the growing fear that, knowing I was alone, Jack the Ripper would pay me a visit. I had escaped his clutches a few times now, and he wasn't getting any less frightening. I also had another fear, one that could be argued was baseless paranoia. Not getting an answer on the phone when I rang Merrick wasn't normal. There was always one member of his family around to answer my call, and then to go upstairs to kick Merrick out of bed for me. To get no response ignited the idea that something had happened, and again, Jack the Ripper came to mind. I tried to convince myself that this wasn't the case, that there were logical reasons for everything. It didn't work that well. What really didn't help was how quiet everywhere was. The streets were empty, and scant cars passed me by, and there was no noise. I almost screamed out when I did hear something, a car reversing out of a driveway. Definitely not my proudest moment.

With Merrick's house ahead of me, I swallowed my courage and knocked on the door. The family's car was still there, which was odd as I knew his dad worked most days, only having days off at the weekend. I listened closely as I heard footsteps. I was relieved to see Merrick's mum open the door.

"Hi, Brennan, what brings you this early? Merrick isn't up yet," she said gently. She had only ever been kind to me, despite what her son had said of her. Merrick had claimed she was controlling and kept pushing him to be better. I'd often suggested to him that he was overreacting, but as always, I had to be wrong.

"It's important. Do you mind if I wake him up?" I returned the gentleness that she'd shown me.

"Be my guest, though don't be put off if you hear him talking in his sleep. He's started doing it a lot lately." I saw in his mum's eyes that she was trying to work out this strange behaviour. I found it surprising that they were only now discovering it.

"Oh! O-okay, I'll keep an eye out of that. Sure it's nothing though!" I don't know how convincing I was. It seemed to placate her though which I would gladly take. I eagerly went upstairs and put my ear to the door, just like I had done on the front door. I heard murmuring and the odd mention of a name here and there. Then I heard my name.

"Brennan! Come in already!" I wasn't sure if he was asleep or not at this point, but I duly entered the room and found that yes, he was still asleep.

"Merrick?" I called out, and this woke him up.

"Bren? Hah, so you were outside the room, just like I dreamt. How messed up is that?" He laughed.

"You dreamt I was outside your room?"

"I saw you stood there, idling, listening to me. I also saw my parents talking about me, how they were worried about my recent behaviour and attitude. They think I'm on drugs, mate!"

"What else have you dreamt about?" I asked cautiously. We still didn't know what form his curse was meant to take. I mean, would you have thought it cursed if you saw things through dreams? Don't answer that, it was meant to be rhetorical.

"I've seen a lot, and even better, I saw something that finally gave me some answers," Merrick swung his legs over the side of his bed, and sat up.

"Answers about what?"

"About why I'm so messed up!"

I had noticed a change in his behaviour. He was more free spirited, putting less value on what other people thought of him. I didn't know if it was good or bad, but it made him... happier?

"What did you want anyway that was so important that you didn't ring?" he asked, tilting his head as he did. Given his dreams, I did wonder if he already knew what I was going to say.

"Riz wants us both. Says he has a job for us to do?" I worded it like a question, as if I was asking him if that sounded right.

"You're asking me? What would I know about what the rat flipping wants! You know, haven't been able to see him anymore, or anything he says. I think he's realised what power I hold. That's why I think he's moved his position to want to cure me!" He spoke while standing. "Can you wait downstairs while I get dressed? Go make some more small talk with my parents, if you're bored."

I nodded and backed out of his room, and before I could turn to close the door, he'd slammed it. With little else to do, I went back downstairs, but I didn't go into the kitchen, where his parents were, I ducked into the living room instead, sitting down in relative silence. I was surrounded by family photos, showing a different kind of life than the one I'd grown up in. He had been part of a large and loving family, aunties and uncles doting on him and his sister, both sets of grandparents around to offer advice. My mind wandered again, making me question how many of them had the curse as well, if they'd ever heard of it.

"You ready or what?" Merrick said, appearing in the doorway.

"Oh, okay, you not having any breakfast?" I jumped to my feet as I spoke.

"Not hungry."

I knew the real reason... he didn't want to interact with his parents.

"Merrick? Where are you going?" his mum asked, as if reading my mind.

"Out! Back later!"

In three short words, he'd pushed me out of the front door and we were away.

"What do you think the rat wants us to do then?" Merrick asked as he left his road.

"I already said he didn't say."

"I know you already said that! I meant, using your imagination, what do you think the job is? You must have some ideas on what it could be."

"I really don't," I said.

"Oh, Bren. Sweet naïve Bren. What are we going to do with you? A poor little soul like you needs protecting."

"Do you have any ideas?" I turned the question onto him, wanting to avoid what he'd said.

"No, not really, but maybe we should talk about something more interesting, like what I discovered about my gift," Merrick said, nose diving from one conversation to another.

"Gift? You mean your curse?"

Merrick stopped moving at the road, and remained deathly still.

"Let me tell you all about it before the rat comes in to ruin our day."

"What?" I asked, but to no avail, as Merrick started his story off.

"My story starts with Adam de Frankton. The location? Wales, the year 1282 to be exact. You see, King Edward wanted to take over the country at that time, but Prince Llywelyn, the last true Prince of Wales, stood against him. The Prince was leading a defence of Wales that was driving the English out. To the Welsh, he was the hero they had been longing for, but someone grassed him up and his army was ambushed."

The story, even as basic as it was sounding, was capturing my attention, and Merrick was fully focused on delivering it.

"In the confusion of the battle, as his kin was getting slaughtered, the Prince and one of his squires tried to retreat, and that's when Sir Adam made a name for himself. He attacked both, leaving them for dead. Later on, he returned to the heavily injured Prince and finished the job, taking his head for a trophy to present to the King."

I felt a shiver run down the length of my spine. It wasn't just what Merrick was saying, it was the way he was saying it.

"Then what?" I said, my voice running faster than I thought.

"He had an unfortunate encounter on his way back from the murder. Well, I say unfortunate, I do wonder if it was fortunate actually. I mean, what would I be if it hadn't happened?"

"An encounter?"

I had different visions in my head how this 'encounter' would have played out then, and where it took place. All the movies had primed my mind to set the scene in a cold, dark and lonely forest. With not even the moonlight providing relief. I imagined a knight on horseback, stopping suddenly.

"W-what was it he encountered?" I said, my words coming out fast again.

"A Hag of the Mist," Merrick spoke slowly, almost to counter the speed that I'd blurted out words.

"A Hag of the Mist," I said back to myself. My mother had covered these, briefly. She informed me that they really didn't care for that name that had been foisted on them. They called themselves Forest Sisters, and had a very unique connection with the land they called home. This had the benefit of making them ageless as their health reflected that of the area. They weren't immortal, mind. "Yeah, so, this hag cursed Adam, with all the retribution that the Welsh would bear down on him. Apparently she could feel the sorrow of the land or some rubbish."

"What did the curse do to him?"

"The curse allowed him to see the truth, that the Prince and his squire had been unarmed. They weren't carrying any weapons, so he had done an unknightly deed and killed them in cold blood."

"That's it?" I questioned.

"You don't get it, Bren! Adam was one of those knightly types, someone who believed in the knight's code so much that his identity was built on it. Killing people in cold blood was a knightly

152

no-no. It drove him mad. Then he heard and saw everyone talking about his disgrace, what he'd done. Every time he tried to sleep, every lapse of consciousness, he was confronted again with the truth." Merrick started walking again, not looking as he crossed the road, oblivious to the cars that were zooming past.

"What happened to Adam then?"

"He died years later, but he'd already passed the curse onto the children he'd sired in those lucid moments of his. Apparently, his ghost is still roaming the place where he died, seeking to restore his honour."

"So that curse is the same one you have?"

Don't judge me too harshly for saying something so painfully obvious.

"Yeah, isn't that fantastic? It's because of this curse though that I saw what happened to Adam. I've lived his life, every dumb decision he made. Then I'm forced to live through every descendent where the curse activated. Every pain-filled memory, every death they caused, and even their demise. I've felt it all, Bren."

I got a good look at his eyes here and saw how bloodshot they were. I could barely imagine what was going on in his head, and everything he'd suffered.

"Merrick, I…" I started to say.

"Don't say anything, Bren. There's literally nothing you can say that will change anything." Merrick laughed as he stretched his arms behind his head.

"That can't be true!" As I spoke, I remembered what Merrick had said before about questioning whether it was a unfortunate or fortunate meeting. "Wait, you said that you thought this might be fortunate?"

"Yeah, because I've got a power in me, one that's been growing as the curse went on and on. The rat doesn't know what he's talking about, Bren. This curse… it can change everything for me."

With that, I stood before my friend and for the first time, realised that I was losing him… and that was something I couldn't allow.

CHAPTER 20
ONE STEP CLOSER

We didn't share a word as we did the rest of the walk to my house. Merrick didn't look like he wanted to keep the conversation going, and I was too afraid to carry it on for what he would say. I'd learned where his curse had come from but I was still light on the details about what it was fully doing to him, and all those ancestors who had suffered with it.

Riz picked up on this mood as we walked into the front room, where he was sat next to the remote, flicking through daytime TV.

"Gud grief, who died? Yer both need ta get out of wateva funk yer in," Riz pointed out, looking at both of us in turn.

"I'm fine, rat. Completely peachy. Not sure what Bren's problem is, but whatever." Merrick sat down on one of the chairs. "You going to tell us what this urgent job is? Why I had to get out of bed so early?"

In case you're wondering, Merrick didn't bother going to college. He'd apparently made this decision as soon as he heard that I was putting it off for a year.

"I'm sure yer get a lot of beauty sleep anyway so gettin up early won't botha yer," Riz said flippantly.

Merrick shot me a glance that said he was about to murder Riz.

"Riz, can you just tell us what you want us to do?" I interrupted, wanting to move on quickly before any hostility could really began to form with these two.

"I've got a plan brewin, one dat will let us take Faine down once nd fer all, but ta do it, I need a place. One dat's bare nd barren. Oh, nd outta site as well," Riz requested.

"Obviously, can't let people see that we hang around with a talking rat after all!" Merrick rolled his eyes as he laughed.

"Wudn't want ta be seen wit a tossa like yerself more like," Riz said under his breath. I'd heard him clearly, and tensed up to see what Merrick would do, but to my relief, he never made any note of it.

"That's all you want us to do?" I asked hopefully. I anticipated that this would be the case, so stood up ready to get Merrick out of there before another argument happened.

"Well yeh, but don't take too long, othawise yer motha will complain at me fer keepin yer too busy."

"So find a place for whatever plan you have? That shouldn't be too hard in Thornaby," I mused. Truth be told, thanks to his description, I already had a place forming in my mind that I knew of that met most, if not all of the rat's specifications.

"What's the plan though?" Merrick asked, sceptical about what Riz wanted. That was one of my concerns, but my anxiety at having these two in such close proximity was getting unbearable. I had to get Merrick away from there.

"I'm sure Riz has that all under control!" I said, gritting my teeth. I had a hunch, what his plan would revolve around, and if even I was only ten percent right, I still didn't want to have to go through that argument at that point. It was like heaping stress into a pressure cooker with faulty parts. It was never a matter of if it would break, but when.

"What? You're actually taking what he said at face value?" Merrick said in surprise, with a flash of anger.

"Let's just go!"

I ended up dragging Merrick out of the room, and out of the house. This was before even my parents knew I'd been back.

"Bren, what the hell was that about?" Merrick demanded, shrugging off my grip. "That rat has a lot to answer for, I know it, you know it, everyone knows it! Why are you defending him? Don't tell me you actually trust that bag of filthy fur!"

"No, it's not that at all! Just I wanted to get this over and done with. I've already got a good place in mind. Sooner we get there, sooner we get back, right?"

My word salad only seemed to confuse my friend more, but he relented and we started walking. The first leg of the journey was to get onto Baysdale Road, and then onto Redcar Road from there. This had taken less then ten minutes, which had all been speechless. I could tell Merrick was focusing on something within his head. I'd learned not to speak during these times as he'd just snap at me for breaking his concentration. It didn't take long for him to start talking again, offering up what he'd been thinking about.

"Bren, seriously, what's your deal with the rat? Nothing is making sense at the moment. Your parents don't seem to be bothered about you dealing with him, despite how long you tried to hide him before. He treats you like crap, went on and on about how important I was to Faine and why he wanted me, but then turns around and messes with me like I'm suddenly worthless. That's including how he won't teach me how to use my curse powers! Then he offers a cure for them! Like what the hell?" Merrick ranted. I hadn't seen him do a long one in a while. He wasn't finished either.

"I mean, I think I've said this before, but can we even trust him? For all we know, he's selling us out to Faine for a small bit of gold, or maybe we're being taught to fear the wrong person. It's not the Fae we need to watch out for, but him!"

These weren't points I could argue against, not brilliantly. The one thing I could point out was that Riz wasn't the one who had allied with Jack the Ripper, a known quantity in this as the inhuman monster who had a brief killing spree in the late nineteenth century. Merrick wouldn't have impressed if I had blurted that out.

"At least he's not trying to kill us all?"

"How do you know he isn't? He's getting us to fight for him, to potentially die for him. Don't you realise how crazy that is?" Merrick stopped to take a look at me. I knew he was trying to read my expression, to work out how I was really feeling. I didn't like it when he did that, as I knew it meant he was working out the best method of attack.

"You're really buying into all of this aren't you? What do you think this is?"

"I'm trying my best," I said, my voice losing its strength. I could feel my self-worth fading just as fast.

By now, we were close to Lanehouse Road, which meant a short trek uphill to where it joined onto Acklam Road.

"Trying your best? What the hell kind of answer is that?"

"What do you want me to say? I know he can't be trusted but look at what's on the other side. We're involved now, and we got to fight for our conscience's sake."

No one should be surprised that I said that.

"Consciences? Seriously? Have you stopped to actually look at what we're doing? Right now we're heading to pick our graveyard! The rat is going to get us killed. He'll run away with no consequences," Merrick laughed.

"Then why are you still here, Merrick? I know you and Riz haven't seen eye to eye lately."

"Lately? When have I ever saw eye to eye with the little git? You treat me like crap, I treat you like crap. That's how it works."

I felt myself getting worked up the more this argument was continuing. Ahead of us now was the turn off that led to the Teesside Park cycle path. It was down there that I'd find the location that I wanted, and one that Riz would approved of. Not that I could think of any of that then. Instead my mind was consumed by what Merrick was saying, and the way his words were eating my resolve away.

"Merrick, please. I know you're better then this! I know you're hurting but just think of what would happen if Faine wins. How many other people will be hurt or worse! You've seen what the Spring Heels are like, you've seen Jack the Ripper! You saved me from them!" I wanted to make him see that there was more to this then just how he was feeling.

"Brennan, you always did have a bleeding heart. No matter

157

what changes, you're still the same as always. I guess you haven't been altered by any of this have you. Always the hopeful dreamer pretending to be a pessimist."

"It's not wrong to want to help people," I said, clumsily.

"It's really cute that you think that any of this is helping people. Or that you clearly class that rat as a person. Then that Valarie."

You could almost feel the distaste in Merrick's mouth as he spoke. I didn't instantly say anything, as I knew I had to be careful with my response.

"She's a good person... I think." I had to add that disclaimer there, as I knew he would have leapt on it otherwise.

"You think?"

"It's just how I feel, alright? It's nice that people want to actually know me."

"Oh? Is that how it is? You're Mr Popular now? Now you got the girl and the rat, you don't want to know me? Charming, Bren, real charming. That why you don't bother sticking up for me with the rat, why you're not pleading my case, get what he promised me?"

A moment after he said that, Merrick pulled his hands across his face, and mouthed a groan.

"See what happens when her name comes up? Let's just drop it for now," he said.

I was ambivalent in my feelings, as I was relieved that the conversation was being dropped, but I was also annoyed at the blame for the argument being fostered onto me. However, like all the rest of my frustrations, it could be pushed away by my desire to not repeat the last few minutes.

"We're almost there anyway, just have to get on the cycle path," I explained.

"There's that haunted house," Merrick mused, stopping me dead in my tracks. I looked at the house that he was pointing at. It was a four storey house that had clearly seen better days. I don't know how long it had been since people had lived there but it'd been long enough for all the rumours and urban legends to spring up. It was these stories that led me and Merrick to both comment on the house whenever we went past it. The house and its next door neighbours, got renovated into cushy apartments a few years ago, which kind of killed the mystique of the place.

"If anything was there, we would be able to handle ourselves now," I said. I was taking a chance here, the fact that Merrick had pointed it out, the fact that he was still walking with me when he could have easily buggered off. I had to keep hold of that thread that was connecting us.

"You're right, one thing the rat actually did well was with these Runes." Merrick pulled out one of the Runes from his pocket, one with a cruder symbol drawn into it than what Riz would ever do. That's how I knew they were homemade.

"You made them?"

"They're easy when you know how. Remember, I see stuff, and I pay attention!" Merrick tapped me on the nose as he said the last part, his finger moving with every syllable. "After the stuff we've seen, a house like that is child's play," he chuckled, not missing a beat.

Within five minutes, we were on the cycle path, and with it, the place I'd chosen to fight Faine.

"This is where you want us to fight Faine? What used to be the race course?" Merrick asked, turning to me, looking as if he wanted to make sure he got all the facts right.

"It's secluded, very open, the wide spaces mean we'd see any threat coming. It's just what Riz wanted." I was quite pleased with myself for thinking of this place, and really it was the only thing of worth I'd done.

"It's fine, I guess. As far as the place we're going to get killed, goes. Does this mean we can go now? I mean, it wasn't a bad way to waste half an hour but there was a lot of better things I could have done with the time." Merrick wasn't impressed with this place, but I wasn't expecting him to be, not after the conversation we'd had on the way.

"Merrick," I said, causing my friend to stop. He had been walking back down the hill, towards the path. "Thank you for standing with me. Through all of this."

"What are friends for…?" Merrick turned his back to me as he answered. "Had it been anyone else, I'd have split long ago. Just remember that."

With that, the two of us went back to Riz, to report on the chosen battlefield. I didn't share with him the talk that I had with Merrick. I didn't know what the rat would say, but I had a hunch that it wouldn't be good. Regardless, we settled on that place, though we were yet to be filled in on the details of Riz's plan…

CHAPTER 21
THE DATE THAT NEVER WAS

It was now October, and we were still no closer to knowing what Riz's grand plan was. If anything, both of my training regimes had increased tenfold. I had never been so grateful for my bed each night. Speaking of my bed, I was actually in it when Valarie knocked on the front door, in her now traditional manner, which was how I knew it was her.

"Wat's dat woman want now?" Riz groaned, from his latest makeshift bed in my t-shirt drawer.

"How the hell would I know?" I was still half asleep as I tore myself away from the sheets that clung to my sore body. Riz's training last night involved throwing rocks at me in an attempt to get me to dodge better. He didn't allow me to heal, like the bastard he is.

"Trust your girlfriend to be the one to get you up!" my dad yelled from downstairs.

I glanced at the clock, which revealed the time to be 9am. I considered this a lie in with due respect to current circumstances.

Valarie was her usual perky self when I opened the door to her.

"Hey, Bren. Did I wake you?" she said, knowing full well that she had.

I followed her gaze and realised I hadn't even got dressed yet. She didn't bat an eyelid though, as she was here on a mission and nothing else mattered.

"Wake me? Nooo, wasn't like I was enjoying a lie in after the pure hell that was Riz's torture sessions, I mean, training."

My snide comment didn't faze her.

"Oh good, I thought you might have had something better to do. Get dressed. We have somewhere to be."

"Where?" I asked, though I was already turning to go and get ready. Yes, even then I had been programmed to obey her. Don't tell her I said that. When I got back upstairs, Riz had already gone back to sleep, but I woke him as I ploughed through the drawer, looking for a t-shirt.

"Wat did she want den?" he asked.

I stopped when I realised I still didn't know, other than she wanted me to go somewhere. I was going to answer when she answered for me.

"Nothing for nosey rodents," Valarie hummed as if it was a rhyme. She had followed me up the stairs, most likely to wind Riz up.

"Fine, like I frickin care neway," Riz said in a huff, he left my drawer and headed to go downstairs. "I'll jus go nd see wat yer dad's watchin, probs more interestin den spendin time wit u."

"Watch too much and you'll get square eyes!" Valarie said with a wink.

"Screw u!" Riz shot back.

I made Valarie leave the room while I finished getting dressed, then once I was ready, we headed back downstairs. So you may be asking yourself, at this point, were we an item? My parents certainly felt we were, and I didn't say anything to discourage that. Officially though, nope, I had made as much leeway into her heart as I had getting in Riz to be politer. A battle I still wage today. You don't know how many times I have to hold him back from biting the clients.

I must have looked like a sad puppy dog to her. As I already pointed out, I was head over heels for her since we met. I don't know what she was thinking, and still don't, but if I was ever a bother, she didn't let me know, and this is a girl that any time Riz says something she doesn't like, she inflicts pain.

"I'm just going to get something to eat. Is that okay?" I

asked, peering round the kitchen door as she made herself comfy on the sofa, rooting through her bag for something. She didn't say anything, and I thought at first that she was just going to disappear as she leaned deeper and deeper into the bag but she suddenly pulled herself out when she realised I'd said something.

"Oh! What did you say?" she asked, looking as if everything was completely normal.

"I-I'm j-just going t-to eat now!" My stutter came back at the wrong time. I didn't stick around long enough to see what she said to that, I just quickly stuffed my face with breakfast, only going into the living room when I was ready.

"You finally ready?" Valarie asked, as she was just sat scanning a file she must have pulled out of her bag, one marked 'Cupid, C', 'For Ministers of Otherworld Business Eyes Only' and complied by 'Z Brooks PhD'. How Valarie had got her hands on it was anyone's guess, and yes, Cupids are real. I don't have time now to go into the details, but here's the cliff notes… most of them are dicks. Want more details? Go look it up for yourselves, I've only had bad experiences with them. As to why she had the file, it's a long story that I won't relate here, besides, that's her tale to tell.

"Right, let's get going then." Valarie shoved the file in her bag and jumped to her feet, and practically dragged me out of the doorway.

There was no time to scream for help.

The morning was your standard October morning, with a chill present, thanks to a wind that had been picking up for the last few days. It was dry at least, that's all that can be said about it.

We'd only gotten out of my street and onto Baysdale when Valarie came in close to me.

"Don't look now, but we've got the government tailing us." She then turned her head towards the black Ford Escort that was slowly shadowing us. A black Ford Escort. The government wasn't breaking the bank when it came to funding the Ministry of Otherworldly Business.

163

"The government? What do they want?" I gasped, trying very hard not to look back.

"Just checking up on me probably. I'm quite a nuisance to them so they like to keep tabs, quite funny actually, you'd think they would have something better to do." She was so nonchalant in the way she spoke about being stalked.

Then again, Valarie always had odd run-ins with different government agencies she came into contact with, regaling me with the encounters. Her best story was the one about two agents from MI5, an older bloke and a younger lass who didn't seem to have a brain cell to share between them. They had tried to commandeer her car to go after someone till the lady went after a double decker bus instead, claiming to already have experience with it. Valarie's strange sight turned stranger fast, when she apparently saw them again, with the bus on its side near the Natural History Museum. Somehow, I've avoided meeting people like that. Instead I'm stuck with Riz, for better and worse. Most of the time it's just worse.

Back to dealing with the overly-curious government agent though…

"Do we just leave them then?" I asked cautiously.

"Yeah, just ignore them. They'll give up soon enough."

Although Valarie was confident in that prediction, the car ended up following us from Baysdale, to Redcar Road, through Diamond Road and then onto Imperial Avenue. A constant shadow that gave off all the threat of a fluffy baby rabbit. Valarie and I were just walking and chatting about irrelevant crap. No, it wasn't an act to fool the driver, we really didn't care. Valarie was absolute in her belief that they wouldn't interfere, and I believed it. Had they wanted to start something, Lionel would have made sure I didn't wake up again in the hospital.

It was when we hit Mandale roundabout that our 'shadow' disappeared, and it was only then that I felt brave enough to find out where we were heading, and why.

"So, what are we doing?" I asked shyly.

"We're going to pick up a package for my uncle. The delivery drivers dumped it at the depot. It's from Riz's favourite person," Valarie replied, acting like she had no cares in the world. From what I know, that was only skin deep.

"Alice?" I asked, not thinking what I'd said. Remember, at this point, Valarie was unaware of my parents' connection to Alice, or if she knew, she'd kept it secret.

"Guess Riz has finally said her name then?"

Hearing that snapped my mind to my slip of the tongue.

"Yeah, he slipped up when he was talking about her." I was also learning to think fast.

"He talks a good game, but he and her go way back. It's also top secret."

"What? You mean we're not supposed to talk about it?"

"No, I mean she won't even talk about it. You ask her, and she laughs and gives you that 'change the subject' stare. You don't mess with that stare, I learned that living with her!" Valarie laughed, revealing that little more about her past. Her story was a blank slate for me. I don't know if it was intentional or just because I hasn't asked the right questions, but I knew next to nothing. I know more now obviously, but we are twenty years removed from that point in time, and neither of us are who we were then. Well, I'm definitely not.

"You actually lived with Alice?" I said in surprise. Alice was getting to be more of an enigma the more I heard about her. Riz's and Mum's stories already threw up a contradiction big enough that it caused a headache whenever I thought about it.

"For a while. My uncle left me in her care when a job with Arty took him abroad." Valarie was so nonchalant about it, it was like she was talking about staying with a cousin for the afternoon. There was also another mention of Arty, which was the shortened name for Artemis, another person you didn't want to get on the bad side of, despite her ditzy cover.

"I've not heard the best of her, Alice, I mean," I specified.

"She's harmless, unless you piss her off. It was from her I first heard of Riz, and his legendary debt!" She laughed.

I laughed as well, but now that I know what it is, and stuck paying it back as well, I only cry.

"I'll say this though, the pair of them, Riz and Alice, they go wayyyy back." Although this isn't the place to say this, the story with Alice and Riz is, well, complicated. Heck, I'm still learning things about the pair and it's been over twenty years since I met her.

"Bren, been meaning to ask, what you going to do when this is all over?"

I stopped walking. Every time someone asked me a question like this then, it got a bit further out, expanding the vision of my future just that little bit further. Leaving home though? That was a step further than I'd considered. Back then, I'd envisioned that I would eventually end up in a shared flat with Merrick, if I ever left home at all. It was a joke that was thrown at me back then, that I'd still be living with my parents by the time I was sixty. Look at me now. I'm living with a talking rat instead.

Seeing that I was lost in my thoughts, Valarie slapped me on the back to snap me out of it.

"Come on, Bren, it's an easy question! You now know there's more to this wonderful world than we can see, what do you want to do?" She smiled as she danced forward.

My stutter decided to pop up and say hello.

"I-I don't k-know! M-maybe I-I guess…"

My brain decided it wanted to stop feeding me words, watching me flounder like a fish out of water. This was how most social events for me worked out, unless I could hide behind Merrick.

"Do you always get this nervous on a date?" Valarie said, taking me by complete surprise. She'd also snuck back up to me, so she was close.

"W-what! I-I-I-I…" I trailed off and she burst out laughing again.

"Relax, I'm just trying to make you smile. You'd look a lot better if you did."

This wasn't new. A lot of people in the past were fixated on getting me to smile. I just never had any reason to, though that did change here. I gave her the best smile I could muster.

"See! Now, keep that on your face as we're going to make this trip fun." Valarie turned and ran off, leaving me blushing and weak in the knees. Yes, it's clichéd but cut me some slack, I was a romantic.

"W-wait! Does this mean... does this m-mean it's a date?" I shouted, chasing after her.

CHAPTER 22
LAST HAPPINESS

By now, we were coming up to Stockton High Street, a place we'd have to walk through to get to the post depot. It was slowly getting busy but luckily wasn't a market day. We'd entered from what I'd nominally call the bottom of the High Street, near the Swallow Hotel. How can I describe this place to you if you've never been to it? All the shops really were on this one long street, which used to be home to the widest street market in the country, though by this point, it was showing signs of fading from its peak. Back then, there was only faint foreshadowing of all the plans that council had, in order to breath new life into the place. As I looked across the faces of everyone we passed, I saw the shroud of naïveté that I had lost. None of these people would have to deal with Jack the Ripper, none of them knew the threat that Faine posed.

Valarie stopped and looked up at the town hall's clock face.

"Great, we've got plenty of time."

She turned on her heels and dragged me back towards the Castlegate Centre, which was the main shopping mall, supposedly built on the site of the old gate of the now torn down Stockton Castle. Boy, can I tell you stories of that place, and the tunnels underneath the town… but that's another tale entirely.

"The post depot is that way!" I said in protest.

"I know, but I want to pick something up first," Valarie said with a little smile, something she'd learned would melt any objections I had. Her new destination was the shop WH Smiths.

It was set to move to a new premises at the other end of the high street, so staff were trying to get things sorted as customers weaved in and out of their way.

"What are you doing?" I asked as she darted inside, leaving me outside.

"I'm just picking up a book I've been after. Reading helps keep your mind keen." She patted me on the head like I was a child then disappeared inside, only poking her head back out to ask another question.

"You don't mind waiting out here, do you?"

"I d-don't mind."

I thought I had rid myself of the stammer, but it was clearly stalking me.

"Good, I didn't want to duct tape you to the wall to make sure you stayed where I left you."

With that she went back in.

"D-duct tape!" I shouted back, but she was gone and it just made people look at me weird, weirder then normal anyways.

Stockton was a place I went to virtually every week, without fail, tagging along with mum and dad's shopping trips. I remember loving it as a kid as it meant I tried my luck to score a toy of some kind, but as I got older, the town didn't have much for me. I no longer fitted in with the place. Why I thought these things while waiting for Valarie to emerge, I still don't know. My thought process is a mystery today as it was then. I'm a master at thinking of the wrong thing at the wrong time.

"Done!" Valarie shouted, waving her new book in my face.

I had just enough time to see that it was a fantasy story called the Child of Light by A R Pearson. Valarie's reading tastes were not too dissimilar from my own, except that she was by far a faster reader than me.

"I've been waiting ages to read this. The first couple of books were fantastic. The author has got tremendous talent. Met her once at a convention, down in London, got her autograph. Really nice person!" she said breathlessly.

Valarie struggled to get her bag open with one hand, not having perfected the method she uses now, which oozes cool when she does it. The bag tipped, allowing some of the contents to spill out. A roll of purple duct tape tumbled out, as did some Rune Stones like the ones Riz had me using. Another book fell out, this one called Bloodlines by P Hartog. It had a handwritten note on the title page, which looked like it was from the author.

"Shouldn't you finish reading a book before starting another?" I asked, picking up the book for her.

"I've read that one countless times already. It stays with me," she said, taking it off me and putting it back in her bag. "The author put a note in the cover for me when me and my family met him on a rare trip to America. He said to follow my instincts and keep reading. That was the last event before it all happened. I keep this…" She pulled Bloodlines out of her bag to illustrate her point. "…with me to remind me of the happy times, before that bug tore everything apart."

I didn't know what to say in response to that. It was a frank admission and one that I didn't have anything to match.

"I'm sorry, I never meant anything by it."

I feel like I've said this before. No wait, I've definitely said that before. It's true, but it's an excuse. I still do it today, speaking when I think I'm being clever, and often putting my foot in my mouth.

"Bren, don't worry. I would be worried if you knew what had happened. Tell you what, I'll lend you the book at some point. It's a cracking read, though he does drop the f-bomb a lot, like, really a lot," Valarie said, putting the book away.

She wasn't kidding. I've never seen the f-word used so many times, and I live with Riz, who swears like no one's business. I wanted to say something, something funny to break the tension I could feel building, but I couldn't think of anything. I don't know if Valarie felt it but she must have felt something as she spoke up.

"This is what I wanted anyway. Time to get my uncle's stuff," she said, prompting a new avenue of conversation to take us away from the serious talk.

"So what is the package then?" I asked, as we started walking up through the Castlegate Centre, leaving it to go back onto the High Street.

"No idea, but knowing my uncle, probably some useless tat, maybe part of a collection he has. He's a hoarder of the highest level."

The conversation moved on to lesser topics as we walked, idle chit chat, that sort of thing. I was still desperate for that golden bullet of a conversation starter. We were only five minutes out from our destination now.

"You asked me what I was going to do, but what exactly are you going to do?"

I managed to get my stammer to bugger off, but the trade was that my voice came out like a squeak. Valarie looked back at me, confused.

"Didn't I already tell you?" she asked.

"No, you didn't," I replied, looking away, but keeping her in my peripheral vision.

"I'll continue onto to my goal."

She put her hands behind her head and faced forward, and I could tell that she was envisioning her future, seemingly in a way I could never see mine. She was optimistic about her chances, a sharp contrast to whenever she was forced to talk about certain aspects of her life, while me, I was pessimistic through and through. What I was doing here, trying to put a positive spin on my apprenticeship with Riz, was bold new ground for me to break.

"What's that then?"

"I'm going to travel and see the world. I want to meet people from everywhere, see the world through their eyes. Eventually, I want to show the world the truth that's been kept from it for so long. To do that though, I need to understand a few things. I don't want to blindly drop truth bombs and wreck lives. I've had enough of dealing with my own."

Valarie stopped short of turning the corner to head to the Post Depot.

"That's a lot. That's a lot to ask anyone to do. Are you sure you can do it?"

I didn't mean for my pessimism to seep out, to try and infect her words, it just happened.

"Am I sure? I won't know till I try. See, you seem to think that everyone knows exactly what's going to happen in their future. That just because they have a plan, that's how everything plays out." Valarie started walking again, this time balancing on the kerb, not allowing her feet to touch anywhere else. "I mean, look at me... I can say my plan is to follow this kerb all the way to the Depot, but..."

She stopped as we came to a crossing, offering four different ways to go, with the road to the right leading to where we wanted to be.

"I can't get over there without stepping off. This means my finely tuned plan is in tatters because of this one change."

The playfulness in her eyes showed that she knew she was taking this to its logical extremes. She admitted as much when I've questioned her about it in the years since.

"To get over there, I'm going to have to admit that my plans are changing. Though I could have saved myself the disappointment by just changing how I view the future."

We crossed when the road was clear, catching the look of a fair few drivers who observed us, probably wondering what the hell we were doing.

"Instead of doing that planning, all I should have said was: I'm going to reach the Depot, by any means necessary. Now I come to an obstacle, I can find a different path around it. I'm not restricted to walking on the kerb. I can choose to walk solely on the pavement, or maybe walk on the cracks in the pavement only."

She started hopping around, even as we approached the gate leading to the Depot.

"That's how I view my future, a place I'm aiming to be, but I'll take every approach I can to get there."

It was a bit cheesy, but what she was saying was effective. I envied the way she looked at things and knew what she wanted. I've never been that articulate with my words. No more was this evident then with what I said next.

172

"I want to help people," I said suddenly, catching even myself by surprise.

Val didn't know what to make of it, and it stopped her in her tracks.

"You want to help people?" she asked, puzzled at what that had to do with the conversation, though I think going back over it, the connection is easy to see.

"I want to be in a position where I can help people who need it, especially in dealing with things like the Fae, or goblins, or-or whatever else lies in the Other!"

Remember, at this point, fairies and goblins were the only creatures I'd encountered so far. I'd no idea about water ghouls, barguests, ashen, true demons, wraiths, worms (not the wiggly earthworm type) and everything else in between. Oh and yetis. Can't forget the yetis.

"So you want to help people? With someone like Riz leading the way?"

A smile formed on Valarie's face, a cheeky one which meant she was testing my newfound belief.

"I need someone to show me the ropes. Besides, he can't be all that bad?"

Yes, it was a question, an open ended one. Riz is a give and take kind of person-thing. He takes my money and gives experience, or he takes my patience and gives me a headache. There are those glimmers, those shining moments where you think to yourself, yeah, there's more here than he lets on. I'll point them out as we come across them.

"All that bad? From my experiences with the rodent, I think you're better off putting him in a hamster ball and letting him roll down a very steep hill. Though your other friend, Merrick, I think I trust him less."

This had just proved what I suspected, but to hear Valarie speak it so bluntly was strange.

"You don't trust him?"

"He's learned that he's perhaps one of the most important guys living in this country right now, because of Faine wanting him. Not all of it makes sense to me, the Curse magic, and all that, but the way he acts, and what you've told me before. I'm curious as to what he wants, what he plans to do with his power. I mean, he's already learning to make his own Rune Stones."

"What he wants…" I repeated the question back to myself. Admittedly, I didn't know the answer back then. I thought I might have known before all this had happened. Then, he would have tried to get on top of whatever social heap he walked into. He'd never talked of a singular profession, having dreams that stretched multiple jobs and desires. All of them had something in common though, the need to free himself from the bonds that he claimed were holding him back. It was easy to think back then that he was just talking about wanting to move out of his parent's house.

"Merrick is…" I had to choose my words carefully here, not an easy task when you don't know what you're saying. "He's… complicated. Ever since I first met him, I knew there was more he was hiding behind the way he talked to everyone. All that work to get on everyone's side, the stress of keeping up all those personas, for the benefit for everyone else."

"Sounds like it was only for his benefit," Valarie said.

"The point I'm trying to make is that he had his moments where all that would go away and you'd see what lay beneath. Those times, I became the target because I saw something I shouldn't have."

"Why do you hang around with him?"

A very good question. One with an answer that was anything but easy.

"He admitted that I was keeping him grounded, giving him an outlet so he didn't break. I was helping him."

As I said the last part, Valarie's eyes shown some flash of recognition, like I'd said something that resonated within her.

"He'll fight alongside us, I know he will. Despite what he says about Riz, what he says about you. There's a good part of him, one trying to prove itself. Me and him started this together, and we'll end it together." I laughed, brushing all the concerns away, hiding my unease under the veneer of laughter, much like Merrick would have done.

"I want you to know that while I don't think you're right in this, like at all, I'll be here to support you. You're one in a million, Brennan." She took my hand as she spoke, giving it a gentle squeeze before letting it go. "Come on, let's go home."

"O-okay!"

And so ended my first ever date, or at least what I classed as a date. We got the box, and its contents didn't matter in the grand scheme of things. Even after Valarie and me went our separate ways, I still cling to this memory of one of the best days I'd had at that point. Halloween was looming though, and on the morning itself, we finally discovered what Riz's plan was, and it was proof that for every good day, there was going to be a torrent to follow it.

CHAPTER 23
HALLOWEEN ARRIVES

With those happy memories behind me, Halloween arrived. Till then, we were completely in the dark over what Riz's master plan was. Valarie and Merrick had their doubts, which they confided in me, though one of them did it quite loudly, and I'll let you work out who that was. If you know me, and are familiar with the rest of my turbulent life, you'll know that I hate Halloween, and often put out the excuse that I find the holiday way too commercial. If you ever thought there was more to it than that, then give yourself a pat on the back.

Riz had me up most of the night before, going over and over in the Rune training, making sure that I knew all the correct pronunciations. Also my mum's teaching sessions had gained an air of desperation about them, as she tried to hurry certain aspects. She wore her worry on her face throughout it all. I was dreading the talk that I knew must be heading my way. What kind of parents would let their only child go head first into such a situation? Because of this, I was on edge most of the time when Riz left me alone with them. As for the rat, when he wasn't torturing me, or watching old TV with my dad, he would disappear to parts unknown. He never explained where he went or what he did, almost as if he was insisting me to trust him.

From when I woke up early that morning till about one in the afternoon, it was like a lucid dream, a malleable experience where nothing felt real. No one mentioned the threat that was looming.

My parents went along their normal routine, treating it like any other day.

This all changed when Merrick arrived at two in the afternoon, shattering the dreamscape and bringing everything back down. Coincidentally, or not, Riz resurfaced, having been missing all morning.

"I hope the rat's plan is a good one," Merrick said after the usual pleasantries.

"Yer know it will be, so stop yer complainin," Riz replied, from his perch atop my drawers. Merrick took a seat on my bed, his facial expression hinting that he wasn't going to take much crap today.

"Guess we're waiting for her to show up?" he asked, pointing out the absence of Valarie.

"She'll be here," I answered.

"She betta, she's got a part ta play in ma masta stroke of a plan!" Riz spat out.

"This the plan you haven't even told us yet, rat?" Merrick turned his barbs on Riz, though I didn't have much problem with what he was saying this time. Nowadays, if I have a plan, I voice it as quick as I have it, and I expect Riz to do the same. This day is why I have that policy. There's been a couple of times where I haven't done it, and both of them, the rat has complained that I kept him out of the loop, completely oblivious to the irony inherent in his grievances.

"I'm plannin on tellin yer in der moment. Jus wait till everyone's ere, moron." Riz's defence was answered with a knock at the door, heralding the arrival of Valarie. "Go let er in, Bren, den I can giv whiney guts ere wat he wants."

"Bren, hurry up, otherwise the rat might be hanging outside your window when you get back upstairs," Merrick growled.

I hurried down to the door, but found Mum already there, opening the door to Valarie.

"Hi, Mrs Landis! Wondered who was going to let me in today!" At least Valarie was her usually cheery self.

"Afternoon, Valarie. I think Bren is already expecting you?" My mum turned as if she knew I was going to be stood there.

"Come on, Val. We're already up here. Riz is about to drop his plan." I summed up what was going on pretty well, while also letting my mum know what was happening.

You might be thinking that this whole event was mad, a talking rat leading three teenagers into an unknown encounter, against a Fae, a whole bunch of goblins probably, and Jack the Ripper. You'd be right, of course, as everything was downright crazy. In an ideal world, a tactical team like you see in the movies would have been meeting this threat head on, bringing all the best expertise and equipment to bear. Me and Merrick, personal circumstances non-withstanding, as far away as possible from events as they unfolded. You notice I left Valarie off from that, well, that's because she was clearly involved in her own business, one that I had no bearing on. This wasn't an ideal world though. This couldn't even reach the mantle of a lofty position of an imperfect world.

Either way, I sat down on my bedroom floor, legs crossed while Merrick sat on my bed, struggling to hide his disgust from sitting next to Valarie. He gave me the side eye and I saw him give me a silent tut. Judging me on a relationship that was basic at best.

"Rite, taday is der day dat we're gonna wreck Faine nd is little posse! Nd I know yer wonderin wat my plan is, ell, now is der time ta tell yer," Riz announced, though it seemed less like he was sharing a plan, and more like giving a grand speech to all three of us.

"Just get on with it!" Merrick said, though he was really saying what I'm sure Valarie and me were thinking. At least, I know I thought it.

"Shuttap! All in gud time yer twats! First off, I'm meetin wit Faine in dat place Brennan found."

"The wasteland near the Teesside Park Cycle Path," I explained, despite Merrick and Valarie being both aware of where the action was going to take place.

"Do I ave ta tell yer ta shuttit again? As next time I'll bite yer soddin arse instead!" I stayed silent, which gave Riz the go ahead to continue. "Now, as I woz sayin, I'm gunna meet wit Faine in order ta hand ova dat twit." Riz pointed to Merrick as he spoke.

They say a picture is worth a thousand words, and the look that Merrick had plastered all over his face was worth triple that.

"I'm sorry, you're going to do what? Hand me over? Are you joking, rat?"

"I ad ta get Faine's attention sumhow, nd I knew dis waz der only way ta get im ta meet face to face instead of hidin behind Jack! I went ta see one of my contacts who runs errands, gettin crap fer Faine, nd told im I wanted a deal, a bit of Aetherite, in exchange fer der twit he wants."

Riz's explanation made too much sense. Don't get me wrong, I was mortified by what he was proposing, even if I thought at that point that he wasn't going to go ahead and give Merrick away, but on the other hand, it was a good way to get the enemy to come to us.

"Don't you think that this Faine will see through your stupid little trap? I mean, you spend this long fighting him, and then you want to cut a deal? I thought you said he was supposed to be clever!" Merrick pointed out.

"Of course, I want im ta think dat, I want im ta plan a double cross! It's der only way I can set up our triple cross," Riz said with a sinister smirk.

"You're going to get us all killed, aren't you?" Merrick said, putting his head in his hands. His frustration was palpable, and I sympathised, though by now, I knew Riz never did things in half measures. Spending the better part of two months with him had given me a little insight, though it was only scratching the surface of the dense void that was the rat's inner workings. Any plan he'd concocted to deal with Faine, someone he was really eager to bring in, I knew was going to be comprehensive.

"Speak up, Bren, you're a part of this! Do you honestly think this is a good idea? What do your parents think?"

I wish he hadn't brought my parents into this. I heard shuffling beyond my door which meant they were listening in to Riz's plan. I looked back to Merrick who was hiding a smile behind his hands, which told me he knew they were there already. I didn't know why he chose that moment to reveal their presence, but I figured it was because of his designation of bait. Riz's treatment of him was coming home to roost, which meant that it fell onto me to try and salvage this. I was going to have to take the initiative for once. I realised that Valarie had also been strangely quiet through all this, but she was sitting listening, her eyes following everyone else present closely.

"Brennan! Stop looking at your bit on the side and talk already!" Merrick shouted, getting agitated.

"Is this the best plan we have?" I said, allowing silence to fall for a moment.

"Unless anyone else haz a brite idea, like Mr Ego ere," Riz said sarcastically.

No one was forthcoming with any other idea.

"Merrick," I started to say.

"Bren! You can't be serious! Think about what you're asking me to be! I'm not bait! I'm your friend! And to me? You're like my brother, the only family I have that I can stand! Even after you meeting that goddamn rat and her! I feel like you've forgetting me in favour of this!"

"It's not like that at all! Merrick, you've got a part to play in this, the biggest part, the best part. You're only the bait to Faine's eyes." From this point on, everything I said was being made up on the fly. I had no idea what Riz's plan actually entailed, but I knew we needed all of us to be on the same page and keeping Merrick on the team meant making some kind of sacrifice. Of course, no one else was stepping up for this.

"What do you mean?" Merrick asked.

I think he had noted that no one else was speaking up about this, which meant all authority about it was being passed to me. Yay me.

"Faine will be expecting Riz to be the one in charge, all of the Fae's planning has revolved around what he will be preparing. He's not going to be expecting us to be led by you. You're a natural leader, Merrick, one that I would gladly follow to the end of the earth. I think you should be in charge of the counter-attack. Faine may think he knows what we're going to do but we can show him what humans can do." As I spoke, I put my hand on Merrick's shoulder, because it felt like the right thing to do. I wanted to show him that I trusted him, that it didn't matter what Riz thought of him, that despite his nature, he could rise above it and become more. You have to admit, it would have been a great irony for Faine to have been beaten by the person he had wanted to capture.

"Wat der ell do yer think yer doin?" Riz said.

I didn't reply to him. I just shot him a look that I had hoped he understood, a very similar one to how I was also looking at Merrick. One of 'please trust me'.

Valarie seemed to have gotten what my intent was, as she looked back to me with a gentle smile.

"I'll follow your lead if you think it's the best," she said, but she worded it in a way so it was hard to make out whether she was talking to me or Merrick, but I got the hint it was aimed at me.

"You really think I can do this?" Merrick asked, in a completely different tone than the one he'd had a few moments earlier.

"I do." My answer seemed to set him at ease, as he nodded and turned back to Riz, and for once didn't act overly hostile to him.

"Riz?" he asked. "What was your plan after you meet up with Faine?"

"Oh, knew yer'd want ta hear der rest of it! Yer a bunch of ejits!" Merrick's kindness was wasted on him. "Fine, I'll ell yer den. See, I know dat Faine will be expectin sumit, nd he'll brin an army of Spring Heels wit im. He'll position dem so dey'll be attackin from behind, wit der real Jack der Rippa wit dat lot."

"The real Jack the Ripper?" Valarie asked.

"Yeh, he'll ave a illusionary one stood next ta im ta hide der fact he's settin up a trap."

"So, then what? We only have Bren and her." Merrick motioned to Valarie. His restored good mood clearly didn't extend to her.

"Nah, fer dis plan, we need im ta think we're all ready before he reveals wat he's hidin. Faine ain't der only one who can make illusions, nd dat's crux of our triple cross. Der ones dat stand up won't be Bren nd Val, dey'll be fakes."

"I see, I see. Well, then I can work with that. What's Faine going to do then, when he realises what's really happened? Will he try and grab me or will he cut and run?" Merrick asked, musing on his options. I knew that the gears must have been turning in his head now. My gambit had worked, though I prayed it lasted long enough to get us all out of the fight alive. I left the three of them to talk, knowing that my role would simply be to blast anything that came near me to kingdom come. I had something else that needed taking care of before we left.

I looked out of my room and into the hallway, and figured that my parents must have retreated into their room after Merrick revealed them. I was trembling at the confrontation I knew was coming, each step towards their room the heaviest I'd ever taken at that point. I reached for the door handle, and turned it, though with my added stress and the tension, it felt like it took hours to open the damn door. Swallowing all of my emotions the best I could, I walked into their room and saw them sitting on their bed. A photo album lay casually open next to them, with my baby pictures on show. The amount of guilt and apprehension was overwhelming. It was enough to make anyone break down into a sobbing mess, but we all held firm.

"M-Mum, D-Dad…" I said with a stressed stutter. "I'll b-be leaving s-soon!" Everything else I wanted to say after that left me.

"We didn't want you to have this kind of life." My mum sighed, as she flicked through the photo album. "Sixteen and off to fight a battle that should never have been yours." There were tears already formed in her eyes, ready to go.

"We were angry when we found out that this life had found you, despite our best efforts, but a lot of that was on ourselves." My dad put his arm around my mum as he spoke, hugging her and keeping her close

"As much as we want to, we can't stop you. Not after what we did when we were your age. What we want you to understand is your father and I, we had to fight every step of the way to escape the life you're part of now. You have to be allowed to follow your own heart, otherwise, we won't be any better than your grandparents who dictated everything about my life."

At that point, she'd spoken more about my grandparents than she had in a decade at least.

"Y-you're trusting R-Riz to bring me back?" I said.

"I wouldn't go that far. He's very dangerous, Brennan. I don't think you appreciate that, Having spoken to Alice about him, we've got a better picture of him, but that one fact doesn't change." My mum's voice became stern as she spoke her warning.

"Th-then why l-let me go?"

"Because of your friends. Also that Riz made a promise to me, and a promise to a banshee isn't broken easily."

This was the first I'd also heard of a promise between my mum and Riz. As to what she was referring to about promises not being easily broken, well that was a special ability for banshees. It was a lot like Contract Breakers, which were Runes made to ensure that all agreements, whether made in good faith or under duress, were adhered to. Breaking any terms of the contract was usually painful, extremely painful. With banshees though, I assumed it had something to do with their screams and the Curse magic that they brought with it. This might have meant hastening the foreseen demise.

"You got him to promise to something?" I said in shock. Even thinking back about it, I still can't believe it.

"Your mum can be very persuasive when she wants to be." There was something in my dad's attitude and behaviour that said he wasn't as okay with this as Mum seemed to be.

"Can I just ask though?" my dad started to say. "Why do you want to do this?"

"Because you taught me what the right thing to do was. If it was only Riz going on about what a threat Faine is, I wouldn't have believed him, but with Valarie vouching for how dangerous he is, I know he's got to be stopped. If it can only be me and a talking rat against him, then that's what's happening." Yes, it's cheesy, but give me a break, I was only sixteen.

"The danger, though… why does it have to be you that goes?"

I think my mum agreed with this sentiment to some degree, as she placed her hand on my dad's shoulder, who now looked moments away from crying, which stabbed me in the heart like a knife. I hated this moment. We were all going to lose something. I could feel the guilt starting to build with every word, every tear that fell.

"I have to do this," I shouted out. "I have to prove this to myself, to prove that the faith that others have put in me isn't misplaced!" I don't think my parents were expecting an outburst of that level. Though I wasn't finished there.

"There's also a lot you haven't explained to me! You mentioned something you did that was similar but never followed through on telling me!" I took a deep breath, before continuing, though with a much calmer head on my shoulders. "I'm not asking you to understand what or why I'm doing, I just want you to trust in what I'm doing. Please," I said. I didn't give my parents many options, so they took the only one really open to them, and they embraced me. I knew from this gesture that I had both their blessings.

"I love you both, and I'll see you tonight. You can count on it," I said, wiping away the tears.

"Don't worry! I'll keep dat ejit alive!" Riz shouted from behind the door, proving that while my parents had been listening in to the plan, he'd been eavesdropping on our private conversation.

"You better get going," my mum said.

My dad nodded in agreement, but didn't say anything. I left the room quickly, not wanting to meet their gazes. I grabbed my gear, and we left as a group. I didn't look back to see if my parents were watching or not, my heart wouldn't take it.

CHAPTER 24
SPRINGING THE TRAP

No one dared talk as we walked towards the Cycle Path. The throes of autumn had given the landscape a golden hue to fight by. I looked at the faces of everyone else, trying to work out what they were thinking, but both Valarie and Merrick might as well have been made of stone. Riz was riding in my pocket, as had become customary. I didn't want to know what he was thinking about, chances are I wouldn't have liked it. Every street we crossed, every path we went down, brought us closer and closer. I got the urge to talk about something, anything.

"Don't say anything, Bren. You'll ruin the moment," Merrick said.

I wasn't sure what gave it away that I was going to talk, though in hindsight, it may have been me opening my mouth like a fish as I thought of what to say. I caught myself trembling again, just like before when I spoke to my parents. Nowadays, I don't so much get that little voice of doubt saying, 'you don't want to do that', as it's evolved into a voice telling me, 'Told you so'. Back then, my internal sense of danger was screaming at me. We hadn't set foot on the Cycle Path yet, but a primal urge in my body was wanting to me to run. As far as I knew then no one else was experiencing this.

My body was still betraying my attempt of a poker face when we walked down the bank towards the Cycle Path, the trees bordering one side of the path blocking the sun from us, and the entrance to the path, loomed like a gateway to another realm.

"Are we dere yet?" Riz spoke up, breaking the atmosphere like a petulant child.

"Why don't you poke your head out and look?" Merrick said, more annoyed than when he had spoken to me.

"I'll poke ma hed out wen I'm gud nd ready! Y don't yer focus! We're bout ta face down Faine nd all dat he can musta against us!" It was very nice of Riz to point out the threat again. It wasn't at all like it was constantly lurking in my mind.

"Bren, are you okay?" Valarie asked, leaving Merrick and Riz to argue amongst themselves. Her hand was gently holding my arm.

"Oh, I'm fine, getting ready to fight, what could be more normal than that?" I didn't buy my sarcasm either.

"You're a terrible liar, Bren. And as cute as that is, it's not going to do you much good here. It's okay to be scared. I was the first time I'd ever done anything like this. But, I wouldn't be here if I didn't go through with it. Also, unlike my first time fighting, you're not alone." It was at this point that Valarie flashed me a smile, and I did feel a little bit reassured.

"Thanks Val," I replied, and there may have been blushing, but again, I was sixteen, cut me some slack. I turned my head, and saw Merrick quickly turning his away. I hadn't even realised that him and Riz had settled their argument.

"Not far now," Merrick muttered.

He wasn't wrong.

Another five minutes passed and we clambered up a hill that allowed access to the wasteland that was next to the path. In a former life, this place had been a dog racing track, but had long since been demolished. For whatever reason, there was a dump of dirt and building materials left over when the retail park was constructed. I had no memories of this place being anything other then what it was now, and it was perfect for our uses. Riz pulled himself from my pocket and crawled up to my shoulder.

"Rite, der set up I waz workin wit meant dat me nd Merrick were gunna stand in der middle, so dat Faine will see us," Riz explained.

"While those two hide and then jump out once Faine has revealed his trump card? I think I can do much better than that." Merrick smiled and looked around. "Yes, I've got a much better plan." He searched his pocket and pulled out some Runes, ones that I'd never seen before. Even Riz had to narrow his eyes as he looked at them.

"Illusion Runes, nd where did yer get dem from?"

"Does it matter? I think Faine is going to be expecting to have them turn up from nearby, and I think we can really trap him, in addition to these Runes." Merrick pulled out more Runes with his other hand. These ones I recognised, sort of. The symbol looked like that of a Blast Rune, but not at the same time. Riz looked over the Runes again, and then back to Merrick.

"Fine, yer got yerself a nice selection I see. Bren! Yer pouch!" In the second that he used to give Merrick praise, he barked an order at me, and I obeyed, not wanting to get bitten before the fighting even started. I held the pouch out and the rat started digging through it, knocking some of them to the ground. Merrick bent down to pick them up for me.

"What's this one? Doesn't look like the rat's handiwork?" Merrick said, holding up one of the ones that my mum had given me when she had taken over my training, one of the more defensive ones as she termed it.

"Oh, that's a Rune my mum gave me, a Shift Spell," I started.

"Yeh, cuz it shifts der planes of reality dat der target is on fer a short time, sorta like a Illusion Trap, but worse since dey don't last dat long," Riz finished.

Merrick looked at it again before handing it back to me.

"Your parents are full of surprises, aren't they?" he said.

"Ah! Dis is der ones we need! Oi! Valarie!" Riz shouted at Val, who was just idly looking around.

"You got a job for me now?" she asked.

"Catch dis!" Riz threw the Rune at her, and she caught it with ease.

"An Area Invisibility Rune? Nice! Where have you been hiding this?"

"Does it frickin matta? Dis is wat yer gunna use ta hide yerself. Guess I'll ave ta get one fer u, won't I, Merrick?" Riz said rolling his eyes.

"No need, I've got my own. Mind if I talk with Bren for a quick moment, before we get to hiding?" Merrick asked.

"Y yer askin me? Wat do I luk like? His flippin keepa?"

"I meant talk to him alone! Don't act so stupid!" Merrick said, his face breaking into a frown.

"Fine, wateva, I'll go nd run thru der plan wit her den." Riz scuttled off my shoulder and down to the ground, then he waddled over to Valarie, though looking like he was hating every second of it.

"Bren, I just want you know, that I treat you like my brother, not just like a little brother, oh no, a blood brother. Like that Papa Roach song. You are the only family that I acknowledge, and I'm not going to let anything happen to you today. I'll keep you safe, just like you've tried to keep me safe. Like that little angel on my shoulder." Merrick put his hands on my shoulders, making it clear how serious he was about all of this. "I've got your back, okay?" He let go of me, and then hugged me. "Let's do this!"

From sentimental Merrick to confident in a blink of an eye. He was giving me emotional whiplash from how he was acting. It was comforting though, knowing that both Valarie and Merrick cared about my well being. The doubt entered my mind that Riz couldn't care less, but I brushed it aside, as I didn't need that. As long as I was with the non rats in this group, then what did he matter? I felt a strong sense of resolve fill me up, reducing my fears, and it was timely as well.

"He's comin! Quick! Get in yer frickin places!" Riz yelled, as he darted over to where I was standing. "Bren! Get one of dose Runes out dat I jus gave ta yer!"

I did as I was told and held up the Invisibility Rune. I expected him to tell me the activation word, but instead, he climbed up me, took the Rune out of my hand and threw it in the air. Using that weird language of his, he activated it. The Rune cracked and turned to dust in the wind.

What happened next is still a pretty nifty memory, even though I've told many people about it. It's just this Rune is super rare to come by, and Riz is a sod because he doesn't like making it. The effect of this Rune was that it felt like a net had landed on me, one that was see-through, but very lightweight. I couldn't see any part of it, but that was the point.

"Stay put!" Riz said, from the other side of the invisible net. From where I was sat, I could see that Valarie had done the same, and Merrick, well, he was setting up the other part of his plan to double trick Faine. Then he pulled the same trick, before appearing next to Riz somehow. I guessed that his must have been the Illusion Rune he mentioned but never went into any detail about. This doppelganger looked the part, but wasn't expressive and sort of swayed into the wind. Everything was set up, and I heard the distant sound of springs getting closer. A whole bunch of them. I made sure to have Blast Runes ready to go in each hand, wanting to hit the ground running as soon as we revealed ourselves, which I think was directly after Faine thought he had the upper hand. My heavy breathing returned, but I did my best to counter it.

It only took a minute for Faine and his group to arrive. There wasn't any surprise that Jack the Ripper was a part of it, nor that he'd brought ten Spring Heels.

Faine was everything I had been told and more. He carried with him an air of nobility that weighed on him. The expression on his face was one of resolve. No doubt, he thought what he was planning was needed. His skin tones were pale, which generally fit in with what I'd learned about them, and read from folklore sources. His hair was messy and unkempt, strands falling at the sides of his face, where deep grooves ran under his eyes. The wings that adorned his back were jagged, with crimson reds and pulsing oranges. His clothes looked like they would have once been regal, but time had worn them down to threads, a frayed scarf fluttering in the wind. At his side, I could just see a sword scabbard, an odd item for a Fae to have, considering their magic.

I gulped as I saw him scanning the area, at one point, staring straight at me. He didn't do anything else though, and turned his full attention to Riz and the illusion Merrick.

"It's good to see that you kept your word and waited here," Faine said. His words, although unimportant, still carried weight.

"Dere's soddin Aetherite involved, I'm not gonna screw around wen dere's dat kind of dosh here," Riz replied, meeting Faine's regal aura with his own brand of uncouthness.

"You protect him and then just give him up at the drop of a hat? You have no sense of loyalty. Yet you continue to defy me? Riz…" Faine looked like he was about to say something else, alongside Riz's name, but the rat butted in.

"Riz is jus fine, prick. I do wat I wanna do, nd nuthin else! Yer got dat? Let's do der trade nd go our separate wayz, fer now." His lie was so convincing then that I did wonder if he was actually doing the proper deal and selling us all out.

"And you? Merrick, I believe that is your name, is it not? Do you have anything to say about this? No, of course you don't…" Faine sighed. "You're only an illusion and thus can't talk." The Fae withdrew his sword and slashed through the fake Merrick, which I guessed was the point Riz made about Faine expecting a double cross.

"Well, yer went along wit it fer a lot longa den I expected, question is, wat re yer gunna do bout it? Yer rite where I want yer! Bringin yer in will do a lot ta help ma standin!" Riz gloated, letting slip his real goal here. Not that any of us were in a position to call him out on it. Luckily though, Faine provided us with a bit more context about that statement.

"You're still chasing after their approval? Do you really think they'll show you lenience for your crimes by pretending to care about what I've done and what I'm trying to achieve? My only crime, as far as you need to know, is that I'm cleaning up your sin against my kind and all others. I know how I'm talked about by those in the Council. Those whose favour you're trying to seek, they call me a monster! For simply throwing away the shackle of the unwieldy laws of engagement that have doomed all Fae kind.

Yet you… you're the true monster here, one that every living being in this realm should unite against."

It was clear that this Fae loved his own voice. Had I been giving Oscars out, he would have been a shoo in. The words resonated with me though. My mum hadn't gone into much detail, but she had mentioned stories that the banshees knew of Riz.

"Yer finished yappin yer gums? Plz, I'm not der one talkin bout wipin out people jus cuz I can't deal wit change, yer loony twat! Do yer worst, as I bet I'll be still standin ere afta it," Riz replied, meeting the challenge head on, just as I had expected him to. Antagonising your enemy was risky but it was a skill that Riz was unmatched in.

"I'm already two moves ahead of you!" Faine snapped his fingers and from the treeline beyond the wasteland more Spring Heels leapt out, their flames scorching the ground near where we were hidden. I held my nerve and stayed put, but watched as Valarie and Merrick appeared, and my own ghostly doppelganger. This was of course what Merrick himself had planned. I held my breath knowing that if the Spring Heels' hearing was good, they would be able to hear the real me, and blow the chance for our surprise attack. I was determined not to let my friends down when they needed me.

"Your plan was too simplistic, as always. You show a lack of foresight, only focusing on short term gain. I don't have that problem. I'm only concerned with the big picture," Faine said, monologuing to himself again.

"Big picture, eh? Well, yer found me out. Nd let me guess, yer gonna talk sum more?" Riz said, standing on his hind legs and crossing his front paws. "I mean, yer were so afraid of meetin me dat yer ad ta brin all yer little clique wit yer, like one of dose American high school mean girls."

Riz was over egging it, and I doubted that Faine would even understand that last insult. From the look on the Fae's face, I was right.

"I hope your allies have it burned into their souls that it was your mouth that made them suffer this way."

Faine clicked his fingers as several Spring Heels came forward. "Kill them all."

"Wait, master!" Jack the Ripper shouted out. "You promised me that I could play with them, or at least one of them! You can't deny me my prize now!"

"Jack, you may torment the rat once they are dead. I've longed to put to test the stories I've heard about his endurance," Faine said. Not that it was my place to say anything, but I think I'd rather meet my end at the claws of a Spring Heel, than Jack.

"Yeh, Jack, yer can come play wit me! Tho I bet yer want ta play wit her, don't yer? She's more yer type afta wat yer did last time. Jus ignore Faine nd go get er. I don't mind waitin fer yer!" Riz teased. I wasn't aware that this was part of the plan, encouraging Jack to go after Valarie. If I had been informed, there's no way I'd have okayed it. I'd later learn it was Valarie's idea herself, and well, you'll see more about that later. At that moment though, I think I'd stopped breathing, watching the Ripper easily give in to Riz's taunting and lunge to Valarie, a few of the Spring Heels taking that as a sign to attack, all of them ignoring Faine and his calls for calm. They should have listened in fairness. After all, those illusions they attacked? Our triple-cross? Merrick had struck up the idea of booby trapping them, with a bit of tinkering by Riz. Jack, by virtue of being the fastest, was the first to learn this, as the Blast Rune detonated in the Valarie illusion. The battle had begun, and I was think it was fair to say that we'd taken the first round...

CHAPTER 25
GOING A LITTLE TOO WELL

You shouldn't be surprised that Jack wasn't too injured by the Blast Rune we'd rigged up to the Valarie Illusion. He was injured, but sadly very much alive. The Spring Heels that went after Merrick's and my illusion? They were blown away completely. Eight of them had foolishly rushed in, and now their remains littered the ground like a disgusting modern art piece.

"What was that?" Jack bellowed in rage, and this was met with a resolute yell by Valarie, who leapt up from her hiding place:

"Tar'Hazdem!"

The Blast Rune in her hand exploded and the energy released found a target in Jack, who was right in front of her. The top hat that, so far, Jack had not been without, was immolated instantly. The goblin himself staggered back, bleeding profusely, his face more horrific as old surgical scars reopened. He retreated back, snarling like a wild beast all the while.

"If you had listened, you wouldn't have been hurt!" Faine lashed out. "Turning your illusions into mines, how clever, I suppose that was your plan all along?" he asked Riz, who rolled his eyes.

"I wish, but that's on im!" Riz shrugged and pointed at Merrick who had leapt from his own hiding place, taking aim at more of the Spring Heels, and uttering the same Breton Activation Word as Valarie, though he did it multiple times, unleashing a torrent of blasts. His target was part of the massed group of Spring Heels that had stupidly stuck too close together. It looked like they hadn't even registered the death of their friends yet. By the time that Merrick's attack had done its worst, Faine's army consisted of a lowly five Spring Heels, and a beaten Jack the Ripper. All in all, it looked like Merrick's plan had worked out. This meant that Faine was still a threat, but the odds were turning to our advantage. The Fae's demeanour didn't change as much as I would have thought though. I expected some annoyance, or, at best, full mental breakdown as he realised how bad things were getting. Instead of any of these things, he looked unmoved, and bored.

"I don't know what should be more annoying to me, that you think my defeat is certain because of how you do your fighting, or that you think I'm affected by any losses you inflict on me. Let me be blunt, I don't care for any of these goblins, those that are alive and cowering or those that you've already killed. Even Jack here is a means to an end."

"Oh, yer think yer so flippin clever, don't yer? Actin all cool nd all, knowin dat yer jus lost ta a bunch of kids nd me!"

More and more, the sound of springs vibrated around us, as more and more dropped out of the sky, bolstering Faine's attitude.

"Do you think I would use all the forces at my disposal straight away? You may think that ten Spring Heels was a trivial amount, but let's see how you handle…" Faine seemed to pause for dramatic effect, a backing chorus of springs filling in the silence. "Thirty Spring Heels," he finished.

That was when they landed, thirty identical looking Spring Heels. Even their moments were in sync with each other, and while the others had looked a bit grubby, these were pristine. Although they were living, breathing creatures, I was loathed to say that they had just popped off the construction line, despite that being the factual truth of the matter. Well, maybe not as you're imagining it but hey-ho. The thirty Spring Heels stayed massed together, seemingly avoiding the temptation to go after us in groups, which would have made things easier. This mass of goblins weaved out of the way as both Merrick and Valarie attempted to kill them, the blasts sailing past harmlessly a target that was there one second, and gone the next. I clutched the Rune in my hand, as I was the only person left to actually do anything. I went to take aim, but my hands were shaking badly, and had I dared utter the word, I'd have probably blasted Merrick or Valarie, which wouldn't have been helpful. I took another deep breath, then left my own hiding place, standing shoulder to shoulder with my friends... well, my human friends anyway, as Riz was still near Faine. I didn't understand then why the rat hadn't attacked in earnest, referring to throw only barbs at the Fae. Even as we faced down the horde of goblins, Riz was still talking himself up.

"Thirty? Is dat it? Yer gunna need more den dat ta stop us from kickin yer arse, yer frickin loser!" He laughed. I heard him quite clearly due to how loud he shouted it over the sound of the Spring Heels jumping around, avoiding every blast meant to blow them apart.

"You're still making the same mistake, the same one you always make! Didn't you learn from your past experiences that pride comes before a fall? It seems to me that your allies can't deal with these smarter reinforcements of mine, and you're too much of a coward to face me in combat. Is it because you know you're at a disadvantage against a full bodied Fae like myself? Or is it that you're going to see how it's going and then try to get in my good graces?" Faine pointed the tip of the sword at Riz, as if he was issuing a challenge.

"Yer challengin me? Ta a fricking fight? Yer dat desperate ta lose, Faine?"

"For too long you have been dogging my heels, so let us settle this!" Faine roared, lunging at Riz. Looking back, it's hard to picture a Fae picking a fight with a rat without laughing. Yet, I wasn't laughing then. No, then I was caught between watching what Riz was doing, and checking to see if Valarie and Merrick had done any damage to that swarm of Spring Heels which were definitely proving harder to hurt.

"Settle dis? Well, yer rite bout dat but yer fergettin one, teensy, wincy, little detail, yer plonker," Riz said, darting about, finally showing off the innate agility that rats can access. "I'm not one fer fightin fair!" Where Riz jumped on the floor, bright spots appeared that erupted into small fountains of energy. The attack seemed the same sort as the Blast Rune but was behaving in a totally different manner. Faine had been focusing on Riz the whole time, so these came as a mighty big surprise to him, as each hit him, burning him.

"You! No wonder they gave you that name!" Faine said, coughing up blood. Despite all those direct hits, he didn't look too bad, his clothes looked a lot worse for wear now, with burnt patches and other holes, but he wasn't physically hurt, but I also noticed something odd, that there was what looked to be crumbling stones falling from the Fae's waistcoat. Riz looked delighted at this development.

"Dat shud take care of dose pesky defences yer were carryin wit ye. I thought yer always hated Runes nd looked down yer freakishly long nose at anyone who used Runes, yer flippin hypocrite!"

I really wanted to pay attention to more of that conversation but Valarie took hold of my and pulled me out of the way as a few Spring Heels dug their claws into the ground where I had been stood.

"Pay attention, Bren!" she reminded me firmly.

Merrick wasn't so calm. "Bren! What the hell you playing at? I told you I had your back!" He glared at Valarie, though the meaning why was lost on me at that point, as the Spring Heels that missed the first time round, decided to have another go of it, leaping towards me, their razor sharp claws reaching out to grab me.

"Together, Bren!" Valarie took hold of my hand that was hold the Blast Rune and she stood shoulder to shoulder with me. "Wait till I say, and remember, I'm here for you," she said quickly. Her words tumbled out quickly, yet I knew what she meant. With the Spring Heels almost upon us, I heard her counting down in between her breaths, from three to one. I instinctively knew that one was going to be our moment, and tried my best to control the shaking, and ready my aim. I felt the heat from their fiery breaths, and I think I may have had a few eyebrow hairs singed.

"Now! Tar'Hazdem!" Valarie shouted out, and I echoed her, my voice coming out strong. The power in the two Runes we held burst outwards and merged into one massive fire ball that the Spring Heels couldn't hope to avoid. They definitely didn't, by the way. The Spring Heels that weren't incinerated were stunned by the rapid reversal in their fortune. To put it in figures, me and Valarie had just toasted fifteen Spring Heels, leaving fifteen left, which needed a new plan.

"Ready to go again, Bren?" Valarie asked me with a devilish wink.

"I won't let you down!" I replied, feeling the strength of my friends bolstering my own resolve. "Merrick! Let's take them!" I yelled at my other friend who had been watching us apparently.

"Godammit, Bren! Just don't get yourself killed!" he said, turning back to the enemies who had now regrouped into three groups of five, wanting to take us on separately. Which seemed the better plan, if you discounted the fact that Merrick and Valarie had already killed several Spring Heels without breaking a sweat.

Not wanting to waste my own momentum, I ran into the group of five Spring Heels. I steeled myself, with Rune in hand, and I aimed, wanting to strike before they could react. I had already thrown them off with running at them.

"Tar'Hazdem!" I fired the Rune off with no hesitation, speaking the words crystal clear and turned the five Spring Heels into two Spring Heels and burnt goblin remains. The remaining two went to attack me, but I moved quickly again, finally putting all that training to some use, not to mention the times I'd had to run away from Riz when the little git was going to bite me. I kept my distance from them, and fired up an Arrow Rune this time. I should have been nervous, after all, the last time I used this one, it did blow my arm off, but as I said, I was riding a wave of self-confidence, one that hadn't crested yet.

"Saezh!" No backlash this time, the Rune broke as it was supposed to, and a thin line of energy, looking just like the arrow that inspired its name, shot forward. My aim was impeccable and the arrow bore its way through the head of one of the Spring

Heels. This left its friend, who had moved away from the one I'd just killed, probably in the mistaken belief that I was going to use a Blast Rune to finish it off. Thinking it had an opportunity to hit me, it reached out, till I revealed what I had hidden in my left hand. Did you guess it? Yup, a second Arrow Rune.

"Saezh!" I said, relishing the feeling. People may think this change in behaviour is unnatural, that I should have remembered that I was just a sixteen-year-old fighting goblins and fairies. I never lost sight of that. I embraced the madness that I was a sixteen-year-old half-banshee/half-human hybrid who was fighting goblins and fairies, with a talking rat nearby. Yes, I think you can say I snapped somewhere around this point. Normal was way past being a distant dream.

"Merrick! Behind you!" I shouted as one of the Spring Heels my friend was fighting was trying to get the drop on him, while he was fending off two in front. The knowledge that I had to be somewhat frugal with my Rune choices was forgotten, mind.

"Tar'Hazdem!" The Blast Rune exploded in my hand, before the energy blast then went and made the Spring Heel explode, moments from hitting Merrick, who didn't seem pleased that I was getting involved with his fight.

"Last warning, Bren! Stay safe! I can't have you putting yourself in danger just to try and hang with us!" I don't know why he added that last part in.

"I know what I'm doing! Speaking of that…" Knowing that I could safely look away from where Valarie and Merrick were putting down the last of the Spring Heels, I gave Riz's fight my full attention. Jack had crawled his way over there from his incident, not that it was going to give Faine any advantage.

"Master! Help me!" Jack pleaded, causing Faine to scowl, but ultimately acquiesce, throwing a Rune down onto the fallen goblin that glowed brightly, then crumbled. Though I didn't see what kind of Rune it was, it wasn't a surprise to anyone to learn that it was a Healing Rune of some description, as Jack stood back up, seemingly revitalised.

"Right! Jack's back!" The goblin laughed, flexing his knife fingers, his gaze locked on me.

"Bren! He's comin at ya, yer daft sod!" Riz broke off from his pursuit of Faine, and ran to me. I wasn't sure of his intent, but he was as shocked as I was when a faint blue glow enveloped us, stopping both of us from moving, which was clear when Riz didn't scarper off.

"You're mine, runt!" Jack laughed, seeing as I was now a sitting duck. He leapt up, using his springs, and came down to stab me. I closed my eyes tight, panic drilling out every other thought.

"Open yer eyes, Bren. We're in deep shit," Riz said, with no emotion in his voice, other than frustration. I did as I was told and saw Jack the Ripper standing through me, his claws in the dirt between my legs. He looked as confused as I was.

"If it ain't one thin, it's anotha…"

CHAPTER 26
THE UNLIKELY TAG TEAM

So, you're probably wondering, what had happened? What was that blue glow? How did I survive Jack's attack? Well, Riz, surprise, surprise, knew the score already.

"We're in an Illusion Trap! Sum bugga haz trapped us! I didn't see Faine or any of is lackey's use one tho…" Riz put his little rat fingers to his mouth as he pondered our situation.

"So what do you mean?" I asked, watching as Jack pulled his hand out and waved it around where I was stood, or where he thought I had been stood. It just passed through me with no resistance, almost like I was dead. Valarie had become aware of my absence, and I heard her call my name. Merrick noticed at this point, but he couldn't do much, as whatever happened seemed to coincide with more Spring Heels coming down, a third wave that was just as numerous as the last. I didn't want to doubt that my friends could handle themselves but it was harder to think that they would have the resources to.

"Ain't it obvious? We're in a different plane of reality ta dem lot! Dat's y Jack's blades cudn't touch yer! Downside ta us bein in ere is dat we're not out dere!" Riz sighed, before his ears pricked up. "Wait a mo, didn't yer mum giv yer a flippin Illusion Trap Rune dat yer jus causally tossed in ta yer bag like it waz nuthin?"

I could feel my cheeks get redder as I looked in the pouch for that Rune, only to discover it wasn't there. How I could have accidentally used it though, without a backlash like my last screw up, was a mystery, but one that wasn't as pressing as getting back to my friends. My thoughts and feelings turned to dismay when I realised that due to my mistake, I had taken away Riz, the best hope of stopping Faine. Valarie was good, but I didn't know if she would be up to taking on him after dealing with all the Spring Heels and Jack the Ripper. Merrick? Given that he only had the same training as me, that didn't bear thinking about. I fell to my knees as all my anxiety came rushing back.

"I screwed up…" I hit the ground as hard as I could.

"Looks like dey've got bigga problems!" Riz pointed to my friends, who had found themselves alone, and Valarie in particular, as Jack had zeroed in to her as a new target.

Jack flexed his clawed fingers, each one catching the dying sunlight. "I kept wondering why I was drawn to attack that stupid illusion of yours earlier, then it hit me. You sorta look like those ladies I killed way back when. A bit younger, but I don't care about that. You all die the same anyway!"

"You don't think I'm scared of you, do you?" Valarie said. "Why would I be scared of animals like you that hurt for pleasure? I've seen crap that'd turn your boss inside out. Compared to the horrors that lurk in my memories, you're nothing but a Halloween reject in a top hat."

Okay, if no one can see why I fell for her, then you have a heart of stone and cloth in your ears. She calmly reached into her pocket and pulled out two Runes.

"Once I'm finished with you," Jack said, "I'll be added to your nightmares. I don't just want you to be scared, I want you to be screaming in pain!" He ran forward, seemingly confident that he could avoid whatever Valarie would throw his way.

"Kordenn! Kordenn!" she called out twice as two rope-like white energy streams shot out of the Runes and she held them like whips. "Always wanted to try these things out."

"Riz, what the hell are they?" I asked in shock. From my admittedly meagre Rune knowledge at the time, I'd not seen anything like them.

"Where der ell did she get Whip Runes from?" Riz seethed.

"Oh! I bet I know where she got dose soddin thins from. Arty probably forged dem. Goddammit."

"Is there a problem with them? Should Valarie be using them?" I said, watching as Valarie twirled them around, almost daring Jack to get closer to her, though he was now showing some hesitancy with his movements.

"It's complicated, nd I'd ratha jus say dat it's not ma fault, nd is one-hundred percent Arty's stupid fault." Riz started pawing around. His paws went through the ground, just as Jack's bladed claws had gone through me. He seemed to be looking for something. I left him to that and watched Valarie launch her attack on Jack as she swept her left handed whip across, before following up with the one in her right hand surging forward, a move that Jack only narrowly avoided.

"Jack! Let the Spring Heels finish her! I need you to secure him!" Faine pointed at Merrick, who was doing his best to stay alive when up against a swarm of Spring Heels, who were all leaping around him wildly. I think it was miraculous that he wasn't roughed up more.

"Screw you! This girl is the only decent prey you've let me go after these past few months! You want him that badly, go get him yourself, or better yet, just stay here and watch me work. You might learn a thing or two," Jack yelled out, causing the bones in his shoulders to creak as he stretched them. He ran at Valarie, jumping over the first whip, and sacrificing his tattered cloak to the second one, jettisoning it with no effort. His hat also fell off at this point, revealing his bald head, that was covered in surgical scars and scraps of metal that had been expertly shoved in there. "Oh, yes, this should be fun," Jack boasted.

Valarie looked disgusted by the attention she was getting, but I saw determination in her eyes, which said that she wasn't giving up. I compared the odds that were stacked against us, and looked back to Riz, who was still searching.

"You can handle me? I don't think so. You couldn't even handle a talking rat!" Valarie sniggered, a clear taunt.

"What? I'm going to make you suffer!" Jack roared, not

noticing the Rune that his opponent had slipped into her hand, holding it alongside the still active Whip Rune.

"You have to hit me first to make me suffer," Valarie winked, which aggregated Jack even more than I thought possible. Like the smaller Spring Heels, there were literal flames coming from his mouth though, almost enough to engulf his head in a blaze.

"Say that after this!" He charged again, the fire showing his trail as he bounced around, evading Valarie's attack's. When it looked like the goblin was about to get close enough to land a hit, and not be hit in the face by a whip, Valarie backed off but dropped the Rune that was hidden in her hand.

"Brumenn!" A mist spread out from where the Rune hit the ground, spreading far. Sadly, it obscured my vision as well, and I lost sight of Valarie, till she ran right through me.

"Valarie!" I called out, before realising my own stupidity.

"Do yer feel betta fer dat?" Riz asked as he still continued to search.

"What are you doing anyway?"

"I'm tryin ta find der Rune yer stupidly activated so we can get outta ere!" Riz sounded exasperated when he turned to me. "Now, yer gunna pine fer yer girlfriend or yer gunna help me already!"

"What about Valarie and Merrick though? That Mist Rune isn't going to last forever."

"I can hear betta den yer can, clearly. As ard as it is ta believe, dose two are workin together," Riz explained.

"What?" I was shell-shocked, and I think after listening to my story for this long, you'd be the same.

"Dey're comin back dis way, so yer can see fer yerself." Riz went back to his searching, shrugging his shoulders at my disbelief. The footsteps behind me confirmed Riz's senses as Merrick and Valarie crept into view and I heard their whispers.

"You sure about this? I don't mind taking on Ripper boy," Merrick said. He stopped moving and aimed a Rune into the mist, just as Spring Heel leapt towards him.

"Tar'Hazdem!" It got blasted for its troubles.

"I don't think you're his type!" Valarie teased. "Besides, Faine wants you and we need to figure out what happened to Bren and the rat."

"It's probably safer where he is then here," Merrick sighed. "Trust them though, to leave all the work to us!" He showed off some more of his trademark charm there, not that Valarie had cared, if I guessed her mood right from her face.

"Either way, we deal with these best we can, then we bring them back. Maybe after, we can figure out what happened. Good luck!" Valarie split away from Merrick, and they went their separate ways. All I heard around us was springs, as I pictured the Spring Heels jumping around in a frenzy as they couldn't work out what to do. I heard Faine's voice over the top of the Spring Heels:

"Jack! Do not follow her! This is a trap! Return to my side at once so we can re-evaluate!" Faine sounded frustrated, which he had no reason to be, not in my humble opinion. He'd lost his rival, and now had two people left to neutralise.

"No! I'm finishing this!" Jack's voice was hard to pinpoint, and I thought it was coming from the right of me.

"Silence! This is an order, Jack!"

The tone of Faine's voice told me that he wasn't liking the tone that Jack was taking with him, or that he was being ignored.

"Leave me to my fun!" Jack laughed.

I saw him moving through the mist, keeping closer to the ground. There were flashes of Rune magic in between the bursts of mist, with Spring Heels getting picked off when the opportunity presented itself.

I kicked the dirt at my feet, but felt like I hit nothing but air. I needed to be out of this trap and helping the pair of them. I wanted to help Valarie gun Jack down, I wanted to help Merrick blast away all the Spring Heels.

"We'll be out in a minute! Yer worryin ova nuthin," Riz said, searching a place he'd only looked at a moment before.

I looked around, thinking through what we'd thought had happened. Where I'd moved from had been carefully marked out by the footprints that we were leaving in this strange realm.

I think if you were at the right height, you'd spot a masterpiece that Riz had drawn. Wouldn't comment on if it was tasteful or not. I hadn't moved much. I worked back to where I'd been standing, and bent down when I saw curious red energy that arched around.

"Riz, what's this?" I pointed out to him. His response came in the form of an "Oh!" sound.

"Well, well, yer found yer cock up! I shud ave us outta ere in a moment." Riz got quieter as he looked at what I'd found.

"Dat's interestin…" He failed to go into any detail over what he was dealing with. "Mite take a bit longa."

I rolled my eyes, not understanding, or caring about anything other then getting back to help my friends. Speaking of which, I heard Jack calling out to Valarie.

"Come on out, girl! I thought you wanted to end me! All those other playthings I've had, they're all rubbish compared to you. Might grant you a small mercy if you meet me face to face!" the serial killer goblin said. From the way his springs were ratcheted up though, he was preparing for her to show up.

"You really know how to tell a story, Jack. You got any more fun tales?" Valarie sang out, as Merrick's blasting gave her a nice backing beat.

"One fun story is what I'll do to you once I catch you! It will be loving and familiar to what I did to all those other ladies. You must be familiar with them. Your culture glorified them for me after all."

A gap in the mist provided me with a look at Valarie, throughout this. It looked liked she was stepping on bugs, or that they were crawling all over her. The killer had been right, about how his victims had been served by history. For all intents, they belonged to him, and were never their own person. Even from the scant months I knew of her, I would have guessed hat she wasn't one to settle for that.

"Mary Ann Nichols, Annie Chapman, Elizabeth Stride, Catherine Eddowes and Mary Jane Kelly." Valarie listed, probably from memory.

"Who?" Jack replied bluntly, searching achingly close to near where she was stood. I could see both of them, but I got the feeling that they couldn't see each other.

"Those were their names. The names of the women you killed. Each one had their own life, their own stories to tell, yet you took it away from them. And why? Because you were just an attack dog," Valarie growled, and I saw her raising her whips, and the crackling energy they gave off, that must have been something that Jack heard, as I saw his ears twitch.

"An attack dog? I'm no one's pet! I killed because I wanted to! If that rat hadn't stopped me, you would have more names to memorise, little girl!"

Can you say hook, line and sinker? Jack lashed out at the sound of the whips. Through his rage filled eyes, Jack just wanted blood, but caught his own as Valarie wrapped one of the whips around the hand that was going for her throat. When the whip tightened, I thought that Jack's arm was going to be ripped from its socket as Valarie swung him round with a strength, that took everyone by surprise. The mist was dissipating now so Faine was able to catch sight of what was happening, as did Merrick, who looked as though he had better things to care about.

"Rite, I think I sorted it," Riz said, before he too took notice. "Now she's jus showin off!" Like Merrick before him, Riz seemed to know something I didn't.

"Can we get out of here now?" I asked.

"Yeh, but we mite wanna move over dere a smidge, yer know, ta avoid bein hit by der flyin gobbo?"

I followed Riz's somewhat helpful suggestion, never taking my eyes off the fight Valarie was having with Jack, though in overpowering him, it wasn't much of a fight, something the goblin must have been aware of.

"Yer ready? In a minute yer will be back out dere, nd we can brin Faine in finally," Riz said, hopping up to my shoulder.

"I'm ready. Merrick and Valarie have done their share. It's my time to step up."

I felt a twitch from Riz when I said Merrick's name there, but didn't question it.

"What trickery is this!" Jack demanded to know, as he was crashed into the floor again.

"Don't you like my Whip Runes? Specially made for me," Valarie asked slyly, as she had both of Jack's arms bound by whips, stretching them apart to breaking point. Jack howled out some swear word, but that was drowned out by the sound of me and Riz re-entering reality.

"Oi, twats! Did yer miss me?" Riz said with glee.

"It's over, Faine!" I shouted out. "Whatever you tried to do, failed. Merrick is on our side and you're about to lose a toy! Just give up already," I said with a bit too much bravado.

The next sound I wanted to hear was Faine cursing his luck, what I didn't want to hear was the sound of the Runes in Valarie's hands breaking, as that red arching light ripped through them, knocking both her and Jack to the ground. I didn't have much time to say anything else as the remaining Spring Heels saw an opportunity...

CHAPTER 27
FRIENDSHIP'S END

Recap: Valarie was now down, I'd lost sight of Merrick as I hid to avoid the Spring Heels that were jumping at me, and to top it off, I'd also misplaced Riz, but that wasn't so bad as out of the corner of my eye, I did think I saw the little blighter running off towards Faine, whose face was the epitome of someone having a bad day. Given the circumstances, my actions were twofold, survive and make sure that Valarie was alright, and what happened with the Runes she was using so expertly to cause the poor Ripper so much suffering. The answer wasn't so much staring me in the face, as it was aiming for my back, while I hid my eyes away from it. I heard Merrick's voice through the confusion, calling me, which I thought was a bit crazy in a hectic moment like this.

"Bren! What the hell, mate! What are you doing? Why would you do that!" He sounded much more panicked than when I went missing, and there was an accusation in his voice that I couldn't put my finger on.

"Riz! Take that twat down!" I shouted out to Riz. It was the least I could do, as I heard springs and saw shadows swoop down on me, and the fight was on me, as two Spring Heels went to stab me.

"Tar'Hazdem!" I yelled, blowing one of them away, and rolling from the other, landing on my feet, which I may or may not have giggled at in my head. I will not confirm or deny this.

Ahead of me, Valarie was moving, and I saw streaks of blood coming from her arms and some splatter on her face, but that looked superficial. I made it to her, and saw that her hands were wrecks, the

Runes that she was so proud of, now mere crumbs embedded in her skin, that same red energy bouncing from the pieces.

"That energy again," I mumbled.

"I'll be fine, just have to get on my feet!" Valarie said through a forced smile.

I wanted to do something to help, but got a kick to my head for my troubles, as the other Spring Heel I hadn't vaporised knocked me back, and didn't let up, using its spring powered legs to propel itself for power blows. A moment after being beaten up, I realised that it hadn't punched me or cut me up, because it no longer had any arms. Seems I got closer to cutting both of them down than I gave myself credit for. Deciding on a different route out of fighting this guy, I felt in the pouch for a different symbol, one that that my mum had taught me. I pulled it out and used it to block the next kick the Spring Heel wanted to deliver to my noggin.

"Kel'ch!" My timing was perfect for this, as the Rune activated the instant the goblin's leg made contact with it. Normally, you would have had to set this to a type of Other, and then you'd be protected for a short while from them as long as you stayed in the circle. My mum, however, taught me this other neat little trick with it, where if your timing was right, you could use it on the spot to create a quick barrier against any threat. In this case, it caused the goblin's leg to break at the join because of the redirected pressure, and the Spring Heel to be sent flying back. I went to run but the sight of that red energy again around the goblin's neck as it had the worst luck ever to land on an outcropping of rocks that severed its head. I looked to see Merrick now just across from me. He was tired, and panting for breath.

"Goddammit, Bren! You sure like making me do all the work!" he moaned.

"I'm back now, and we can finish this! You need to look after Valarie while I help Riz in taking down the rest of these Spring Heels!"

"What? You want me to look after her? Why the hell should I do that?" Merrick questioned.

"You've both done more than your fair share. Just leave it to me and Riz now. We can end this!" I knew he was going to say something else, but I didn't want to hear him. I turned and ran to where Riz had already re-engaged Faine, the pair of them going at it like a rat and a Fae. Which totally wasn't weird, if you could have seen it. Being of small stature, Riz wasn't able to hold many Runes, like, he could only have ever held one and still been able to move somewhat freely. His plan was to have several stashed on the ground, and just run to use them. This was what he had done early on in the battle, and despite the side-track of being whisked to another reality, he was able to pick up what he'd started.

"Ey kid! Yer got more Runes ta giv me, den throw dem down! Den bugga off! I've got dis, yer run away wit yer pals," Riz said in between dashes for his stockpiles.

"Why must this happen every time we fight! How are you able to claw back victory from defeat! And you do so by abusing those Runes! Was it not you who told us to be careful about these in the first place? Was it not you who encouraged us to rely on our own types of magic?" Faine shouted.

"Yer usin Runes, yer cheatin bastard! Besides we all know wat wud happen if I didn't use dem! Nd dat wudn't be fair wud it! Think of dis as me goin easy on yer!" Riz retorted. In the meantime of them arguing, I had rolled a few extra Runes into Riz's path, and this of course caught Faine's eye.

"And you, the head human lackey of this despicable being. I hope you're happy with the company you've made! For all they call of me, I am a legend next to him! You're nothing but a spineless worm that hastens its own destruction! The being that kills him will be sung about till the end of time! You will not even be a footnote!"

Faine was really going all out on the insults, which largely flew over my head at the time. I wanted to attack him, and there seemed to be plenty of openings for me to do so, but given how hard Riz was working, I knew it best not to, besides, there was still the rest of the Spring Heels to deal with, hence I left Riz to the bigger threat. I had hoped to turn my head and see Merrick and Valarie leading an orderly retreat, something that I could have linked up to and worked with, healing Valarie of course, to kill the last of the Spring Heels that would of course target us. I didn't even think about the fact that I had lost sight of Jack the Ripper. I'll let you tell me how stupid that was in a moment.

What I saw instead was Merrick as far away as possible from Valarie, dealing with three Springs Heels, fending them off with odd actions, while Valarie was at the mercy of a disabled Jack and another Spring Heel who seemed to be doing everything its boss couldn't do, on account of all the injuries that he'd received from the erstwhile Valarie Turner. I had one Blast Rune ready, and I could hit one of them now. Despite all of that adrenaline pumping through my body as that heady charge took over, I froze like a deer in headlights. Here was the biggest moment in my life till now, and one that that would shape everything that was to come, including why I hated this time of year, because really, I hated myself. Even before I did anything, thought anything, I blamed myself for this coming to pass. I knew that different choices would have led to better outcomes than this... if I had just used my brain a bit more efficiently, or even listened to what was going on around me, then I wouldn't have been faced with this choice, and had to live with the consequences. About now, you might have guessed what was going to happen, what my choice was going to be, and to that, I say, congratulations on being able to put together everything I had to live through. Hindsight is a bitch, and one that I have to live with every day, though most days I do call him by his proper name of Riz.

Anyway, with my breathing slowed right down, and having worked through my choices of targets, I went with my gut, and fired.

"Tar'Hazdem!" I yelled, with all my heart and soul, and the blast went flying towards that Spring Heel that held Valarie, trying to make her an easier target for Jack the Ripper who was mustering his strength to raise a clawed finger against her. The attack killed the target, allowing Valarie to roll over, and onto her dropped bag, which armed her with a Rune that she then used on Jack. From what I thought I heard, I think it was another Lightning Rune, a family favourite, or so I'm told. Jack was sent electrifyingly backwards, towards where Riz and Faine were fighting. I ran to her and checked to see if she was okay, getting a weak smile from her as a reward. I turned to see how I could best help Merrick, assuming he was still being pressured by the Spring Heels.

I assumed wrong.

"You had a choice, Brennan. You always had the fucking choice. And you chose wrong, again! Every time, you muck it up, mate. It must be a special skill that you have, I can't believe it myself," Merrick said, shaking his head in disbelief, as he walked towards me, callously stepping on the neck of a Spring Heel as it tried to retreat, its legs broken. It, and its brethren were laid low, dying or already dead. The same red energy arching over their bodies.

"Merrick, what did you do?" I asked. I had intended it to come out softly, but my fear got in the way, so it came out cold.

"I cursed them, what does it look like? I cursed them to be so clumsy that they would kill each other? The same I cursed her Runes to break so that we'd have the chance to be rid of her. The same way I cursed that Rune of yours to protect you!"

Welcome to ground zero.

"Wh-what?" I stammered. Momentary confusion entered my brain and made a nest as everything I was striving to think about just turned to mush.

"I put you in that Illusion Trap? Yeah, I put you in there to protect you! Didn't plan on the rodent getting in there, but if it made you happy, then sod it. Then of course, you go and mess it up!"

"You can thank Riz for that, I think he figured out what you'd done and un-did it," I replied.

"Screw him, I hope Faine steps on him! He's the reason you're like this! Him, and her!" Merrick motioned towards Valarie, who still seemed in pain and wasn't moving. "I thought I was your brother, Bren! I thought we were bros for life!" Merrick sounded more maniacal. "Yet, you chose her over me, someone you've known for all of your fucking life... her... someone you've known for, like, a month. What am I to you, Bren?"

All the questions that Merrick was bombarding me with, I didn't have any answers to, at least, not then. Not when my mind was being ripped apart by his accusations.

"Merrick! Please, this isn't the time for us to fight! Faine is just there, we can take him down, then we can help you!" I shouted out at him, desperately wanting him to turn back from whatever precipice he was standing on.

"Help me? Why would I want to be helped now?"

"What? What are you saying?"

"Bren, what I'm saying is... I don't need help! For too long, I've ignored my true self, always been told that I was cursed, and that I needed helping. Riz treated me like I was the problem, something for his ego to fix without a second glance. Well, now, I'm finished with that line of thinking!"

I didn't have a retort for that at hand, so I looked away absently, catching Riz's duel with Faine in my peripheral. Of course, the rat was holding his own, even when he appeared to doing things without the Runes. Merrick caught my gaze.

"See! Even now, you're more concerned with him then me! I'm standing here and you look to him for guidance! The rat that ruined everything! This is why I need to get away from this. I need to learn who I really am." His voice changed as he finished his little speech, calming himself like a self-help guru. I saw a range of emotions on my friend's face, each one passing in the space of a second or less. He'd jumped the gulf from rage to apathy, all the way back to acceptance. Maybe with his gift, he'd seen this possibility and prepared himself.

"Bren! Wat's goin on? Yer a sittin duck dere!" Riz shouted out as he went paw to toe with Faine. I would have thought that with his big ears that he would have heard some of the argument I was having with Merrick, but no, he wanted Faine dead, and that took all his focus.

"Go! Run to the rat, do whatever he wants you to do. I know

how things are. I know where I'm going to be better treated! But first…" There was a flash in his eyes and my feet sank into the ground.

"Merrick! What are you doing? Where did you learn this?" I questioned, trying not to think that I was trapped with dangerous goblins springing around me.

"I picked a few things up from what I've seen, things I've spoken to, but I'm not about to say their names yet, I'm not that stupid. Don't you worry though! The Spring Heels won't hurt you, but I can't just leave her and the rat unscathed. No, I'm pissed off and for once, you won't stop me from doing what I want!"

"I've got Runes too, remember!"

"Will you really use a Rune against me? Bren?" Merrick stood arms open, a Rune in his hand aimed at Valarie's prone form. "You're a soft touch, Bren. Most predictable thing about you is that you won't fire that at me."

"He might not, but nothing is stopping me!" Valarie said, bursting into life as she fired out the Blast Rune she had hidden in her damaged hands.

"Tar'Hazdem!"

The blast shot upwards, and Merrick had no choice but to dash backwards to avoid it, not that he managed it completely as part of him was engulfed and he screamed out in pain, something that I can still hear if I close my eyes and remember.

Valarie jumped up and ran to me, helping me out of the ground as the Spring Heels were almost on top of us. The pair of us were ready for them, using Runes to blast them to kingdom come. Seeing as there was now only a pitiful number of them left, the survivors had second thoughts about rushing in to face off against us.

"How? You were finished!" Merrick said, in pain, staggering forward, holding his own ruined body.

"When I checked on her, I dropped my Healing Rune onto her," I said, "as well as a Blast Rune. I knew she would do something clever with it. Just as I knew deep down that you were connected to my Rune back-firing. Merrick, it's not too late. Come quietly and we can discuss this like adults." I held my hand out. "I know you're angry, but that's not going to do you any good in the long run."

Merrick looked at my hand, and then spat out some blood.

"Sorry, I'm not going back now. That halcyon past you want no longer exists. You chose your path, and it's not one I'm on."

"Well, appears to me you don't have a lot of options then," Valarie said. It was clear to see where she was coming from. Faine's forces had been decimated. Jack? Well, I didn't know if he was alive or dead at this point and I pretty much didn't care.

"I've always got options," Merrick grinned, wiping blood away, his eyes glowing red, and I saw the unhinged glare that I'd only ever seen hinted at in my friend's worst moments.

"I'm not letting you go!" I went to grab him, but I tripped up, Merrick using his power once against me. Valarie managed to stop me from hitting the ground, where a set of Spring Heels claws were perilously placed to have torn my throat out.

Merrick, despite his injuries, was already where Faine and Riz were fighting. I tried to shout out to Riz, to warn him about Merrick, but it was too late, and there was a bright red flash, followed by a massive crack of thunder that threatened to tear the sky open. When my vision returned, all I could see at the top of the hill was Riz lying in a crater. What had transpired, I didn't know. It was a fair assumption that Merrick had brought all his curse powers to bear in that instant, wanting to pay the rat back for everything that he'd blamed him for.

"Goddammit," Riz wheezed. He rolled over, and rubbed some of the dirt off. "Almost ad der bastard! Den dat twat shows up!"

"You okay, Riz?" I asked nervously.

You might be sitting there, yelling at me that this wasn't my fault, and that there was no possible way that I could blame myself for anything. In the kindest, most polite manner I can muster, shut up. I wanted to drop to my knees then, looking at the battlefield, and seeing nothing but the pointlessness of it all staring me in the face. Faine was nowhere to be seen, neither was Merrick or Jack. I'd promised to help Riz, but only succeeded in making it worse. Valarie put her arm around my shoulder, offering comfort but I was too numb to take it in. All the consequences of what had transpired that night started hitting me. I was the last person to see Merrick alive. He would become a missing person's case. The guilt when I couldn't tell his family what happened to him...

"I think we're dun ere, kidz," Riz sighed, his words hitting the hardest. "Let's go before der twerps from der government get involved. No reason ta stick around..."

Following Riz's sage advice, we left, and headed for home, cementing my abhorrence for Halloween. One that would last the ages.

CHAPTER 28
THE COLD NOVEMBER

On a plus note about that evening, my parents were thrilled to see that I was home and in one piece, my reluctance to talk, or Riz's sullen mood having no bearing on their own happiness. My mum in particular even joked about how close she was to venturing out to aid us. They only discovered the outcome after a bit more prodding and Riz told them in no uncertain terms that he needed a strong drink to wash away the foul smell of Faine's escape. Valarie kindly filled them in with the rest of the sordid details.

"So, yeah…" Valarie said, as she finished explaining, drinking the last of her strongly brewed tea. My parents were in silence and I think they were both calculating what it meant that I had come home alive, but also failed to do what I set out to do. It was kind of Valarie to leave out the details about how one of my mum's Runes had caused a scene when Merrick made it backfire.

"Where's Merrick now?" my dad asked, putting his cup down.

"No idea, nd fer all dat twat's dun, he can stay where eva der ell it is! Go ta all dis effort ta help im, keep im away from Faine nd wat does dat twit do? Run straight ta im as soon as he runs inta a bit of botha!" That wasn't how I would have described the events that had transpired but Riz did have a way with words that sometimes bypassed actual reality.

"I thought he was cursed though? How was he able to do all of that? That isn't how that magic type works," my mum asked with eyebrows raised.

"Dat waz der thin I didn't get till lata, wen I realised dat sumit

217

waz wrong. Fer sumone ta be dat strong wit curse magic, nd dem be cursed on top of it, dat don't happen normally."

My dad graciously handed Riz a bottle of one of the cheaper beers, and the rat ungratefully snatched it, downing it in one breath.

"And what do you think did it?" my mum pressed further.

"No idea, nd rite now, I don't much care." Riz retreated into his gloomy misdemeanour. This soured the conversation, and dented the joyous mood that my return had created.

"Would you look at the time!" Valarie said. "Thanks for the drink!" She gently placed her mug down and went to leave, but I reached out to stop her.

"Wait! You can't just go!"

"Bren, right now, I think you need to get some sleep. I've still got my own things to sort out, but don't worry, I'm not going anywhere." She winked, and kissed my head. "Bye!"

Valarie left, and I couldn't have been more despondent. However, she had been right about one thing, I wanted my bed, and I needed to close the book on this horrible day.

Sleep came easily enough despite my uneasy head, but I was still awoken in the middle of the night by the sound of my window opening. When the origin of the noise became apparent, I bolted awake, and sat straight up, looking at Riz as he was halfway onto the window ledge.

"Ah, bugga, yer awake..." he said, somewhat sheepishly.

"Riz?"

"Dis ain't easy ta say, but I'm gonna ave ta get goin." Riz wouldn't look at me during this.

"Wait, you're just leaving me?" I tried to keep my voice down, in fear of waking my parents, but I was understandably confused and angry.

"Dere's thins I gotz ta do. Thins I can't involve yer in. I'm not doin dis ta be a twat nd leave yer hangin!"

"Really? Because it looks like you failed to get what you want, and now you're cutting your losses and running."

"Bren, don't be a twit, rite now, we're on a break. Faine ain't gunna do anythin fer a while. Yer bastard of a friend is off doin who knows wat. Dere's nuthin fer me ta do now, so I gotz otha thins ta do!" Riz tried to explain his stance again, by not explaining anything. You could argue that he didn't have to tell me, we weren't a partnership at this point. I should have felt lucky that he had stayed as long as he already had. Anything I was feeling was clearly alien to the rat. I doubt it crossed his mind that I'd just lost my closest friend a scant few hours ago. Valarie walked away from me, offering little closure for what had happened. It was entirely possible that I would never see any of them again.

Since that day at the beck, my world had revolved around these three in some fashion, and now, they were all torn away. No one seemed to care about how I feel.

"I'll be back in a few dayz alrite? Yer keep doin… wateva it is yer doin. Got it, kid?" Riz showed no compassion in how he spoke to me, treating me like a child that was stopping him from doing what he wanted.

"But where are you going?" I asked, reaching out to grab Riz, without thinking about what the results of that would be. In case you wondered, he bit me. Big surprise there. I recoiled in pain, and Riz took the opportunity to get the other side of the window.

"Ain't important where I'm goin, kid. Won't do yer any favours if yer knew."

My emotions were getting the better of me, and I felt like crying, tears of frustration, of sadness, mixed in with the rage of no one listening.

"So, that's it? I'm supposed to be fine with you leaving? I'm supposed to just wave as you waltz out of here, after turning everything upside down?"

"A bit excessive, ain't it? All yer ave ta do is jus say bye." Riz cocked his head, proving once and for all that he wasn't thinking about me.

"Bye?" I repeated what he said, and the word made him wave in response.

"Bye! Don't do anythin I wudn't do!" Riz said, his words undercutting the situation.

"No! Riz!"

My words fell on deaf ears as he left without saying anything else. Like that, I was completely alone in my bedroom. I didn't bother trying to go back to sleep that night. I knew it was just going to evade me.

The next day, I informed my parents that Riz had gone, and it was met with a mixed reaction. Mostly, they were happy that the rat had gone, seeing him as a danger magnet that I didn't need around me.

"As long as you're okay." My mum hugged me. "From the stories I've heard, it was a good thing that the rat left. We've got enough on our plate regarding what we are."

I hung my head low, not wanting to cause an argument with Mum at that time. Learning from Mum would be the only vestige of the life I had before that cursed Halloween encounter. My attention span was devastated, and I found it hard to concentrate on anything. Be it my mum's lessons, or Dad choice's about what to watch on TV. Despite the fact that I knew the secret behind my bloodline, my parents were quick to push for things to go back to normal. They even dropped in hints of what I could be studying soon enough, and I didn't care. All I wanted was for something to remind me that things weren't necessarily so bleak. I think you can guess the tone of what happened next...

CHAPTER 29
THE MASK FALLS

As November gave way to December, I woke up to a morning light of a rainy dawn, the steady beat of raindrops on the window taunting me. I got up and repeated my morning routine, feeling nothing but stillness. I didn't know if I was coming or going, and as a result, I generally stayed in my room. My parents had accepted this. At first. It eventually got to the point where they pestered me to get some fresh air, to go for a small walk. Hence why, on the first of December, I gave in to their demands, when the rain calmed down my mind. I wasn't happy with the nagging, but that paled to how I was feeling about myself.

I took a deep breath and set off down the road, wandering aimlessly. You could argue it was fate or just my guilt that my feet led me to Thorntree Road, and to a shop I used to frequent when visiting Merrick. I had some small change, so popped in, determined to get something for my troubles. It was here that the latest twist to my life unfurled, as I overhead the staff talking to another customer.

"That's awful that. How did you hear about it?" the cashier said, taking their sweet time in scanning the items, just to prolong the conversation.

"I live over the road, heard the screams last night, and saw the police flood the place. They're still there actually," the customer replied, with the glee of someone more than happy to share their gossip.

"Any idea what happened?" There was the nervous twitch to

the cashier's voice that made it clear that they were a bit of afraid of asking, in case they got an answer they weren't prepared for.

"Well, when I was walking the dog, I spoke to an officer outside, who told me that he couldn't tell me anything. Just that it was an active crime scene."

"Oh, that's not exciting."

"It gets better. I walk slowly, and I can overhear him talking to someone else on his walkie talkie, saying they need more people to clean the rooms up, once forensics have collected all the parts..."

"Parts?" the cashier said with shock. "As in body parts?"

"That's what my gut tells me. Poor sods, first their kid goes missing and then this. That family must be cursed or something."

When the customer said that, I had the horrible realisation of who they were talking about, and my guilt got sharper. I put my would-be purchases back on the shelves and ran out of the shop, and down the road to Merrick's house. From the end of the road, I saw the police vans, and my heart plunged, cutting my breath short. My fast pace slowed to a crawl till I plodded in full view of the house. There were police officers everywhere, and forensic specialists combing the property.

"Can I help you?" an officer asked, walking towards me.

"Oh! Erm, yeah! I know the family..." I mumbled my reply. It wasn't what I really wanted to say, but I don't think the officer would have understood what I wanted to say. If anything, it might have made them look at me with suspicion. As it turned out, there was someone else there who was already looking at me with an eye for uncovering what I knew.

"I'm sorry, but this is an active crime scene. There's nothing you can do here. You'd be better off going home..." the officer started, before a hatefully, familiar voice stopped him.

"Officer! I'll take over here, this boy does have a link into this case. Go get a nice cup of tea." Lionel stepped out of the closest van, smiling.

I stiffened, remembering what he was threatening to do to me. The police officer I'd been talking to gave Lionel a look, before shrugging his shoulders as he walked away.

"What are you doing here?" I said, backing up slightly.

"Working. Your friend has made quite a mess, but you wouldn't know anything about that would you?"

"I've only just heard…"

While I wasn't lying, Lionel tilted his head, and I could see his devilish mind working overtime, probably thinking of how he could entrap me in this case. I wish I could have believed it was because he genuinely thought I was hiding something, and not at all that it was petty revenge for Riz embarrassing him.

"Oh, so you don't know the full details then? It was quite a scene actually, the first responders had to be sent home, stoic individuals reduced to quivering wrecks. Want to see the photos? I think you'll find something interesting on one of them." Lionel didn't give me chance to say no, grabbing my arm in a vice-like grip.

He dragged me towards the van, so I was away from the view of any onlookers. Once he thought I was safely obscured, he forced a handful of photos in my hand, and gestured me to look through them. It was a good thing that Lionel and his bosses were pretty much above the law, as the way he was acting should have gotten him fired.

I didn't want to look at the photos. I could have guessed what they were depicting, but I couldn't stop myself from looking. Call it morbid curiosity or whatever, but my eyes were drawn to the photographs and to the horrors lurking within them.

Carnage wasn't a strong enough word for what had occurred in that house. They weren't just killed, Merrick's family had been desecrated, pulled apart, put back together. Pins and other fasteners had been used to stick their joints back together, turning them into marionettes. They had been left suspended from the ceiling, and at their feet was a crudely made smaller puppet, one that stood out because it wasn't made from flesh. This one had its strings cut. I blacked out for a moment in shock, and judging from Lionel's shoes when I woke again, I must have thrown up. It was absurdly amusing to hear that this was the fourth time it'd happened that day.

The homemade puppets weren't the only thing the killer left... no, they also went to the trouble of leaving a message on the walls. One that sent chills down my spine as I knew he was talking to me. The message read: 'Is this subtle enough for you?' It was written in blood, because of course it was.

"Do you know what he's talking about?" Lionel asked, with a knowing look on his face. What he thought he knew, I had no idea, as my mind was whirling with what had happened, and I kept imagining what Merrick's family had gone through. I shook my head at his question though, and instead asked one of my own.

"He?"

"Oh, I must have forgot to include that photo,"

Lionel pulled another polaroid from his pocket and handed it over. This one was another message. Its meaning was straight forward and got straight to the point.

'Merrick is dead, long live Gallows.'

"I mean, we're not looking for anyone else in relation to this crime, just your friend and two accomplices. Any ideas on them?" Lionel leant back on the van, and again, he seemed to be waiting for my reaction. I didn't say anything, but my reaction gave me away as I connected the dots and thought of the two most likely suspects who would be with Merrick now.

"I warn you, withholding information from me, means I get to use my tools against you..." Lionel smiled. "Tell me who they are."

I tried to back away, but Lionel followed me step for step.

"I'm also aware that your guardian rat isn't with you, so no last minute saves, boy. I suggest you co-operate before I haul you in as a suspect, and make you disappear for a long, long time."

The smile on his face was sadistic, and reinforced the idea that he was doing this for revenge.

"You can't! I have nothing to do with this!"

"You're withholding information from me. You escaped last time but now it's just pathetic old you."

I fumbled with my hands out of nervousness, running them over my pockets but in doing so, I found something I could use.

A Rune, left over from Halloween, the last time I wore this coat. Without giving away the fact I had the Rune, I plunged both hands into my pockets, playing it off as more anxiety. I even forced a stammer to help the act.

"I-I don't k-know anything!"

The Rune in question was a Barrier Rune, one which would force something away from me, giving me a protected space for a moment, though there was an issue in that it had to have a type to go with it, so it knew what it was supposed to be repelling. Lionel was a human, but so was I, and it could easily backfire on me, and either throw me into Lionel, or try and make me share the same space as the van's metal frame. I knew enough about physics to know I didn't want that.

Not having much of an option, I had to go for a riskier approach, use the Rune undefined. My mum had said it was possible, an observation agreed by Riz, but the effect would be lessened greatly. Seeing I didn't have much of a choice, I went with that.

"I think you know a lot more then you let on, not just about this case, but about the rat, about that other pain in our arse, and others. I want to get all the information." Lionel got closer and closer to me.

"I-in that c-case then, all I've g-got to say is one thing. Kel'ch!" I allowed my stammer to fade out, before yelling out the activation word, much to Lionel's surprise.

As the Rune in my hand broke apart, a bright light forced me and Lionel apart, knocking him over. I now had the perfect opportunity to leg it, which I did with gusto. I was almost at the police ticker tape when Lionel shouted at me.

"Stop! I'm not done talking to you yet!" This worked against him though as a police officer poked his head out of the front door to Merrick's house.

"Excuse me, who do you think you're talking to?" the officer asked, directing the question at Lionel, who had to bite his tongue. As much as Lionel was in control, he still couldn't reveal too much about the Others, so for now, he had to let me go. Being on the other side of the police tape gave me some relief, but not a lot. I still had chest pains, as I recalled those photographs, and what would have been the beginning of my interrogation session. I ran home, losing the strength to do so a bit up Humber Road, but I continued to push my legs to do so.

I collapsed near the front doorstep, managing to build enough strength to feebly knock on the door. My mum answered and gasped when she saw the state of me. She helped me inside, and I started to tell her what had happened.

By the time I had finished, I could see the pain on my mum's face. Through my friendship with Merrick, she had tried to get along better with his mother. They didn't see eye to eye on everything, but just enough to be friendly towards each other. She was visibly shaken, and that's considering I had left out the manner of their death and how the police found the bodies. I was also a bit vague on my meeting with Lionel, having to report the deaths of a family we knew was bad enough, to add an attempted torture session on that would have just been uncalled for. Mum shook her head as she left me in my bedroom, figuring I'd need some time to myself. It was a good call as I did need some headspace.

An hour or so later, I heard the phone ringing. My parents had one of those systems in place where there were actually three handsets for the whole house, one of them being in my room, one in their room and one in the living room. So when someone rang, you could hear it everywhere. I was going to let my parents deal with it, but I'm glad now I didn't. I reached over in a daze and answered the call.

"Bren, it's good to hear you," came the voice down the other end.

Merrick, his voice was unmistakeable.

"Merrick! What are you doing?" Those were the first words I could think to say with the muddle in my mind, and had I known he was going to call, I would have said some far more 'choice' words.

"I'm checking in on you, that's what I think I'm doing.

You also need to stop using that name, man. I've been reborn, and I'm going with a much classier name now."

"A classier name?" Here I was, on the phone with my ex-best friend, a murderer, and all I could do was parrot back.

"Gallows. Pretty cool, don't you think, much better for me. Don't play coy with me though, I'm sure you've heard about what's happened now. Thornaby isn't that big a place, even you in your sheltered bubble should have heard." He sighed.

I could hear his breath down the phone as if he was standing right next to me.

"I killed them, Bren. I finally put my money where my mouth is, and I killed them. I've never felt more free."

The conversation went as dark as I expected it. I knew he would bring it up if I didn't mention it first.

"You killed them?" I played dumb. While he was expecting me to have known already, I wanted to keep my cards close to my chest.

"Yes, and it was bloody brilliant. This past month, I've learned so much. Faine and Jack, they've both helped me to improve, and connect with myself. That's why I did what I did to the bodies. Not sure if you would have heard about that part, but if you haven't, you should definitely find out, as I'm proud of that."

"Proud? How can you be proud of killing your family!"

"Because it means I had the strength to take my freedom back, and in doing so, I now know what I'm here to do. Bren, I'm going to bring freedom to everyone! A world free of rules and restrictions. To free us from the strings that stop us being who we were meant to be!"

"This is crazy…" I muttered.

"No, it isn't. You see, Bren, all my life I've bent myself into different shapes to appease other people, to be who they wanted me to be at whatever instance they want. Well, no more! I'm finally free, and I'm going to share the feeling with the world, both worlds, in fact. I don't know how yet, but I'm sure it will come to me." Merrick rambled on. Whatever was left of my friend was now gone. I'd say it was the ranting of a madman, but that would be hurtful to an actual madman. Gallows, as Merrick

227

was wanting to be known, was so far removed from that now, I didn't know what to think, and still don't.

"Now, this brings me back to you. Bren, it's been a month, but I think I'm ready to forgive you for what happened. I know you must have been beating yourself up about it. Let bygones be bygones, and come and help me out! There's a lot of fun to be had in the world I'm going to build."

I was far quicker with my words this time when he asked me. "No!"

"What?" Merrick was genuinely surprised.

"Why would I help you kill people? I'm not a murderer, Merrick! I want to help people, not kill them!"

I heard another sigh at the other end of the line.

"I see," Merrick laughed. "You still need a little bit more motivation. Not to worry! I was already planning on this! I'll release you from your strings, don't worry. See you soon, Bren."

The line went dead. I frantically called 1471 to find out what number he was using, but that proved to be fruitless, as it had already been disconnected.

I was shaking now, and I looked out of the window nervously, half expecting to see Merrick standing there. Given what he'd said to me, what he did to his own family... The threat couldn't have been clearer to me, and it made me sick to my stomach. Thankfully, there was no one out there. I pulled my curtains closed and went into the foetal position. In my mind, matters had gone from bad to worse. All my fears had been realised. Merrick had thrown his lot in with Faine and Jack, and now the three of them were going after me and my parents. It was times like this where I needed a friend.

As if by cue, there came a tapping at the window. A light rapping that was slow and deliberate. I let it continue for a few seconds just to make sure I wasn't hearing things.

Knowing it was real, I slowly peeked behind the curtain to see...

"Riz!"

"Yer gunna let me in? It's freezin out ere!"

CHAPTER 30
SEASON'S GREETINGS

"Riz! You're back!" I shouted. I couldn't open the window fast enough to let him in.

"Godammit, y don't yer ave yer heatin on?" Riz moaned, trying to warm himself up with my blanket. I hugged him, which is something I'd never done before, and have only done a couple of times since. He can testify to that.

"Wat do yer think yer doin? Put me down!" he pleaded, so I did.

"I'm so happy that you're back." I started crying at this point, which must have unsettled Riz, a lot, because he backed off.

"Wat der ell is wrong wit u?" Riz asked, looking very disturbed.

I took a deep breath then rushed through what had happened to Merrick's family, the interrogation with Lionel, and the phone call that Merrick had made to me. I'll point out now, to avoid any confusion later, while I still referred to him as Merrick, Riz, and Valarie both adopted the Gallows name for him. So from this point on, the name is interchangeable. Sorry for any confusion.

Having explained everything to Riz, I waited to see what he would say. The rat nodded to himself before replying.

"Oh," he said at first, before continuing. "Dat's messed up, dat is."

The understatement of the year.

"Tell me about it. I'm worried about what he's going to do."

"Clearly, he's gunna torture yer."

229

"That's not helpful, and of course, Faine and Jack are involved…"

"Yeh, dat I knew already. Wen I left ere, I went ta ground again, rootin around my contacts ta see wat dose pricks were gunna do next. Guess I gotz ma answer, don't I? Tho dis is y I'm back, nd dis time, dere isn't gunna be any screw ups, yer got dat?"

I nodded, and looked away.

"Nd stop mopin already! Wat's dun is dun, nd we can't change der soddin past. Yer luk at wat yer did, nd yer try not ta do it again. Dat's how I lived ma life ta der fullest." Riz stood on his hind legs to berate me a bit more. I spun through different words in my head, trying to think of the right thing to say, but none of them really stood out in contrast to what the rat had said.

"Ne wayz, quit feelin sorry fer yerself, as now we ave ta think of sumit we can do bout dis mess. So get ta sleep already, as tomorra, we prepare fer war!"

"You expect me to sleep in a situation like this?" I questioned.

"Get ta sleep, Bren, or I'll bite u."

"Guess I'm going to sleep then."

Riz could be very persuasive. Not wanting to get bitten, I did lay down, as the rat went and recreated a nest in my clothes drawers, finding comfort in the newly washed clothes in there.

"Lik I've neva been away," he said before he started snoring.

The next morning was an odd one as my parents had actually been busy during the time I had been upstairs. Riz's mouth was slack and hung open as he took the sight in.

"Wat der heck is dis…?" he said.

I never told the rat how crazy my family was for this time of year. It was heartwarming to see, mind. Like my parents, I too loved Christmas and all its trappings. It didn't hurt that my birthday was this month as well, making it a double whammy of a celebration. The house was decked out in hues of golds, silvers and greens, with festive red adding to the mix. The usual pictures on the walls were swapped out, becoming pleasing Christmas scenes of snow and cosy cottages. To top it off, a large tree was placed in the living room, decorated to the extreme with baubles, crystal ornaments, lights of every colour and a golden star on top. When it came to Christmas, my parents didn't know the meaning of the word overboard. To add to the scene, festive music blared out from the CD player. All this added to Riz's horror. This balanced my dislike of Halloween, I thought. It even affected what got played on the CD player, and shown on TV, much to Riz's horror. While I had never been one for Halloween, Christmas was Riz's bugbear.

"Now I get y dat prick want's yer family ded," Riz said,

"Is that really appropriate?" I said, trying to work through what I was going to tell my parents.

"Bren, would you like a cup of tea?" my mum asked, coming out of the kitchen, and stopping when she saw Riz on my shoulder. "Oh, you're back." She didn't hide her disappointment.

"I'd luv a cuppa, thanks," Riz replied, ignoring her reaction.

"When did you return?" my mum asked, rubbing her forehead.

"Last nite, nd yer gunna want ta get yer husband as I gotz news, nd it ain't gud."

"Is it related to what happened yesterday?" My mum took a more stoic pose, steeling her eyes, which slowly moved from Riz, to me.

"Yes, yes it is." Riz hopped to the settee.

"Will, you're going to want to come in. Riz is back," my mum yelled back through the kitchen. I didn't hear what he said, but knowing my dad, it was some outburst. He walked in and stood beside my mum, the pair of them waiting to see what Riz had to say.

I'll save you the conversation, as it was mostly repeating what had already happened. Going back over the fate that befell Merrick's family, and his threats against us. The only new bit of information was that about Faine and Jack.

"I knew it wasn't over…" my mum said softly, prompting my dad to put his arm around her.

"This is just par for the course now, isn't it?" my dad sighed. "We better sort things out to run then."

"Not on yer life," Riz spoke up. "Runnin ain't gunna solve anythin. Gallows ain't like der Others yer ad before. He gets visions of conversations, so he'll know where yer gunna run. Our best bet is ta fite, nd end der threat!" Riz was resolute in what he was saying, even if the words were akin to madness. It was no wonder he didn't want to tell me the plan the last night, as I would have told him where to shove it. The look on my parents faces though, was in sharp contrast to my own, as they seemed to be considering what the rat had said.

"You sure he'll be able to find us?" my mum asked.

"Yup, as I sed, runnin ain't an option."

"I am tired of running…" my mum admitted.

"Me too, and we do have those Runes of yours, and I guess the rat will pitch in," my dad added.

I couldn't believe what I was hearing.

"No! I can't have you risking your lives because of my mistake!" I yelled out.

"I'll deal wit dis," Riz said to my parents, before biting me. "Wat did I tell yer last nite, yer ejit! Wat's dun is frickin dun. No point lettin it stew ova wen we gotz ta deal wit wat's happenin now. In case yer wanted ta know, wat's happenin now is we're gunna beat Gallows, nd Faine, nd dere attack dog, Jack, inta der ground nd bury dem!"

I think Riz had swallowed his own bravado.

"Mum, Dad, you can't be serious about going along with this!" I said, staring at them.

"Riz is right," my dad said, uttering the words that sting me to this day, no matter who was saying them.

"Bren, believe me, we can handle ourselves in these matters, if it comes to it," my mum said.

"Nd it's commin ta it," Riz added unhelpfully.

So there I was sitting amidst a Christmas wonderland, listening to the confirmation that my parents were going to listen to Riz's advice, and fight against Merrick and company. It was exactly as crazy as it sounds. The thing that I didn't understand was how hard they'd tried to stop me going into this sort of life, yet here they were embracing it so easily. I still had a lot to learn about what they'd experienced before I was born.

Anyway, with the matter settled, Riz wasted no time in getting us prepared for the ordeal to come. Of course, the looming threat wasn't the only thing to cause arguments, as the love of Christmas was getting to the rat.

"Y? Y dis of all seasons? Y is dis der season dat yer family ave ta go completely crazy ova? Dis is maddening!" he shouted at me one morning, I think it was early in the month, round about the third. He had woken me up to rant, and I didn't appreciate it, especially since he'd had me up till two in the morning again, brainstorming ways to cure a curse.

"What's the problem again?" I mumbled.

"Yer know wat der problem is! Yer folks woke me up again wit dere music! Mistletoe nd Wine isn't der thin I want ta hear first thin in der mornin!"

"And I don't want to be woken up by a rat moaning on at me. Guess this is where we are."

This little routine was repeated regularly, and Riz constantly threatened to move out of my room and house, begging for my family to ease up on its celebrations.

Was it wrong that I was full of glee that we kept on celebrating? Why it bothered him so much is still an ongoing thing, though I doubt there's some deep reason behind it, I think he just doesn't do Christmas, and I don't care.

Riz decided to mix things up every now and again, by throwing training drills at me and my family, simulating the fact that Merrick could strike at any time. I had my doubts that it would have been completely at random, as I knew my friend and he did have a dramatic streak. A usual training regime went something like this:

Riz would shout, "He's ere! Move it! Move it!" at the top of his lungs, while also blowing an air horn that he got from somewhere. He never did tell me where it came from. This was him raising the alarm, and making us all move quickly, heading to an agreed point outside the house, underneath the clear, frozen skies. Riz would time us to see how fast it was we could move, and most times, he found it lacking.

"Nice. Yer all dead still, by der way. It shudn't take yer all five minutes ta get from yer beds ta down ere!"

"Riz, I thought the idea was for us to fight back against them, not run into the back field," my dad questioned.

"It is, but yer know wat else is gunna be important? Learnin ta listen nd act wen yer flippin told ta!" Riz yelled, before heading back to the house, muttering to himself.

I shared the same expression that my dad had, and I wondered who was going to be the first to attack Riz and shove him in a sack till we were ready to deal with his nonsense. We all hauled our exhausted bodies back to bed.

The days on the calendar flicked by, with little variation in events, and through it all, Merrick never attempted to get into contact again.

We were now coming up to my birthday, the fifteenth of the month. Or as I thought of it back then, the most glorious day of the year. This was one of the days I had pegged for Merrick to show up. Luckily, I was wrong.

I woke up that morning with Riz ready to greet me.

"So yer anotha year older, big whoop. Happy Birthday, kid, yer made it to seventeen."

This was as cheery as a birthday message got when coming from him. No, he didn't get me a present either. My mum was a lot more enthusiastic, giving me a hug when I came downstairs. Riz rolled his eyes as he trotted off into the kitchen.

"Happy Birthday, Bren," she said with a warm smile. I don't know if it was just because it was my birthday, or if it was also the season, as she was always happy this time of year. I said before that both my parents liked Christmas, but she was always its heart. It was always said that I took after her most, and I'm not going to deny that. When I was younger, she was my world, and I always listened as she sought to explain the season to me, and what Christmas meant. To her, Christmas was that time when we could show what we were capable of, in our generosity and willingness to help each other. She said that I should try and embody these things all year round, and not just for one month a year. In my own way, I like to think that I succeeded, just sometimes Riz makes everything harder than he should. Though, it could be argued that I stuck with Riz because of those values. I'll let you draw your own conclusions on that one.

To my surprise though, Riz did give me the day off our studies and training. Although I never shared my belief with him that Merrick might have chosen this date, I was relieved to have had Riz come out and say that he didn't think it fit the 'profile' of Merrick.

My dad gave me the same birthday message as my mum and we settled in for a day together, any worry about being ambushed pushed to the side, and I got to celebrate. While it was destined to be a memorable day, there was one last thing surprise for me, and it came via a knock on the door. With Riz's assurance that he hadn't detected anything, I gingerly opened the front door, as I couldn't tell who was the other side of it. To my relief and joy, I opened the door to see Valarie standing there, with a present and a card.

"Room for one more?" she asked as she stepped in.

I couldn't speak.

"Sorry for not being in contact, but I've had a very crazy past few weeks. Me and my uncle had to travel to Greece to sort a few things out, amongst other things. I knew I couldn't miss your birthday though!" She hugged me, and gave me a little kiss on the cheek.

"Valarie!" I said finally. "I've missed you so much!" I could feel myself starting to cry as my mind made me relive everything that had happened. "Merrick! H-he killed his family! He calls himself Gallows now! He's working with Faine and Jack and he wants to kill my parents!" I rushed all the words out, knowing that Valarie would be able to make some sense out of them all.

"I heard about his family, but Gallows? What a weird name to choose… So many better options out there!" Valarie joked. I think she wanted to see me with a smile. "Also he wants to kill your family? Over my dead body!" she declared. What she'd said had caught Riz's attention, and he poked his head through the door to see what was going on.

"I'm sure ova yer ded body can be arranged," Riz said, baring his teeth at Valarie, who brushed off the rat's attitude.

"And I'm sure you'll try your hardest!" she beamed. She seemed to have gotten hold of the fact that Riz couldn't stand unbridled optimism. "Anyway, Bren, I really am sorry about ghosting you."

"I'm guessing you can't tell me?" I said, already knowing the answer.

"Sorry, we've all got our secrets…"

"I can live with that. I'm just thankful that you're here now."

Valarie took my hand in hers.

"After what happened at Halloween, I'm here to see it through to the end with you. I'll always be there to help you."

"Thank you," I said. I may have been crying, or it may have been raining. Either is a distinct possibility. As it was, with Valarie back in the fold, we were at our strongest, which was just as well, as Christmas was now close, and with it, Merrick's planned assault.

CHAPTER 31
A BLOODY CHRISTMAS EVE

So it came to Christmas Eve, the one that Riz had guessed Merrick would choose. Despite seeing my parents, Riz and Valarie working together in an effort to stop Merrick, anxiety riddled my brain. The atmosphere in the house was different than it had been in years past. Gone was the frivolity of preparing for Christmas Day, instead replaced with the preparations for whatever Merrick would throw at us. I hadn't told anyone, but I still wanted to try and reason with him again, an act of insanity some might say, but I had to try. Avoiding a fight was always worth the effort. My mum played her violin, as hauntingly as always. The revelation of our family's banshee heritage added a whole new dimension to her music, while also explaining why it drew everyone in and conveyed emotion so readily. Me, Riz and Valarie waited in my room, listening to the violin music, which was more akin to a funeral dirge, quite fitting considering we were all waiting for the inevitable.

I gave a thought for the families around us, who were going about innocently, not having any care in the wold. I was worried that Merrick might involve our neighbours, treating them as disposable hostages to use against me. Valarie voiced some reason against this though, arguing that his focus was squarely on me, and that his goal was to make me like him, and using hostages wouldn't accomplish that. I didn't have the heart to tell her that Merrick wasn't really on talking terms with logic like that at the moment.

Our first hint that something was up was at eleven o'clock, when all the clocks in the house rang out, and then were silenced. Riz's ears picked up and he turned to me.

"Bren. Check outside," he said, in a serious tone.

"Okay," I said, my body tense, the hair on my arms standing on end, as if an electric current was being passed through me. I carefully opened the curtains and peered out. It was dark and raining, but nothing out of the ordinary. I then squinted at the top of the street where I spotted half a car parked in front of the flats there. I say half a car, it was more like a visual effect had caused part of it to disappear. I felt a knot in my gut, and looked around the street, seeing more oddities like that car, including an indistinct person, frozen in time.

"It's the same as before," I said, turning to Riz, who nodded.

"Yup, dose cleva dicks. Dey put us in a Illusion Trap, tho dis time he didn't curse any of our Runes, which means he's leaned how ta do dem, probably wit der help of Faine," Riz pointed out as he joined me in looking out the window.

"Can't we just break out of it then?" Valarie asked.

"Duh, but dat's wat I waz hopin fer anyway," Riz explained.

"You wanted them to trap us in another dimension that would make escape almost impossible?" I asked incredulously. From the way Valarie nodded, I think I had beaten her to the punch in asking that question first.

"Yup, as now I can use watevar dey're usin ta power dis Illusion Trap to super charge a Rune ta bypass all Faine's defences and lock im bak in der Fae realm, so dey can deal wit im."

"You needed a supercharge Rune to do that? There was me thinking you were supposed to be somewhat of a genius with Runes," Valarie said mischievously.

"If it were dat easy, we wudn't be in dis mess, but no, Faine haz defences dat he uses ta stop me jus banishin im," Riz snapped.

"Guys, I can't hear Mum's violin anymore," I interrupted. It was odd as I thought she had still been playing even when we discovered the trap, for it to cut off with no reason was an ill omen.

"I don't hear anything," Valarie added, noting the stillness. I went to the door, grabbing the handle, which shifted as though it was made of rubber. Although harder to turn, I forced it open to find a kaleidoscope of hallways.

"I think we know the form the trap took then," I said, turning to Riz and Valarie. It wasn't as if it looked like a different place, the wallpaper matched our landing, the doors, all hundred of them, looked like ours. It was like that someone had copy and pasted everything. I couldn't even see the stairs anymore, as if this dimension hadn't even bothered to contain them. Across from my door was another, one that I could reach without leaving the safety of my room. It opened easily enough and inside was a darkened mirror of my front room, except for shadows that revealed themselves to be the puppets that Merrick had made out of his family. They were dancing merrily, grins etched into their lifeless faces. I slammed the door shut, before closing my own.

"Dat waz different," Riz said, rubbing his chin.

My heart was racing, and that was all the git could say.

"So, it's not just a maze we're dealing with then. Gallows wants to give us nightmares as well," Valarie said, her hand on my shoulder, showing me some comfort for reliving the ghastly sight of my friend's handiwork.

"We're gunna ave ta be really careful, tho jus member that most thin's yer see will be jus illusions. Der only real thins dat'll be ere re dose three pricks! So don't be a wuss."

You have to love Riz's fantastic advice. Ordinarily our task would be an easy one, link up with my parents in a finite space. This trap and the illusions made it all the more difficult.

"How are we going to do this then? All three of us move from room to room till we find them?" I asked, looking at the choices before us, wondering how lucky we would have to be to find my parents through the first door we chose.

"Three of us? Nah, yer alrite. I'm gunna stay ere ta make sure der plan works, while yer nd Valarie can bugga off ta find yer parents before dat twat Gallows does."

Whatever work Riz was on about doing, he'd started, or at

least, I think he had. He was huddled over several Runes, some of which I didn't recognise as the symbol seemed a completely different style compared to the others I'd used.

"Get goin!" Riz shouted impatiently.

"You ready for this, Bren?" Valarie asked me. She straightened the bag on her shoulder, her hand already clutching a Rune, showing that she was expecting some trouble. The sight of the Rune reminded me to grab my own Runes. I wasn't looking forward to the idea of using them in my own home, but if it needed doing, then I would do it if it meant protecting my parents.

"As ready as I'm ever going to be."

As the pair of us walked out of my room, a threatening presence swept through me, and I felt eyes on me.

"That normal?" I asked Valarie. I don't know how I expected her to know what I was on about.

"Sometimes?" Valarie didn't sound sure of her answer.

"Which door...?" I cast my eyes over the never ending doors, wondering which to start with.

Valarie forced the choice back to me. "I'll follow your lead, Bren."

I took a deep breath and pointed, choosing a door that was two to the left of where we stood. I didn't exhale till my hand was on the handle, opening the door.

Inside this room was my dining room, looking quite normal. There wasn't anything monstrous waiting for us, no ghastly vision, but through the front window, for the briefest of moments, I saw Merrick. He just stood smiling and waving at me, then I blinked, and he vanished. From the lack of reaction from Valarie, I guessed that she didn't see him.

"An empty room on your first try. Could have been worse!" Valarie said, shutting the door on the scene. "How about I pick the next one?"

I nodded, hoping that she would have better luck then me.

"This one."

She chose her door, but didn't get to open it herself, as it was flung open, and my blood-covered father burst out of it. Stricken and bedazzled, his face was scratched, and he looked like he was trying to stop the bleeding on a large wound in his side.

"Dad! What happened!" I said in a panic, my heart rising to my throat.

He collapsed towards me, but his body faded as it fell.

"An illusion?" Valarie said, taking a look in the room he staggered from, but found only a black emptiness. Still shaken, I closed the door but then opened again. My dad was standing there, in front of the fire place, looking just as I last saw him before Merrick had sprung his trap.

"Ah, Bren! There you are!" He took a step forward when a knife flew from the kitchen and hit him in the neck, spraying blood around the room. I couldn't move, for the second time in just as many minutes, prompting Valarie to stand in front of me.

In from the kitchen came someone I was hoping not to meet yet. Jack, looking more skeletal and ghoulish then Halloween. There was plenty of evidence of the wounds he'd suffered, but his flesh was now a pallid and sickly white. His stance was more hunched and there was a sharp contrast with how he looked and the smile he had. While I got the strong impression that my dad in this room was as fake as the other one, Jack was all too real.

"All I've had to kill is these illusions of your father… practice is practice but I'd rather tear the flesh off your bones…" His gaze was solely on me, till he noticed Valarie, who was leaving nothing to chance. "Though you'll be my prized kill." Jack went to take a massive stride towards us.

"Tar'Hazdem!" Valarie roared, the Rune aimed at Jack.

The energy from the Rune surged forward, and from his appearance a direct hit should have snapped him in half, but the room shifted in the middle of it, with Jack being swallowed by a wall, so the attack did nothing.

"Sorry about that, Bren!" Merrick said, his voice rebounding off all the surfaces in the room. "Jack was just getting some practice in before he found your parents. I moved him away for now. Don't want you getting hurt in all this! Your girlfriend though… next time, Jack can have her."

"Send him back if you want, Gallows!" Valarie challenged. "We all know I would have broken him with that shot! You just don't like me breaking your toys!"

"How astute. Maybe you should spend less time talking, and more time thinking about where Bren's parents are."

"Can't we settle this without them!" I yelled.

"Bren," Merrick said with a pause. "I can't do that, it would spoil the surprise I'm planning for you."

"You're planning on killing them, aren't you?" Valarie pointed out, as the pair of us started edging towards the door.

"Oh well, you know the surprise, but I'm still going to do it. You just wait and see," Merrick boasted.

There was some good news, that being we knew that Merrick wasn't going to let Jack near me, which meant that out of all us trapped here, he wanted me alive. It remained to be seen at the time if Merrick was going to be able to keep Jack away from me and keep the illusions under control.

With some renewed strength and urgency, me and Valarie went and tried a different door. Through this one, we saw that it opened into a dark dense forest, where three Spring Heels were jumping towards us, their bodies horribly twisted, their limbs lengthened, skewing their proportions. My first instinct was to slam the door shut, providing a barrier between us and them. I figured I'd get an answer to if they were illusions or not if they tried to get through the door, which they did, as I had to move my head out of the way when razor sharp knife claws ripped through the wooden doors, trying to break them apart. I grabbed the door handle that was next to me. Me and Valarie rushed through, wanting to put distance between us and the Spring Heels. The room that this led us to was another version of my living room, with both my parents lying dead in front of the fireplace. Their eyes were fixed on me and Valarie, and both bodies started to rise, changing to resemble the puppets that Merrick turned his family into. The mouth of each puppet started to chatter, with inhuman voices singing out.

"This was always your fault! Even from when you were born!"

I tried to drown the voices out in my head. It was obvious these were just more of Merrick's illusions, designed to torment me, but what hurt was that I felt what they were saying. Their taunts lined up with what I believed about myself.

"Bren, let's try another room. We're not going to find them here," Valarie said, grabbing my arm.

I nodded, but before we could get near the exit, we heard the rattling of the kitchen door handle. It slowly opened, but neither me or Valarie could see who was on the other side. The possibility existed that this was just another part of the illusion, that from this door more nightmare fodder would come forth. At the very least, I knew that it wasn't likely to be Jack, given that Merrick wanted to keep him away from me. The puppets of my parents were still dangling there, hurling insults at me. If they were even aware that the other door had opened, then they didn't show it. A kitchen knife flew across the room, and hit the puppet of my dad, causing the head to shatter like wood, making it drop to the floor. The mum puppet just faded from view.

A hand grasped the door, and then my Dad pulled himself forward. He looked like he'd been through hell and back, clothes torn in places and bloody scratches everywhere. He saw me with wild eyes and made his way at me. I didn't know what to do, and Valarie went to do something, but I instinctively stopped her, as my dad put his hands on my shoulders, and stared at my face.

"Bren, please tell me that it's you. I mean, it's really you." I noticed that his usual clean-shaven look was gone, as there was a few day's worth of stubble there. Which didn't make any sense to me, it hadn't been that long since the trap had fallen on us.

"Dad? Are you okay?" I replied, and he hugged me. Again, making me question the time difference.

"Brennan, I thought I would never see you again! Especially when that person started chasing me, then. I had to. I had to…" My dad broke down crying. It was a shock to see him like this. He had always been a stoic figure.

"How long has it been since you last saw us?" Valarie asked.

"Two days," my dad replied, without even looking at her. "That's how long I've been wandering through this place."

"Dad, it's only been, like an hour. It's still Christmas Eve."

My statement caused Dad to laugh.

"No! It's the 27th!"

"Bren's right," Valarie said. "The trap fell, and we started searching for you and your wife. This is like the fourth or fifth door we've been in."

"So this place is also messing with time? How did Merrick pull this off?" I questioned.

"Merrick? You mean Gallows? He's been stalking me, him and that Jack. There was some other guy as well… I saw them kill me, I saw them kill your mother. Can you imagine what that is like? To see your family murdered in front of you, over and over again." My dad dropped to his knees, his trauma fresh. He looked back at me, but straight through me.

"Come on, we have to find Mum." I nodded at Valarie, and motioned to her to help me, as I grabbed my dad's arm. Me and Valarie together hauled him to feet. It may seem like I was being callous to what my dad had experienced, but there was never going to be a way for me to discover what he'd gone through or what he'd seen. It made me feel terrible, adding to my already palpable guilt, but it was what it was.

We made it back into hallway, and I shut the door, knowing that if I opened it again, it would have changed like the rest, an infinite roulette wheel of danger. Knowing that Merrick could mess with time in here was alarming, but it added to something that had been said earlier, about how much effort he must be exerting to keep everything under control. I kept a hold of this fact, wanting to believe that it may come in handy later on.

"Where's Riz, Bren?" my dad asked, probably realising how quiet it was.

"He's in my room, somewhere." I also realised that Riz was also technically lost here. He wouldn't have seen it that way himself but from our perspective, yeah, it would be next to impossible to find him again.

"Why didn't he come with you? Wouldn't that have been the sensible thing?"

My dad had spent more or less four months with Riz by this time, it was amazing he hadn't learnt much of his personality, and that sensible in Riz's vocabulary meant what made sense to do in regards to his well being and no one else's.

"Riz is a selfish prick who rather we do all the hard work so he can swoop in and take the credit."

Valarie, on the other hand, she had the measure of him down to a tee. I wanted to say something encouraging about Riz, but I couldn't think of anything. Nor did I get any time to say anything, as a bloodcurdling scream rippled through the hallways, one that I hadn't heard before except in fever dreams. The voice was unmistakeably my mother's but there was a special quality to it that I hadn't heard before, though it should have been obvious in hindsight.

"Mara!" my dad shouted. "She must be in trouble. We have to find her!" He must have found a new source of energy within himself as he sprinted down the ever-growing corridor, leaving me and Valarie with no choice but to follow him.

CHAPTER 32
REUNITED

We tried each and every door we could to find the source of the scream, but we had no luck. My dad was getting desperate, you could tell from the way he opened the doors, practically pulling them off the hinges. When we cleared one room, it was back to the hallway to regroup. To make it clear, all three of us were trying different doors. Just as it must have been for dad, I was having trouble with keeping up with how much time was passing, relying on Valarie, and her watch, to keep track of it all.

Around us, the trap was creating, and trying to suffocate us with its dark presence. I could feel a sense of despair and dread rising within me, draining me of the strength I was relying on to find my mother. I took a step back from trying doors and sat down, staring at the ceiling, my mind drifting to the impossibility of working out how all this existed in space. I wanted to say something to my dad, who was also taking a breather. No words came to mind. Valarie hadn't stopped though, but she had stopped telling us what she was looking at in each room. Through our mad rush to find Mum, and why she was screaming, we had seen all sorts. It seemed there was no end to Merrick's creativity.

"Ready?" my dad asked, standing again, eager to carry on the search.

I couldn't help but think there must have been a better way to go about this, one that didn't require us to search till the end of time. I wracked my brain, going at it from every angle, seeing if

Merrick might have overlooked something. Of course, we still hadn't encountered Jack or Faine.

Faine being in here with us was an interesting thought. From the way he acted before, I couldn't see him coming in here voluntarily, not just to target my parents and me. That's what Jack the Ripper was for.

Following my dad's lead, I also resumed my search, opening more doors and encountering more strange sights. In the room I just ventured in to, I found mutilated bodies hanging like meat. They hung before a warped interpretation of the living room, with esoteric angles and perspectives. There were no straight lines, and the shapes were off just enough to make you question it.

I shut the door and moved on to the next one, which proved to be even worse. This one looked like a blank room, not one that had ever been in my house. When I first entered, I thought I heard something, and it turned into to a slow whine that occasionally spiked. The grey walls pulsed with white vines that appeared to creep across their surfaces. As I stood trying to figure out what was going on, there was a screech added to the ambient noise. While freaky at first, I knew it wasn't human. I figured it was part of the uneasiness that was emanating from the room. Then I noticed what appeared to be cuts on the wall.

Valarie and my dad came in to see what I'd found, and they looked just as puzzled as I was. Larger cracks appeared in the wall as my fingers touched it, so I pulled back, yet the cracks kept on coming.

"Brennan! Get back from there!" my dad said. He reached forward and practically pulled me back with a forceful grip on my shoulder. The cracks joined up to each other, and the wall shattered like glass, but the sound that accompanied it was a multitude of screams. I recognised some of these screams as being my mum, my own and even those of Merrick's family. Through the collapsed wall there was an abyss, but then Jack pulled himself into the room.

"Gallows can try and keep you from me all he wants but he also told me to hunt down your family. Not my fault you're standing together!" He smiled. "I'll sell this as an accident, I mean, even master Faine understands and approves of my wants and needs."

"Fine by me!" Valarie said, aiming a Rune at him. "I'm going to finish what I started back at Halloween!"

"Try it!" Jack launched himself into the room. "I wanted to kill you first anyhow!" He sounded ecstatic at the turn of events. I didn't understand what must have changed for Jack to have been able to reach us, despite Merrick's interference. The room vibrated as we heard someone shouting. The voice, although distorted, belonged to Merrick, who didn't sound happy.

"Jack! Stop it!" His tone was anger, but Jack didn't care as he avoided the Blast Rune that Valarie had fired towards him.

"I almost had your mum, boy!" Jack said through gritted, broken teeth. "She got away from me thanks to that scream of hers. None of you will have that luck!"

At least we knew what the source of that scream was now, and it was the first instance I had of my mum using her banshee powers. Jack moved in a zig-zag pattern, wanting to get close, even though we spread out. The door had ended up behind me, and that was our exit point. If we could get out and shut it while Jack remained in here, it would give us a lot of breathing room.

"Dad! Get back in to the hallway!" I told him. It was loud enough for Jack to hear and react to, but that was the point. I wanted him to come after my dad, as that would give Valarie the chance to move. It would have been even better if I could have made him focus on me, but I don't think he was even that bothered by me, not as much as Valarie or my father.

"I'm not letting any of you go!" Jack howled. To my surprise, and Jack's, my dad rushed forward and grappled him, holding his bloody fingers high. I could see flames starting to build up in Jack's mouth, so now my turn had come to act, though I acted on instinct. I ran forward and punched the skeletal goblin in the face, causing the flames to dissipate with the shock of the blow. My dad was then able to overpower the confused Jack, and push him away, which gave us a clear shot at an escape.

"Move it, Bren!" my dad said, which made me stop and realise that my plan had been turned on its head, but I gave the quickest of shrugs, as I wasn't going to look a gift horse in the mouth. Me, Valarie and Dad made a break for it. You would think that being the size of a small room, it would have taken all of a microsecond to escape. What we found was that the room stretched. We were getting further and further from Jack, but no closer to the door.

"I thought Gallows didn't want you to be in the same room as that freak!" Valarie shouted.

A thought occurred that this was the work of someone else… Faine. I didn't have any evidence that he was behind this, just a gut feeling, which I've learned in the following years was enough. The simplest answer is often the right one after all. Unless Riz is involved, then all bets are off.

"Faine?" I said, giving word to my thoughts.

"Faine interfering with what Gallows wants? That would put a cat among the pigeons."

"This isn't working!" My dad was near enough out of breath at this point.

"Where do you think you're going!" Jack heckled. He was back on his feet, and gunning for us.

What we needed was a new plan, or something that could alter the dynamics of this fight in our favour.

"Why don't you try shooting me again?" Jack's laugh was more of a hiss, and he was right on top of us, when the wall next to us bulged. The goblin noticed it far too late, and could only turn to look as the wall blew out, sending chunks of it at his face, knocking him down again. A sight I never expected to see greeted us. My mother, looking very pissed off, stepped over the rubble of the wall. Like my father, she was scratched and battered, but had a fire in her eyes, and her hair seemed to move on its own, spreading outwards. She took one look at Jack, and the goblin cowered for a second, hesitant as to what was about to come his way, when she screamed at him, the same as we'd heard before. I understood now that my mum wasn't screaming in pain, but more in anger, and Jack was knocked backwards even more, with no help being granted by Merrick.

"You try to hurt my family… and you think you can just walk away?"

This was a different side to my mum, one that made me wonder more about the other side of the family that I hadn't met at that point.

"Brennan, Will. I'll deal with this monster. Wait outside."

"We would love to Mara, but Bren and Valarie think that Faine is messing with this place now. We've been trying to get to that door for ages!" my dad replied.

A sinister laugh interrupted us, as Jack creaked to his feet. He snapped his jaw back into position as he did.

"You're not the masters of this realm! You are slaves to Master Faine, and to that upstart Gallows." Jack's mouth was twisted, the remnants of his face raised.

"Masters or not, your life ends here," my mother hissed.

"Looks like it's going to be a woman who ends your life after all!" Valarie smiled, throwing the peace symbol at Jack, which caused his smile to shift to a scowl.

"Do not look down on me!" You could see the rage entering his eyes, as the flames billowed from his mouth. He took a deep breath and then exhaled as if he was a massive flame thrower.

"Kel'ch!" I shouted, copying what I did when I was faced with Lionel, throwing a Circle Rune into the path of the flames. The flames were redirected from us, and when Jack was finished, he looked up into the eyes of my mum, who took her own big breath. The scream that she subsequently unleashed was more then enough to knock Jack to his knees again, and as he tried to claw his way towards her, one of his arms snapped. The goblin screamed back in rage, but that was lost to the void as the scream of a banshee was too much for him, and he broke down into dust, his body too broken to continue in the face of her power.

I think the feeling that we ought to celebrate the end of the infamous Jack the Ripper was shared between those that stood there, but no one said anything to mark the occasion. We were down one threat, but there was still Faine and Merrick. Both of who could change the nature of this place. I also got the impression that because of Faine's actions already, we may get caught up in some kind of lover's feud between that pair.

My dad approached my mum cautiously, and carefully put his arms around her. I knew how long Dad had said it had been since he last saw us, but I had no idea on how long it'd been for mum. As foolish as it sounded, I prayed that it wasn't long, that we'd all spent more time searching than she had.

For a moment, no one moved, till my mum reciprocated the hug. Valarie even put her hand on my shoulder, sharing a smile and a sigh with me.

"We have to go now. There's some one else coming. I think it might be Faine," my mum said ominously.

"Then, I guess we have to go and get Riz," I suggested.

We were all back together again, and by now, I figured that it must have been time to enact whatever the rat was planning.

"Can't we just leave him here?" Valarie teased.

"We're going to need him, and put up with him boasting about how we needed him," I laughed half-heartedly.

"Yeh, keep talkin like dat. Tho yer can stand ta grovel a bit more!" Riz's voice came through like an announcement on a PA system.

"Where are you?" I asked, looking around.

"Try lookin behind yer."

Following his instructions, we all turned to see him standing in the open doorway, holding a Rune that had little sticks poking out of it. He spoke into it like a microphone.

"As yer can see, I'm ere ta save all yer arses, before Faine comes nd screws everythin up."

"I'm sorry but Bren's mum just nuked Jack the Ripper. You need to show the proper respect!" Valarie gave a sly smile.

"Oh yer were der one who took im out? Gud on yer, dat twat refused ta flippin die. Knew yer banshees weren't all talk."

"Is that a compliment?" my mum asked.

"Nicest thing he's ever said. Just take it and run with it," I suggested.

"Rite, enuff wit all dis talkin! Time ta end dis illusion, nd send Faine nd Gallows packin fer all der frickin trouble dey've caused."

CHAPTER 33
NIGHT'S END

"How do we do that then?" my mum asked. We'd all moved back into the hallway by this point. Our mood was elated, as with Jack finally dead as a doornail, we seemed to be down a major threat. You might think this odd since Faine and Merrick were still active and trying to mess us around, but Jack was the only one who liked to get his hands dirty as it were. Even if Faine did try anything, I believed that Riz would have risen to the challenge of keeping him at bay.

"It's easy. I'm gunna use dis Rune ta drain all der energy from der trap, den, I'm gunna use it ta power dis Rune ta send Faine, nd Gallows ta a far away place where dere's a nice prison waiting fer dem so dey can spend eternity gettin ta know each otha," Riz said, holding the two Runes that were essential for his plan.

"Then what are you waiting for?" my dad said, shocked that Riz hadn't used it yet. "Is this another moment where you want us to swoon over you?"

"How dare u! Fer yer information, yer shud alwayz be swoonin ova me! Besides, I adn't used it yet cuz I ad ta meet wit u lot first! Yer know, so yer didn't end up havin yer bodies turned inta spaghetti a get thru der dimensional pressures wen dis place breaks down."

It was comforting to know then that Riz did care about us enough that he didn't want to see us die.

"If yer all were gunna die, dat wud ruin ma plans fer how ta make a crap ton of cash exploitin yer'll lata."

253

I think Riz should have stopped talking before that sentence.

"Rat, up to now I've been patient with your disrespect, believing some of what I've learned about you," my mum explained in no uncertain terms. "However, you dare think that I'm going to let you use my family in any of your get rich quick scams, then you have another thing coming."

"Dis is a gud point. Okay! Scratch all dat I sed den, let's jus get dis ova wit, before we get any more visitors!"

As soon as Riz uttered those words, I felt a shudder that stretched from me to the hallway around us, as each door shattered into a storm of splinters, each one leaving a void that only opened to a pitch darkness.

"You had to say that, didn't you, rat?" Valarie said, face palming.

"Where do you think you're going?"

The voice belonged to Faine, and it sounded like it was close by instead of how it sounded when Merrick did it. This meant he was in here with us, and closing in.

"Rite! Guess I'm doin dis now den!"

Riz took the Rune he was holding, the one with what looked like rods sticking out of it like whiskers, and jammed it into the ground. He then took the other Rune he carried, and stuck it to one of the rods.

"Hurry up!" my dad said, as we spied an object coming towards us down the hallway, a distinctly humanoid shape that could only belong to Faine, unless Merrick had grown wings. I learned something about Fae magic here. Namely, that their magic has a range. This was proved as the Fae only started his attack when he was close enough for us to see the mad expression he was wearing.

"I've had enough of your meddling!" Faine yelled, and at his command, fire leapt up from beneath us, forcing us back, though the flames followed. I heard a whistling sound from behind and narrowly avoided a fragment of wood from impaling my eye. That was only the first of the storm that the Fae inflicted on us, as he caused all the splinters of wood to dive at us.

"Oi! I'm tryin ta fukin focus ere!" Riz said as he went back to whispering in that funny language of his.

"What are we supposed to do?" I said.

"Duh, fite im off! Gawd do I ave ta think of everythin," Riz complained, and I could have throttled him myself, but no, there was a furious Fae to deal with. I turned as Valarie was already taking aim best she could, getting scratched to pieces in the trade off.

"Tar'Hazdem!" she yelled, but was dismayed to see the part of the wall tear itself off to absorb the blast, similar to what had happened when she tried to hurt Jack earlier.

My mum stepped up next, and she screamed, the force of her voice breaking all the shards of wood into even tinier, harmless fragments. Faine was hit by her efforts, seemingly being unable to deflect this kind of attack unlike the Rune magic, but he was undeterred in his approach, and was practically upon us. In preparation for this, he drew his sword from the scabbard, the blade having a haunted sheen on it, one that hinted that we really didn't want to be cut by it, even more so than any sane person would ever want to be hurt by a flipping sword.

"A banshee? Marrying a human? What nonsense is this? You should be helping me," Faine said, more visibly annoyed than ever.

My mum's response to this was to scream again and again. Each attempt pushed Faine back that little bit further, but for every inch of ground he lost, he advanced twice as much. I saw desperation in my dad's face. While I had Rune magic to try and then this around, my dad didn't even have that.

"Riz! Are you finished yet?" I quickly snapped

"I wud be if yer jus let me get on wit it." Riz seemed oblivious to what was going on around him. Which wasn't that surprising, to be fair.

I darted over to Valarie, and held up the Rune in my hand, without saying anything. I knew she would get what I wanted to do, and the pair of us waited till my mother paused in her attacks. Without anything to compare her to, I got the impression that she was a pretty strong banshee by the space between breaths and what she was able to do. All she needed was to hit an unguarded Faine, and this was where me and Valarie came into things.

We found the pause and completely in sync, we set to work. Valarie pulled another Blast Rune out of her now empty looking bag, as I did. We knew that if we attacked blindly, Faine would manipulate the trap again like before, but this was all part of the plan. Acting out of necessity, the Fae pre-empted our move by having another part of the wall pull itself free to block what Faine thought was incoming. He got what was coming to him, alright. Instead of firing the Blast Rune, like Faine anticipated, Me and Valarie raised our hands, and in one motion, we thrust them forward.

"Tar'Hazdem!"

As predicted the bit of wall took the shot, and was pulverised for the privilege. Faine smirked, as though we had both wasted our shot. Well, he was half right.

"Tar'Hazdem!" I shouted, not more then a split second after Valarie's. The fae didn't have the time to alter the surroundings in a pitiful attempt to save himself, and the blast hit him hard, knocking him back, and hurting him.

"You'll need to do more than that human," Faine said, gritting his teeth.

"I know, but aren't you forgetting someone?" I pointed to my mum who was already in the process of screaming again, and while the Fae had braced himself for the attack before, he didn't have that luxury this time, and was sent hurtling back.

"Rite, now we're cookin! Hold on ta sumit, cuz ere we soddin go!" Riz yelled as the hallway started to stretch even more and became distorted. Then tears opened up as the dimension collapsed around us.

I had to close my eyes at this point, as they were assaulted by colours that I'm not sure I was even supposed to be able to perceive. When I opened them again, we were on top of the landing. Faine was nowhere to be seen, and the house looked like everything was as it should be.

"Now what?" my dad asked.

"Now, we get der ell out of ere!" Riz helpfully suggested, clutching the other Rune as he hopped up onto my shoulder. He didn't need to explain any more than that as we all raced down the stairs, accompanied by the sound I could only describe as a dimension tearing itself a new one. If you haven't heard it already, then don't wish to.

Following this, we heard Faine once again, only angrier than when we last saw him. Luckily for us, we were already out of the front door. I don't think we even stopped to look back till we reached the field.

Riz had always planned for this to be the final battleground, regardless of what Merrick and company had in store. Why? Because of the wide open spaces it offered. I think Riz's idea now was to use the Rune he'd powered up to deal with Faine and Merrick before they could cover the ground to get to us.

"It's midnight," my dad said, glancing at his watch. Despite everything he'd been through, he seemed taken with the fact hat it had still been Christmas Eve for the rest of us, and the rest of the world. "Merry Christmas, everyone!" he announced. If I had to, I'd say that he was the one out of all of us that believed the danger was over.

"Merry Christmas! Mum, Dad," I replied, allowing myself to think we were through the worst of it too.

My mum didn't respond at first. She had a look about her, which didn't sit well with me, but I was too afraid at the time to question it. I didn't want to question it.

"Merry Christmas, Bren," she said finally, before returning the greeting to my dad with a wary smile.

"Don't forget me!" Valarie said with her usual smile. "Merry Christmas!"

"Merry Christmas, Val," Me, and my parents repeated.

The only one of us who didn't give seasons greetings was, of course, Riz, who was rolling his little eyes at our little display of feelings.

"Dis is a serious thin we're doin, so can yer shut up wit all dat Christmas rubbish," he snapped.

In the middle of all this, Faine reappeared, fluttering out from our back garden, cast in a reddish haze.

"How many plans have you interfered with? How many times do you have to doom us to extinction? You, who put this burden onto us in the first place!" Faine ranted. His words made no sense to us, but given how Riz sank his shoulders a little bit, I guessed who they were really meant for. The Fae's eyes glinted in the darkness, and the earth beneath us started to shift, pulling itself apart.

"I've been waitin fer dis!" Riz said with some glee, but before he could raise his Rune, I saw red energy spread out from his feet.

"Riz!" I shouted, trying to get his attention.

I wasn't quick enough though, and I saw Riz fall as the ground underneath him just gave way. I jumped across from where I was standing, trying to reach him, thinking that he may have been clinging on for dear life. I felt someone haul me back though. I turned, expecting to see Valarie or one of my parents, but instead, I stared straight into the face of Merrick, who was looking more demented than I would have expected. His eyes were bloodshot and had heavy shadows under them, like he hadn't been to sleep in a long time. The corners of his mouth were swept up to the ears.

"I'm so glad you made it through all that alive! I should never have trusted Jack. Sending him in was a huge mistake. But now, I can oversee the end of this. Best you just run along, me and Faine can deal with this!" Merrick said, a lot of words coming out in a short space of time.

"No! Merrick, I don't want to have to fight you. Call this off!" I pleaded. I then realised I couldn't see my parents or Valarie anymore, as a red mist had risen from the cracked earth. I even lost track of the position where Riz had fell.

"Not going to say it again. Just leave and everything will get better for you. Consider this my Christmas present to you. More freedom than you'll realise you needed." Merrick stepped back, so that the mist overtook him.

My panic rose, and I dived into the mist after him, and strained my ears, wanting to hear some sign that my parents and Valarie were fine. I knew they could handle themselves normally, but this wasn't going to be a normal situation.

As I wandered blindly, I did come across one figure, who also looked to be searching. Only after I approached them, did I remember that Faine would also be here, and just my luck that I encountered him.

"You..." Faine whispered. "I'm not supposed to touch you, but I think that rat has taken such a shine to you that even the eyes of the 'Others' are on you now." He advanced on me.

"I believe in you," I said. "I believe in the Fae. I'm not a problem." My reasoning here wasn't the best.

"Wrong, and I don't care what Gallows thinks. You are a problem, and if I let you go, you'll only become a bigger problem. You can be the first of your family to die tonight."

His threats at least revealed to me that the others were safe for now.

"Merrick doesn't want you to touch me." I used the last argument I had left.

"I'll simply claim you got in the way as I was killing the others. You do seem the type to throw your life away on a whim. Like why you even decided to involve yourself in our affairs to begin with."

"You wanted to commit genocide!"

"To save my people from the actions taken by the rat. You think me a monster? You know nothing of your close friend." Faine took a step closer, and drew his sword. "There is no rat to save you now, and you lack the magic of your banshee mother. What can you do against me?"

I had let Faine run his mouth. I'd hoped that when he looked at me, he only saw someone quaking with fear, and that he wouldn't see me prepare a Rune. I wanted to make sure that I had the element of surprise.

"Wh-what can-n I do?" I said, pretending to have a quiver of fear in my voice.

"That is what I said, I don't need you to repeat that."

The annoyance he was feeling hung on his words. I don't know if he truly hated me then, but it would have been a given if I'd kept the act up for longer.

"R-r-repeat w-what?" I played dumb. I had the Rune I wanted in my hand, and I grasped it tightly, waiting for my moment.

"I don't normally take pleasure in the murder of creatures beneath me, but I'll make the exception in your case!"

Clearly, whatever was holding him back from striking me down the instant he saw me, had broken, which is what I wanted. An angry enemy is an unfocused enemy. Nowadays I also know that an angry enemy is also sometimes an unpredictable enemy, but I was only at the beginning of my journey here. Faine charged in with his sword drawn, and had I done nothing, he would have sliced me in half. I pulled the Rune out and cleared my voice.

Before I could say anything though, Faine was punched in the face, my dad's fist proudly embedded in the Fae's mouth and nose.

"Bren! Run!" he said, not realising what I'd planned. I was stunned to see him take that kind of action, or even how he knew where I was in this mist. It wasn't like I'd been shouting out. Faine recovered quick, but as he turned to face my dad, he got another blow, and another. There was no finesse to the moves my dad threw, or to the way he poised himself. My dad was the epitome of someone fighting wild. It was then that I saw the red energy streaks that were running along the ground. Given their placement, I gathered that someone had led my dad to where I was, knowing that he'd step in to save me, had he thought that I was in danger. I cursed Merrick, despite me knowing that such an act was pointless.

I had my Rune primed, and ready to use, but I wasn't about to sacrifice my dad to get a good hit on the Fae.

"Dad! Get away from him!" I screamed.

"What? No, you get away from here!" my dad replied, taking his eyes off Faine for the slightest of seconds.

That was all the Fae needed. Faine recovered enough to catch my dad's next punch, holding his fist in place. With this, Faine had the moment he needed and slashed my dad diagonally with his sword. My world started to break, as I cried out for my dad, but I can't remember if there was any sound or not. I ran to him, paying no attention to Faine, who was readying his sword for another swing, this time at me.

"Dad! Stay with me!" I pleaded. As I held him, my hands became slick with his blood. I struggled to get a Healing Rune out of the little bag, knowing that it was his only hope.

"Don't cry. You'll be with him soon enough!" Faine laughed.

A scream blew away the mist, and hit Faine hard, causing him to drop his sword and stagger backwards. My mum, with tears in her eyes, knelt down next to me, and she took my dad's hands.

"No, Will, don't go, don't leave me!"

It was too late though, my dad was gone. I wanted to cry, the burning stench of failure clinging to me.

"One down!" Faine laughed as he stood again. He snapped his fingers and the sword flew back into his waiting grasp. With one swing, he threw off the blood that stained the blade. I glanced at my mum and saw the sadness exchanged with pure rage. She gently let my dad's body rest on the broken earth, as she turned to the Fae, and screamed with all her might. Given that he had time to prepare this time, Faine did something that resulted in a shield that formed, one that took the initial force of the scream, letting him walk forward towards us. I allowed my own anger to take hold, and despite knowing better, I threw all caution to the wind.

"Tar'Hazdem!" I shouted, forgoing my original plan against Faine, for one that offered instant gratification. The blast was nullified by the Fae's shield, but with a renewed scream from my mother, the shield broke. It wasn't going to stop Faine though, as he braced himself and pushed forward.

"Tar'Hazdem!" Valarie re-joined the fray, copying my attack with one of her own. Her aim was true, and she didn't have to worry about any defence the Fae had, but even a direct hit to his chest, one that severely damaged the armour he was wearing, didn't stop him.

"Another pest that's come to die," Faine said. A fire ignited in his eyes that he spread to the ground with a whisper. The flames roared and shot towards us like lightning bolts, forcing me, Valarie and my mother away from each other, and away from my dad, the flames licking at his body, starting to consume it. I wanted to split apart. My father was dead, and yet, I had to continue, I had to keep fighting. I held no illusion that after this was all said and done, I would just collapse in a broken heap. More red energy was sparking around, growing darker in colour, and I caught sight of Merrick, and noted his appearance, crying blood tears of his own. He looked like he might keel over at any point, the crimson aura that was around him, matching what was around us.

"Watch out! Merrick is planning something!" I yelled out at the top of my voice. Yet, I didn't hear anything, not even a whisper escaped my lips. I put my hands to my throat, pulling them away to see the swirls of my former friend's magic tracing out from my fingertips. I tried to call out again. I saw Valarie similarly struggling, and I realised that with this, Merrick had cut our offensive power away. Me and Valarie couldn't use our Runes, and my mother couldn't use her voice. I was struck by fear when I worked out that me and Valarie becoming powerless was a nice side effect. The true target, was, and always had been, my mother. When I turned my head to face where she had been standing, I saw her attempting to scream as Faine rounded on her, his single-minded purpose keeping him focused. Not being able to shout out, I ran towards my mum, arm outstretched, but the ground beneath me turned to mud, and I fell, only able to watch as Faine struck my mother down the same way as my father.

Silently, I cried. If I'd had my voice, I would have become hoarse till nothing came out but blood.

Faine turned to me, and charged, not satisfied with the kills he'd already claimed. There wasn't much I could have done to stop him, but to my surprise and his, the crimson aura around me evaporated, allowing me to use my voice to full effect.

"Saezh!"

The Rune did its thing and blasted Faine backwards, sending him crashing through the garden fence and into the house. I turned to see Merrick, who shook his head, rolling his eyes. I didn't have time to question why. I crawled through the mud, towards my mum.

262

"Bren. Is t-that… i-is that you?" she asked weakly.

"It's me, Mum, I'm sorry! I'm so sorry. Please don't leave me!" I held onto her right hand, and although I didn't have the time to do so with my father, I fumbled for my Healing Rune.

My mother stopped me, putting her other hand on mine

"It won't work, Bren… I'm not human, remember? You need… to edit it, to change the type…"

Even dying, she was still trying to teach me things.

"I want you… to do something for me," she said.

"Anything," I cried.

"Don't change. You're a kind boy. People need that. No matter what… no matter what you do… stay kind… help people…" She smiled, while coughing up blood.

"I don't understand."

I really didn't understand. I had just witnessed both of my parents die in front of me, murdered to a plan by my ex-friend, who had got what he wanted. No one could be expected to come out the other side of this unchanged.

"I'll… I'll make it… easier for you. Love Christmas… like you do now…"

Out of all the things she could have said, this was the one that got me the most.

"What? But how can I?"

"That spirit… of good will… of helping people. Please, Bren, Christmas is… when… me and your… father met."

I felt her pulse getting weaker, and I knew this was it.

"Okay, I promise."

Riz hates me for this, I must add, but I don't care. I never got a response, as my mum breathed her last. Like that, I was alone.

Everything turned oppressive for me in that instant. The houses were overbearing before, but now they were on top of me, taunting me. The air was heavy and thick with despair. I looked up through the tears and saw Faine, standing again. The Arrow Rune had blasted through his armour but had done no damage to him.

"First time I've killed a banshee. Quite boring really," the Fae said, his eyes falling on me. "Where's the rat?"

I knew he was asking me, but I was too numb to answer. I summoned up every ounce of willpower I had, standing back up. My whole body was shaking, and the part of me that wanted to run, was the loudest it'd ever been.

"You're making it very easy to kill you," Faine threatened, as he walked menacingly towards me.

"And you're making it very easy to kill you," Valarie said. She went to fire her Rune at the Fae, but he charged her, turning away from me. I did the only thing I could do, which was chase after him. I grabbed his wings, which made him stop dead in his tracks.

"Now, Val! Incinerate this twat!" I yelled, my eyes closed with tears welling up.

"Go on, woman. Do your worst! Or not, as I've studied you humans enough to know that your feelings and emotions are your weak points. Fear dominates you, and in this case your fear of hurting this worm, all because you love him," Faine explained, though no one asked.

Valarie stared at him, and it made me wonder if she was going to attack or not. I wanted her to, as that's all it would have taken.

"You're not going to do it, are you? You're not going to risk his life!" Faine laughed as he started to fight back against me.

"I don't need to do it. I'm leaving it up to the rat, since he's been waiting so long to do this," Valarie teased.

"The rat?" Faine's confusion quickly turned to panic as he stared at Riz, who'd climbed out of the hole he fell down. He was still holding that special Rune he'd created in the house.

"Oh, yer dun it now! Get ready, prick!" Riz boldly ordered. "Kid, get out of dere!"

I could have let go, and run, but that wasn't enough. I put my foot against his Faine's back, and pushed off. Remember, I was still holding on to his wings. Can you guess which broke first? The Fae's wings ripped off, seemingly easy, leaving bloody remnants. Faine fell forward, yelling out as he did. He clutched at the stumps and became a sitting duck for Riz's Rune, which he held up, taunting the Fae in his ancient language. A line formed from the Rune to Faine, hitting him square in the chest, and he was instantly paralysed.

Merrick stepped out of the shadows, standing with his arms crossed, an expression of murder on his face.

"Gallows! Do something!" the Fae cried out.

"Oh? You're asking me for something? Just like how I asked you not to do something? Hmm?" Merrick asked, directing the question to Faine, whose face alternated between anger and terror.

"What?" Faine replied, flabbergasted.

"I expected it off that useless Jack, but you? I thought you were better than to succumb to bloodlust. I'm not happy, Faine, I'm not fucking happy."

"I made you who you are now! You owe me!" Faine's words were pained as the Rune that Riz hit him with seemed to be taking effect as the wind picked up, blowing around him, and overhead, a crack in the sky formed.

"I owe you nothing, Faine. Now I'll bid you adieu, I'm done here." Merrick turned on his heel and put his back to the Fae. "See you around, Bren! Oh, and Merry Christmas! Hope you enjoyed your present."

Like that, he walked away.

I would have run after him, but there was still Faine, and an odd sound, like nails on a chalkboard backed up by a rusted pipe dragged over a cattle grid combined filled the air.

"Rat! What's going on!" Valarie said as she fought past the winds to stand next me.

"Dis Rune! It's messin up! Dats wats goin on! It's supposed ta only send im bak ta der Seeley Council, so does twats cud deal wit im!" Riz explained as he tried to keep the Rune in his hand steady. "Der energy from dat Illusion Trap haz screwed summit up."

I saw Riz's eyes widen as the hole above Faine opened more, big enough to see what was om the other side. I tried to look at it. Given what Riz had said, I thought that I would be looking at the Other for the first time, the home of the Fae. My eyes burned as

I tried to peek. The glimpse I got was of a cosmos, one that was consumed by shifting shades of eldritch fire, and of a darkness darker then black. I felt the Healing Rune kick in, as my eyes slowly started to heal.

"Yer frickin ejit! Who told yer ta look? Jus stand bak while I deal wit dis," Riz chastised. As if he was ever one to listen to rules.

"What is that place?" I said, seeing only grey blobs in darkness.

"Eh, betta if yer don't know, let's jus say its not where I wanted im ta go but he's probably not gunna enjoy it eitha… Soz bout yer parents by der way," Riz went from explaining some mystical, horrific place to sheepishly acknowledging the death of my parents, something that I was still processing.

"Don't think you've won!" Faine called over. "I don't care where I end up, I'll return, and I will deliver vengeance on you both! I'm the saviour of the Fae, the only one who can stop the rot that you placed at the heart of our world. No, not even the Beyond will stop me!"

Faine screamed the last part as he was sucked up into the hole, which closed itself with a crack of thunder, which faded into silence. This left me, Valarie and Riz on the grass, on a cold Christmas morning.

With nothing left to focus on, I collapsed to the floor, finding the mud had hardened with Merrick's departure. The freezing weather started to bite but I didn't care. The full weight of my parents' death hit me, and I cried. I cried my heart out. Riz kept his distance, so I found comfort in Valarie's embrace. Faine was gone but his actions had left scars. Scars, which still hurt me today.

CHAPTER 34
THE END OF THE STORY

Here we reach the end of this little tale, but I guess I should expand on what happened next. At least in terms of what we did next. Otherwise, I'd have to give a full rundown of what I've been doing for the past twenty years plus. I don't think you want that. Anyway, Valarie informed the proper authorities, with my permission, and the Ministry of Otherworldly Business soon arrived to begin their clean up. Thankfully, they didn't send Lionel, as that would have been the last thing I needed. When they arrived, tents were thrown up around my parents' bodies, and a bigger one that I was escorted into. I had to give a statement on what happened, and any interrogation was negated by the presence of Valarie and Riz, the former seemed to hold some authority over the Ministry. I didn't question it back then.

"Right, you're free to go," the agent who'd been questioning me said. His composure told me that this wasn't his first time doing this. He sighed a lot and kept looking back at his watch, nothing that he was doing was adding anything to this life. I thought how different I was than that guy. Even as I sat there, having lost everything.

"Free to go?" I asked, absently paying attention.

"Yes, we got everything we need off you. Just stay away from the house as that's an active crime scene. We need to document everything in there. You'll be able to return sometime in March." The agent didn't even look at me as he spoke, treating me as less important than the note book he was focusing on.

"But that's my home. Where am I supposed to go?" I asked. The agent had already turned his back on me, walking away to another task.

"Honestly, I don't care, that's not my job."

I left the makeshift tent while other members of the Ministry ran around, getting rid of any trace of last night's events. I had noticed my neighbours' faces at the windows. I could only imagine what they'd be saying. The gossip they would be spreading as soon as they felt comfortable leaving the safety of their homes. None of them would have witnessed what happened, none of them would have believed the truth. I also had no idea of what story was going to get spun to the local authorities. The more I thought about it, the more I realised that Merrick would still get the blame, even with much of the means erased from the official narrative. After all, the Ministry still allowed him to be named as the suspect in his family's murders, so adding my parents to that total wouldn't change anything.

"Bren!" Valarie called me over. She'd just gotten all her gear back, as the Ministry had confiscated all of her bags as a precautionary measure. I was too afraid as to ask why, even though the implications spoke for themselves. "You okay?" she asked, noting the look on my face. I think deep down she knew it was a silly question, but it was one that always had to be asked at a time like this.

"I don't have anywhere to stay. They say I can't come back here till March, and even then…" I cast a look behind me at the building, made with bricks and tainted memories, what been my family home for the past seventeen years. "I'm not sure that I'll be able to. Not after what happened, and of course, if I could even afford it."

"Me and my uncle can take you in for a little while, even if just till you figure out what you're doing. Plus, while I doubt the rat has been talking about you, I've been talking to Alice, and she's very interested in meeting you," Valarie said, trying to put on a cheery face.

"I don't even know your uncle." I wasn't trying to sound hostile to her offer, but I felt like I had to say it.

"Oh, don't be like that. He's great, and you'll get to try lots of Greek food. He's great at cooking food from the motherland as he calls it."

Valarie's attempt to sweeten the deal went over my head. I'm not great at trying new food.

"Dese buggas don't like givin anythin back, do dey?" Riz said in a huff. He was dragging my Rune pouch behind him, presumably having fought to get it back.

"I thought you would have legged it by now," Valarie said, rolling her eyes. "I mean, haven't you done everything you set out to do?"

"Shows wat u know! Besides, me nd Bren, we're a team!" He grinned at me, and I thought for a second that I was staring at the Beyond again. He nudged me in the elbow.

"We are?" I couldn't hide my surprise. Like Valarie, I had thought that this was the end of our partnership, despite everything that was said previously. Given how secretive he was, I didn't trust much of what he said, and thought everything else had an ulterior motive.

"Course we are! Yer flippin ejit! We're goin ta stick togetha! Nd first, we're gunna find a nice cheap dive fer yer to move to while we figure out money."

Riz clearly had it all figured out.

"Or, Bren, you can take me up on my offer and take time to recover and mourn over this tragic loss."

I think Valarie saw through what Riz was trying to pull then as well. Given I knew both choices now, it was easy to pick one. Yes, I know that, technically, I could have gone off on my own, to try and live a normal life, but I had a feeling that was never going to happen. Not with Merrick being out there.

"Okay, Val, can you introduce me to your uncle?" I asked, humbly.

"Wat, yer want us ta move in wit er!" Riz was outraged, but it didn't last long, not when I made it abundantly clear that I wasn't going to entertain his idea. "Fine, wat eva."

"You're just lucky that I'm letting you in the house!" Valarie glared.

"Yer sure bout dis, Bren? Know a place down south we can go ta," Riz whispered. I say whispered, as I think that's what he was trying to do. Me and Valarie stared at him, and he bowed his head.

"Can we jus get sumit ta eat now?"

There's more to tell from this point, but I think I've said enough. There were repercussions still to be felt from Faine's defeat. There were even repercussions from meeting more of Valarie's family, but these are all things for another time. It took me a long time to finally come to terms with my parents' deaths, and it did hang over me like an executioner's axe. It complicated my thoughts about Merrick, and if I could truly get my friend back, or if I was finally seeing what I'd been too blind to see before. As for Merrick himself, he'd kept quiet for quite a while at first, and I'd imagine that it was all because he was finding time to get to know himself, and what he was capable of. There was something else interesting that Riz shared with me, a belief that his Rune should have worked, but it was hijacked. He never went into any more detail than that, and I think it was because he was afraid of whatever it was he suspected of being behind the hijacking. That alone made me nervous.

Anyway, with that story at an end, I had other urgent matters to attend to...

CHAPTER 35
GALLOWS REUNION

The present day…

Back to where we left off.

My calculations had been accurate, as by the time I reached Thornaby Beck, night had fallen. I reckon I must have proved quite a sight to anyone driving past me, or to those who stood gawking out of their windows as I ran past. I was so out of breath that my second wind had peaked after its own second wind. Luck was with me for once, as the only sound coming from the beck was trickling water, and not the sound of teenagers drinking themselves stupid, though truth be told, I could have gone in on that now. Dealing with Merrick had that effect on me. In case you were still wondering at this point, after dealing with him multiple more times, I used his Gallows name when with Riz and Valarie. I think they assumed that I'd finally given up on the idea of rehabilitating him. They didn't know the depths of my guilt over that Halloween night, though they should by now.

Being that I was at the beck, in night time, on a cloudy night, there wasn't a lot of light around. I couldn't use my phone, as I'd already turned that off to stop being bombarded from calls from Valarie and Riz, who no doubt would be equal parts pissed off and worried. Riz certainly, as I had the wallet with all the money we had in it. That may as well have been a sacred artefact as far as the rat was concerned. I stood still, soaking in the atmosphere, and heard the little sounds that people take for granted, the shuffling of the smallest wildlife, the chirping of crickets, and the footsteps of someone walking on the other side over the shallow stream of water.

"I'm here, Merrick! Alone!" I shouted out, disrupting the quiet, which returned swiftly, but there was a different presence in the air, one of menace, yet with a wave of serenity that followed in its wake.

"Alone? You're never alone, Bren. Where's the rat? Or that girl? What was she called again? Verruca?" Merrick joked as he emerged from the undergrowth.

Without any light, I was saved from having to see him grinning at me, though I could imagine it easy enough.

"They're not here, and I didn't tell them where I was going," I said, even going so far as to put my hands up, palms facing outwards so that anyone could see they were empty. Assuming they could see them in the first place.

"Well, that is a surprise. Getting any time or space to talk to you in private has been a massive time sink these past few years, yet I kill a few useless people and you come to me! If only I'd thought of it earlier," Merrick laughed.

He had thought of it earlier. I had a case file back in my office as thick as a phone book that's all him. He's only ever gotten better at killing.

"It doesn't have to be this way," I said, though I knew I wasting my breath.

"Oh, there you go again, pretending I'm just another case for you to solve. Bren, have you learned nothing? Do I need to resurrect your parents and kill them again for you to get the lesson through that thick skull of yours?" Merrick said as he paced backwards and forwards across from me.

"You didn't do that to teach me a lesson, you did that because you thought that I needed to be free like you were," I fired back.

"Aren't you? Think about your life ever since I organised that present for you. It was a good thing, wasn't it? I don't mind that you never thanked me for it, but you can at least admit that your life since then has been better! How much you've lived since then!" Merrick got excited as he spoke, a shadow of how our conversations over the past few years had gone every time I confronted him.

"I'm not going to answer that," I said, having rehearsed these feelings and thoughts. I knew what he wanted me to say, and I wasn't playing his game. Yes, I'm here now because they died, but who's to say that even if they lived things might not have turned out the same. They still had their own secrets that they took with them. My mum was a banshee, for crying out loud. Nothing was going to be the same after that, not with Riz and Valarie being part of my life.

"Still in denial then? Well, if you won't answer that, answer this then. What did you think of my little message?" Merrick brought the conversation back to focus.

"Did all those people have to die?"

"How else would I have said hello?"

"Like normal people, sending me a letter or making an appointment."

He wasn't likely to do any of those things, but they wouldn't have involved anyone being murdered.

"That's no fun, besides, I was in a killing mood."

For someone who loves freedom so much, he was very good at taking it away from people. His answer for this was that in a clash of wills, the strongest wins, and he just applied that logic to everything.

"And the fairy statue?"

It was my turn to get to the point.

"That was the most important message of all. Didn't you understand what I meant? I tried so hard to make sure people got it, now are you're going to tell me that no one realised what I meant?" Merrick put on a sad tone as he finished speaking.

"A fairy statue in someone's stomach isn't the most easy thing to decipher, so why don't you just spell it out for me," I sighed. I didn't like having to act like this with him. Felt like I was giving him too much control again.

"Fine, I'll be boring and give it in simple terms. He's back,"

Merrick said, and again, though I didn't see his face, I knew he was serious. His playfulness was drained away.

"He's back? Who's he?" I asked, wanting more information than two words.

"You don't understand who I'm on about? There's only one 'he' I would mention. Have you blanked him from your memory?"

I thought hard, and the answer slowly revealed itself to me, and I bit my lip.

"You mean Faine?"

"Yes, Faine is back." Merrick's composure was tense. "And we're his targets Bren. You, me, the rat, Valarie. He wants us all dead."

"Big surprise there. How did he come back? I thought it was impossible to come back from there."

The wind changed direction, blowing against me, almost as if it didn't want me talking to Merrick, or hearing what he had to say.

"I heard whispers of conversations, snippets of words that if uttered in full would render people mad," Merrick said. "You wanna know what I heard?"

I was almost afraid to ask.

Though I still asked anyway, my curiosity was peaked, and knowledge could enlighten just as much as it could condemn. "What did you hear?"

"I heard something talking to Faine, and that something opened the door for Faine to come back here. And that something? Came through with him. Isn't that exciting?" Merrick let out a small laugh, one that it could be argued sounded more concerned then mocking.

I gritted my teeth as I processed the information. Faine being back was a threat but unless something happened to him, he was just a Fae. He could be dealt with. Who freed him on the other hand… that was terrifying.

"Got nothing to say?" Merrick asked. "Well, that's rude but you do you. I think you'll appreciate it if I skedaddle. Don't want you trying to play the game 'handcuff Gallows' again."

"Wait! Merrick!" I shouted but it was no use. He was gone before I could finish. I'd let him slip through my fingers. I wanted him to stop what he was doing, to stop hurting innocent people based on his whims. Every showdown we had made it clear that he had no intention of stopping. I had all his victims' blood on my hands. I had created this monster but, as Riz would point out, I lacked the will to do what needed to be done. The rat talked about killing as if it was the easiest decisions to make.

"Shud of killed im den, Bren!" he'd said after one previous encounter with Merrick. I had tried to explain my reluctance but it got me nowhere.

I stood on the bank of the beck and stared off into the darkness, knowing I was now alone. That was until Riz and Valarie caught up with me.

"Bren! Dere yer re yer daft bastard!" Riz yelled, running over to me faster than if I'd waved a wad of cash at him. He didn't hug me or anything, instead he sank his teeth into my leg, showing his displeasure. The pain did act as a distraction but I had to pry him off all the same.

"I did what I did so he'd speak to me. And from what I learned, you'll be glad I did as well," I tried to make my tone as serious as I could, to make Riz realise what I saying. It flew over the rat's head, of course.

"And what did he have to say?' Valarie asked. She seemed to understand the severity in my voice. She'd walked up casually, though she didn't look best pleased. A mood that was guaranteed not to improve once she knew what I knew.

"Told me that Faine has returned," I said, finally prying my arm out of Riz's jaws.

"What?" Valarie said in shock.

"Dat's impossible! Yet don't come bak from dat place, not fer sumit like im," Riz argued.

"No, Faine is back and he wasn't alone, something else came back with him. And he wants us all dead."

"Sumit came bak wit im?" Riz visibly shivered. "Dis ain't gunna be gud."

Riz never shivered, unless he was worried about his wealth. For him to react like this made me shudder as well.

"Can we trust him?" Valarie asked, apprehension in her voice.

"Gallows has never lied before. He taunts with the truth, knowing the damage it will cause," I reminded her. I wished it was a lie, far easier to dismiss the emerging threat.

"So taking it at face value, what do we do with this information?" Valarie changed tack.

"Duh, we prepare fer der worst."

"So, I should get the rocket launcher from the lock up then?"

This may sound like Valarie was making a joke, but she wasn't. She was being serious, deadly serious. I once got lost in her lock up.

"I reckon we got time before Faine makes is move, till den we mak sure we can deal wit watevar came bak wit im. Faine is jus a lousy Fae, know lotz of wayz ta deal wit im."

"And dealing with the other thing?" I inquired.

"I don't wanna think bout it, der forces from der Beyond nd further den dat, we mite ave ta kill godz…"

Riz's ominous words served as a full stop. From then on, every mysterious report that came in of an unidentified threat, masqueraded as Faine's initial strike. Not that they turned out that way but it was that fear which spurred us on. Even Riz seemed to have some urgency now as he worried about Faine's benefactor.

Word even spread to the 'Other' world and with it, tears appeared in the fragile peace between the Seeley and Unseeley, something I had played a part in securing.

Of course, how I did that is another story…

THE BUGLE IN
THE GRAVEYARD

There are relatively few truly odd moments in my life. Not the thing you'd expect me to say probably, especially if you know my profession. At the same time, it is because of my profession that I've seen or experienced odd moments. You've run away from one ghost, you've run away from them all. You dealt with one tribe of goblins, then you've got a good handle to deal with the multitudes and multitudes of other tribes out there. I'm getting off point here, but at this moment I'm being chased around Acklam Cemetery by an unhealthy mix of ghosts, skeletons, and the odd zombie. I hate zombies, not necessary to this current misadventure, but I just wanted it on record. Why am I being chased? Well, I owe this turn of events to Riz. No one should be surprised by that.

All this had started yesterday morning when Riz woke me up with excited news.

"I bloomin ell did it! Yer can start praisin me wen yer want," Riz said, folding his paws and standing on my chest. For context, I'd only been asleep a couple of hours, having been working the night before.

"Why should I do that?" I groaned, pushing Riz off me.

"Cuz I jus got us a gud payin job," Riz answered.

I don't know if he expected that to suffice for me, but, shock and horror, it didn't.

"We had a good paying job last night remember? We shouldn't be out of money that fast."

"Den yer shudn't ave left yer phone in ma reach den shud yer, nd also yer need a new password, yer current one is easy peasy ta hack."

I was going to murder him. I could put his body in the rubbish bin and no one would know that anything had happened. I'm sure that no one would blame me if the truth got out. Certain people might even give me a medal for it. However, I was numb to these antics, they'd been played out so many times already. I could even guess what he'd bought with the money.

"What's this new paying job then, and why are people dealing with you at this time in the morning?" I replied, downtrodden, yet I still found the spirit to add a touch of sass.

"It's cuz dis old guy jus put der job up dis mornin. He's pissed off wit der bugle music wakin im up every day, nd now wants rid of der pest. Payin big money ta get der job down today. Aint it perfect? Get rid of der ghost nd walk away wit a big pay day!"

"One that I'm not letting you waste."

"Try nd stop me!"

Despite Riz's joke, what he said did make me question something.

"How do you know that it's a ghost?"

"Cuz der music is comin from a graveyard. Wat else wud be in a place like dat, yer plonker."

"You neglected that information. Heck, you haven't even told me where we're going for his job!"

"Rite, if yer gunna be a baby bout it. Der client wants us ta deal wit der bugle player in Acklam Cemetery, by wateva means necessary."

"I'm guessing as long as it doesn't interfere with the location itself as I can't see him getting the permission of the council to send us in."

We had a mixed track record when dealing with the council, any council. More often than not, it quickly devolved into a blame game contest. Then there were the times where we hadn't been paid, yet the times we owed them money, they hounded us more than the things we were sent to deal with. They owed us on the other hand? Well, the phrase 'can't get blood from a stone' comes to mind. I digress again. So, yeah, we were off to Middlesbrough.

Riz didn't waste any time in getting me ready, biting me whenever I paused to do something.

"If yer don't want me bitin yer, jus get ready quickly!"

With that, he scurried off, back into the office. I presumed he was going to start daydreaming again while I pulled some clothes on. I thought about purposely going slow, but I didn't need any more teeth marks on my ankles, so I thought better of it.

Within the hour, we were on our way. Getting to Acklam Cemetery was exceedingly simple, the only thing about this case that was. We had driven all the way up Acklam Road in Thornaby, crossing over the busy motorways, and then turned right once we reached the Coronation pub, then we continued along till we came across the expansive cemetery on the left. Riz informed me that our client lived opposite. As much as I wanted the job being over with, I sighed, knowing it was only right to go and speak to the client. Riz was as much against it as I was, but for the fact that it was at this point I found the clients were more of a problem than what they hired us for. I'm sure Riz keeps a ledger of all the jobs I've cost him this way.

The client in question was a retiree called Mr Swale. He never gave me a first name to call him by.

"Every morning since I moved back ere, that blasted bugle player wakes me up! I don't sleep well at the best of times, Mr…" He paused his explanation to try and pull more information out of me, which was not going to happen.

"It's just Brennan, no need for the mister part."

At this point, and after looking around, I noticed how much of the house was ordered. Nothing was out of place. Even Mr Swale was smartly dressed, without a single crease in his clothing to ruin his appearance. He stood with his hands behind his back, his beady eyes watching me through the lenses of his thick rimmed glasses.

"Brennan? No, that won't do, Mr Brennan, this bugle player has to go. I know you and that twice-dammed rat are the ones to do it!"

That was a surprise. Normally during this phase of the case, Riz either hides in the car or rides in style in my coat pocket. I'm not lying, he's set it up like his home away from home. Yes, I do have to clean it out regularly. It isn't fun.

"Oh, yer used ta work fer der soddin Ministry, didn't yer? Dat explains ow an old coot who lives in a place like dis can afford wat yer willin ta pay me!" Riz said as he poked his head out of my pocket.

"Yes, hence why I knew you were the one to contact. Your love of money is legendary," Mr Swale said, raising an eyebrow. "Now may I continue explaining what I want you to do?"

"Wats der point? Yer want us ta get rid of der ghost, so yer can get sum sleep, not much ta explain is it? We don't need yer frickin life story!"

As much as I said that I was a cause for lost jobs, Riz had sunk more. While I wouldn't have been too bothered not to do this job, I knew it would affect our already low reputation.

"Riz," I muttered, catching the rat's attention.

"Wat?"

"Knock it off alright?"

"Fine, wateva. Can we jus get ta work already?"

"A bit pointless, the darn player only plays the music in the early hours of the morning. You won't find him now," Mr Swale pointed out. Information that could have been passed on through the phone.

"What else can you tell us about this bugle player? Anything that might help?" I said as I clamped down on Riz's mouth to stop him from talking.

"My neighbours call him 'Jimmy'." Mr Swale didn't hide his

disgust with that information, which made me think that he and his neighbours didn't get along, at least, behind his back. "Other than that, scant little is known about him, Mr… Brennan, despite the limit you have to work under, I expect you to have this done in a timely fashion. I will not accept excuses. I want that ghost moved from this world. By choice or by force, I don't really care. I will not have my peace and quiet disturbed by a musically inclined ghost! Now if you'll excuse me, this meeting has already gone on long enough! Please vacate these premises!"

Like that, Mr Swale had thrown us out… not literally, as I think lifting me would give him a hernia.

"Well, let's get on wit it," Riz muttered, crawling back into my pocket, the motion he used almost serpentine.

"No, we're going to the cemetery later. Much later. I want to know what everyone else thinks of Jimmy the ghost bugle player," I explained as I marched out of Mr Swale's garden, knowing full well I was under his watchful eye. I'm sure he was probably still watching me as I went from house to house speaking to anyone and everyone I could. As I suspected from his tone, his outlook on the bugle player was the outlier amongst everyone else. All those I spoke to, who responded to me and didn't act I was a shifty door to door salesmen, spoke fondly of Jimmy and his comforting music. Some had been in the cemetery as he was playing. Pressing them for more information netted me a couple of theories of who he actually was. Both involved the First World War, and him being a local. Where they differed was age.

One spoke of him as a child who'd tragically lost his family, and another said that he was a soldier. Not that these details mattered too much as where I could connect to the spirit was the love of music. All the stories shared the bugle that he played whenever he could.

All of that chatting and running around brought us to the onset of evening, the objectives now getting something to eat, and then like old times, sleep in my car till it was go time. For now though, we had an impromptu meeting in said car.

"Yer don't wanna do it now, do yer?" Riz asked, sighing. He knew me so well.

"Considering there's only one guy with a problem, yeah, I've got doubts about doing this job."

"We need der cash!"

"Oh! Now it's 'we'? Back there it was only you. With that 'pay me' comment. Don't think I didn't hear that."

Good thing that we were in my car, otherwise people would think I was a raving lunatic.

"Look, can't we plz jus keep dis simple! We find der ghost, we cross im ova, everybody's happy!" Riz said, standing on the dashboard so he could reach up and grab the lapels of my coat.

"Everybody?"

"Yeh, all dose old folk yer talked ta, dey'll all forget der soddin ghost before too long, den he'll just be an old tale like all dose otha ones we helped! Wat makes dis one so fukin special?"

"Maybe the fact that this one isn't doing any harm?"

When I said this, Riz let go of me and pulled at his eyelids, stretching them before letting them snap back.

"Yer frustratin! Gah!" he screeched before sitting with his back to me, staring out of the windows like he was one of those nodding dogs. "Don't talk ta me until food time!"

Well, that was one perk of this… a nice bit of peace and quiet. If I could have gotten away with it, I'd have dispensed with eating altogether.

After food, I tried to rest, not that the car or Riz made it easy, but I watched the clock tick away. I sometimes get asked what I think about before a case, and the answer is: everything. I try to control the flow of my thoughts, get a bit of meditation going. I've seen so many insane things in my life, and they all try to come through my head in a mad rush. That was when I first heard it. The sound of the bugle. The tune itself was what I'd describe as comforting happiness. It also carried nostalgia, of a sort. From what I heard, it cemented the fact that this ghost wasn't a threat.

However, that didn't mean I didn't want to meet him.

"Riz, wake up! He's playing!" I opened the glove box and pulled the rat out.

"Wat! Who's playin? Y did yer wake me up!" As was the case when I woke him up early, he went to bite me, but I threw him into the passenger seat.

"Jimmy the bugle player, that's who. Let's find him now!"

"Find im? Oh, yer came ta yer senses, did yer, nd decided ta zap im so we can collect?" Riz asked, presuming he knew what was going on. He clearly didn't.

"No. You know what? I'll explain it to you once we're in there."

Riz leapt to my shoulder, and we got out of the car and raced towards the gate. Which, of course, was shut. I didn't like to do it, as it could cause a bit of trouble if security found us.

"Riz, do your thing," I said, looking away.

"Now we're talkin!" Riz went to work, and it was a long-standing deal that I never saw what he did, and it's one that I was happy to continue with. Plausible deniability and all that.

That out of the way, we slipped in, and Riz undid whatever it was that he did in the first place. As a child, I always thought that cemeteries were creepy places, especially when my parents used to drive us past Thornaby Cemetery at night. That feeling still stays strong with me, despite having been in more graveyards at night than I would ever care to admit. This was my first time in Acklam Cemetery though, and all too late I knew we should have done a circuit of this place in daylight. It was night time with zero visibility, and we were hunting a ghost. Not the best of starts. The bugle music had been playing all this time, but Riz hadn't commented on it. Turns out that was because he had something else to comment on.

"So we're lookin fer der bugle playa rite?"

"Yeah?"

"Looks like is fans re out in force."

When Riz said this, I for some reason expected to see actual living people hiding out here. No, that was not the case, why would I ever have thought that would have been the case? What

Riz had pointed out was all the other ghosts that were standing by grave makers, or milling around, and all of them staring at us.

"Bren, I think dey've spotted yer," Riz added. Unhelpfully, I might add.

I took his sarcasm and fired it back at him. "What was your first clue?"

The ghosts around us kept their distance. It was weird though, seeing all these ghosts in one place. In case you were wondering, I was not going to be sending all these ghosts to the afterlife. For one thing, I didn't have that many Runes that I could use on them all. The other reason was that they weren't doing anything. In all the other jobs we've done that involve ghosts, they'd been making a nuisance of themselves in some fashion. They're had been a few one-off cases where I did it to harmless spirits, but that was far more complicated and I really doubted that any of these spirits would fit the sane criteria they did.

"Y cudn't dese twats jus move on already? Neva mind, let's find Jimmy, nd finish dis job!" Riz shouted, far louder than he should have. The spirits were already glaring at us, and with the announcement of our intent, well, that was it! They all started drifting towards us, hands out stretched and I didn't want to find out what they had in store for us.

"Next time, keep your trap shut," I said as I took off down the path. The ghostly luminescence of the spirits gave me a little advantage here, as it meant I could see the ones ahead coming. The ones behind me were a different story, but I trusted Riz would inform me if they were getting too close. I turned my head slightly to see what he was doing, and found myself face to face with a skeletal hand that waved at me. I took one look at it and then threw it back on the ground. It didn't take long for its owner to appear, holding itself together with the lightest of spiritual power. Now this was new. We all know ghosts can possess people, but I'd only heard recently at that point of ghosts being able to possess their own earthly remains. It couldn't be done straight away, time had to be taken to learn the skill. Yet, here were these Jimmy fans, taking their old bones for a walk.

"Bren! Get yer arse over ere, yer twat!"

I heard Riz's insult from the left. I wasn't going to even try and guess at what point we'd got separated. Without slowing down, I turned in that direction which meant I was going to do something I don't normally end up doing. Jumping over graves. I offered a silent apology to whoever it was in each grave, hoping that they weren't one of the ones chasing me, and I leapt over them like they were hurdles on sports day. Hopping over three grave markers brought me to rendezvous with Riz, and he leapt back up to me as I passed him, just as another skeletal hand burst from the ground. There was going to have to be some explaining done either way, it seemed.

"Rite, turn dat way!" Riz pointed.

"Where the hell are you taking me?" I asked. I still ran in the direction he indicated. I had nothing to lose at this point.

"I've got betta hearin den u! Jimmy is still playin nd we're gonna find im! Now run like yer life depended on it!"

He didn't have to tell me twice but the decomposing body that had emerged from the ground in front of us, did well to put me off that route. The smell radiating off it was enough to knock you out, and would have laid me low except I've smelt much worse in my partnership with Riz.

"Gimme more directions, Riz!" I did a sharp turn away from the moving corpse and I was running out of places to, well, run to.

"Yer want more directions? I'll giv dem ta yer! Not dat way, not dat way, nd deffo not dat way!"

"How is that helping right now!" I had to do another sudden turn as a skeleton, with some force behind it, jumped through the ground.

"I'm tryin ta keep yer alive! Maybe it's time ta start fightin back, I mean dere only flippin ghosts, fer cryin out loud!" Riz yelled right into my ear.

"No! That'll just make things worse! And you call me an idiot…" I muttered, jumping over a couple more headstones to get away from the skeleton eager to see my bones.

"U're an ejit!"

"This is not my fault."

"Dis is entirely yer fault!"

"How?"

"I don't know yet but wen I figur it out I'll bite yer!"

All the time me and Riz were arguing, I was going as fast as I could, throwing all sense of direction to the wind in an effort to avoid our pursuers.

"Watch out!" Riz yelled as he twisted my head to face to the right where a zombie, hidden behind a tree jumped on us. I could easily push it off, after all its legs fell off when we collided. But this was the distraction that all the others had been waiting for.

"Riz, your inability to sense ghosts directly really, really sucks." I rolled my eyes as the spirits had us surrounded. As things fell silent, Jimmy's music seemed to get louder, now seemingly in stark contrast to the scene we were in. Our captors formed a circle around us, ensuring no escape, unless I started blasting them.

"C'mon! Let's jus zap dem already! It's us or dem, nd it's deffo not gunna be me!" he snarled in a way that I think he meant to be threatening, but certainly didn't come off like that. We should have been at their mercy. I'll stress the 'should have been' part. The ghosts stood still – incorporeal, skeletal – and the zombie glared at me. I could tell they wanted something off me, and I had an inkling as to what it was.

I raised my hands to show my peaceful intent. "I only want to speak to Jimmy. I'm not here to hurt him or take him away from any of you."

"Wat der ell re yer doin? Wat bout der job? We need dat cash!" Riz obviously protested.

"I think they need Jimmy more than you need a bit more useless tat!" I snapped in a hushed tone, only tilting my head towards him rather then turning to face him.

"Ow dare yer say dat of my gold rat collection!"

A sharp blast of a bugle broke our argument up, and the ghosts parted. A spirit floated towards us, carrying a spectral bugle, its colour shifting in luminous hues.

"You wanted to speak to me, mister?"

No points for guessing that this was Jimmy.

"Yer were controllin dem wit dat blasted bugle der whole time, weren't yer!" Riz accused with his wagging finger pose. This was his favourite if he thought he had the best of you. Which was quite often.

"Huh? I can't control anything with this. I just like playing it!" Jimmy said bashfully. It was also often that the rat would be wrong completely, and was never not amusing, even in life-or-death situations.

"And a dammed fine musician at that," one of the other spirits said, a man with a rather large pipe held to his lips.

"His musical talents do bring a smile to these old ears," an elderly woman joined in the praise and within a moment there was a chorus of the dead, all paying compliments and lavishing praise on the young bugle player. It was a very wholesome scene, until you remembered that some of these were cadavers missing flesh and other body parts.

"Enuff wit all der pleasantries, fer flips sake! If he weren't controllin yer, den you did yer do all dis! We cud ave sent yer where eva we wanted yer! I cud ave dun even nastier thins!" Riz fumed. I almost saw steam coming out of his ears. I also sighed at what he was saying we were capable of. In the short timespan we'd spent here, there wouldn't have been enough time to make any Runes capable of what he described.

"Because we don't want to lose him, isn't that obvious?" a ghost of a young woman said, floating in the air, her lower body nothing but a whispy trail. "His music helps us to remember our lives and the happiness we had, instead of us focusing only on what we lost."

"Dats all fine nd dandy, but y don't yer jus move on den?"

I started to think that I was going to have to grab his snout to stop him talking before we started another pointless fight.

"Why should we? We're not into scaring people, and we've got a nice community here. Can't you just respect our wishes?" the ghost with the smoking pipe asked.

I dived in with an answer before Riz could. "As long as you're not causing any harm, then it's not a problem at all. I just wanted to speak to Jimmy to find out why be was still playing after all these years. By my reckoning, you've been here over a hundred years easy."

"Wat? We've got a job ta do yer twat!" Riz shouted out, and I followed through with my threat to hold his mouth shut.

"Der cash!" he managed to squeak out through my fingers.

"It's been a hundred years, has it? Time flies, guess I adn't noticed it. Not when I've been practising every day." Jimmy laughed, ignoring what Riz had said.

"That practising has been worth it, you play a mean bugle," I added my compliments to the rest the ghost had received. I saw why everyone but Mr Swale was more than happy for the playing to continue.

"Sure is nice to hear that, mister."

"How come you didn't cross over with your family?" I asked. Something had kept him here, when everyone else in his family had already gone.

"Oh, I wanted to at first but they told me to stay and play my music. Said a gift like mine needs to be heard, that I could do more good this side than over there," Jimmy humbly said, while scratching his head, or at least mimicking the action.

"Who told yer dat? Yer family?" Riz piped up, having taken a sudden interest in the conversation.

"My family? Nah, it weren't them, they'd already gone by that point. This was just a voice I heard as I floated around."

"Rite…"

Riz then hopped off my shoulder and, with us all watching him, went to the nearest tree. When he got there, he head butted it at such a force, that it broke part of the bark of the tree off. Then, he headed back our way.

"Fine, yer win, Bren."

He crossed his arms in a huff. Jimmy looked at me for an explanation, but I had none to give.

"I win?"

"Yeh, so finish yer conversation so we can get der heck outta ere. Alrite?"

Figuring that was all that I could get out of him, I thought it best to move the conversation on.

"What did the voice sound like?"

This revelation, plus Riz's odd behaviour, put a whole new spin on what happened. Of course, I thought that the rat knew more then what he was letting on, but I also knew that not all of the secrets he kept were bad. Don't get me wrong, most were, but there were a couple rattling around in his head that could be considered good.

Jimmy didn't answer straight away, and if I had to guess, he was trying to remember the inciting incident.

"They sounded... nice? I guess? I'm afraid I can't give you more than that!" He laughed off the lack of information. As frustrating as it was, there was times like this where tantalising knowledge was always out of reach, as here with the identity of the mysterious voice.

"Well, thanks for all the information. I'm glad I got to hear you playing for myself," I said smiling.

Riz face-palmed.

"You mean, you really don't want to hurt him?" one of the other ghosts asked. If it was possible for a spirit to show signs of relief, they were all attempting it.

"It wasn't really my intention when I came in here." I looked down at Riz as I spoke, inferring what he wanted to happen. "I had my own questions to ask, and you've answered them, thank you for your time. Maybe I'll have to come back in the future and jam with you."

"Jam?" Jimmy questioned with a raised eyebrow. I forgot that some of the words I used may have been confusing for him. I pictured the spirit thinking of the spreadable kind of jam in his head.

"Oh, I meant I'll bring my saxophone and we can play together," I blurted out.

"I'd like that very much!" Jimmy beamed. He held his hand out. I didn't know if he knew it or not, that you couldn't really shake hands with a ghost, so I copied his gesture regardless. My hand did feel warm where it met his but that was the extent of it. "Are you going now or can you stay a bit longer to hear more?" he added on.

Really, I wanted to go to sleep, my body craving that relief that only a goodnight's rest could provide. I wasn't going to get that though, either way. Additionally, it was hard to turn down the offer, and it was rare to be in the presence of ghosts and not be trying to blast them to God knows where.

"I've got time, friend. Play on."

At this point, Riz buried himself in my pocket, in a mood that he'd get himself out of over time. This gave me an opportunity to text Valarie and ask for her to run something over when she had a moment.

By the time the sun had come up, the light reacting beautifully with Jimmy's bugle, I think everyone was ready for a rest. The spirits returned to their graves, as did the skeletons and zombies. They still left the holes they made in their pursuit of me but, as callous as this sounds, that wasn't my problem. Unless they caught me here. Then it would be my problem. It was a risk I was willing to take on account of the music I was privileged to hear.

I said my goodbyes to Jimmy and promised to return. You'd think that this would be the end of the story, right? I'd turned my back on the job we were hired to do and made an acquaintance out of Jimmy, the bugle player of Acklam Cemetery. Job done, case closed and all that razzle dazzle. But no, there was still one thing left to take care of...

"I heard that bugle player again! I thought you were getting rid of that annoying waste of ectoplasm!" Mr Swale said in an exacerbated tone. He really didn't look happy to see me and Riz.

"I decided that the best course of action was to leave him be. You were the only one with a problem and he kept the other spirits in the cemetery at bay as well," I stated, noting that the elderly gentleman was getting redder and redder.

"Oh? And what about my problems then? I can't sleep when he's playing that racket!"

This is where the item that I had Valarie bring me came into play. She'd left it under my car for me, so it'd been easy to retrieve. I playfully threw a pair of noise cancelling headphones at him.

"These will fix you right up, put them on and you won't have to worry about that music, or any other sound waking you up again," I explained with some detachment. If you get the impression that I didn't want to deal with him anymore, then well done.

"You don't expect me to pay you for not doing the job, do you?"

Mr Swale had reacted as I anticipated, showing no gratitude for me even thinking of a different solution. One that was obvious in hindsight. The fact he jumped to the extreme option of getting rid of the bugle player said a lot about him really.

"Keep your money. I'll survive like I normally do, and I can go and listen to that music you hate whenever I want." I turned away from him.

"This is ridiculous! I asked you one thing!"

"And if you really wanted it, you should have done it yourself!"

You may have noticed that Riz was awfully quiet during this entire exchange. This is because I told him in no uncertain terms before I knocked on the door that if he dared speak or make any snide comment that his precious rat statues would find their way to pawn shops. It was not a threat I made lightly. So he was sitting in my pocket, sulking.

I heard the door slam behind me, which I was grateful for, as it served as the ending to this job.

I returned to the car, with a feeling of contentment which only seemed to happen on missions like these. Riz crawled out my pocket and pulled out a wallet that I had no idea was in there.

"Whose wallet is that?"

My contentment faded a little.

"It's dat twats! I took it wen we first met wit im. How did yer think I figured out he waz ex-Ministry? I wanted ta make sure we got paid! Shud ave known yer wud screw it up," Riz shouted, then after a moment of silence, he spoke again. "Yer gunna mak me giv it back, aren't yer?"

I thought to myself, coming up with an answer within a split second. I grabbed it, got out of the car, went to his house and threw it over the fence so it landed in the back garden. When I sat back down in the driver's seat, I turned to Riz.

"He'll find it. Let's go and get breakfast."

"First thing yer sed dat I agreed wit since yesta-day!"

There would always be more jobs out there...

Find Peter James Martin on Twitter @ Brennan_and_Riz